Primal Mirror

Primal Mirror

A PSY-CHANGELING TRINITY NOVEL

NALINI SINGH

BERKLEY
New York

BERKLEY
An imprint of Penguin Random House LLC
penguinrandomhouse.com

Copyright © 2024 by Nalini Singh
Penguin Random House supports copyright. Copyright fuels creativity, encourages diverse
voices, promotes free speech, and creates a vibrant culture. Thank you for buying an authorized
edition of this book and for complying with copyright laws by not reproducing, scanning,
or distributing any part of it in any form without permission. You are supporting writers
and allowing Penguin Random House to continue to publish books for every reader.

BERKLEY and the BERKLEY & B colophon are registered trademarks of
Penguin Random House LLC.

Library of Congress Cataloging-in-Publication Data

Names: Singh, Nalini, 1977- author.
Title: Primal mirror / Nalini Singh.
Description: New York : Berkley, 2024. | Series: Psy-changeling trinity novel
Identifiers: LCCN 2023058315 (print) | LCCN 2023058316 (ebook) |
ISBN 9780593440735 (hardcover) | ISBN 9780593440759 (e-book) |
Subjects: LCGFT: Paranormal fiction. | Romance fiction. | Fantasy fiction. | Novels.
Classification: LCC PR9639.4.S566 P75 2024 (print) |
LCC PR9639.4.S566 (ebook) | DDC 823/.92—dc23/eng/20240117
LC record available at https://lccn.loc.gov/2023058315
LC ebook record available at https://lccn.loc.gov/2023058316

Printed in the United States of America
1st Printing

This is a work of fiction. Names, characters, places, and incidents either are the product
of the author's imagination or are used fictitiously, and any resemblance to actual persons,
living or dead, business establishments, events, or locales is entirely coincidental.

For the ones who are always there.

Primal Mirror

Bloodlines

GENETIC INTEGRITY.

A cold ideal, but one to which certain Psy families committed during Silence. It was believed that the more intensely curated the genetic line, the more powerful the abilities of the children born into that line. As such, potential partners in the creation of the next generation were investigated for any and all anomalies, only the most tightly controlled of the other genetic lines in the PsyNet allowed to intermingle with theirs.

It worked.

Over the more than one hundred years since the inception of the Silence Protocol and the subsequent elimination of emotion from Psy lives, this subgroup of families have refined their bloodlines to such genetic perfection that *all* their children are high-Gradients. Their cells carry no "extraneous" material that could initiate an unexpected result. There are no genetic leaps, no extraordinary new gifts, but on the flip side, there are no low-Gradients who will be a drain on the family's resources.

Unfortunately, these families did not allow for a trifecta of wild cards.

First: the unpredictability of nature.

Second: the continued inability of the Psy race to pinpoint the exact genesis of their mental abilities on a biological level.

And third: the interference of those who believe themselves better than their fellow Psy—their own families included. Because for a *super* minority within this "flawless" minority, genetic perfection isn't enough. A high-Gradient child isn't enough. Even power far beyond that of the vast majority of the population isn't enough.

Dominion over all sentient beings is what they crave.

Power so unqualified that it is a drug.

FIVE MONTHS AGO

Chapter 1

"Stand down. I have your squadmate in the truck."

—Remington Denier, alpha of RainFire, to Aden Kai, leader of
the Arrow Squad, one storm-lashed night (9 April 2082)

REMI SWORE UNDER his breath.

He'd been hoping that what he'd picked up hadn't been conscious movement, merely branches breaking in the aftermath of the rainstorm that had passed over this part of the Smoky Mountains an hour earlier.

But what was happening on the land adjacent to his pack's northernmost border had nothing to do with nature. Remi and his people, as well as their very dangerous friends, the Arrow Squad, had been attempting to trace the ownership of that land since two senior Arrows had woken up badly wounded in the single building that sat on the land: a flat square bunker created of old-fashioned concrete.

Back then, it had been draped in camouflage netting and dead foliage. These days, the walls were covered with moss and lichen, the concrete itself dirty and marked by exposure to the elements. Two or three more decades, and the creeping tendrils of the forest would overpower it until nothing of the bunker showed to the naked eye.

Remi would've been fine with that—though he'd much rather have found the owner. The Arrows knew who'd been behind their capture, but they hadn't been able to tie any member of that group to this land. At first, it appeared the trail ended with the name of a deceased five-year-old child, but that had turned out to be just another misdirection.

Last Remi had heard, the squad's civilian specialist had landed on another faceless shell corporation. "Whoever did the paperwork to hide ownership," Tamar had muttered, "they were good, did all the same things I would have. Trail's circular and eats its own tail."

As it was, the Arrows had had to shelve the search for the time being. The PsyNet, the psychic network that connected the majority of the Psy on the planet and that the other race needed to survive, was breaking down at a catastrophic rate. The squad had focused their power and attention on that looming threat to millions of lives.

"As it is," the leader of the squad—and Remi's friend—Aden Kai had said, "we've poisoned that location for the owner, regardless. No way to run black ops out of it anymore, not when they know it's in our crosshairs."

Now, eyes narrowed, Remi leaned one shoulder against a mature yellow birch, its spring-green leaves a falling rain around him, and watched the small gathering in the clearing in front of the bunker: two women, three men, all of them in suits a little too lightweight for the temperature at this elevation.

The older woman—maybe in her early fifties—was a tall and very thin brunette with skin of pale brown and eyes that appeared dark from this distance. She looked to be in charge, the three men listening intently to whatever it was that she was saying.

The younger woman stood apart, her possibly curly black hair viciously contained in a knot at the back of her head, her skin an ebony that glowed even in the cloud-heavy light. She was on the taller side for a woman, maybe five eight, and wore a black skirt suit paired with a white shirt, her black heels so unsuitable for this terrain that it was laughable.

That wasn't what caught his attention.

It was that the woman wasn't simply silent and uninvolved in the discussion. She didn't appear to be *present*, her expression seeming lax as she stared into the distance away from both Remi and the other group. Though all he could see of her was her profile, the way she stood—her arms loose at her sides, her body swaying the slightest amount—confirmed that something wasn't quite right.

Shifting his attention off her because she wasn't the threat, he zeroed in on the brunette. But no matter how much he strained, he couldn't pick up on the conversation. The group was just a fraction too far away for even his leopard's acute hearing.

Which left him with only one real choice.

He straightened, and was about to prowl out of the trees when the younger woman jerked her head in his precise direction.

Her eyes were a hauntingly eerie blue, moonstone made liquid.

Remi sucked in a breath. His leopard surged to the surface of his skin at the same time, Remi's own eyes shifting to the yellow-green of the primal creature that was the other half of his self.

The cat's response wasn't, however, aggressive. It was . . . more complicated. As if the cat was compelled and repelled by her in equal measures. The animal within Remi had belatedly realized the same thing the human part of him already had: she might be strikingly beautiful, but even with her expression no longer distant and vacant, her body held with tension, something about her raised his hackles.

Still, aware that he couldn't afford to scare her, Remi allowed the human side of him to rise to the surface once again as the woman began to walk toward him. The others didn't look to be paying attention to her, but, soon, the most heavyset of the men turned to follow her.

Then the older woman called out to him, and the man returned to the huddle around her without giving the blue-eyed woman a second glance.

Not worried. Why should they be?

After all, they were meant to be alone in the wilderness.

In truth, they *should* have been alone. The heart of RainFire's territory lay a significant distance away—but that didn't mean Remi and his packmates didn't patrol this area on a regular basis. It would've been stupid in the extreme to leave an unguarded threat on their border.

No one came after the younger woman even when she walked into the trees, but Remi stepped forward so she wouldn't come too far. Right now, given the shadows thrown by the other trees immediately around them—a mix of maple and beech along with a stand of poplar—the others would still be able to see the back of her body but would have no chance of spotting Remi.

"Good morning," he said as he took a deep inhale of her scent in an instinctive changeling act.

Scents could tell you a lot about a person.

Hers was . . . problematic. Erratic in the most abnormal way he'd ever sensed. He'd never usually use that term about a person—each person's normal was their own, scent a very unique marker—but it was the only one that suited this specific situation.

Her scent fit *none* of the parameters for a sentient being. Had it been formed of light, he'd have said the rays were reflecting off a funhouse mirror that distorted everything. Muddy and sluggish and with too many pieces to it, it made his leopard snarl.

Those extraordinary eyes—such a striking translucent hue—held his for a split second before drifting away.

He didn't mistake it for an act of submission.

Lost in her own world, this woman likely didn't hold anyone's eyes.

It would've been easy to peg her as neurologically atypical, but that didn't sit right, either. Not when her scent was so *wrong*. He'd interacted with others through the years who wouldn't meet his eyes in the same way, but their scents had read as natural nonetheless.

Never had he met *anyone* with such a fragmented and unsettled scent . . . almost as if she wasn't a whole person at all, rather a collection of disparate pieces that clashed and broke against each other.

The hairs on his nape prickled.

Yet he didn't do anything to stop her when she reached for his hand.

He couldn't, however, keep his leopard's claws from pushing out of his skin or his eyes from shifting back to those of his cat. That cat's initial fascination with her had turned into a confused protectiveness: it didn't want to hurt her, seeing her as wounded, but it also didn't want her too close.

She didn't pause or stare at his clawed hands, continuing on her trajectory until her fingers grazed the face of his mobile comm unit. Small as an ordinary watch, the thing was pristine even more than ten years after its purchase . . . because Remi had never been able to make himself use it except for this one day every year.

Her birthday.

"I know you'll never spend this kind of money on yourself," his mother had said with a smile right before the end, when she'd insisted he take it. "You and your dragon's hoard."

All those years he'd been denying his instincts to nurture and protect a pack, determined he'd never be an alpha, he'd still hardly spent anything. He'd told himself he was saving for retirement . . . even when he'd believed with every fiber of his being that he'd fuck up his life well before then.

"Rem-Rem." A whisper of a word from the woman with the muddy scent.

One that kicked him right in the gut.

"So tired." She swayed left and right. "My wrist is so thin this is falling off. Wonder if my Rem-Rem will figure out I bought it for him in the first place."

Remi fought not to lash out, not to react in a rage of grief. Because she couldn't be reading his mind. Changeling shields were too powerful. She'd have had to launch a violent telepathic assault before she could have ever gotten to his memories—and such an assault would've probably destroyed his brain in the process.

Whatever this was, it wasn't mind reading.

"It's my mother's," he said, his voice harsh. "She left it to me." She was also the only person in the entire world who'd called him Rem-Rem.

But only when they were alone together. Because it was a little boy's name, and "oh my Rem-Rem, what a man you've become"—words she'd spoken to him more than once, her eyes shining with love.

But the blue-eyed woman who knew his deepest memories was listening only to her own internal voice. "One last gift." Her face softened. "My boy, I'm so proud of you." Her lashes quivered, her eyes staring hard into nothing. "Cake. Brown cake. Small brown cakes."

"Chocolate cupcakes." His mother's favorite; she'd baked them at least once a week.

Later, after she was too sick, he'd baked them for her.

"Pieces of color. Tiny pieces of color on the small brown cakes." A blink that appeared to have been forced by her watering eyes. "It hurts." She pressed a hand to her stomach. "Oh, it hurts." Then she made soft sounds . . . that were an exact mimicry of his mother's small heart monitor signaling an emergency alert.

Remi jerked away his hand.

She stumbled, swayed.

Feeling like shit, though his face was hot, his grief tangled with anger at the intrusion into the most painful part of his past, he gripped her upper arm to stabilize her. A jolt under him before her head shifted, her eerie, beautiful eyes meeting him head-on.

At that instant, there was no lack of clarity to her, no fuzziness to the edges of her.

And no muddiness in her scent.

It was complex, and bright, and intoxicating.

"She was happy the last time she wore that watch." Clear words, the intent in them potent. "No pain, just comfort at being with you, at lying by the window in the sun, with the forest just outside.

"She was so proud of what she'd accomplished in life. *You* were her greatest pride . . ." Gaze turning dull and unfocused, her eyes drifting away, her muscles going slack under his grip . . . and her scent twisting once more in that funhouse mirror.

Shaken, he released her.

She turned and walked back the way she'd come, until she stood in the same spot as when he'd first seen her. But she'd left carnage in her wake.

Bending down, his hands on his thighs, he gulped in lungfuls of air as his mind filled with memories of the mother who'd brought him up with love and heart and courage. She'd also held his feet to the fire when needed, especially during his teenage years, when he'd wanted to rage at the entire world.

"You sit your ass down, Remington, and we'll have this out until I know what's hurting you." Fierce eyes of palest brown locked with his, her leopard a golden glow on the edges of her irises. "No son of mine is going to go off the rails because he's got a fear inside him that he's allowing to fester."

Her strong, capable hands cupping his face, holding him in place. "You are not only your father's son, Rem-Rem, you are also your *mother's* son. Don't you *ever* forget that."

You were her greatest pride . . .

His throat closed up. How could a Psy know to say that? How could a Psy understand what a blow it struck to his weathered but never-forgotten grief to know that his mother had died proud of the man he'd become?

In the sun, in her favorite chair, in the little cottage he'd built for her when she got too tired and sick to get up to her aerie. She'd wanted to die at home, not in the antiseptic environs of a hospital. "I'm dying anyway, baby boy." A husky whisper of memory. "I'd rather spend my last days surrounded by the green that's always fed my wild heart."

So he'd brought her home, and when she'd asked, he'd carried her outside, into the trees. But she'd been content to spend most days in her favorite armchair, next to an open window from where she could watch the world while the sun caressed her face.

She'd shifted in that sunlight one last time right before the end: a leopard who was too thin, whose bones stuck out against her pelt. But who'd sighed in contentment as her eyes closed, her head placed on her forelegs as if she was just taking a lazy afternoon nap. His last memory of his mother, sunbeams dancing over the black and gold of her.

. . . lying by the window in the sun . . .

How could this strange Psy with the broken scent know *any* of that?

It took effort for him to rise to his full height, even more effort for him to retract his claws into his body. His leopard was right at the forefront of his mind, and he knew his eyes hadn't yet returned to their human shade.

He had to get that under control if he was going to talk to the group. Because he was certain the woman with the unnerving presence that disturbed both man and leopard on a fundamental level hadn't said a thing to them about him, telepathically or otherwise. They remained in the exact same positions, while she stood there rocking back and forth, her arms hugging her curvy body.

It was several minutes later that he emerged out of the forest, his stride easy and his expression friendly. He'd moved so that he arrived from a different direction to where the woman had entered the trees. It had also been long enough since then that the others shouldn't connect the two incidents.

The entire group froze—and two of the men did so in a way that told him they had tactical training. He lifted a hand, keeping it casual and lazy through sheer effort of will. "Remi, your neighbor."

When the young woman locked her gaze with his again, his gut tensed.

The brunette crossed over to him even as the blue-eyed one blinked, then looked away.

"Good morning." The greeting was flat, but the brunette came close enough that they could talk without strain—while her guards followed, two besuited shadows. The third man shifted closer to the woman who'd told Remi things she had no way of knowing.

"I am Charisma Wai, executive personal assistant to Auden Scott"— a nod toward the silent younger woman—"the new owner of this land."

Chapter 2

"Remi Denier quietly bought up a piece of land in the Smokies and set up a territory with a bunch of loners he met while roaming. Just heard he's sent out the call for others to join the pack."

"So he finally accepted it? I knew he was meant to be an alpha the first time I ran across him—and he was determined to break his neck on a racetrack at the time."

"I've had my eye on him for around the same amount of time. Figured I might one day have a problem on my hands—Remi's too dominant to be prowling around without a pack."

"You think he's willing to listen to advice that might make the entire thing easier?"

"I'm going to make the offer. But I like what I'm seeing so far—I don't think it's chance that he bought land right up against the border of a fallow territory under trust control."

"Smart. He holds that ragtag pack together for a full year, and he's in position to apply for a land grant. I don't like cats as a rule, but yeah, I hope he makes it."

"I mean, if we can put up with a bunch of mangy wolves, anything's possible."

—Conversation between Lucas Hunter: alpha, DarkRiver leopards and
Hawke Snow: alpha, SnowDancer wolves (27 January 2080)

. . .

REMI HAD NEVER heard of Auden, but he did know the last name Scott. Few years back, a couple with that name had been on the comm channels all the time as representatives of the now-defunct Psy Council.

The husband had been big, with skin the hue of mahogany and a military bearing, his face carved of aristocratic lines that shouted breeding. His wife, slender and fine-boned with cool white skin and ice-blue eyes, had carried the same air of contempt. Oh, they'd been clever about acting the perfect, refined Councilors, but Remi had always had a good bullshit detector.

Henry and Shoshanna Scott, that was it.

The skin and eye coloring had altered in Auden, become more intense on both fronts, but no doubt about it, those two had to be her parents. Her height was close to her mother's, but her face held her father's aristocratic bones on a feminine frame.

"Well now." Remi folded his arms, and added a kick of charm to his smile, even though he knew it was wasted on most Psy. But no harm in trying. "I've been attempting to get in touch with the owner of this land for quite a while. All trails led to dead ends. You mind telling me how Ms. Scott managed to track them down?"

Auden Scott remained silent, her unseeing gaze on the trees.

Her assistant could've told him it was none of his business, and she'd have been right. Instead, she said, "Auden inherited it from her father. The records were lost after his passing—and it appears from the unauthorized structure on the land that someone made use of that oversight. Do you have any knowledge of the people who trespassed here?"

Remi's leopard growled within, not particularly interested in talking to this woman whose scent was off, too, but not like Auden's. Charisma's had that metallic undertone present in the scents of a percentage of Psy.

It wasn't as bad as before the empaths had returned to the PsyNet, but it was still bad enough. Changelings who'd had more contact with Psy than Remi had told him that the metallic edge came from those who had no real emotion in them, their growth permanently stunted by the program called Silence that had ruled Psy lives until the very recent past.

The three men carried a faint glimmer of the same scent.

Auden Scott, this woman who'd just torn him to pieces, shifted on her heel.

His cat drew in another breath, snarled. What the fuck *was* that in her scent? Some kind of sedative? He'd smelled nothing medicinal when close to her, and he could've sworn that Psy didn't deal much with those types of drugs—multiple Arrows had told him it messed with their psychic abilities.

Forcing his attention off her, he answered Charisma Wai's question. "Paramilitary-type unit," he said, wondering if she was as clueless as she was making herself out to be.

Everyone knew what had happened to Councilor Henry Scott— he'd picked a fight with the biggest wolf pack in the country and lost. Man had mingled with exactly the type of people who'd abducted, then brutally operated on Aden and Zaira. The two would've died if Remi hadn't been prowling around with the intent to spy on the activity up here; next thing he knew, he had two bleeding Arrows in his vehicle. "Whole unit cleared out one day roughly a year and a half ago and haven't been back since."

Aden had told him the squad was certain the unit was linked to a group called the Consortium. "They've gone quiet of late," he'd said more recently, while the two of them were scaling a sheer rock face. "Kaleb mentioned to me that while he's never been able to prove it, he's always suspected Shoshanna of being part of the Consortium, maybe even the central figure."

So whichever way you sliced it, the Scotts had been involved in all kinds of deadly games. They were likely to have been in this up to their necks.

"I see." Charisma Wai made a note in the thin computronic organizer in her hand. "Do you have any further details?"

"Nope." Remi glanced once again at Auden Scott. "Funny."

Auden focused on him, staring in an unblinking way that his leopard would've read as a challenge at any other time. Today, he was disturbed by that stare—because he was near certain she wasn't seeing him at all, her gaze directed at some sight beyond his senses.

"What is funny?" Charisma Wai asked after a glance at her boss.

Who blinked several times before her gaze turned fuzzy once more, the abnormal tones back in her scent.

A growl threatened to rumble inside Remi's chest; he fought it back because Psy would take it as a threat. "Losing track of a whole piece of land."

"Councilor Scott's passing was unexpected." A smile so false that it looked like a skeletal rictus to his eyes. "And, to be quite frank, he was wealthy on a level you can't hope to understand. This little tract of land was but an afterthought."

"Oh, ouch." Remi's grin was real. "That put me in my place."

"No offense was intended."

"Rich people things, huh?" Remi lifted one shoulder in an easy shrug to take any sting out of his words. "So, you interested in selling?"

Charisma Wai glanced down at the organizer. "We're in the preliminary inspection process, so I can't promise anything, but yes, there is a possibility the parcel will be up for sale."

Well, *that* he hadn't expected. And while he wanted to talk to Auden Scott, this was more important—it was pack business, was part of his duty as alpha of RainFire. That duty came first.

No one had ever had to tell him that. He'd known from day one.

"I'd appreciate a heads-up if you do decide to put it on the market." RainFire wasn't rich, far from it, but this particular parcel was so isolated and remote that it was unlikely there'd be other takers. The pack might be able to negotiate their way to it by dint of being the only interested party.

"Of course. Do you have a comm code I can contact you on?"

Remi recited it, then directed his next question to Auden. "You have any idea why your father bought this land in the first place, Ms. Scott?" he asked, to see if he could get a response out of her. "And why he hid it under so many shell corporations and false identities?"

Auden Scott ignored him.

Her mouthpiece graced him with that nauseatingly fake smile once again. "The Councilor's records indicate he purchased it when he was young," she told him. "He might've been building a property portfolio before realizing this region wasn't the most valuable in terms of future capital value. As for the rest . . . he *was* a Councilor."

Remi nodded. Even though she'd given him nothing solid, what she had said could be the actual truth. Psy generally didn't make any attempt to own property in remote areas—unless of course, they were a Councilor up to nefarious business. Nice to have a secret getaway where you could torture prisoners without anyone hearing them scream. Also made sense that he'd structured the ownership so it couldn't be traced back to him unless he allowed it.

Until, of course, an upstart pack set up shop here and ruined the whole operation.

"You have official proof of ownership?" he said. "I don't want to be a stupid changeling taking you at your word." Every changeling in the world knew that Psy like Charisma Wai thought themselves better than humans or changelings.

Humans were considered too weak, changelings too feral.

The executive assistant showed him the deed on her organizer screen. Looked official, with the transfer to Auden Scott noted as occurring three weeks earlier. If it was legit, then whoever was settling Henry's estate *had* lost track of this land for some time.

"I'll send you a copy at your comm code so you can verify it with the relevant authorities," Ms. Wai said. "I understand your wariness given the rogue military unit you mentioned."

Sometimes, the whole logic-is-best thing Silent Psy had going on actually worked to make them straightforward. Not often enough to balance out the other crap they pulled, but it was a small positive.

It could, however, also be used as a shield.

"Appreciate that," he said aloud. "You know where the borders are? I don't want any of your people startling my sentinels into aggressive behavior." His senior people were far too smart to attack without thought, but Remi needed Wai to see them as a threat, so neither she—nor anyone else in the Scott camp—would start getting any ideas.

Another tap at her organizer before she flipped it so he could see the map on the screen. The boundaries glowed red. "Does this align with your understanding?"

"Looks good," he said after a thorough scan. "My people have become used to running through here while it was uninhabited—I'll tell them to back off, stay within our boundaries."

"That would be appreciated." Another smile that put him in mind of a cobra changeling he'd met—man's blood really had run cold. Good thing cobra changelings were so rare that no one else he knew had ever come across one. "I wouldn't wish our security to be startled into aggressive behavior."

He gave her a small smile. "Got it." After another glance at Auden Scott, who hadn't spoken a single word to anyone the entire time, he melted back into the trees.

But he didn't go far—just far enough that there was no way they could see him. It was possible the security team was doing telepathic scans, but his Arrow friends had told him that most security specialists didn't bother with the draining task unless they were in a high-risk situation.

"Arrows do it as a matter of course," a senior member of the squad had said, "but Arrows have more psychic power than ninety-nine percent of people."

As it was, Remi could make things even harder for them.

Stripping in the shadow of the trees, he cached his clothes on a lower branch that wasn't too wet from the rainstorm, then shifted. His body broke into a million pinpricks of light before coalescing into the leopard that was his other form. The change took a heartbeat, the agony and the ecstasy of it singing through his bones.

It was pain beyond the imaginable, and it was pleasure untold.

Shaking his body to settle his new skin in place, he jumped up onto the trunk with muscular feline grace before making his way to a thick upper branch from where he could watch his new neighbors even if they were once again out of hearing range. His tail twitched lazily, but there was nothing lazy about his eyes or his mind. A mind that Charisma Wai and her security goons could no longer spot—it was Zaira who'd told him that.

Lethal assassin, Aden's lover, and the unexpected heart of the place the squad had made their home, she'd said, "You have a shield in either form, but I've noticed that once in animal form, your shield doesn't feel like a shield. I can only sense changelings in animal form because I know so many of you. To most telepaths, you'd read as an animal."

That suited Remi just fine.

So he wasn't prepared for Auden Scott to do it again: jerk her head in his exact direction and stare at the trees as if she could see through the wall of dark green to the shadowed golden pelt of the creature that stalked her little group . . . as if she felt the same primal compulsion that had driven Remi to keep trying to get a response from her, find out the truth of her.

He stared back, the two of them locked in a battle invisible to the world.

Chapter 3

Given the previously noted circumstances, as certified by qualified counsel, I hereby remove Auden Jackson as my legal heir. She no longer has any claim on my estate beyond any specific bequests in this amended document.

To clarify, no penalty is to be paid by Shoshanna Scott for her family's adoption of Auden into their bloodline. The matter has been negotiated satisfactorily between Shoshanna and I, and no debts remain.

—Amendment to the Last Will and Testament
of Henry Ignatius Scott (9 March 2076)

AUDEN'S HEAD FELT heavy, her vision foggy, but she couldn't stop staring at the trees. At the man who wore a comm thick with memories that hadn't hurt her. The person who'd worn that watch before him . . . had been a good person. Auden had few parameters for what words like "good" meant, but she thought the lack of pain associated with her read of the device must be a link to goodness.

Her thoughts splintered without warning, the edges fraying until she couldn't remember why she was looking at the soaring trees with their dark green limbs and thick trunks marked by natural patterns and textures she could almost sense against her palm. Just like she couldn't remember why she'd woken with bruises on her hip and thigh today.

They ached.

"Auden." Charisma's crisp voice.

It took a second or two to penetrate, but once it did, Auden forced herself to look away from the trees and to the older woman who had been her mother's right hand for so long that she was present in Auden's earliest memories.

Charisma Wai was intelligent, rigid in her views on Psy perfection and the importance of bloodlines, and excellent at her job. She'd also been long enough in Auden's life that Auden never forgot Charisma, even when the rest of her memories fractured.

"That was unexpected," the other woman said while Auden fought the compulsion to stare once more into the shadowy green of this place so different from the pristine lawns and precise hedges of her childhood.

"Yes," she said at last, because Charisma was waiting for her to reply. The truth was that Auden didn't know what she was replying to, had already lost track of the conversation.

"The male was a changeling." Curt words from Charisma, whose eyes were on her organizer. "He made an offer on this land."

Auden stayed silent.

"Normally," Charisma continued, "I'd advise against a sale. It can be useful to have a hidden location that can be utilized for more covert matters."

Auden had retained the thread of the conversation this time around. "But?" she said, trying to read the face of this woman who had been a peripheral part of her existence since the day she was born. It hadn't mattered that Auden had spent most of her time in her father's house-hold, among his people. She'd nonetheless always understood Charisma's importance to her mother.

"I wasn't aware until now that this parcel was so close to a pack." Charisma's lips tightened. "Many of the packs are intensely insular and keep to themselves, but given that the male approached us, I don't think we can rely on that—whatever his animal is, it isn't the kind to mind its own business."

Auden's brain fired, a fragment of memory crashing inside her temporal lobe: a man with eyes like the topaz stone she'd seen once, so clear and striated with light. His hair had been cut messily, countless shades of brown within it, his skin a gold that seemed warm and touchable.

No, his eyes had been yellow-green, argued another part of her mind.

"Both," she whispered under her breath. "They were both." Because he was changeling.

A cat of some kind.

It confused her that Charisma, with a mind that was undamaged and whole, hadn't worked that out. It had been obvious in the slow prowl of his walk, the languid fluidity of his muscles.

"I think . . ." she said loud enough for Charisma to hear. "I think I'd like a house here. A quiet place. Like . . . Father used to have."

I go to my quiet places to think, Auden. That's why you can't come. When I'm with you, I think only about you because you are my daughter and my heir.

Charisma's gaze sharpened. "Can you solve this equation?" She flipped the organizer toward Auden.

The numbers blurred and swirled, but Auden found her hand lifting, found herself inputting numbers that formed in her head in a soft glow. Ghosts created by her fully functional visual cortex.

Charisma sucked in a quick breath.

"I do believe," the older woman murmured, "it's time we go back to Dr. Verhoeven. As for the land, I see your point. But think it over. I'm not fully aware of your father's more private residences but your mother's were in locations with no watchful neighbors. Furthermore, there is no road to this godforsaken place. You'd be reliant on air vehicles or teleports."

Auden's eyelids came down, rose up again. The streamers of her

thoughts attempted to fly away. But, for the first time in . . . an endless
nothingness of being, when she extended her psychic hand and gripped
at the streamers, she managed to keep hold of them.

The transport issue: that could be a good thing.

Before the fogged brain and the broken thoughts, she'd done something. What had she done?

*Congratulations on your graduation from flight school. To have passed the
testing at fourteen, that brings great honor to the family.*

Controls under her hands, the sensation of lifting off the earth.

Fly. She could fly things. Small things. A private jet-chopper. Her
father had given her one, she was sure of it. A sleek black machine, a
present on her graduation. Shoshanna hadn't been pleased, she remembered, had said Auden was too young.

"As for the changeling pack," Charisma said, her gaze once more on
the organizer that was an extension of her body, "they have next to no
footprint on the Internet. Some packs work hard to achieve that, so we
can't assume they're small or weak.

"I believe I have the name at least—RainFire. I was able to find it
in a search of property records. The pack purchased the block of land
against our border outright just over three and a half years ago now;
they also have changeling rights to land in public ownership. But the
main chunk of their private territory comes out of the Peace Accord
Land Trust."

Auden stared at the older woman, her brain struggling to comprehend the shape of Charisma's words. "What?"

"I don't know what that is, either." Charisma's rounded eyes had a tilt
at the very corners, and now it seemed as if those corners twitched in
frustration.

Auden knew that was her own imagination—or a glitch in her mental processing of the image. Charisma's Silence was without flaw.

"I'll run a quick search on the PsyNet," Charisma said.

Auden knew she should be able to run her own identical search but
she couldn't figure out how to enter the PsyNet, her brain refusing to

give up that knowledge. It was *right there*, just beyond her grasp, a thing so basic that it should've been second nature. It was like forgetting how to walk.

"Ah," Charisma said, "the trust was set up in the aftermath of the Territorial Wars in the eighteenth century. It holds the lands of dead packs in trust until they can be passed on to a living pack that meets the criteria."

None of that meant anything to Auden, the streamers of her thoughts sliding out of her suddenly slack grip. She swayed back and forth.

Gripping her shoulder, Charisma spoke to someone other than Auden, her tone clipped. "Teleport us to the medical facility."

Auden didn't feel the teleport, but she was soon standing in a crisp white room that held a white examination chair covered in leather-synth, along with countless monitors hooked up to computronic machinery.

The air smelled sterile, no damp green, no ozone in every breath.

She'd been here before. Many times. When Charisma nudged her into the chair with wide arms and a clear top part that came down over her face and head while the body of the chair reclined so that she lay supine on it, she didn't resist.

"Charisma." A male voice, movement at the door. "Show me the equation you had her solve."

Dr. Verhoeven, Auden's brain supplied, putting a face to the name, the voice. Pink-tinged skin with scars from childhood acne outbreaks that had either been left untreated or not treated well, brownish-red hair he kept short and combed in neat lines, and a compact body on a frame shorter and stockier than Charisma's.

"Yes," he murmured. "An encouraging sign."

Screens lit up around Auden as the doctor started the . . . scan. Yes, that's what this was, a scan.

She faded into her mind, her thoughts filled with the most fascinating thing she'd seen today: the changeling who moved like a cat. But what kind of cat? Not a house cat. She didn't think any changelings shifted into house cats.

A jungle cat then.

Leopard. Tiger. Jaguar. Lynx. Puma.

Were there others?

The lights flickered around her, bringing her back to the present day.

". . . working." The doctor's voice was higher than usual. "Intensification of neural activity to levels we haven't seen since the initial failure."

"I wonder why today. I've been taking her on various site inspections and other low-risk private business matters for the past two months, ever since you advised that she was beginning to show signs of neural regeneration. Shoshanna is intrigued by the change and wants to see if the external stimulation will progress it further."

"It's possible it's just time. Despite what we like to think, there's still a lot we don't know about how Psy brains work."

"How will this impact the other medical situation?"

"I can't predict it. Is she even aware that she's pregnant?"

Auden's mind faded out again, her thoughts filled with images of large jungle cats . . . and flashes of things she'd done for which she had only snapshots, no context to the memories. Was that her? Sitting at a meeting table? Being hooked up to a machine that scanned her belly? Lying on a table while . . . while . . .

Almost all her thoughts slipped out of her grasp.

Only one remained.

A large, shimmering fragment that rippled with a single word: *pregnant*.

Then the word vanished, forgotten, while another memory floated to the surface: a comm call with a business associate. She'd attended it. Not today, or yesterday, or even two weeks ago. But at some point.

She hadn't had to do much, mostly just show her face while Charisma undertook the negotiations. Her job, she'd understood, was to ensure the cutthroat businessman believed that the family had a powerful heir waiting in the wings.

Not her father's family. Her mother's.

Scott was her mother's last name. Henry had used it publicly to foster the image of unity he and Shoshanna had agreed to portray as part of their agreement to work together. He'd been a Jackson by birth: Henry Ignatius Jackson.

"A Scott must lead these negotiations," Charisma had told her. "A direct line descendant. Not a secondary branch as applies to your uncle and cousin. You are from the first bloodline, and it's important that you start to become visible now that you're in your twenties. It will assure a smooth transfer of power in the future."

Auden didn't know why any of that mattered when Shoshanna ran everything, but her brain hadn't been working well enough for her to ask Charisma to explain. So she'd played her part, spoken the words that Charisma telepathed her to speak during the introduction phase, and then she'd sat back.

No one had trusted her to actually undertake the negotiations.

"Won't he be insulted I'm not interacting with him?" Auden had asked Charisma in a rare moment of clarity.

The other woman had stared straight at her. "Astonishing. Your mind truly is returning to its previous acuity." Then she'd answered Auden's question. "No. It is understood that you are a young woman who is learning the ropes.

"Your presence, however, makes it clear that you *do* intend to take over when your mother is ready to retire—and they are used to dealing with me as her proxy, so there is nothing unusual in that. Everyone understands that the former Councilor is a very busy woman."

Auden's mind had begun to fade in and out toward the end of the meeting, and she'd had to fight to hold on to reality with a grip as sharp and hard as the claws of the man to whom she'd spoken in the forest today.

Topaz. Feral yellow-green. Glints of gold in that tumbled hair.

Big frame . . . but fluid movements. Feline.

Was this a memory? How could it be a memory? What reason would she have to stand face-to-face with a changeling in a forest? Her upper arm pulsed, an echo of fingers hot and strong holding on to her.

Threads unraveling, the memory being eaten away at the edges.

A faint growl, those yellow-green eyes following her into nothingness.

Chapter 4

Failure is total. The malfunction has burned lesions into her brain.
Probability of full recovery is negligible.

—Dr. Nils Verhoeven in report to Shoshanna
and Henry Scott (11 November 2075)

AUDEN WOKE IN her bed, dressed in a nightgown of plain white that reminded her of a hospital smock. Looking at her bedside table, she took in the date and time as projected by the small device attached to the wall just above.

Three days since the day she might've come face-to-face with a feline changeling.

Auden was used to losing time, but of late, since she'd begun to regain a semblance of coherence, she usually had basic awareness of what she'd done through the day. Fuzzy and faded and confused memories, but *memories*.

But when she looked back through the past three days, all she got was a blank.

Yet her legs and arms ached as she got up, as she moved. Not the ache of pain. The ache of exercise.

Rising, she padded across the carpet and into her bathroom suite.

Her arm brushed the inside left wall to bring up a soft light even as she continued on to stand in front of the mirror. Her hair was in braids tight to her skull. The work was clean and precise, intricate; it would've taken three hours at the very least.

Yet she had no memory of strands tugging at her scalp.

As she had no memory of making the decision to adopt this style. It wasn't her. Her father's mother had taught her that it was an excellent option to protect her hair from breakage, and had made her wear her hair that way through her childhood.

No choice. No discussion.

Perhaps that was why adult Auden never utilized it. She liked to pull her hair back into a single knot, or—when she was at home, with no outsiders around—to leave it out but pushed back from her face using sleek hairclips.

A vague awareness of *something* inside her mind . . . but she wasn't afraid.

A surge of protectiveness washed over her instead, and she found herself touching her abdomen. There was no protuberance, but she'd lost her slightly concave shape.

"I'm pregnant."

She felt no surprise at that. What she didn't understand was *why* she was pregnant. Even at only a quarter away from twenty-four, she was too young by the standards of Psy society, and *far* too young per the standards of her family. The Jacksons weighed each individual on their merits, but the Scotts had a firm rule: no reproduction contracts until at least thirty. The family—her *mother*—simply would not support any earlier applications.

And the Scotts, Shoshanna, were her family now. She wasn't and would never be a Jackson again.

Information so embedded in her memories that she remembered it as rote.

Charisma . . . had told her something, but Auden couldn't remember what now. However, while that lack of memory was blurry, today and yesterday and the day before were a total blank. Suddenly remembering what else Charisma had told her, she returned to her bedside table to pick up the pocket organizer that lay beside a bottle of water.

"I'll create a diary for you on this." Charisma's voice coming into focus in Auden's thoughts. "You can make entries in it of course, but I'll also enter information on the days when you aren't fully mentally present. That way, you can read back and see what occurred over the day. Dr. Verhoeven believes it may help you maintain longer periods of coherence."

The last entry glowed on the screen the instant she scanned it open using her voiceprint. Charisma's name and familial code pulsed at the very top.

Auden, you decided you needed to exercise. As Dr. Verhoeven's colleague in obstetrics has encouraged appropriate exercise during the pregnancy, I took you to the private gym set up in the household security HQ after calling in a personal trainer under contract to the family. (He has signed an ironclad NDA and knows the penalty for any breach will be severe in the extreme.)

Your mother authorized these actions during her short twenty-four-hour visit.

You exercised with him for an hour, and he took care to ease you into it, and to not permit you to do anything too strenuous all at once. You were breathing hard by the end, but completed the exercises he set. The trainer has suggested you make this a daily routine so that you can build up the strength you've lost in the years since the initial failure.

I didn't confirm or reject the plan—that's up to you. But I have placed the trainer in a rental residence in the adjacent town so that you can utilize his services as required.

Auden tried to remember lifting weights, tried to remember walking or doing stretches, or even seeing Charisma's slender form and dark hair, and came up against that same blank wall. But . . . no, the wall wasn't *quite* blank. There was a taste on her tongue, a slickness of metal that made her wonder if she'd cut herself, was tasting her own blood.

But when she checked in the mirror, she had no cuts inside her mouth.

Yet the taste of metal persisted. It also came back four days later, and with it, another—larger—blank in her memories. She brought it up to Charisma at that point, and the other woman had Dr. Verhoeven check her over.

His conclusion was that her brain was burning itself out as it functioned at full capacity again for periods. "It'll settle down," he promised her. "Right now, it looks like you're going into a variation of the ordinary psychic flameout. In this state, your mind can no longer create memories for a period. You had major neural damage—such hiccups are to be expected."

That didn't sound right to Auden, especially when Charisma's notes in the diary indicated that Auden was coherent and determined to proceed with her self-assigned tasks during those same periods, but she didn't have the words to argue back. Not then, and not in the weeks that followed, as the memory blackouts grew in volume until the metal on her tongue was a taste so strong that she threw up from it one night.

Her cheek on cold tile. Her throat choking. Her body spasming.

Baby. My baby!

Alarms going off.

A rush of feet.

A pink-red face over her. "—overload! Get her to—"

Later, snatches of a room with machines that hummed and beeped, fine tubes going from her body and outward.

"—stop for the—" Charisma's sharp voice, fading in and out of her consciousness. "—won't be—"

"It could've caused a miscarriage. You must convince her to limit—"

Nothing, her thoughts as tangled and as soft as snarled wool.

The taste of metal was gone when Auden surfaced the next time, and though she waited, it didn't return in the days that followed. She still lost time, but those memories were present, just fragmented and blurry. No chunks of blankness, more as if an omnipotent being had taken a bad eraser to penciled-in thoughts and left behind a mess of smudges.

Yellow-green eyes wild and hot with anger.

Claws hard and deadly.

A touch that burned.

That false memory would not fade, would not vanish. It haunted her in her dreams, through which prowled a big cat whose form she couldn't quite pinpoint. All she could see were his eyes glowing in the darkness . . .

Chapter 5

Sir, the effect of the last attempt was deleterious, with significant risk of a miscarriage. Dr. Verhoeven has strongly advised that you make no further attempts to test the theory until the fetus is born. I'm attaching his recommendation, as well as notes on Auden's medical status.

—Charisma Wai to Shoshanna Scott (21 June 2083)

THE WOMAN WHO had once been a Councilor and was now a being far more powerful, took note of Charisma's message, but put the documents aside until she'd dealt with a more pressing matter.

After she finally had a chance to sit down and go over the medical reports on both the fetus and Auden, she had to agree with Verhoeven's recommendation. Auden was expendable, but Shoshanna had spent far too much time and money on the infant to put it at risk now.

Well, no matter. She could wait a few more months to test her theory again—after all, she'd waited for years already, since the day the biograft burned her daughter's mind to cinders.

Leaning back in her chair, Shoshanna took a sip from a glass of clear liquid designed to refuel her brain. In the back of which whispered the word "mother" spoken by her true children, her Scarabs.

Soon, she promised them. *My reign draws near. Soon you will be where you were always meant to be: at the apex of the Psy race.*

PRESENT DAY

Chapter 6

While I do not wish to have her out of my sight, I believe we must permit this to ensure her continued cooperation. We cannot reinitiate any of the previous measures, not at this late stage. The risk to the fetus is too high.

The most important thing is to keep her calm—and the risk is manageable if she wears the biomonitors I've supplied. We can teleport to her if she shows any signs of medical distress.

—Private message from Dr. Nils Verhoeven to Charisma Wai (48 hours ago)

IT WAS LARK who spotted the small black jet-chopper passing over RainFire lands deep into the night hours. She was also close enough to the far northern border that she saw that same chopper come down on the small landing pad that had been put into place on their neighbor's land a month ago—on the heels of the construction of a one-bedroom insulated cabin.

The Scotts hadn't bothered to remove the bunker already on the other side of the property—probably too much work and effort.

"I didn't wake you," Lark said to Remi the next morning, "because it was just the one person. Pilot." Biting off a piece of buttered toast, she chewed and swallowed.

The two of them were sitting at a table with Angel, another one of Remi's sentinels. The dining aerie was fairly quiet, filled mostly with packmates coming off the night shift—it tended to be a mix of security and infirmary crew, with the odd other individual thrown in, depending on their duties.

The majority of those filling plates from the mixed dinner/breakfast spread just lifted a hand in a wave before taking their plates to find solitary corners—or tables with other cats who also didn't want to talk just yet.

With cats, you had to respect the need for time alone.

Then there was Lark, who had obviously been a bear in a past life. Elfin face, petite frame, midnight skin, and a delicate pixie cap of hair that was a vibrant pink today thanks to her wholesale love of dyes that didn't last through a change into leopard form, Lark loved company as much as she loved sharing gossip.

"I couldn't get any specifics," she added now, "because of the way our neighbors constructed the landing pad right behind the house. Pilot got out and walked straight in via the back door."

Remi didn't scowl at the idea of sleeping through a possible threat; a good alpha trusted the people he put into senior positions. An alpha who tried to micromanage predators like those in RainFire would soon find himself alpha of nothing. Cats did not fuck around with idiots who wanted to put them on a leash.

Considering Lark's intel, he took a drink of his orange juice. "You sure it was only one person?"

"Yep. They were piloting one of those tiny hoppers meant for short-distance flights. Clear glass dome. Only space for two inside, and I saw a single silhouette."

"They probably took off from the outskirts of Sunset Falls," Angel murmured, his black hair tumbled after the night and his cheekbones as striking as ever. "There's that small hangar and attached runway where out-of-region folks can park private air vehicles for when they visit this part of the Smokies."

Remi nodded at the mention of the nearest township as Rina Monaghan slid into the seat next to him with her own breakfast. Tall and curvaceous, the blond sentinel wore her hair in a high ponytail and could separate your head from your body if you pissed her off.

His leopard had snarled in pride when she'd asked to join his pack.

Despite his excitement at having attracted such a strong young leopard to RainFire, however, the first thing he'd done was ask Lucas what he thought about losing Rina. He'd known she must've already spoken to her alpha, but it would've been a bad move on his part not to have that discussion himself.

The last thing RainFire needed was to make an enemy of the powerful pack that had been the first to call them friend. Lucas had been beyond generous in his support of Remi's bid for the position of alpha, had even lent Remi some of his own people for the initial construction of RainFire's aeries.

A gift from one alpha to another, an offer of friendship that Remi did not take lightly.

"Now that she's fully mature," Luc had said, "Rina's too strong and well-trained to be anything but a sentinel, but we already have the max number we need. The only reason we haven't already lost her is that she's fucking loyal to her own." A tightening of his jaw. "I don't want to let her go, but it's time. She'll be an asset to your pack."

As it was, RainFire was top-heavy in terms of dominants—an emergent pack needed more sentinels and senior soldiers than an established one. They also needed energy of the kind that prowled under Rina's skin, hungry and wild. She'd no doubt been a nightmare as a teen, but adult Rina had mastered iron discipline over her furious instincts.

"What're we discussing?" she asked. "Anything I need to know for the morning shift?"

Once Lark had caught her up, Remi said, "Lark, you able to tell if the pilot was a man or a woman?" His mind filled with an image of the eerie eyes of moonstone blue that he'd seen five months earlier, but the woman with those eyes had been in no state to pilot anything.

"Nah." Lark yawned. "Pilot's head didn't touch the top of the hopper's dome is about all I can tell you, but those domes are high enough to fit you or Angel, so it isn't much."

"Don't worry." Angel's distinctive ultramarine eyes shifted to tiger gold, the gleam in them amused. "Remi's going to go up there to satisfy his curiosity anyway. You might not have noticed, but our alpha has a *slight* interest in our neighbors."

Remi gave their resident tiger the finger. Angel was the quietest of the sentinels, but he'd also known Remi the longest, a blood brother who'd always intended to walk the path of a loner—until Remi asked him to help set up a new pack. The other man had pinpointed Remi's fascination with Auden Scott the first time Remi mentioned the strange interaction.

"As if you're not as curious." He shoved a hand through his shower-damp hair. "I'm also pissed off, in case you failed to notice. I thought we had a real shot at getting that land." All else aside, he hated having a possible threat on his border. "Why would a Psy even want a place like that when they know they can't use it for shadow ops?"

Lark shrugged after swallowing a forkful of scrambled eggs. "I dunno. Some of them are reclusive. I mean, have you met your Arrow bestie?"

"Aden isn't reclusive. He lives in the Valley with other Arrows." A place to which Remi had been invited, to attend the squad's first-ever high school graduation ceremony. The invitation had been a symbol of trust between their two groups—as RainFire's agreement to allow playdates between their cubs and Arrow children was a symbol from their end.

"Krychek then." Lark pointed her fork at him, while Rina—never talkative in the mornings—ate a bacon roll and listened. "*Wild Woman* reported that he lives in the boonies with his mate, and my Moscow bear friends on the forum confirmed it."

"Ah, *Wild Woman*," Angel said after a leisurely sip of his coffee, "that bastion of investigative reporting."

"Fuck you, Stripes." Mild words. "Try to borrow my copy next month and see where it gets you."

A tinge of red on Angel's cheekbones that had Remi's shoulders shaking and Rina looking over with a *very* interested expression on her face.

"Oh, do tell, Angel," he said, poking at his friend. "Secret fan?"

"This is why I was a loner," Angel grumped before throwing back his coffee. "I hate people."

Remi and Lark both laughed, while Rina smiled a slow smile.

Their newest sentinel rose soon afterward. "I want to do a full sweep today, through all quadrants."

"Wait for me." Lark scrambled up, too. "I'm going to get into my pjs and catch up on the latest episode of *Primal Lives & Private Secrets*. Yesterday's episode ended on a cliff-hanger. Writers had the main protagonist get kidnapped by her human billionaire enemy—with whom she has tons of sexual tension."

She fanned herself for a second before scowling. "On second thought, I hope she rips off his pretty face. I mean, she *is* meant to be a wolf alpha. No one kidnaps an *alpha* and lives to tell the tale. I'll stop watching if they make her act like it's romantic."

Shaking her head, Rina picked up her plate and cup to return to the counter. "Feather, last month you had me watch the episode where one twin pretended to be the other twin and no one caught on even though it was meant to be a pack of bears with hypersensitive noses."

"I know, I *know*, Reens." Lark scrunched up her face. "I'm an *addict*." She grabbed her own dirty dishes before the two sentinels walked off together.

Of all the friendships in the pack, that one struck Remi as the most unexpected. Where Rina was driven and ambitious with a fiery temper, Lark was all sunny temperament, cheerful delight in the world, and an ability to forge bonds that was unparalleled.

He was fucking lucky to call them his own.

Angel waited until he and Remi were alone to say, "You doing okay?"

A direct gaze from the only person in the world who understood the relevance of today's date.

It wasn't that Remi didn't trust the others; they just hadn't been around when he lost his mother. Angel alone had witnessed his grief. Their friendship had only been of six months' duration at that point, born when they'd ended up working the shutdown shift of the last operating oil rig in the world.

You'd never usually find a changeling on a site like that, but they'd both had their reasons to choose work that hurt their very nature. And, despite the nascent character of their friendship, the then-nineteen-year-old tiger had come home with a similar-aged Remi when Remi's mother realized she was sick in a way nothing could fix.

Angel, the boy who'd walked alone since he was sixteen, had then stayed with Remi and Gina for seven months . . . all the way to the end. Gina had hardly slept toward her final rest, and the tiger had sat up with her during the times when she'd ordered Remi to sleep. He didn't know what they'd talked about, but they'd had their private jokes neither would explain to him.

His friend had made his mother laugh in her last days and it was a gift Remi would never forget. Angel had also been one of Gina Denier's pallbearers on the day they'd laid her to rest in a sunny meadow, with no headstone or other sign to mark her grave.

It was the changeling way and what she'd wanted.

"Close to the earth, Rem-Rem. So that my body nourishes the flowers that bloom in the spring."

The other pallbearers had been his mother's closest friends, four women who'd wanted to mother Remi in the aftermath because that was their way. But Remi had only ever had one mother, and he couldn't accept their kindness. After doing the last thing his mother had ever asked of him and laying her to rest in that field eleven years ago today, he'd left with Angel—because Angel let him grieve and run and rage without trying to make it better.

"Just remembering her," Remi said today, and though his sorrow would forever be a part of him, the loss had long ago stopped being an open wound. He could remember the good times now, laugh about how often she'd allowed him to think he was getting away with mischief as a cub. "Thinking how she would've been the warm core of RainFire had she had the chance."

"Yeah, your mom knew how to love with open arms. I miss her."

Angel rarely made such emotional statements; he'd come too late into Gina's life for Gina to bathe him in maternal love as she'd wanted to do, Angel already closed off, remote. Yet there had been the laughter, and the nights when they'd spoken of things that made Gina squeeze Angel's hand while she shook her head in affectionate denial.

Remi had never asked Angel what his mother had told him not to do, what his friend had shared with Gina between them alone.

"I'm thankful every day that she was my mom." Feeling a rustle under the table, Remi reached in without looking and grabbed a cub in leopard form by the scruff of his neck.

"Snuck away from your parents, did you?" he said with a grin, and nipped the cub on the nose before cuddling him against his abdomen. Asher wasn't much more than a year old, all soft edges and playfulness and affection.

"She told me you'd be an amazing alpha if you'd only give yourself the chance," Angel said, his eyes on the cub who was currently trying to chew the tongue of Remi's belt. "Did I ever tell you that?"

You were her greatest pride.

Remi's entire body stiffened at the memory of Auden Scott's whispered words. "No. But I knew what she thought." He let the cub put small paws on the edge of the table so the boy could peer at Angel. "I just didn't believe her."

Angel reached over to tug on the cub's ear, making Asher emit happy sounds. "She'd be so proud of you, Remi. For the pack you've built, the family you've created for all of us—this asshole included."

With that, Angel pushed away from the table to head off for his sleep cycle. Pretty standard for the tiger. He could only do so much emotion before he had to hit the cutoff valve. Remi knew some of why, but he had the feeling that perhaps Angel had told his mother all of it.

As for Remi . . .

He touched the mobile comm he'd put on again today. He'd started wearing it more often after his encounter with Auden Scott. Wasn't that a kicker, that it had taken a Psy with haunted eyes and an uncanny way of staring into forever to make him accept the final gift his mother had ever brought for him?

Chapter 7

RainStone: 27 survivors, including 12 minors, no alpha, no sentinels. Seniormost-ranking survivor a young maternal; she has advised the Peace Accord Resettlement Board of the survivors' unanimous decision to join the new amalgamate pack, SkyDawn.

Any remaining RainStone funds to be added to SkyDawn's. RainStone lands to be surrendered to the trust in return for a compensatory addition to SkyDawn's newly assigned territory.

Transfer signed off by the Resettlement Board in conjunction with all adult survivors of RainStone (see appendix 21C for documents).

—Handwritten entry made in August 1781 in the Changeling Historical Codex, maintained by the Peace Accord Land Trust

"COME ON," REMI said to the escapee in his lap. "Let's get you back to your table."

After chatting with the pajama-clad family, he exited out onto one of the canopy walkways. This early, the world was rich green and darkest gray shrouded in diaphanous mist. Light glowed from the windows of the aeries that perched in the branches of the massive trees that formed the heart of his pack, a scattered string of jewels.

RainFire's small size and disproportionate number of young members was why the aeries remained snugged together in this area, multiple homes perched in the branches of each tree—trees that had been planted long ago by another pack. RainStone hadn't survived as a pack after the Territorial Wars, but it had left the gift of these incredible trees for the future.

It had felt right to incorporate part of the old pack's name in theirs.

Now, he used the high walkways to do the rounds, greeting those who were awake, and ensuring that those who slept were safe. Peace reigned, the only sounds that of the light morning wind—and the quiet movements of leopards on their own business, their bodies whispers of stealth in the mist.

After spotting motion inside the large plas-enclosed activity area that they had on the ground, he jumped to the forest pathway with feline grace and made his way inside.

"Remi!" Little Jojo, her fourth birthday soon on the horizon, ran in his direction.

All glowing brown skin and the yellow-gold eyes of her leopard, her face bearing clawlike markings on the right-hand side of her face, she wasn't wearing her favorite purple corduroy overalls today.

She asked her doting aunt to make a bigger version of her most treasured item of clothing each time she outgrew a pair. He had the feeling he'd one day be seeing an adult Jojo in the same overalls.

The idea made him grin.

Today, however, she'd chosen a sparkly black jumpsuit with golden paw prints all over it. He knew she'd chosen it because Jojo had been opinionated about her fashion choices since the day she could make those wishes known. Her sneakers were a matching gold, her curly black hair pulled into lots of tiny knots all over her head, each knot anchored with a golden hair tie.

"Miss Jojo." Grabbing her racing body before she could run headlong into his legs, he threw her up into the air.

The cub shrieked with laughter before settling into his arms, her legs at his hip, one arm around his back and the other lifting up in a questioning motion. "What's up?"

Man and leopard both grinned. "I should be asking you that. It's dawn o'clock. Why are you awake and playing?" The play area was otherwise deserted of children, though three adults and one juvenile were making use of the climbing frames—and had no doubt kept an eye on Jojo.

"JD's babysitting me," she said with a huge smile. "No rules for Jojo!"

Remi glanced over to where Jayden a.k.a. JD—age sixteen—was making his way up the climbing frame. "I guess that's the prerogative of a big brother. He do your hair?"

"Yup." She tilted her head this way and that to display the tiny knots. "I love JD." The words were innocent in their sincerity.

"He's a good brother." And a young male Remi knew would be a future core member of the pack. "Want to do the rounds with me?"

An enthusiastic nod from the little girl in his arms.

After alerting Jayden that he was taking Jojo with him, Remi put her on the ground. Where she stalked next to him, her tiny hands in the pockets of her jumpsuit. Unlike most young cubs, Jojo *never* forgot to take off her good clothes before shifting. He'd seen her literally growling at her more impatient friends who were yelling at her to just shift.

When they stopped by the kitchen aerie—connected to the dining aerie by a covered walkway—his tiny shadow stood there with a serious listening expression on her face through his entire discussion with Fabien's team.

The trained French chef was one of the founding members of Rain-Fire. Remi had run into the other man—ten years older than him—during his years on the racetrack; he'd soon discovered that Fabien never stayed put in one place long. The same restlessness that drove most loners had led the chef to do stints in five-star restaurants around the world.

When Remi had asked Fabien to help him kick off his new pack for the princely sum of no actual salary but all the hard work he could stand, the tall and rangy "silver fox" of a chef—per Lark—had said he could give him six months.

Turned out grim and temperamental Fabien liked the challenge of setting up a new pack—and he had a soft spot for all the "ferals" Remi had collected into RainFire. Today, he threw Jojo a wink while he stood with his arms folded against the side of a counter. Many an adult woman would've died for that wink, Remi thought in amusement.

Afterward, once they were on the ground again, on their way to the infirmary, his little assistant gave him a proud look. "I was good for a whole hour!"

Remi's leopard huffed inside him at that highly inaccurate gauge of the time involved. "Yes, you did a great job." He tugged at one of her knots, careful not to dislodge it.

"Can I have a cookie now?" A plaintive look. "Fabin always gives me cookies."

The cubs alone could get away with butchering Fabien's name, of which he was very proud, passed down as it had been from his grand-père.

"Strong dominants have a good breakfast," he reminded her. "Cookies are for an afternoon snack."

She sighed. "*Maaaaan.*"

He had to squeeze his eyes shut not to burst out laughing at that mournful exclamation. He had no idea who she'd picked that up from, but it sounded just like an adult except in a pip-squeak voice.

Talking of pip-squeaks, he said, "How's your friend Pip?" The little Arrow boy and Jojo were as thick as thieves, with Pip now having enough control over his psychic abilities that he'd been permitted to overnight with RainFire a couple of times.

Never alone, of course. Kid was too strong. But his Arrow babysitters made it seem as if they were also having a sleepover with a friend—while keeping Pip within their psychic shields. The last babysitter had been an Arrow with gray in his hair who was so obviously out of his element that it would've been funny if it wasn't so touching.

The Arrows, raised without love, without tenderness, without play, were trying so *fucking hard* for their children.

RainFire would always be there for them. Even if it meant handling older Arrows who sat around stiff as mannequins and awkward as all fuck. Last time around, Finn was the one who'd made a breakthrough, talking the gray-haired Arrow into a card game after stating it was about strategy.

Then there was twenty-three-year-old Zinnia. Remi was pretty sure the bubbly and confident maternal—a brunette with *all* the curves— had initiated more than one Arrow into skin privileges. Since Aden hadn't come to Remi with complaints about shell-shocked no-longer-virgin Arrows, he'd left her to it.

A virgin could do a lot worse than an affectionate maternal who liked taking care of people and knew how to be gentle.

"Oh, oh!" Jojo jumped up and down. "Pip's gonna come!" She held up three pudgy little fingers. "In one, two, three"—a little tap on each finger—"days!"

"Is that right?" he said, though he was well aware of the scheduled visit. "You speak on the comm every day?"

"Yup. Every day. Mama says rain or shine, Pip and Jojo gonna talk up a storm." Jojo's tiny hand tucked into his as they walked down the path to RainFire's infirmary "cubes," her smile when she looked up at him a sunbeam of trust.

Kid was going to blow up his heart one day, he knew it. Probably go off roaming when she turned eighteen. Because if Remi had a flaw, it was that he wanted to hover over all his people and keep them safe. But to do that to a pack of predators would be to destroy them.

So he'd learned to deal.

Didn't mean the urge had gone away.

"Yo." Finn raised his hand in a casual hello from where he sat at his desk in the main cube of the three that made up the infirmary. All three were connected in a chain but had biohazard doors and other protocols that meant each could be cut off to create an isolation zone if needed. Painted camouflage green on the outside so they didn't stick out against the trees, the cubes were pristine white on the inside.

The setup had eaten a significant chunk of the pack's budget, but this far out from a major hospital, they needed their own medical care—Remi hoped no one in his pack would ever face the same choice as his mother, but if the worst happened, he wanted them to be able to stay home, near the pack.

"I see you brought along a future sentinel." Finn, the fine strands of his light brown hair pushed back from his face, bumped a fist with Jojo's tiny one.

"Any broken bones or other injuries overnight?" Remi asked.

"Nope. To my great shock." Finn helped Jojo clamber into his lap. Pressing a kiss to her temple, he rubbed her back as she propped her elbows on his desk, her chin in her hands as she looked at the medical charts on the screen with a squint of concentration.

"I hear we have a new neighbor." Leaf green eyes met Remi's.

Remi wasn't surprised at his knowledge—Finn had been on night shift, too, and was their third-in-command. "I'm going to scope out the situation now that I've done my morning walk-through. Just have to walk Jojo back, and have a quick meeting with the junior soldiers."

Part of building a strong young pack was ensuring his packmates knew they had the right to their alpha's attention and time. No adult or cub in RainFire would *ever* feel as if they had to beg for crumbs of attention.

Because Remi was his *mother's* son.

His father's DNA could rot in hell for all he cared.

"I can walk back with Miss Jojo." Finn nuzzled at her cheek. "How about it? You and me and breakfast?"

Jojo's stomach rumbled on cue. "We gotta get JD, too," she said loyally.

Remi rubbed the back of his hand over her cheek. "You did a great job as my assistant today."

Her beaming face stayed with him when he left the pack twenty minutes later, after meeting with the group of shiny-faced new soldiers who were training under pretty much the entire senior team—RainFire didn't have enough people yet to have specialists, so each of them led classes whenever possible.

Today, he left the youths in the care of Jojo's thirty-one-year-old aunt, Serenity. Look at her in her grim-faced senior soldier avatar and you'd never peg her as the same Aunt Sisi who sewed Jojo's clothes and who'd been known to play princess tea parties with her behind closed doors.

Remi left to the sound of her ordering the trainees to fall in line for a "wake up your lazy butts run." He'd decided to make his journey on foot, too—and had made the call to stay in human form on the off chance that he needed to speak to the new resident.

Several familiar scents brushed over his skin as he passed, the lingering echo of his people coming and going. Those scents thinned out the farther he ran, until by the time he reached the border with the Scotts, he couldn't scent anything but the myriad tones of a forest clothed in the colors of fall. That didn't mean a soldier hadn't come by during a regular security run, just that enough time had come that the scent had dissipated.

Chest heaving after the pace he'd set himself, he stood in the trees and took in the cabin. Prefabricated, the contractors had put it up in a day, but it was a good imitation of a real log cabin. Mist curled around the edges of it, the morning light muted. Clouds had grayed out the sunrise, the mountain in a moody frame of mind.

Light against the nearest window, a yellow rectangle in the gray.

The front door opened before he could decide on his next move.

Auden Scott stepped out, her hands cupped around a mug of something that sent tendrils of steam into the air, curls of white against the cloud-shadowed fall foliage in the background. She was dressed in black tights and an oversize sweatshirt in the same dark hue. Clothing flexible enough to accommodate a belly that could mean only one thing.

Auden Scott was very, very pregnant.

Chapter 8

We've authorized the severance experiment by a unanimous vote. I hate keeping secrets from our people, but I had to agree with Payal's suggestion that we keep this information on a need-to-know basis for now. No general public notice.

Threads of fear hum through the Honeycomb on a continuous basis these days. Everyone is so scared. Telling them we've decided to consciously tear the PsyNet into pieces risks catastrophic panic.

—Message from Ivy Jane Zen, president, Empathic Collective, to Vasic Zen, Arrow (27 August 2083)

KALEB HAD ALWAYS thought he'd be the one at the center of the breakaway PsyNet island the Ruling Coalition had been planning since it became clear that the vast sprawl of the PsyNet was fragmenting at an unstoppable pace. He was the strongest, a dual cardinal who could hold the island together through brute power alone.

"That's the problem," Payal had pointed out during the decisive meeting where they'd agreed to this attempt. "We have only one Kaleb Krychek. For the plan to work, the psychic island has to be maintained by ordinary people."

So here they were, about to gamble a hundred volunteer lives on the shoulders of those same volunteers. The group stood on a large football field where medics and empaths could monitor them with ease, and where their physical reactions could be recorded by multiple watchful cameras.

Others stood ready on the psychic plane, prepared to make note of every tiny fact.

Each volunteer had spent the past month interacting on the psychic plane with the others so that they could create a temporary net of their own if the separation from the main body of the PsyNet led to their complete fall from the network all Psy needed to survive. Lose the bio-feedback and they'd die in a matter of minutes if not less.

There were no children in the experimental group. The risk was too high and children could not consent. Kaleb would've vetoed the idea had anyone floated it, but he'd forgotten that the Ruling Coalition was no Psy Council. For one, the President of the Empathic Collective was a member of the Coalition—Ivy Jane Zen's mere presence meant certain things were simply off the table as a matter of course.

Today, he sent one last telepathic message: *I am linked to all of you, and can literally throw you back into another part of the PsyNet if the experiment fails. Do not panic.*

Their agreement was a murmur of voices at the back of his mind. And maybe it was Sahara's influence, but he found himself following up what should've been his final statement with: *You should be proud of your courage. Today, you fight for the survival of our very people.*

Because if the PsyNet failed with no alternative in sight, the vast majority of Psy would die. It was that simple.

The people in the field stood straighter at his words.

Brace, he warned, then began his task: to deliberately isolate the solid area of the PsyNet to which the volunteers were linked. It didn't take much energy—he and the others had chosen this section for the experiment because it was a single undamaged piece surrounded by thin patches prone to failure.

The medics sent him continuous updates as he worked, as did Payal on behalf of the anchor responsible for this region.

Stable.

Stable.

Stable.

Kaleb cut the island's final link to the PsyNet, and was almost at the point of believing it would work when a shout went up from multiple M-Psy: *Physical collapse! Neural shutdown in progress! Activate emergency procedure!*

Kaleb was ahead of them, had already wrenched the experimental group into another part of the Net—one that remained connected to the larger whole, for all that the whole was badly damaged.

Status?

Stabilizing rapidly, was the response of the head medic. *They didn't lose their connection to their piece of the PsyNet at any time, so I don't know why their brains began to shut down. Not enough biofeedback perhaps?*

That can't be it, Kaleb said, *not when the LaurenNet was much smaller.* He'd asked Judd's permission before sharing the full details of the Lauren family's successful defection from the PsyNet.

"Share it if it helps," the other man had said after quickly confirming with the other adults involved. "We understand the consequences if you can't figure out a solution to the collapse."

Annihilation.

Millions of minds dead, ninety-nine percent of the Psy race erased from the planet.

The reminder of his discussion with Judd made him reconsider their plan. *A hundred was the wrong place to start,* he telepathed Payal. *We need to begin small, and work our way up to the maximum viable number.*

Possible. But the more we fragment, the less certain I am that my anchors can service these islands. The LaurenNet had no anchor, but was heavily skewed toward high-Gradients—including a cardinal. I was hoping we'd balance that out with the larger group.

Kaleb had hoped the same. *We need to try regardless.*

Agreed. But we need to check with Ivy Jane on the advised recovery period for the volunteers.

The answer was two weeks.

I know it's a long time with the increased degradation of the Net, the empath said, *but this definitely won't work if our volunteers are exhausted.*

A rapid-fire exchange between all the members of the Coalition, and the time for the next attempt was set for fourteen days hence.

Dropping out of the PsyNet after helping with the aftermath, Kaleb opened his eyes in his Moscow office. When he turned to the floor-to-ceiling window that faced the square below the building, it was to a misty rain and a brilliant array of umbrellas.

Lenik, he telepathed. *I am no longer offline.*

A knock on his office door, before his junior aide walked in. His senior aide was at present doing a historical deep dive into the PsyNet, to ensure they hadn't overlooked any possible solutions.

"Sir," Lenik said, far more confident these days than he'd been back when he'd started working for Kaleb. "I have the report you requested on the Scott family's new base in Sunset Falls, Tennessee."

A more unusual place for the HQ of a major Psy family, Kaleb couldn't imagine. Built in the shadow of the Great Smoky Mountains, the town had about forty thousand majority-human residents scattered across a large area, with the town center not much more than a single main street with the odd offshoot.

Trees and other foliage dominated, with not a skyscraper in sight. From the images Sahara had pulled up online when he'd mentioned the anomaly to her the other night, the place was awash in fall color at this time of year, the vivid reds, glowing oranges, and intense yellows of the tree leaves living up to the town's name.

"How stunning." His lover's face had lit up. "I'm dragging you there the next time we can take a break. But I see what you mean—it's not exactly London, Milan, or Las Vegas, is it?"

Those were just three of the metropolitan cities where the Scotts had a presence.

Yet it was to this remote location that the Scotts had moved their center of operations after the death of their matriarch Shoshanna roughly two months ago. The Scotts had owned the small compound for twenty years—but Kaleb understood it to have been used as a training ground for younger members of the family.

Now, and though the family had made no announcement about the shift in HQ, it was the residence of Auden Scott, the official Scott CEO. That made it their HQ, no matter how many shiny buildings they owned or occupied in major centers. "Summary?"

"No information anywhere as to the reason for the move, but I was able to confirm Auden Scott's residence at the location. She was spotted in a vehicle that passed through the main street."

Lenik showed him an image that was blurred at the edges from how quickly it had been snapped, but there was no doubt: that was Henry and Shoshanna's daughter.

"The same vehicle has since been at the compound," Lenik added. "We can't rule out travel via teleportation, and I did pick up a rumor of a jet-chopper at the compound, but I've been unable to track down any sightings of her at their other properties, so chances are high that she's still in that region."

"Thank you, Lenik," Kaleb said, his eyes on the report.

Lenik left to return to his desk.

The data was as thin as the aide had warned. Nothing in it even came close to addressing the question of *why* the Scott CEO had moved to a location more suitable for changelings than Psy.

It only added to the mystery of the enigma who was Shoshanna's unlikely successor: barely twenty-four years of age, and—*critically*—with no indication that she'd been handed some of the reins at an earlier age in preparation for the move, Auden Scott should not have been in the CEO position.

This wasn't the same as the situation with Pax Marshall, another young CEO. Kaleb had known of and negotiated with Pax as Marshall Hyde's proxy prior to Pax's takeover of the Marshall Group. Auden Scott, in contrast, had been functionally invisible until she'd emerged as a full-fledged CEO. He'd heard she'd sat in on a few negotiations led by Shoshanna's chief aide, but that was about it.

Of course, Shoshanna hadn't intended to die so young.

And, given the cold purity of the gaze that had held Kaleb's during a negotiation soon after Shoshanna's death, Auden had more of Shoshanna in her than might be indicated by her age.

That made her dangerous.

Chapter 9

Silence was a program instituted by our people from 1979 to the end of 2081. During the existence of that program, we, the Psy, conditioned all emotion out of ourselves and our children.

We believed that such conditioning would help our people control the side effects of our abilities. These side effects include minor to major mental instability, uncontrollable rage, and homicidal acts done without intent.

The aim of this essay is to discuss Silence in the context of the ongoing fragmentation and possible catastrophic collapse of the PsyNet. The question is whether Silence is the reason for the damage to the PsyNet—or if a return to Silence is the answer.

—Essay by Catalina NightStar (16), for Modern History module II

THE AIR WAS clean and icy in Auden's lungs, the steam from her heated nutrient drink a welcome balm against her face. Color caught her eye everywhere she looked, the forest ablaze in such brilliant hues as she'd never imagined.

A bump inside her, a sudden shocking reminder of the life within. Shifting her mug to a one-handed grip, she cradled her belly with the other, for the first time feeling as if she could show what she felt without it being used against her. "You're safe," she murmured to the child who shouldn't exist—but whom she would defend to her last breath.

No one would do to this child what had been done to her. Was still being done to her.

A rustle in the trees.

She jerked up her head . . . and wasn't the least surprised when the cat prowled out of the shadows, pure, taut power and languid motion. All she felt was a knee-trembling relief. He was *real*. She hadn't imagined him in the fragmented landscape that had been her mind until four weeks ago, when the last of the pieces had finally come together and *stayed* together.

"Which cat?" she found herself saying when he was close enough to hear her, her breath a puff of white in the air.

"Leopard." A rumble of a voice that rolled over her in a tactile brush.

She continued to cradle her stomach, even as her heart accelerated. She knew it was rude to stare as she was doing, but she'd lost a lot of her social filters during the years when she hadn't been present. "I thought I imagined you."

He held up his forearm, muscular and with visible veins. "Do you remember?"

Her gaze hooked on the streamlined black comm device.

Fingers gripping her upper arm, eyes that weren't human looking into hers.

"Did I read the device?" she asked. "I'm sorry, I have no memory of it."

Eyes narrowing, he dropped his arm. "You were pretty out of it that day. Medicated?"

"Something like that." Auden wished it was that simple, wished she'd just been sedated—because the truth was far worse.

Charisma had fought with her about her decision to come here, reminding her that she was in the most vulnerable state of her life, but Auden had needed time to think, to *decide*. She couldn't do that in

Shoshanna's house, her mother's influence in every mind that worked there, embedded into the very walls of the building.

Part of Auden had expected Charisma to stop her—because whatever it might say on paper, the truth was that Auden wasn't in charge in that house. Neither was Hayward, Shoshanna's younger brother, and the supposed second-in-command. Auden still had no idea why Charisma had folded at last, but no doubt the older woman was playing a deep game.

Regardless, Auden had made it here.

Still, now she questioned her stubbornness. She had her reasons. Very good reasons. Deadly reasons. But as a result of her own decision, she was now face-to-face with a predator while all alone on a mountain, far from any source of help that could arrive fast enough to stop a leopard's strike.

It wasn't as if her psychometric ability could help her here—she'd heard that some Ps-Psy could turn what they read against a target, literally take violent energy and channel it, but she'd never seen a concrete example.

It sounded like a myth made up by young psychometrics to her. As far as she was concerned, Ps abilities were among the most passive in the Psy race. That she was a 9.4 didn't make any difference. Neither did the fact that she had a basic level of telepathy—a bare 2 on the Gradient.

Nothing enough to take on changeling shields should this leopard turn aggressive.

"You sure you should be up here alone?" His eyes, such a clear topaz, darkened. "Cubs have been known to come early." A nod at her belly.

Auden's spine stiffened. "I've been told that asking about a woman's pregnancy without invitation is a social faux pas among the emotional races."

He shrugged those big shoulders. "Usually. But these are exigent circumstances—specifically that you are an *extremely* pregnant woman in a cabin on my border. I'm going to feel responsible if anything goes wrong."

Auden didn't soften her stance.

Care, she'd come to learn, even *true* care, could be a front for terrible ugliness. Never would she have believed that her father would go along with her mutilation. He'd spoiled her as much as any child could be spoiled in Silence. In her secret heart, Auden had believed he loved her.

Yet he'd hurt her in a way brutal and permanent.

"I'm only just past the seven-month mark, with no indicators of a possible early birth."

The leopard's gaze flashed to that inhuman green-gold, making her skin prickle in warning. "Did Ms. Wai give you my comm code? Name's Remi."

Remi. She either hadn't known that or hadn't remembered it.

"If anything does happen," he continued, "we have a qualified doctor in the pack. He recently completed a unit on treating Psy patients, too."

Auden wondered why a changeling healer in an isolated pack would want to know how to treat Psy patients, but she had the feeling Remi wouldn't answer that particular question. "Is your full name Remington Denier? If so, I have your code."

Charisma had included that information as part of the packet for Auden's "time in the wilderness"—though Auden'd had no idea to whom it related until this moment, when the leopard nodded, but added, "Call me Remington at your own peril." Easy words, but his eyes were primal in their intensity.

The hairs rose on her arms, fear a frigid whisper on the back of her neck. "What?"

"You're not like when I first met you. If not medication, then what?"

Auden's blood ran cold. "I was recovering from a head injury," she said, the cover story one Charisma had devised for her. "I really shouldn't have come out, but I made a miscalculation as to my health status."

SHE was lying to him. Remi knew that as well as he knew that he'd been more than rude in his bluntness. But that was the thing with Psy who clung to Silence as so many of them did so close to the fall of the Protocol—you had to be in their face to get any kind of an answer.

Give them any wiggle room and they'd take it.

His leopard prowled against his skin, intrigued by the cub growing inside Auden. That was an alpha thing. The cat liked to keep an eye on the pregnant members of its pack. Apparently, the same feline had decided to extend its protectiveness to this non-packmate because she was alone while in a deeply vulnerable state.

"Auden Scott," Zaira had said when he'd asked the Arrows for intel, "is peculiarly little known for being the child of not one, but two Councilors. Political dynasty aside, she should be sitting on dual financial empires except that it appears Henry chose a different heir some years prior to his death. It's odd, because she was raised in his household, not Shoshanna's."

"Is she Shoshanna's official heir?"

A nod. "The two must've agreed on that, with Henry giving up rights for some unknown reason."

All that financial power and still, Auden remained a cipher, unknown and unseen. Per Zaira, even the squad hadn't been able to confirm her specific psychic ability, but if the rumors they'd picked up were right, then Auden Scott had no offensive capabilities.

"Possible high-Gradient psychometric," Zaira had said.

She'd been leaning back against a majestic sugar maple at the time, one booted foot braced on the distinctive bark of the trunk as she peeled an orange for a cub who'd handed it to her. She'd been using a razor-sharp throwing knife to do it.

Psychometric.

"Those are Psy who can pick up information from objects?" Remi had asked, to be certain.

"Yes. How much and the exact parameters of what they can pick up depends on the specific psychometric, but in general, it's considered an academic ability. A rare few are attached to search and rescue teams on the tracking end, but most work for museums and other institutions.

Can't have been easy being born a psychometric in a family like the Scotts. They're known for aggressive telepaths."

And today here was this Ps-Psy, seven months pregnant in an inimical environment.

Remi was now responsible for her. It didn't matter if she told him she could look after herself. A human might call that overbearing male chauvinism, but a female alpha would've had the exact same reaction.

It was built into their DNA.

"You have enough food, nutrients for your stay?" he asked, a niggling sense of having missed something important gnawing at him.

Her expression didn't alter. She was giving a good impression of being a remote machine, when the woman who'd read his comm had done so with tears shimmering in her eyes. "Yes. If I need more, I can fly myself out anytime I please."

"Make sure you check the weather every single time, even if it looks clear." He wondered if he'd only gotten that glimpse of emotion on their first meeting due to her head injury—*this* woman with her frigid expression was a Scott, had to be the real Auden. "Mountains can be changeable as a rule."

"I appreciate the data." Those piercing eyes wouldn't look away from his in what at any other time he'd have taken as an act of dominance.

Today, he brushed it off, his leopard's protective instincts overwhelming any sense of aggression. "Stay safe."

He could feel her eyes between his shoulder blades until he was deep into the trees.

A shiver rocking him, he looked back once he was far enough into the forest that there was no way she could track him . . . to see her staring after him, her gaze along the exact line he'd taken. Just a Ps? He narrowed his eyes. Maybe. And maybe, she had more of a hunter's instincts than was public knowledge.

It wasn't until he was some distance away, the wind rushing past his body in a familiar cascade of rich earth, and the intoxicating "green" that was the forest no matter what the season that he realized what had been bothering him—her *scent*. It wasn't a muddy funhouse mirror any-more, was instead a lush complexity as enticing as a delicate caress across his bare skin.

Whatever had happened to Auden Scott, she was now out on the other side.

Chapter 10

A9: I've experienced increased sensitivity the deeper I get into my pregnancy. I can still sleep in my bed, but I think that's only because I've had it for three years. I tried to use a new piece of mass-produced furniture yesterday and nearly had an aneurysm from the scream of voices inside my head. Am I going insane?

—Post on Psycho & Metrics: A forum for Ps-Psy (26 September 2083)

HER INTERACTION WITH Remington Denier—Remi—was at the forefront of Auden's mind when she finally walked back inside the cabin. The tip of her nose felt like ice, but her skin was invigorated and her mind alive with fascination.

She knew that Remi likely wasn't worried about her at all, that the entire conversation had been a clever game of chess to gain more information from her, but regardless . . . it had been odd, how he'd looked at her.

As if he wanted to strangle her for being out here on her own.

Frowning, Auden shook off the thought. Remington Denier had given no indication of any urge to take such violent action. That was just her making things up to fill the gaps in her knowledge of how normal people were meant to behave.

Because if there was one thing Auden knew, it was that she wasn't normal.

She ran her hand over the small chair she'd made herself using materials she'd fabricated with her own three-dimensional printer. It was badly done. Crooked joins, scratches where she'd slipped with a tool, and no real aesthetic to its chunky frame, but to her, it was as precious as gold because when she touched it, she tasted no one else's memories, no one else's leftover emotions.

It was hers to use, with no ghost hanging off it.

The same with the seat cushion she'd sewn herself. Of course others had handled the fabric, the stuffing, but no one tended to get particularly emotional about a bolt of fabric, or a packet of needles, or a bag of stuffing. In general, the material needed to create an item received less handling than the completed object—and the imprint usually faded if she set the materials aside for a month or so.

Imprints on completed objects tended to be "stickier." Whether because the object was an emotive thing in itself—an example might be a cradle handcrafted for a beloved child—or because of the person who'd utilized it.

One of the Ps-Psy in the small but active online group of which Auden was a member under a pseudonym had once gone to a relative's home and sat in a chair . . . only to be jolted with images of blood dripping off a blade. His relative had found the chair at a secondhand shop, and it had no provenance.

Now that psychometric couldn't sit on any chair without suffering a panic attack.

Auden had previously relied on mass-produced items, which usually only held a background murmur that faded within a matter of days or weeks, but her pregnancy had pushed her ability into hyperdrive. She'd asked about it in the group, received commiserations from several other members. It turned out that pregnancy-related sensitivity was a known side effect for a minority of the group.

Kellie99 (Admin): I almost ended up locked in a psych ward—gee, that sure would've helped!

Sl8q: What helped me was sourcing goods made by empaths. They're rare because Es are needed in other capacities, but so worth the peace they bring. (p.s. Kellie99, is that the reason behind the name of this forum?)

Kellie99 (Admin): Ding ding! I set up the forum the day after I escaped incarceration by PsyMed. Rest of our own damn race can't be bothered to know anything about us or how our brains function. Sorry you're having to deal with this A9. You'd think they'd have figured out a solution by now.

Hive2907: I found it helpful to use natural materials that I—or my mother—gathered. My mother is a calm individual who tends not to leave "busy" imprints, and while neither one of us is very handy, we managed to put together a few rough bits of furniture between us.

B2cc: I suggest an investment in a 3D printer. (p.s. Kellie99, I thought the forum name was funny even when I was pretending to be Silent. Heh!)

Auden had tried for the E-sourced items at first, but they were snapped up at the speed of light by other Ps-Psy in the same position—and financially speaking, she had far more resources than many of her fellow psychometrics. She hadn't attempted to outbid them.

Instead, she'd gone for the printing option. Only . . .

"This chair will collapse if I sit on it." She sighed as she accepted the truth; it wasn't the object's fault she'd put it together with such a lack of skill or finesse.

At least her cabin was usable. Soon as her mind had begun to function well enough to consider her options, she'd ordered this build—a build that was machine prefabricated. The contractors who'd put it together had done so using heavy-duty gloves, under secondary shielding provided by a Scott security team.

She'd then left the cabin "fallow" for a month.

So far, she'd only picked up the odd "ghost" in the materials, mostly faint echoes of a detail-oriented machine operator. It helped that she had a habit of wearing socks most of the time.

It wasn't, however, psychometric tripwires alone about which Auden had to worry.

Utilizing financial sleight of hand that she'd learned at her father's knee, she'd secretly purchased a small but high-spec surveillance detection device. She'd run the first scan upon her arrival, discovered two cameras and three listening devices, but would do another scan today to confirm she'd eliminated the bugs. After that, she'd check the bunker for any hidden threats—just in case.

Then she'd consider how to create a foolproof exit strategy for the child in her womb.

For now, she needed to put up her feet—and with the chair out of the question, it would have to be the futon laid directly on the floor. An impractical bed for a woman in her state; getting either down to it, or up from it was a major operation.

It was also the only option.

"I haven't slept for the past week," she'd told Charisma when the other woman balked at Auden's refusal to even consider a bed frame. "I've started to sense details from the workers who assembled my bed here at the house, and I've had that for years."

Charisma's pupils had expanded. "Your sensitivity is that intense?"

"Unfortunately."

The futon itself was borrowed from B2cc, a fellow psychometric who'd offered it to pregnant designation-mates.

B2cc: I've given birth and my imprint sensing is back to normal. This
will carry my imprint, but I've heard that Ps-Psy leave weak imprints
as a rule, so if anyone wants to test it, you're welcome.

Auden, sleep-deprived and desperate, had taken the invitation. And
would report back that the woman who'd offered the futon had been
right. She could sense the other Ps-Psy, but it was a fuzzy knowing at
best. No hard edges. No intrusiveness.

Even though they'd never met, Auden trusted her fellow anonymous psychometrics in a way she trusted no one else. They wanted
nothing from her except information—the same thing she wanted from
them in return. The kindness shown by B2cc . . . it had been an unexpected and generous gift, and Auden intended to pay that kindness
forward.

Because Ps-Psy were on their own.

No one had ever studied psychometrics. Likely because they were no
threat to anyone. Despite the legends, there was no evidence that a
psychometric had ever killed someone using their ability.

Even empaths could wound or kill people with their ability. It hurt
the E to do so, but at least they *had* an offensive tool in their toolbox.
Could be that was where the legends of "assassin psychometrics" had
come from—because while the Council had left Ps-Psy alone during
their attempted purge of empaths, psychometrics were as tied to emotion
as empaths.

The big difference, however, was that Ps-Psy could distance themselves by only working with objects old enough that the emotional resonance was so faded as to be negligible. Empaths had no such choice.
Es also came into *direct* contact with violent emotions, the reason why
they could utilize it as a weapon in exigent circumstances.

Prior to the fall of Silence, Auden and others like her had only experienced emotion thirdhand. Other people's emotions, other people's
memories. Imprinted onto the objects they'd left behind. Add in the

passage of time as occurred with most items handled in museums and Ps-Psy had never been a threat to the protocol.

Especially since they'd never been one of the more numerous designations. Their numbers had continued to decline in Silence because it was only the odd academic family that bred for a psychometric. Families like Auden's wanted offensive powers. If not that, then at least a designation like F, which would add to the family coffers.

Instead, her parents—two telepaths who were both beyond 9 on the Gradient—had produced a 9.4 psychometric.

Older psychometrics on the forum said that back during their time, they used to believe the NetMind was the reason for rogue psychometric births. That the neosentience that was the librarian and guardian of the Net was balancing out the psychic ecosystem to stop the extinction of their designation.

Auden had never come into contact with the NetMind and word on the Net was that it was dead, driven mad then murdered by the horrific ongoing breakdown of the PsyNet.

She rubbed a fisted hand over her heart.

"Thank you," she whispered. "If you're the reason I'm me."

Being a psychometric was all that had saved her from becoming a mirror of her father and mother. She had touched emotion all her life, even if it had been muted, and it had forever altered her. She'd never treat any sentient being as disposable. And she'd *never* hurt her child in the pursuit of power.

"I'll protect you," she said as she levered herself down to the futon by bracing one hand atop a short bedside dresser she'd placed there for just this purpose. "I'll find a way."

Because while she could protect her child's mind inside her own, she couldn't protect their body. That didn't even take the devastation in the PsyNet into account. Her baby was going to be born into a world where her life hung by a psychic thread—and into a house where people were far *too* interested in a pregnancy that should never have happened.

Her mouth tightened.

Exhaling after she was settled on the futon, she reached into the last drawer of the dresser to retrieve a small and narrow black box. When she opened it, it was to reveal a gleaming black laser weapon.

Small enough to fit into her palm.

Three settings, including a stun that could kill.

A gift from her father on her fifteenth birthday.

"Secrets can be power, Auden," he'd told her, his big hand warm on her shoulder. "This weapon is our secret. It's recorded nowhere, and has no history. It can never be traced back to you."

"The imprints, Father?"

"It's new, machine fabricated with only minor handling. Leave it aside for a year to eighteen months to ensure no imprints remain, then I'll take you shooting."

He never had done the latter. Because Auden hadn't been Auden by then.

She still couldn't bring herself to touch the weapon. Her stomach lurched at the very idea, disturbing the child growing inside her.

Slamming the lid shut, she used her telepathy to soothe the mind that was yet amorphous.

She'd get to the gun, just not today.

Today, she'd sit in this cabin far from the dangers of the Scott household, and she'd work on how to protect the baby her mother had wanted so much that she'd consented to it in her role as the person with authority over an impaired Auden.

Now Charisma and Dr. Verhoeven would carry out her ruthless and brilliant mother's orders. Their loyalty to Shoshanna was a truth unshakable—and no matter the lip service paid to Auden's role as CEO, or her uncle's role as head of the family, Charisma was the one in charge, the one to whom Shoshanna had entrusted the codes needed to run the entire Scott operation.

And two days ago, Charisma had ordered an intensive brain scan of Auden's baby—even though her unborn child didn't even *have* a fully formed brain. Auden had permitted it only because it had been noninvasive and caused her baby no distress. She'd had to grit her teeth throughout, however; remind herself that she was playing the long game.

Her silent rage had been a heat scalding enough to start a forest fire.

She turned to the box that held the gun, picked it up again. It didn't matter what it did to her to handle a weapon, didn't matter if doing violence would destroy a piece of her. This wasn't about her. She was already damaged in ways nothing would heal, but her baby? Her baby had a chance to live a life free of pain and fear.

Auden opened the box.

Chapter 11

REMI USUALLY NEVER hesitated to share data with the Arrows; Rain-Fire and the squad were friends as well as allies. But he had no intention of doing so when it came to Auden's pregnancy. His leopard growled at the idea of it, the human half in full agreement. It went against every ounce of honor in his body to pass on a truth so private.

"It's not like her pregnancy is a security threat," he said to Finn the next morning—because he *had* told their healer; Finn needed to be prepared in case shit went wrong.

"No," Finn agreed as he danced out of the way of a kick from Remi.

Like most healers, Finn hated violence. But also like most healers, he had a protective streak so wide it was a six-lane highway. Add in the fact that he was conscious of RainFire being a small and isolated pack, and here they were.

"I want to be trained," he'd declared. "I'm an adult in good condition. I need to be able to protect our vulnerable."

He was right.

Despite knowing that, Remi had to force himself to carry through on any strikes that might land—alphas just *did not* hurt their healers unless they were unhinged assholes.

It helped that Finn hadn't started out green as grass. He'd picked up bits and pieces during his sojourn as a relief healer in other packs, but had never done the full course intended to arm noncombatants in a pack.

Remi and his sentinels had fixed that.

The weekly sessions were to ensure he didn't forget.

"And," Finn said, his chest heaving as they circled each other in the small clearing they used as a practice ground, "I'd say it's her personal business unless she makes it ours. Woman's just minding her own right now.

"Plus, we've got no hard evidence that she was involved in what happened to Aden and Zaira in that bunker—didn't Aden say she doesn't appear to have had much power until after Shoshanna's death?"

Remi launched another attack.

Finn kicked forest floor debris right up into his face before spraying him with a disgusting smelling spray that he'd pulled from his back jeans pocket. Because with Finn, they often trained as if he'd been attacked while at work in the infirmary. Today, that meant jeans and an old blue shirt with the sleeves rolled up.

And the foul spray.

Fuck, that was rank.

"What the hell?" Remi choked on the stink, his forearm raised to his face in a vain attempt at blocking it.

Finn backed off, coughing—while somehow grinning at the same time, his leopard a glow in the green of his eyes. "You and Angel both told me to play to my strengths. Lots of toxic stuff to throw and spray in an infirmary. Don't worry, this one is just stinky."

Healers. Smart and smartasses with it.

His leopard proud even as it wanted to bring down curses on Finn's smart head, Remi held up his hands. "I surrender. Let's get the hell away before that stench sinks into our skin."

A smug Finn put away his dastardly concoction and did a graceful bow. "I accept your defeat." His face broke out into another huge grin as he rose up from the bow. "I also plan to tell everyone."

Remi growled without any real threat in it; it was good to see Finn happy. "I'm going to run up to the cabin again today," he said after they escaped the biohazard area. "Check she's doing all right."

Finn pressed his lips together. "To be honest," he said, hands on his hips, "I'd feel better if you did. She must have a senior M-Psy on speed dial, but that won't help if she trips and falls and knocks herself unconscious."

"Great, thanks for that image." Which would now haunt him every hour that Auden was in that remote cabin. It didn't matter that he barely knew her; protectiveness was built into his nature.

She was happy the last time she wore that watch. No pain, just comfort at being with you, at lying by the window in the sun, with the forest just outside.

His chest clenched. Because yeah, there *was* a little of the personal between them. Whatever had been wrong with Auden that first day, whether she was lying or not about the brain injury, she'd given him a gift beyond price when she'd spoken of his mother's last days, leaving him with an image of a leopard at peace, happy and warm.

He owed her in a way he'd never forget.

"Welcome to the inside of a healer's brain." Finn's voice brought him back to the now. "I am ever haunted by thoughts of future calamity."

A clear ping of sound.

Glancing down, Finn grimaced at the message that had popped up on the mobile comm he never took off; the pack had funded that because, quite frankly, he needed it given their limited numbers and the youthful skew of their population.

"Talking of which," the healer muttered, "possible broken ribs in a group of juveniles who decided they wanted to practice sparring without oversight. They're about a thirty-minute run away."

"How serious? You need me?" Remi was tied to Finn by a bond of blood, the act an intense and private one between alpha and healer that made Finn one of Remi's in a way that had left Finn in tears for the closing of a circle that had been open too long in his life. It also meant Finn could pull the pack's energy from Remi during a complicated healing.

But Finn shook his head. "At least one of the juveniles has completed the first aid course and thinks it might just be heavy bruising, but he isn't comfortable making that call." He changed direction toward the infirmary, no doubt to grab his medical kit, his chest reverberating with his leopard's grumble. "How our young survive to adulthood, I have no idea."

Remi grabbed the back of the healer's neck without aggression, squeezed. "A combination of dumb luck and strong changeling bones."

Finn's cat continued to grumble, but he didn't shake off Remi's touch. Which Remi had initiated on purpose—because Finn was getting grumpier with each day that passed and contact with his alpha would calm his cat.

Touch was the cornerstone of the relationships in a pack.

Remi knew the reason behind Finn's behavior. Healers loved family, loved children, and while being the healer of a small and close pack like RainFire helped feed some of that need, what Finn really needed was a long-term lover or mate.

That was simply how healers worked.

They liked to pair bond and often did so earlier than other change-lings. Finn's closest healer friend, Tamsyn, had mated at only nineteen years of age, and while she was an outlier in terms of how early she'd found her mate, *all* of Finn's healer friends of a similar age were happily settled.

Unfortunately, Finn had never found anyone with whom he wanted to tangle on a more than friendly basis. A worried Remi had even tried to play matchmaker by sending Finn off to conferences for changeling healers, in the hope that he'd find love among his peers, but all Finn had found were interesting new medical techniques.

While he did have friends in RainFire and other packs with which he exchanged skin privileges, that was getting rare enough to con-cern Remi. Changelings needed contact, affection, touch, to be at their best. Dominants got aggressive without it, but healers? Healers got sad and . . . broken.

"You need skin-to-skin contact," he said now, after another squeeze. "None of the single women in the pack would turn you down." Finn wasn't just liked, he was loved. A heart piece, without which the pack would never quite function right.

The other man's eyes shone wet when they met Remi's. "It's not enough anymore." A raw confession. "I keep thinking what's wrong with me that I can't make that bond? I'm a *healer*. We bond as easily as we breathe."

This was one of the things no one could teach you about being alpha. Protection was one thing, care quite another. "There's nothing wrong with you, Finn," he said, holding those leaf green eyes to drill that home. "You just haven't found your forever yet. She's probably pissed off about it, too."

A snort of laughter from Finn before he looked away for a second.

Only healers could do that in a pack—just break an alpha's gaze. But he turned back, and didn't avoid the embrace Remi gave him.

Just because Finn was strong and intelligent and held it together no matter what the emergency didn't mean he didn't also need his alpha. "I know it's not enough," Remi murmured, "but take the gift of skin privileges your friends want to give you. It'll help you maintain until you find the one who's meant to be yours."

Finn's arms clenched around Remi for a moment before he pulled back and gave a small nod. "You'd tell me if I was falling down on the job, wouldn't you?"

"Finn, that's the one thing about which I never worry—you'd be dying but still trying to help people." He tapped one palm against the other man's cheek. "But if it makes you feel better, yes, I would kick your skinny ass if you weren't living up to your promise to the pack. Message me once you've seen the juveniles."

Finn's lips curved before he turned and jogged the rest of the way to the infirmary. Right before he pulled open the door, he yelled, "My ass is prime, I'll have you know! Had an entire hunting party of bridesmaids tell me so last time I visited San Francisco!"

Chuckling as the healer vanished inside the infirmary cube, Remi turned on his heel to check up on the current biggest pain in his neck. The juveniles' antics, at least, he could predict. Auden Scott? Fucking nightmare of a problem that technically had nothing to do with him— and that would gnaw at him every second she was in his vicinity.

So *of course* he reached their border to discover her holding a deadly little gun all wrong while facing a homemade target—a piece of card stuck to a big stick that she'd poked into the ground. On the card was a wonky hand-drawn bull's-eye.

Then she shot and it went so wide of the mark that it wasn't even in the same galaxy.

His leopard hung its head in reflected shame.

Groaning, Remi deliberately made a lot of noise as he walked out so that she wouldn't shoot him by accident—though her chances of hitting him were so low as to be miniscule. When she swung around with the gun pointed, he held up his own hands. "I mean, you have a point one percent chance of actually hitting me, but don't shoot."

A glare.

Yes, a definite glare, before she smoothed it over with the ice-coated exterior of Silent perfection she'd shown him yesterday. His heart kicked anyway, his leopard on the hunt.

There you are, the cat purred.

"I apologize." She lowered the weapon and the movement disturbed the air currents, sending more of her luscious scent in his direction. "I didn't intend to convey aggression . . . but you did sneak up on me."

His body stirred in a way unexpected, as drawn to this Auden as he had been disturbed by the woman he'd first met. "I made enough noise for a herd of drunk bears."

This time, she looked like she *really* wanted to shoot him.

Amused, he nodded at her target before she could give in to her rage. "Let me guess—your first time with a laser weapon?"

A pause and he knew her training was telling her to lie—according to what he'd picked up from hanging out with Arrows, powerful Psy were taught to cover any and all vulnerabilities. Or they had been under Silence. Who knew how long it would take for that to change, or if it ever would. A century of indoctrination wasn't exactly easy to shrug off.

Auden finally seemed to realize there was no point in lying when he'd witnessed her stumbling attempted shot. "Yes," she said at last. "It's probably not safe for you to be close by." A grudging warning.

His cat, contrary feline that it was, liked her better for being aggravated by his teasing. "I can't leave you here with that." He sighed to further nudge up her anger, to better see *her*. "I'll lose my mind worrying that you'd lasered off your foot or blasted your cheekbone."

Her eyes went black.

Remi stayed relaxed, his hands on his hips—he'd seen other Psy eyes do that when in the grip of great power—or great emotion. Auden Scott was becoming more fascinating with every second that passed.

"I," she said in the most precise diction he'd ever heard, "know not to turn the weapon toward myself."

Remi stopped playing. "You're on the lowest setting. Highest setting, that thing kicks like a horse. You could accidentally trigger it in a direction you don't want."

The black didn't retreat.

Well, hell, now he'd pissed her off. But no way was he leaving before assuring himself of her safety. "I can show you how to hit your target."

Her fingers tightening on the weapon as her hand came to her belly, she took a small step back.

Shit.

Remi wanted to kick himself. He'd gotten so caught up in her clear ability to go toe-to-toe with him that he'd forgotten her vulnerable state. To Auden Scott, he wasn't Remi, her alpha who'd die to protect her; no, he was a stranger, bigger and stronger than her.

"You can keep hold of the weapon," he said. "I can direct you from a distance." Changelings might be tactile by nature, but skin privileges were just that: *privileges*. No changeling with any honor would just take that precious gift, no matter the context.

"First," he said when she remained silent, "you need to learn the stance. You're standing wrong for your current balance."

He showed her the standard stance, then modified it for her present center of gravity, and after a long moment, she tried to copy it.

"Yeah, you almost have it." Eyes on her legs so he could judge how well she was doing, he gave her step-by-step instructions to get her into the exact stance—it went painfully slowly, but at least she was willing to listen.

"It doesn't feel right," she muttered at one point, the steely facade falling to expose a woman with soft features and even softer lips.

"It will," he said, shoving aside the unexpected spark of attraction for this woman who was an enigma in more ways than one; Remi couldn't risk lowering his guard with her, not when he was responsible for an entire pack. "First, put the weapon away in your pocket, then lift your hands as if you're holding it."

It took her a long minute to follow his instruction, but once they got going, she proved a fast study. Sharp. Quick on her feet for a woman seven months into a pregnancy. "You've had training," he said when they came to a stop. "In movement, if not in shooting."

"Standard drills to help me evade kidnappers if I was ever in that position."

He raised an eyebrow. "Not what I thought you were going to say." But it made sense; she was the only child of two Councilors. A certain caliber of person would've seen her as a payday.

She retrieved the weapon from her pocket, her eyes shining in a way that was surprisingly adorable. "Can I shoot now?"

"Let's go through the settings first." Once they had, he told her to choose the lowest. "It'll give you experience with the smaller recoils before trying to handle the big one."

After doing as he'd suggested, she took the stance he'd taught her, sighted down the barrel as they'd practiced . . . and shot.

The beam hit the wall of the bunker behind the sign.

Her face fell.

He wanted to cuddle her, the response instinctive. "You singed your target," he said, while reminding himself more harshly that he couldn't take anything about Auden at face value. Even if it was fucking hard to remember that with her looking so dejected. "That means you're two meters closer than when you started out."

Walking over to the target, she peered at the left edge, her eyes in a squint. "You're telling the truth!" She turned with a lightness to her step, appearing so young and innocent that it punched him in the gut that she hadn't even hit her mid-twenties. He'd still been racing cars and battling to control his screwed up emotions when he was her age.

Six years and a lifetime ago.

Auden pointed at the spot with the singe mark. "I almost hit it!"

Remi's leopard huffed on a surge of affection strong enough to bypass his wariness. "Almost," he agreed, though that was the most generous interpretation of the word he'd ever heard.

"Let me try again," she said, that new brightness lingering in eyes that had shifted back to a luminous blue during their lesson.

Then, as if forgetting she wasn't alone, she stroked a hand over her stomach to cradle it, a faint curve to her lips as she looked down at her bump. The love and tenderness in her expression? He'd stake his life on it being genuine.

Who was the real Auden Scott?

Chapter 12

PsyNet disintegration has picked up speed at levels we can't explain, given known factors. The time remaining has compressed to six months—but if the compression is cumulative, that estimate is useless.

—Report to the Ruling Coalition and EmNet from PsyNet Research Group Alpha (1 September 2083)

THE STATE OF her brain aside, the Auden with whom Remi spent the next half hour was the same one who'd come to him in the trees and spoken to him of his mother with an openness that was raw and without sophistication.

She was a wild and quixotic creature who argued with him over millimeters when he eyeballed how close she'd come with a shot, and who—at one point—asked if it hurt if someone stepped on his tail while he was in leopard form.

"I'm too fast for that to ever happen," he growled back in insult.

A sly look. "I bet I could do it. Not step on it. Catch it."

Remi stared at her. "Are you daring the alpha of a predatory changeling pack?"

"No." She took aim. "Just making a statement."

She fired.

This Auden, Remi realized with a sense of the portentous hanging over his head, could be far more dangerous to him than either of the avatars he'd previously met.

The question was, was she real . . . or a mask created with him as a target in mind? "I have to head back," he said and it wasn't a lie. He also, however, needed space to think.

Her face fell. "Of course." The quicksilver faded. "Thank you for the lesson."

Remi found himself hesitating, once more viscerally conscious of her aloneness. "I can help carry the target inside for you. Might rain overnight."

"No." A stiff look, the corners of her soft mouth pinched. "No, I prefer to do it myself."

Remi thought of her fingers on his comm device, the way she'd clutched at her abdomen as she whimpered that it hurt, and realized he had no idea how her psychometric abilities impacted her daily life. But from the guarded way she was looking at him, she didn't plan on sharing anything with him on the point.

He could've left it, but that didn't sit right, especially when her reticence was going to roadblock things he could do to help her. "Psychometric stuff?"

A rapid blink, a long pause.

"I have friends in the PsyNet," he added. "Rumor is you're a Ps-Psy, and I know that's right because of what you did with my comm. No one knows your Gradient, but guesses are 7 or higher, because of your parents." Remi made a face. "I don't get grading people that way, but I guess it works for the Psy."

Narrowed eyes, the stiffness eroding under a flash of irritation she couldn't conceal. "From what I know, changelings do the same."

It was his turn to scowl. Folding his arms, he set his feet apart. "You'll have to explain that to me, Deadshot."

She folded her own arms, and held his gaze with the moonstone blue of her own. "Your grading scale goes from dominance to sub-mission."

Remi opened, then shut his mouth. "Well, damn." Shoving his hand through his hair, he said, "Point to you, Ms. Auden Scott." She was wrong in putting submissives on the end of the "grading" scale—submissives weren't automatically less important in the hierarchy of a pack—but that there was a hierarchy was the salient point.

Her lips parted, her shoulders easing, and for a single heartbeat, he thought she might even smile. But a pulse later, the mask swept over her features, the Auden who'd dared say she could catch his tail retreating beneath the veneer of Psy ice. "I appreciate the time you took out of your day to give me the lesson."

Remi didn't want to leave, especially not when he'd begun to get a glimmer of the woman behind the mask, but he had vows to uphold. And unlike his father, he took his vows dead seriously.

"My pleasure," he said, and shot her a playful salute.

He'd already half turned on his heel when a sudden thought made him freeze. "Don't go in that bunker." Shifting, he locked his gaze to hers again, his leopard in the growl of his voice. "Did Ms. Wai tell you about the paramilitary team that last used it? They hurt people in there. I don't know how long stuff lasts in terms of your ability to pick it up, but you should know the risk."

From the way she flinched, it was clear Charisma Wai had forgotten to warn her.

"You understand?" The words came out rough with the leopard's protective streak—a streak that was so intense and so deep-rooted that Remi had to fight it to allow those under his care freedom.

Given free rein, that part of Remi could turn him into a controlling dictator and he knew it. That was why he surrounded himself with peo-ple who'd haul him back if he ever got too close to the brutal edge, and, if necessary, who had no trouble getting in his face about it.

Auden Scott, for all her current physical vulnerability, had the same titanium spine. His cat liked that. A whole dangerous lot.

. . .

AUDEN nodded to acknowledge Remi's warning about the bunker, but the man who'd made her forget all the rules for the past hour—and whose eyes had shifted to a feral yellow-gold before his curt words— still hesitated for several long seconds before loping off into the trees with that feline grace of his. She continued to stare after him long past the time she should've turned away.

Aloneness enclosed her in wings of soft black.

Shivering, she hugged her arms around herself, and stared at the bunker.

Auden didn't believe Charisma's omission had been malicious. Charisma was well aware of the risk to the baby should Auden come into unprepared contact with a surface with a violent past.

In her present state, it could trigger preterm labor.

Charisma would never risk that; she was very, very invested in Auden's child.

Auden cradled her belly, her heart racing and skin ice. Her shields, shields her father had helped design when she'd still thought him a good man, a good person, held her emotions inside, away from the betraying darkness of the PsyNet. Auden's Silence had never been flawless—as with most psychometrics she'd *just* skated through the tests, basically by ensuring she never tried to read anything that might be saturated with emotion.

Easy enough to do in Shoshanna's and Henry's homes.

She had, however, had trouble maintaining around Remi. Probably because he was a creature of open emotion, untamed in a way that triggered the part of her that was embarrassingly imperfect by Psy standards.

Auden couldn't believe she'd told him she could catch his tail.

Her cheeks flushing, she patted at her belly. "That was fun, though, wasn't it? *He's* fun . . . and wild and deadly in a way that makes me want to be stupid." Never in her life had she met anyone whose energy prowled so close to the surface of his skin. It had taken all she had not to touch him, feel if that energy had a tactile form.

Was it like his leopard's fur? A soft enticement before the predator snarled?

Her fingers curled into her palm.

She could think such primal thoughts here, safe in this landscape far from those who watched her and who monitored her baby with voracious intent.

Charisma wanted the child in her womb. Auden just didn't know why.

"They won't get to you, won't *ever* do to you what they did to me," she promised again, the words trembling with a rage that had built and built from the first moment when she returned to true consciousness. "I'll bring down their entire precious empire first."

Because, no matter how much she might wish it otherwise, Auden was her parents' daughter. But where they had used their ability to strategize and game the system to grow their power and brutalize those who were weaker, Auden's actions were shaped by her all-encompassing love for the child in her womb. Her mother had no idea what she'd unleashed when she'd permitted Auden to be impregnated.

Two months.

That was how long she had to set everything in place. And to pull it off, she needed data, the most important piece of which was why Charisma was so focused on her pregnancy—and why Shoshanna had taken the step of leaving her aide in effective charge of Scott operations.

The official word, per the private family-only document Shoshanna had left behind to be opened in the event of her sudden death or disability, was that Hayward didn't have the capability or the personality to lead the family. It said a lot about how effectively Shoshanna had psychologically destroyed her brother that Auden's uncle had just accepted that slight.

The transfer of power document hadn't ended there:

AUDEN IS INCAPACITATED AND NOT IN THE LINE OF
SUCCESSION EXCEPT IN TERMS OF PUBLIC PERCEPTION.
HOWEVER, IF SHE IS ABLE TO MAINTAIN FOR PERIODS
OF TIME, SHE SHOULD BE USED AS THE FACE OF THE
SCOTTS. ONLY IF THAT IS ABSOLUTELY IMPOSSIBLE
SHOULD HAYWARD STEP IN AS THE FACE.

THIS TEMPORARY STATE OF AFFAIRS WILL END WITH
DEVLIN SCOTT REACHING HIS MAJORITY AT TWENTY-
FIVE YEARS OF AGE. CHARISMA WILL TAKE OVER HIS
TRAINING FROM THE TIME OF MY DEMISE OR DISABILITY,
AND ENSURE HE'S READY TO STEP IN AS FULL CEO AT
TWENTY-FIVE.

Hayward's son, Devlin, was only sixteen right now, but he was already turning into a cold and calculating creature. Auden still felt sorry for him—the boy had to spend many hours a day with Charisma, his future mapped out for him, choice not even a question. Yet despite him being the official heir apparent, Auden couldn't shake off the feeling that she and Devlin were both pawns in a bigger game.

Something just wasn't right in the entire setup.

But no one could challenge the status quo while Charisma held the control codes. Hayward couldn't get into the main systems, and neither could Auden. Young Devlin would only get the codes when he turned twenty-five.

Charisma held the keys to the kingdom and that kingdom was rife with secrets.

Auden's eyes landed on the bunker dark green with algae and mold.

Another secret. Another mystery.

Breath catching and throat dry, she began to walk toward it. Her heart thudded louder and louder with each step she took. But she wasn't a little girl anymore. She knew how to control the input into her circuits when it came to rapid "test" reads—pregnancy hadn't eliminated those walls.

When warned, she could and did protect herself.

Stopping a foot away from the external wall, she raised a hand and touched the tip of her pinky finger to the lichen green plascrete. External walls tended to be safer for the most part—unless they were on the ground floor and had street frontage, people didn't much make contact with them. And this external wall was in a remote area.

—fur—

—shouts, dulled by time—

—cold, contained power—

—gold and black—

—a handprint in blood—

Jerking back her finger, she nonetheless stood in place. That last image had been vivid, but still . . . distant. Whoever had created that handprint had done so long enough ago that time and the elements had scrubbed most of it.

The strongest impressions *hadn't* been of violence. She'd felt the softness of fur, seen colors black and gold that rippled with life, heard a throaty growl. "Leopards," she whispered, realizing RainFire cats must've been prowling around and through this land on a regular basis.

She was glad for that, for them.

For *him.*

She'd never before had an opportunity to touch a changeling imprint, but the people in her group who had experienced them had mentioned that they had a different impact from Psy or human imprints. Likely because of the nature of changeling shields. Today, all she'd sensed was an intense awareness of their surroundings—under paws, against fur, in the air—entwined with a wild curiosity.

She wondered if a Ps-Psy had ever been inside a changeling den. And she found herself searching desperately for something Remi might've touched.

So she could see him, *know* him.

But he'd been scrupulous in keeping his distance, and now he was gone, just another feline shadow in the trees.

. . .

REMI dreamed of Auden Scott, an eerie dream in which her face kept switching. One face was frigid and remote, while another laughed, another cried.

And the final one . . . it screamed.

Jolting up in bed, he didn't fight his instincts and, shifting into his leopard form, ran full tilt to her cabin. All seemed peaceful within, no sign of any trouble. No hint of anyone's scent but hers and those of his packmates.

He was tempted to wake her up nonetheless, see her with his own eyes, but he knew that was irrational, would disturb rest she needed. But he couldn't make himself leave, so he jumped up onto a branch of a tree that overlooked her cabin, and napped there. Lights came on in the cabin with the break of dawn, and not long afterward, he spotted Auden's form pass in front of her window.

Remi growled softly in satisfaction before jumping off the branch to run back to his pack—and to the vows he'd taken to protect and shelter each and every individual within it. Those same vows meant he couldn't get back to the cabin the rest of that day, or the next. Having foreseen that, however, he'd ordered his people to do extra sweeps, keep an eye on her from afar and make sure she was safe.

Then Theo reported that Auden had flown out in her jet-chopper, and that was that.

Or it should've been.

Those moonstone blue eyes haunted Remi . . . as did the strange dream born of his leopard's memory of her funhouse mirror of a scent. It made Remi wonder if the cat had seen something the man had missed, if the woman who'd said she could catch his tail—and had instead caught his interest—had been the best mask of all.

Chapter 13

A9: I've recently come into contact with a changeling group and had an opportunity to sense an old changeling imprint. It was less . . . visceral than other imprints of a similar age on the same surface. I'd like to hear further from those of you with experience with changeling imprints. Is this normal?

Jervois: I've never had the chance, but I'm curious to hear from the others, too. My family is considering a business venture with a small changeling group, so I might come into contact with their imprints. I would like to be prepared.

TNS: I've had multiple opportunities to sense changeling imprints. A9, your experience is similar to mine. We can still read them, but not at the depth we can Psy or human. And in passive mode, I find that I'm not discomforted at all in even heavily changeling-imprinted spaces. I've theorized it's as a result of their natural shields.

Jervois: That is intriguing to me. After all, Psy have heavy shields, too. Why are we impacted so strongly by our own race then? Humans, it makes sense, since their natural shields are paper thin.

A9: Perhaps we are sensitized to other Psy in a genetic sense? Or perhaps it's because a changeling has a dual aspect to their nature, which might somehow scramble our senses.

TNS: Valid theories—perhaps one day one of us can get a grant to study the phenomenon. Though, A9—I see from your profile that you've posted in the pregnancy subforum—I can't tell you anything about how your current physical status will impact the effect of changeling imprints. It's not something with which I've ever had—or will have—any experience.

A9: Hopefully another one of us can chime in with more knowledge.

Enna: It's been seven hours. Does no one have more information? This is the most interesting thread we've had in forever.

—Thread on Psycho & Metrics: A Forum for Ps-Psy

REMI SPENT THE next nine excruciating days pressing the flesh and schmoozing with potential business partners, Theo at his side. They had to fly for some of it and damn it to hell he hated planes, but at least he was back at their Sunset Falls HQ for the last hellish day of face-to-face business meetings.

"I hate this," he growled as he pulled at the pale gray of his tie after another mind-numbing negotiation.

At least he'd had the satisfaction of booting the previous party onto the street while their eyes bugged out. Those particular asses had thought they could take advantage of RainFire because they were just "dumb animals"—he'd literally *heard* one of them say that while leaning down to whisper to his associate.

Who the fuck went into a meeting without looking up the abilities of the other side?

He'd have expected such behavior from a certain caliber of Psy, but turned out there were pockets of humans who thought the same superior way. It had given him great pleasure to purr, "This dumb animal isn't interested in your offer" as he allowed his eyes to shift.

He'd then risen to his feet with a smile that held pure death. "Let me show you to the door."

He hadn't made a single violent move, had kept up his smile the entire time—and they'd almost shit their pants as they scrambled to get the fuck away. Theo had cracked up afterward. "That's one hell of a smile, Remi. You ever look at me like that, I'm running away and never coming back."

Mliss Phan, the head of their public HQ, meanwhile, had just said, "I'm going to find their most dangerous competitor and offer them the deal of their lives, just to screw with these bastards."

Remi liked the way his chief operating officer thought.

Now, having already hung the dark gray of his suit jacket on the back of the chair, he rolled up the sleeves of his lighter gray shirt as he took a seat at the break room table. "No one warned me about CEO bullshit when I said I wanted to be an alpha."

Mliss raised a perfectly arched eyebrow underneath asymmetrical razor-cut black bangs that framed an elegant face with wide cheekbones and full lips against tanned olive skin. "What? You thought it'd be all dominance fights and chest-beating?"

The tall COO puffed out her cheeks and squared her slim shoulders before beating her fists against the white silk of her shirt. "Me alpha man, hear me roar."

"Why the fuck am I surrounded by assholes?"

"This asshole made you coffee to take the edge off *and* is plotting vengeance against that one group, so stop with the snarling." She placed the mug on the table, her scent a comforting mix of pack and the threads that were just her, including a faint undertone of roses that came from her favorite soap.

Intelligent, a tough negotiator, and much better at public relations than Remi, Mliss's "grade" in the pack, if he was to use Auden's terminology, was senior maternal. As such, she had significant dominance. Maternals ran the gamut from deeply submissive to dominant enough to face off against a soldier, and, despite the name, weren't only women. It just happened to be the one term that had stuck in the changeling world.

In a pack, maternals generally took charge of everything from organizing the education of the cubs, to disciplining their young, and ensuring a pack felt like a home. Maternals were why their older kids had just aced a set of countrywide exams, why the dining aerie was set up like a cozy room in someone's private aerie, and why Remi's aerie had curtains that suited his personality.

Maternals were also some of, if not *the* most ruthlessly organized people in a pack. Add that to Mliss's MBA and other qualifications, and she'd been a slam dunk to be the head of operations of their public HQ.

He'd borrowed the idea of a public HQ from DarkRiver. It not only permitted RainFire to keep their territorial lands private, a bland public office also removed the intimidation factor when it came to humans and Psy who'd never before interacted with changelings.

While some idiots thought them dumb, others expected Remi's kind to go around clawing off people's faces, rending them limb from limb, then dragging their bodies off into the forest to feast on. It didn't help that certain juveniles found it the height of hilarity to spread exactly those rumors online. The last one Remi had seen was a solemn account of how a SnowDancer wolf had made a cape out of an intruder's skin.

Juveniles were punks, but at least they'd picked the right pack for that little fantasy. SnowDancers didn't play if you encroached on their territory. Neither did Remi, his leopard vicious in defense of his own.

But today, he wasn't dealing with a threat to the pack. He was with his own, people who trusted his far more dominant and deadly leopard to keep them safe. Mliss wouldn't stand a chance against Remi in a rage. Neither would built-like-a-linebacker Theo. Their bond was a thing of trust and loyalty.

"Me alpha," he snarled. "Me drink coffee."

Mliss, standing with her back against the counter, snorted coffee out of her nose and down her shirt. Even as she cursed him, she was laughing until tears rolled down her face.

Theo, who'd been an invaluable help over the entire interminable nine-day odyssey, all of it designed to build RainFire's business network, poked his head inside to see what was going on. He still wore his chocolate brown suit, complete with an unmolested silk tie and a pristine white shirt. "Oh, Liiiiissy," he said in a singsong way, "how are you going to explain that stain to your big sister, hmm? Didn't she buy that for you in some fancy schmancy boutique in Paris?"

Mliss stopped laughing long enough to glare daggers at him. "You snitch to her and I'll bite off your face, Theo 'I can't mind my own business' Ortiz."

The big sentinel held up his hands, palms out. "Hey, I was just making a comment." He glanced at his wrist. "Forty minutes till our next meeting, Remi. You want a briefing or you up to speed?"

"I read the notes," Remi grumbled before giving the sentinel a narrow-eyed look. "Why do all these meetings not drive you nuts?" Man's eyes were still shining and even the loose curls of his hair looked bouncy.

Theo shrugged. "I dunno. I like chess. Business is like chess."

Mliss, who'd given up on dabbing away the coffee from her top, came over to sit in the seat opposite Remi. She brought a tin of cookies with her—because she *was* a maternal, even if of the hard-ass variety. "Eat and stop being a sourpuss."

Remi begrudgingly ate four cookies, while Theo inhaled half the tin. Remi's brain, however, wasn't focused on the cookies studded with nuts and topped with sugar crystals. "You think you could deal with being out here on a more regular basis?" he asked Theo, who was propping open the door while he ate cookie after cookie.

"Yeah, sure. It's not that far to the nearest forest if I want to shift and run."

It was Mliss's turn to make a sour face. "Do not saddle me with Teddy here."

"Call me Teddy again and I'll definitely snitch. *With* pictures of the scene of the crime."

Mliss's claws hissed out to carve furrows onto the wooden table. Look at her like this and you'd never imagine her as the cool, calm, and controlled center of their business operations.

"Now, now, children," Remi drawled, wondering when these two would finally tear off each other's clothes and put themselves out of their clear misery. He had no idea what the problem was; both were single, and with Mliss being a senior maternal to Theo's sentinel, there was no power imbalance.

Mliss snarled at him, but backed off. Theo, meanwhile, finished off his final cookie and said, "You want me to handle more stuff here?"

Mliss answered before Remi could reply—and this time, she was in her COO avatar. "Won't work. Not yet—not with the meetings anyway. Has to be you, Remi."

Mliss had come to RainFire from a small pack built around a sprawling family—all the adults left at some point, to find mates and experience life in other packs. Some returned to their familial pack, bringing their mates with them, while others stayed put in their new packs.

Remi had all his digits crossed that Mliss would stick with RainFire long-term, because the other thing about that familial pack was that they punched *way* above their weight in the business world. In this sphere, Mliss had more knowledge in her pinky finger than the rest of them combined.

Which was why Remi didn't argue with her statement, just said, "Why?"

"Because we're not DarkRiver or SnowDancer with their decades-long track records. In business circles, while their alphas are respected and considered dangerous adversaries, *DarkRiver* and *SnowDancer* are the brand—exactly as it should be for any pack that wants to stay healthy for generations."

Claws retracted, Mliss used a finger to worry absently at one of the grooves she'd created on the tabletop. "We're new, and our track record is so thin as to be nonexistent. Right now, people want to deal with the boss, put a face to the pack, build a personal connection. You're Rain-Fire's first alpha, Remi—you're the one who has to turn it into a brand. But to do so, you have to act as the foundation."

Dark eyes meeting his. "And, fact is, while you might hate the schmoozing, you're good at putting others at ease. I see you at these meetings and I understand the string of deluded women who call you charming."

"Damn it." Remi could feel his eyes shifting. "How long will it take before you or Theo can take over?"

"Not for years yet." Mliss closed her hand over his fist, her fingers long and her nails polished an opalescent pink. "Right now, RainFire doesn't exist without you. The first alpha, or the first alpha who comes in after a bad period for the pack, is always the brand for at least a decade—it's around that point that, if you've done your job right, we can distribute the weight among the pack."

Groaning, Remi shoved both hands through his hair. He knew she was right. It took time to create the kind of business reputation enjoyed by DarkRiver and SnowDancer. He didn't know much about the history of the wolves, but he knew DarkRiver hadn't done it overnight, either. It had taken years and years of hard grind.

"Our job," Lucas had said to him during his mentorship of Remi, "is to leave the pack better than when we took over. It isn't about us. It's about the pack."

"Oh, by the way," Mliss said, her clear voice mingling with the memory of Luc's. "Lark mentioned the Scott up at the cabin, so I poked around a bit—their compound just out of town has gone into serious overdrive over the past eight months. Prior to that, it was closed up for most of the year."

Remi's abdomen clenched.

Eight months.

Longer than Auden's pregnancy, but not by much. Preparation for the eventuality?

A rustle in the doorway, young Phoebe poking her head in. "Um," the teen intern whispered, her cheeks pink and soft brown eyes rounded, "there's a leopard at reception? He says he's come to visit his sister?"

"Name?" Mliss asked, no-nonsense but not unkind.

Phoebe, who worshipped the ground Mliss walked on, went bright red before looking down. "I didn't get his name. I'm so sorry, Mliss."

"It's all right, kitten," Mliss said with a smile. "That's why you're here. To learn."

Remi pushed up to his feet. "You two carry on. I'll go with Phoebe." When he tumbled the juvenile's fine blond hair, she leaned into him with a trust that made Remi's throat close.

This, this was what he wanted to create with RainFire. A home. A safe place.

No cub of Remi's would ever feel lost and unwanted.

Phoebe was old enough that she hadn't been born into the pack, had entered RainFire at age twelve when her adventurous parents decided to throw in their lot with Remi right back at the genesis of the pack. That Remi had managed to earn the trust of her young heart? It meant a fucking lot.

For some odd reason, it also made him think of Auden. Whom, he wondered, did she trust? Clearly not anyone she could ask to teach her how to shoot. Unless, of course, that had all been a game, a way to play him.

For what reason?

That was where he got stuck. Because he couldn't think of a good one for Auden Scott, part of the hugely influential Scott family, to bother ensnaring the alpha of a newborn changeling pack.

"I forgot," Phoebe whispered. "To ask his name, I mean. I got distracted."

"Come on." He put his arm around her shoulders, cuddling her close. "Show me to our guest."

Snarky muttering started up behind him the second he left Mliss and Theo alone. Smirking, Phoebe whispered, "Jeez, get a room."

Remi grinned. "Shh. We suspect nothing."

Phoebe mimed zipping her lips closed.

Funny kid. And a kid who was usually onto it—one of the reasons she'd been selected for this internship. Yet she'd forgotten to get their visitor's name.

That she'd left the visitor alone in reception didn't matter as much;

Remi had chosen an office space with a secure door behind reception, which meant guests had to be walked in by one of the pack. It also meant RainFire didn't have to assign a security team here on a day-to-day basis.

Reception itself was protected inside a spacious and bulletproof glass cubicle that backed onto another door leading to the back. Their designer had made it seem a feature, complete with water falling down one side of the cubicle and thriving greenery everywhere.

The entire thing had cost an arm, a leg, and both of Remi's kidneys—but it had already paid itself off by setting his dominants free from having to stand guard. That was the better look, but they were too small to spread their manpower so thin. This way, the pack appeared polished and professional, while making sure their receptionist—whether it was Phoebe doing her intern hours, or their official receptionist—was protected against any threat.

Remi might not have thought of threats a decade before, but the past few years had been full of unrest. Pure Psy, the group with which Auden's father had been associated, had vanished out of existence in terms of a public presence, but word was that malcontents who blamed changelings for the changes in the Psy race were still floating around.

Then there were the usual idiots who might think to target a small pack in the hope they could kidnap and hold a packmate for ransom.

Not happening under Remi's watch. "Let's go find out our mysterious visitor's identity." He pulled open the secure door.

Chapter 14

"You're no alpha. You're a coward!"

—Gina Denier to Rhett Farley, alpha, WhiteMountain
(defunct) (9 April 2070)

"THERE HE IS," Phoebe whispered, her cheeks going pink again.

Remi saw at once why she'd been distracted. The young male was tall and muscled, with thick auburn hair that he'd had cut neatly along the sides, but left long enough up top that it held a wave. The naturally cream tone of his skin held the slightest golden tan, and his jawline was square, his eyes a rich dark blue, his smile bright and engaging. And poor Phoebe was a juvenile running on hormones.

Their visitor was also a *powerful* dominant.

Leaving Phoebe just outside the door, Remi walked over, hand outstretched. "I recognize that familial scent thread. Kit Monaghan, right?" Around twenty-three years of age if Remi was correctly remembering what Rina had said.

Kit's smile deepened. "That's me." He threw Phoebe a sheepish glance. "Sorry I didn't introduce myself."

The blushing teenager shuffled her feet.

Deciding to save her from melting into the floor, Remi nodded at her to return to her post. She drew out her short journey, throwing little glances back at Kit the entire time. Man was going to cause carnage among the single women of the pack.

"Rina's told me a lot about you," Remi said after they broke their handshake.

"She's been telling me about RainFire, too. I hope it's okay for me to drop by?"

"Of course it's fine. Have you checked in with Lucas?" Rina's younger brother was part of DarkRiver, a youth with the scent of a future alpha who'd gone roaming to stretch his wings, figure out who he wanted to be.

DarkRiver had made it clear to Kit that he didn't have to take up the mantle of being an alpha if that didn't suit him. Lucas had become alpha too young for ugly reasons, and though he'd been ready and willing to step into the role, he also understood what it did to a young man to carry that much weight on his shoulders.

"Kit's one of mine," the other alpha had said to Remi. "He'll always have a home here, never be forced into a choice."

He'd held Remi's gaze with the panther green of his own. "What your pack did to you was unacceptable. You were a *cub*, younger than Kit by years—any threat your alpha felt from you was due to his own inadequacies. You need to not only understand that but internalize it, so you're never at risk of repeating the mistake."

Remi had appreciated the blunt talking-to, even though he was well aware his flaw was a protectiveness that could turn into a cage. He wasn't one to push any child out of the nest. But Luc's job had been to ensure Remi ended up a good alpha. That meant making sure he was aware of his own shit.

It wasn't until now that Remi realized a part of him had worried that he *would* react negatively to a young alpha in his pack, that he'd been fundamentally damaged by his own alpha's decision to kick him out at a bare seventeen years of age. Instead, his leopard prowled against the surface of his skin, intrigued by Kit's strength—and painfully aware of his youth.

For the first time, he really got it, understood how fucked up the WhiteMountain alpha's actions had been. Because Kit was a gift to DarkRiver, a strong male loyal and true, who might one day extend their circle of allies to an entirely new pack. But right this moment? He was still young, needed guidance and support as he grew into his skin and his power.

Remi slapped the younger man on the shoulder after Kit confirmed that he'd alerted Lucas he was back in the country. "I'll introduce you to the others here. We're not heading up to pack territory until late tomorrow. You okay to wait? You can stay with us—we have some simple sleeping quarters on the second floor for the short term." Mliss and her official staff of three had proper apartments next door.

"No problem. But can you not tell Rina?" Kit's leopard gleamed in his eyes. "I want to see the look on her face when I walk out of the trees."

"I'm a cat. Of course I'm good with startling her."

Kit's laughter made poor Phoebe all but combust on the spot before Remi took their visitor through to the back to introduce him to the others. Yet as he watched Kit win them over with the generous warmth of a leopard who'd been raised in the heart of a healthy and loving pack, he found himself thinking of Auden again.

His claws pricked his skin, his leopard's lip curling in a snarl.

He had to let that little obsession go. Because the chances of Auden returning to the cabin anytime soon were close to nil. That she'd come even once while so heavily pregnant, though . . . it made Remi wonder. Why would a woman leave her home at such a critical time if that home was a safe place for her?

AUDEN sat in her office staring at her computer. She hadn't done much on it . . . ever. She hadn't even *had* an office until she was moved into her mother's care.

Why she'd been given one, she didn't know.

Perhaps as a backdrop to a meeting, should it be necessary. Because at that point, she hadn't had enough mental capacity to utilize any of the systems. Oh, she could pretend for brief fragments of time, but nothing sustained.

That history did, however, mean that this computer was unlikely to be monitored by anything aside from the generic Scott security system that kept out hackers and the like. She hadn't had a chance to test it yet, having done any prior computronic work on an organizer given to her as a young teen that was clear of any bugs because, quite frankly, it was too old and clunky to run the software.

Unfortunately, its age also meant she could no longer really use it except perhaps to visit the forum. As for the *other* organizer she'd managed to source, the one with specs high enough for everything, she had no plans to link it to the Scott system—at least not until she was ready to sacrifice the device. For now, it was clean, and she intended to keep it that way.

So it would have to be this computer. Inhaling a long breath, she started up a security check using what she'd learned as a teenager prior to the neural damage. Computronic security had been a necessary part of her studies.

"We might exist on the PsyNet," her father had said, "but we can't do business on the Net alone. For one, not all data can be stored there. You must know how to secure your devices."

That advice had ended up prescient, given the continued fragmentation of the PsyNet. With the foundation in the midst of a mass collapse, nothing stored in its psychic fabric was safe, not even the most well-constructed vault.

Her computer proved clear of babysitters or spies.

She remained circumspect in her research into RainFire. Nothing that couldn't be explained away as her attempting to educate herself about her neighbors. There were no pictures of the pack members online, but she did find a small article in a business journal about their indi-mech arm.

Per the journalist, RainFire Mech was "an increasingly strong player in the lucrative and underserved niche." It also looked like their current clientele—the ones the journalist had been able to interview anyway—were very happy with their work.

She checked her mother's holdings, the information available on their unrestricted internal network. She'd remembered correctly: Shoshanna had bought a majority stake in a company that needed individualized pieces of mech on a regular basis. And from the look of things, their current supplier was charging above market rates, likely because they were entrenched and believed they had no competition.

Her heartbeat kicked up a notch.

"Auden?" Charisma stood in the doorway, a strange expression on her face. "I thought I imagined you there."

"I haven't been here often, have I?" Auden said lightly, because she needed to keep Charisma on her side while she set up her plan. "I barely fit behind the desk as it is." She indicated her belly, careful not to cradle it, careful to be the perfect Scott.

"Why are you putting yourself to such discomfort?" Charisma walked over. "I could have provided you with a new organizer."

"I was curious about the RainFire leopards."

Charisma went motionless. "Did they approach you?"

Auden found herself saying, "No." Then she played up her naiveté, leaning into how Charisma had viewed her for years. "I just saw the information in the dossier you gave me."

"Oh yes, of course." Charisma's spine relaxed. "I do recall looking the pack up. They're fairly insignificant."

"Yes, but read this." She called Charisma around to her side of the desk and indicated the article.

"Hmm," Charisma murmured. "Interesting area for changelings."

"That's what I thought. Then I remembered a deal of Mother's, and glanced over the files. See the latest invoices on this work?"

Charisma examined the paperwork, then gave Auden a long and penetrating glance. "Your memory is excellent," she said in an eerie tone that Auden couldn't pinpoint.

It took effort to keep her voice even, to not give in to the shiver that threatened to rock over her. "Mother took me to tour a warehouse once, a long time ago. We didn't often do things together, so I remembered." A wholesale lie, but one Charisma had no way to check—not after so many years.

The other woman's attention was back on the screen. "I see what you mean on the pricing. Our supplier is getting too comfortable, isn't he? I need to get the general manager there to tighten the negotiating screws."

"I was thinking we switch to RainFire," Auden said before she could second-guess herself.

Charisma's eyes were unblinking when they looked at her. "Scotts have never worked with changelings."

"It's strategy." The words fell off Auden's tongue with a speed that made her blood run ice-cold. "We give one contract to the cats and our prior supplier will come crawling to us with a better deal than we could ever negotiate. *If* we even want to stick with them, because here's what else I found."

She showed Charisma another four-paragraph article that most people would've missed; it spoke about the innovations RainFire had made for another company that had led to increased output and a resulting rise in profit.

The CEO had nothing but glowing praise for the leopard pack.

"I don't think our current supplier is doing any R&D," she said. "We contract RainFire before anyone else of our size or caliber finds them, and we can monopolize their skills while our competitors rely on companies with outdated methods of design and composition. Doesn't matter if they're changeling, human or Psy, the family needs to control the market on the components in order to surge ahead."

Charisma didn't smile—she had been too deep into Silence for too long, but her expression warmed in a way that was as close to a smile as she might ever get. "That's the same call your mother would've made," she said, a whisper of awe in her tone. "Small, intelligent moves with the long term in mind. Brilliant, Auden."

Her cheeks frigid, Auden closed down the computer. "Thank you."

"I'll action it." Charisma made a note in her organizer. "Per the file I just pulled up, our old contract expires within the month, so we'll have to move fast—and hope the pack has enough capacity to accommodate us."

"I think they'll make the capacity with a contract this large." Pushing back from the chair, she rose to her feet to stretch her back. "Since I discovered this, what do you think about me dealing with the cats?"

"I'm afraid you're in too exposed a state," Charisma said, her voice gentle. "We can't have you at risk."

"We could meet here." Auden didn't back down. "I really do need to start doing things, Charisma. I know I'm not the intended heir, but I am meant to be our face for the time being—and I appear to have full cognitive abilities at this point."

Charisma's pupils expanded. "Yes"—a soft voice—"and you are the direct line descendent. Your cousin is a substandard replacement."

This is it. The fault line.

The voice inside Auden's head was cold and manipulative . . . and not her own.

Her gorge threatened to rise.

"Yes, and if I'm no longer disqualified by the state of my brain, then no one in the family will argue against a deviation from the transfer document," Auden pointed out past the churning in her gut, because this was about her baby, about the innocent life she'd promised to protect. "I was created for and trained for this position by both my parents."

"Yes, you're right." A firm nod. "Yes, Devlin has had nowhere near your level of training—and you were Shoshanna's chosen heir before . . ."

Auden waved that off before Charisma could walk herself back from her decision. "It would've been a useful thing had the experiment worked," she said. "As it is, it proved a temporary problem, and I'm now at full capacity."

"What about your physical status? It's not safe for that to be made public."

That risk wasn't imagined. The Scotts had made a lot of enemies, many of whom wouldn't hesitate at acting against a pregnant woman. "We make RainFire sign a confidentiality clause backed up by the promise of a ruinous financial penalty." Once again, the words came from a part of her that felt colder and more mercenary than she'd ever believed herself to be. "They don't have enough money to risk it."

"I should've thought of that," Charisma said, but it was with something akin to pride in her tone. "You truly are your mother's daughter. She would be proud."

Auden was going to throw up any second. "So we're agreed?" she managed to say. "I'll deal with RainFire?"

"Yes—but not here," Charisma said. "We have a public building we can utilize. And to assure there is no attempt at interference from inside the house, I'll make it so neither Hayward nor Devlin knows about the meeting until it is fait accompli."

They have no real power, Charisma telepathed, *but they could cause you physical harm. Especially as neither ever thought to come so close to the throne.*

Auden nodded. *You are a true soldier, someone on whom I can rely.*

Charisma's spine grew straighter in front of her, her face aglow. "I'll start work on this now, sir."

Auden barely managed to wait until after the aide had pulled the office door shut behind herself before she ran to the private toilet attached to the office, and threw up the contents of her stomach. The shudders that wracked her were hard and raw and she worried that they were hurting her baby.

Which was why, after she'd cleaned up, she went and saw Dr. Verhoeven.

"Nausea at this stage of the pregnancy is unusual, but it does happen," he told her. "As for the fetus, its readings are within the normal parameters. You should, however, hydrate yourself with nutrient-enriched water."

After thanking him, Auden grabbed a bottle of the prescribed water, then made her way out to the back of the property. The air was crisp and cold, the manicured lawn a bright green that seemed unreal, the trees at the back neat and tidy.

Not even a hint of the wild forests of the place RainFire called home. That Remi called home.

She tried to focus on that, on the fleeting peace she'd found at the cabin, but all she could think about was how those words, those *manipulations* had come so quickly to her tongue. Her father hadn't been like that, and he was the one who'd raised her for the most part. Even though she knew he'd hidden a lot of his evil from her, she wasn't wrong in her judgment of his overall personality.

Henry's household had been more martial, less political. He hadn't been the one with the silver tongue in his partnership with Shoshanna. That had been Auden's mother. And today, that had been Auden.

So slick, so cold, so nauseatingly serpentine.

Realizing she was in danger of hyperventilating, she began a slow walk across the lawn. She wanted to cradle her bump, wanted to reassure her baby with loving contact, but all she could do in this place where others might be watching was touch her baby's mind. *I'm here. I'm your mama. You're safe.*

The baby's brain wasn't yet developed enough to understand those words, but Auden hoped it would understand the emotion behind them. Because Auden wasn't hiding anything when it came to the child in her womb. Her baby would never wonder if she was loved—Auden would drench her world in love.

But to do that, she had to stay healthy and in control. She couldn't let her distaste of how efficiently she'd just manipulated Charisma get to her. The pregnancy had awakened some primitive part of her brain, she told herself, a part that was ready to use every tool at its disposal— including Auden's memories of her mother.

Because while Shoshanna hadn't been part of her day-to-day life, Auden *had* spent time with her in her teen years. She'd seen her mother work, seen how she made people do what she wanted without making any demands. Something inside her had clearly filed away those memories for an instance when they'd be needed.

Now they were.

Auden wasn't going to flinch from using them.

"I'll do anything for you," she whispered to her child. "Cross every line without hesitation."

Auden would fight for her as no one had ever fought for Auden.

Even if that meant playing a dangerous game with an alpha leopard with eyes of a primal yellow-green.

Chapter 15

"You are going to be the most dominant person in the room a lot of your life, Rem-Rem. That doesn't mean you will be the most important. The coward we once called alpha has forgotten that; he thinks he's the only one who matters. An alpha who thinks that way? He'll crush his pack's heart under his boot."

—Gina Denier to Remi Denier (circa 2070)

MLISS RAN INTO the meeting room just as a T-shirt-and-jeans-clad Remi finished writing up his final set of notes before he could head home. "You will *never* believe this!" His calm and cool COO was literally dancing in her high heels.

Fascinated, Remi tried to come up with the most outlandish answer possible. "Nikita Duncan wants to hire us."

Mliss's grin was feline all right—of the Cheshire cat variety. "Not Duncan. *Scott.*"

He all but ripped away the piece of paper in her hand. It took him two read-throughs to confirm it said what he thought. "They want us to send in a bid for *all* their indi-mech needs?"

"Yes! Within the next two weeks, though they're willing to extend the time period a fraction, since they understand this is an enormous ask."

Remi's heart thundered, his leopard prowling to the surface of his skin. The human part of his mind, however, was calculating the odds of this being a coincidence and coming up with no fucking way.

He couldn't, however, see the time he'd spent with Auden as any reason to be suspicious—likely she'd started to research RainFire, stumbled across their mech arm, and decided the pack might be useful to the Scott group of companies.

"No ethical considerations, either," Mliss said. "At least not on the associated projects—I know the Scotts have a rep so I dug hard, but every one of these operations seems above board and routine."

"Send me all the details." It didn't matter that business wasn't second nature to Remi. He had to stay on top of everything with which the pack was associated. RainFire was too young to take any risk that could affect their reputation.

All final calls in the pack were his, good or bad.

As Mliss had said, the Scotts had more than one skeleton in their closet—but from what he'd picked up through the Arrows, most of those skeletons had to do with politics and power. Their business enterprises were prosaic enough, and included significant holdings in computronic and mech fields.

On top of that, Shoshanna was no longer in charge.

I bet I could do it. Not step on it. Catch it.

She was happy the last time she wore that watch.

Can I shoot now?

Remi growled silently at himself. Because despite that strange hour he'd spent with Auden, he didn't know her. Not as anything but a woman who couldn't shoot and who cradled her pregnant belly with a near-feral protectiveness. He'd stake his life on that being real, even if every other thing about her was false.

Auden Scott would battle to the death to protect her child.

"Can we fulfill their needs?" he asked Mliss through the chaos of his thoughts. "Do we have the capacity?" A huge deal like this could pay off their business loans within the year, but *only* if they could produce the goods.

"I don't know. We'll have to do a breakdown."

"Get everyone in this room. We'll figure it out before I head home."

Two hours and a ton of calculations later, the consensus was that it was doable if they trained five to seven more of their people on the low-level work. Remi knew they'd get volunteers for that gig from younger packmates keen to get experience on the floor.

"Do it," he told Mliss. "Work with Theo to put together a draft proposal, then send it to me. I'll put out the word that we have openings and ask for applications to be sent to you, Ru."

Having joined in from the factory floor, Rulinda Bay, their head of engineering, gave a quick nod. Her silver hair shimmered in the overhead light, the lines on the pale skin of her face speaking of a lifetime of experience. RainFire had gained her expertise because she'd decided to move packs to stay close to Asher and her two other grandcubs; she'd brought her mate—a robotics expert—along with her.

"It's going to be tight." Mliss was already typing on her organizer. "The deadline. But I don't want to ask them to push it—first impressions and all that."

"I'll send you a couple of senior people to cover your usual duties for the duration." Remi was already reaching for his phone. "I know you like to keep an eye across the board, but nothing else on your slate is as important as this."

Mliss blew out a breath that made her bangs dance. "Agreed. Send me Byron. I'm trying to lure him away from managing the pack's various needs anyway."

Remi grinned. "I'll call him in, but there's not a chance I'm letting you steal him." Byron Castille was a sweet, shy submissive; he was also the quiet engine behind the scheduling and ordering and operations that kept RainFire functioning smoothly day to day.

"I have faith in my persuasive skills," Mliss said, but it was an absent comment, her attention focused on the draft quote in front of her.

Leaving Mliss and her team to it, Remi met Kit at reception.

The auburn-haired young male, his duffel over his shoulder, lifted a hand toward Phoebe. "Bye, Bee."

The girl went bright red but waved back with enthusiasm before Remi and Kit walked out to the rugged all-terrain vehicle that would take them a considerable way into home territory, after which they'd stretch out their legs and run.

Remi usually shifted for the latter, but with Kit having his gear with him, they'd keep to human form. "So," he said after they were on their way, "do anything interesting during your roaming?"

"Worked with BlackSea." He stretched out his legs. "Played with them, too."

Remi's leopard huffed at that smug tone in Kit's voice. "I hope you made allies and not enemies with your play friends."

"Definite allies. Invited back anytime." Kit rolled down the window so he could draw in the air. "I also got drunk with bears one time. Just *one* time. And nearly ended up arrested."

Remi grinned. "I've been there, my young friend. I woke up naked in a cave in the forest with not a bear in sight and a note in lipstick on my chest that said 10/10. All I remember about that night is that I had a damn good time—and it's possible I wore a bear suit to blend in at some point."

Kit's laughter was young and bright. "I wonder if Lucas has a bear story?" he mused. "I've always been too chicken to ask him." A considering look Remi could almost feel. "You're a fellow alpha. You could ask him."

Remi decided he really liked Kit Monaghan.

Conversation flowed between them with ease, and when it came time for the run, Kit proved fast enough to keep up with Remi even through the falling darkness that muted the spectacular dance of color that was the fall foliage in daytime. No light remained in the world by the time they reached the heart of pack territory.

"We're on the periphery," Remi said, bringing them down to a jog. "You want to lurk while I go lure Rina out?"

Kit's grin was huge. "Absolutely." Waiting until they'd reached the very edge of the aerie trees, the twinkling lights of the homes perched in the branches showing from between the leaves, he dropped his duffel to the side. "You'll bring her so I'm upwind?"

Remi nodded. "Won't be long. I checked with Finn before we started our run—he's our healer, by the way—and she's in the dining aerie shooting the shit with the other sentinels and senior soldiers over dinner."

"Wait." Kit frowned. "Sandy hair, green eyes, that Finn? I think I met him at Tammy's."

"Same one," Remi said. "He's friends with your healer. Back soon."

After Remi stepped out of the trees, however, he first had to react with lightning speed to catch a tiny cub who'd jumped into his arms from a branch. Growling, he nipped the culprit's ear. "You should be in bed, Jasper."

The cub nuzzled his chin, patting at his chest with tiny paws.

Remi scratched the baby's head, but dropped him off with his parents. Play was encouraged among the pack, but so was safety. Before handing him back to his parents, he held the cub up by the scruff of his neck and said, "No sneaking out after dark." He used his alpha voice.

The cub made a mournful growling sound.

"Yes, you *are* in trouble." He nipped the cub's nose. "The rules exist for a reason." Leopard cubs were curious to the nth degree—without those rules, they'd never make it to adulthood.

The cub hung his head.

Bringing him against his chest, Remi petted him. "You're one of mine, and I want you safe," he said, gentling his tone now that the message had gotten through.

Being alpha meant walking a fine line when it came to the cubs. Discipline had to stand alongside affection and love. One without the other would damage their fierce and curious hearts. "It's too dangerous for you to be out alone after dark. Do you understand?"

The cub lifted its head, its ears pricked, and nodded.

Remi nipped his nose again, this time more playfully. The cub batted at him with unclawed paws. Laughing, he handed the boy over to his frazzled parents. Zion's hair was sticking up in spikes and he had suitcases under his eyes.

He and his mate not only had Jasper, but a newborn cub.

"We turned our backs for *one* second," the man grumbled, throwing the cub over his shoulder. "It's like they're made of pure grease—just slide out under doors."

Leopard in full agreement, Remi left the two to wrangle their cubs, then made his way along the pack's treetop highway to the dining aerie. "Rina!" he called out from the door.

When she glanced over, spoon paused above her dessert, he motioned her across. "Can I grab you for a sec?"

"You need me, too?" Lark asked, looking up from a truly enormous bowl of ice cream.

"No, just Rina."

He'd jumped down to the forest floor by the time Rina made it outside. Seeing that he wasn't on the balcony, she made the jump, too, her ponytail a blond banner behind her. It wasn't a jump any human would ever make, the trees goliaths—and even Remi's cats wouldn't chance the jump from the very top, but the dining aerie was in the lower branches.

"What's up?" the sentinel asked once she was beside him.

"Walk with me. I have some—good—personal news for you."

Reaching up, she fixed her ponytail as she fell into a walk by his side. "Yeah?" A smile. "Don't tell me. My baby brother sent another postcard from a random location."

"Something like that," Remi said, just as Rina's head snapped up, her eyes nightglow as she stared at the trees to their right.

She was running full tilt in that direction a heartbeat later, having obviously picked up her brother's scent despite Remi's upwind approach.

Kit emerged from the trees to catch her and lift her off her feet as she slammed into him like a small tornado. The young male was laughing as Rina hugged his neck and yelled at him for not letting her know he was in the country. At this point, Kit far outweighed Rina both physically and in dominance, but you wouldn't know it from the joyous familiarity of their big sister–little brother interaction.

Delighted for the sibling pair, Remi bowed out and returned to the dining aerie.

Lark was still working her way through the ice cream bowl as big as her head. "What happened to Rina?"

"You'll see." After grabbing a plate of food, he slid in beside the sentinel, two of his senior soldiers across from them. "Where's Angel?"

"Security shift," senior soldier Ihaka said, then scrunched up his nose. "You smell of a cat I don't know . . . though there's something about it that's niggling at me."

"I've had a torturous number of meetings with all kinds of people." He buttered a warm bread roll from the fresh basket one of Fabien's juvenile helpers had just placed on the table. "Thanks, Jack."

"I hate kitchen duty," the juvenile muttered before slouching off—but he made sure to brush his body against Remi's as he did so. Because even big cubs just needed contact with their alpha sometimes—even if they were too moody to admit it.

"Ah, teenagers," Felipe, the older of the senior soldiers, said. "Beaming balls of sunshine and light."

"Kitchen duty is a pack rite of passage," Ihaka added. "He can't just be going out on runs all day like he wants to do."

"I get him." Lark poured more chocolate syrup over her ice cream. "I hated kitchen duty, too, but mostly because our cook was a grizzled old leopard who thought children should be lightly sautéed and served up on a platter."

Remi allowed the conversation to flow around him, his cat happy to be in the heart of his pack. But even so, part of his mind couldn't stop thinking about eyes of moonstone blue and a woman who was an enigma.

Which Auden would he meet the next time around? The quicksilver delight of a woman who fascinated him, the eerie psychometric who'd been there without being there . . . or the ice sculpture whose face gave nothing away.

"Holy drunk bears!" Lark's low whistle emerged into a sudden silence.

Having already caught their scents, Remi wasn't surprised to see Rina standing in the doorway with her arm proudly around her taller sibling. "Everyone! My brother, Kit!"

Kit, his skin flushed with happiness, held up a hand in a wave.

Lark, meanwhile, was waving a hand in front of her face and whispering, "Can you suffer an attack of heat wave at night, because, wow, I'm burning up."

Her reaction was restrained in comparison to another one of their packmates, who yelled, "Is he single? Because if he is, I call dibs!"

From there, it dissolved into friendly chaos, with the young leopard welcomed with slaps on the back and a few kisses on the lips. Remi kept an eye on the situation, but it was clear that Kit could handle himself.

Ignoring the flirts with a natural and warm charm, he slid in at a table that held several soldiers around his own age, and was soon chatting away with the group. That he'd integrated so quickly with his own age group despite his overwhelming dominance was the mark of a damn good leopard.

Rina went off to catch up with a few people she was training.

"Hmm." Lark narrowed her eyes. "He's a dominant. A *really* fucking strong dominant." Glancing at Remi, she raised an eyebrow. "Are we planning to try to keep him?"

"Let's make an effort not to pick a fight with the most powerful leopard pack in the country, hmm, Lark? Especially since they like us right now." But he'd have been lying if he'd said the thought hadn't crossed his own mind.

He even had the perfect argument for it: he had not a single doubt in his mind that Kit *would* one day be an alpha. How better to train for that than to help Remi and his people build their own pack? Then, even if he walked into a position as the alpha of an already existing pack, he'd understand what it was to grow a pack from the foundations, know all the basics.

The young leopard looked over at him just then, raising a mug of beer in his direction in a silent thank-you for the welcome into Rain-Fire. Remi, who'd been passed a beer of his own at some point, raised one back. Whatever happened, RainFire would always be tied to Kit through Rina, which was another small bond in the network the pack was building around itself.

Now, it looked like they might even build a business connection with the Psy.

Translucent blue eyes in his mind. A woman of quicksilver and ice and mystery.

His skin tightened, his pulse rapid—and his leopard ready to play a game for which the rules might be murky, but which Remi's instincts said was dangerously real.

Chapter 16

Abort! Abort! Abort!

—Medical alert during the second attempt at
creating a PsyNet island (19 October 2083)

FIVE DAYS LATER, and Remi's leopard woke up grumpy after another sleepless night dreaming of a woman who thought she could catch his tail that he most definitely could *not* trust. He was guzzling a giant mug of coffee when Lark—still chipper after her night shift—wandered over. "Wow, did you fall out of your aerie or something?"

"Didn't sleep much," he grumbled as he waited for the coffee to take effect. "That was a big rainstorm."

Chewing the bite of her breakfast bagel, Lark nodded sagely. "Uh-huh," she said after she'd swallowed the bite. "Not like you enjoy the rain or anything."

"Go away."

She smirked. "Worried about our resident-with-cub neighbor?"

He froze. "She's there?"

"Uh-huh. Arrived last night. Piloted in right before the storm broke. Smooth as silk." Lark grabbed coffee, then bumped her shoulder against his arm. "She's fine. Still way too pregnant to be up there on her own, but otherwise okay."

"Why the fuck is she so alone at this time?" Leopards could be loners, but pregnant packmates *always* had a support structure. Even if it was just friends who dropped off food while ducking the soon-to-be-mama's wrath.

"I dunno." Lark swallowed another bite. "I remember my cousin, Petunia, one time she said she wanted to claw off everyone's faces because they were all up in hers, so she banned visitors from her aerie for ten days. Only exception was her mate. Petunia threatened to shoot anyone else who came near her door. Maybe our neighbor visits the cabin when she's in one of those moods."

Somehow, Remi didn't think so. Auden Scott wore an air of aloneness that he found difficult to put into words. It wasn't the kind of contained isolation that he'd sensed in fellow loners when he'd walked that road himself; this was an aloneness so profound it made his soul ache.

Which was why, even though he barely knew her, he put together a package of food that wasn't as much about nutrition as it was comfort, then drove up as far as he could. It made sense with the food, and because he had multiple comm meetings today for which he couldn't afford to be late.

That included his monthly check-in with the alphas in this region, where they passed on relevant intel and shared news. None of the others were feline, and he actively disliked the pompous eagle wingleader, but changelings had learned how important it was to communicate after the Psy tried to play them against each other a while back.

So they gritted their teeth and kept any growls to a minimum. At least the closest wolf alpha wasn't an ass, and Remi genuinely appreciated the brash black bear alpha who'd once muttered that certain eagles should get their feathers plucked—this had been while only she and Remi had been on the call.

The fifth member of their group was from a herd of horses. Calm and even-tempered, and with enough grit to hold his own against a bunch of snarling predators. It helped that the entire group never met in person. Less chance of a personality conflict leading to posturing.

After that headache, he had a scheduled call with Aden. With the two of them so busy, he hadn't seen the Arrow leader in person for a couple of months, but they never let a week go by without speaking. Other than Angel, Remi considered Aden his closest friend. The other man was an alpha, too, albeit of a different kind—but unlike with the area group, Aden was an alpha with whom Remi had no trouble dropping his shields.

When they talked, it was the real deal, complete with hard edges and private worries.

Once he'd parked, he made his way to the cabin on foot—and wasn't the least surprised when a tiger prowled out of the trees to shadow him. "Shut up," he said to his best friend. "She's out here all alone. I'm just being a good neighbor."

The tiger made vocalizations that sounded suspiciously like choked laughter. You'd never know that Angel was one of the quietest members of the pack, the one who'd intended to be a loner all his life—until Remi talked him into being part of RainFire. Angel had only initially signed on for a year out of loyalty to Remi.

"I'll take off after," he'd warned.

But he hadn't left.

He'd committed. Even if he questioned his sanity in doing so at times, Angel never flinched from the duty he'd taken on. For one, Jojo and her posse often talked him into playing hide-and-seek and Angel would gamely pretend he didn't see their tiny butts sticking out of their hiding places, or pick up their scents, or see their tails swishing as they hid in the "bestest" spots.

It was to Angel's credit that he pulled it off with such aplomb that he was their favorite hide-and-seek playmate. Kids had a way of seeing right through his scowl to the heart of the boy who'd first become Remi's friend. Angel had survived hell, had once told Remi he'd lost his soul in the process.

He'd been wrong. Angel's soul might be scarred over, but it stood wild and strong.

This morning, Remi's best friend nudged at his legs in a silent question. "I don't know," Remi said. "But I don't think it matters whether we can trust her or not—we still have to look after her."

A human or Psy might not have understood, but they were changeling. More specifically, they were RainFire, a pack that held protecting the weak as a core tenet of their honor. Never would Remi's pack be like WhiteMountain, a noxious place that had seen nothing wrong with a fight-or-die mentality.

In the end, it had been the pack that had died.

If Auden didn't want company, he'd back off—but his people would continue to do discreet runs past her place, and he'd continue to drop off food. That was their way.

Growling an acknowledgement, Angel broke off to the left to complete his security sweep.

And Remi walked out into the clearing in front of the cabin. It was still damp from the night's rain, though the sun was starting to spear through the clouds. The soft morning light made Auden's skin glow as she opened her front door to step out and for a moment, he was stunned by her radiant beauty.

Then he saw her eyes. Frigid. Hard. Flat.

"What are you doing on my property?"

He went motionless at the unwelcoming question asked in a voice that was "off" in a way that made his claws prick at his skin. "Being neighborly."

"I have no need of company." She stared at him with an eerie lack of recognition on her face.

Spine locking as he thought of her vacant stare on their first meeting and of how she'd told him of a head injury, he said, "Do you know who I am?"

"I assume you must be a changeling to be so at home in these feral surroundings." She looked around, almost as if she didn't know what she was doing here herself.

Inside his skin, Remi's leopard opened its mouth, its incisors glinting. A reaction to her scent . . . to the teeth-aching *metal* in it.

Metal that hadn't been present the last time they'd met. It wasn't a contact scent, either. This was *hers*—except how could it be? A person's true scent—the one created of the total sum of their parts—didn't change in a matter of days. It wasn't like perfume that could be washed off or applied at will.

"Why haven't you left?" the woman with Auden's face demanded. "I've made it clear I don't want your presence on my land."

Every instinct Remi had screamed that something was wrong.

Holding up the cooler as he considered his next action, he said, "A gift from the pack, to establish friendly relations."

"I have all the nutrients I need, so I'm unlikely to consume anything within if the gift is of food, but I appreciate the gesture." Words so encased in frost that they raised the hairs on his arms—and made his leopard pace in dislike and confusion both.

Much as he'd prefer an easy explanation, this wasn't another woman, a secret twin. She *did* carry Auden's scent except that it was mangled and altered on a level he'd never before experienced.

Could the change be a sign of serious mental instability in Psy?

Hit by a sense of loss for something he'd never possessed, every muscle in his body threatened to turn rock-hard. "I'll leave it with you anyway. My cook included high-energy items that might come in useful if we get another storm and you run out of supplies." A total lie; he'd packed the cooler himself, and he'd brought treats for the vulnerable woman who carried aloneness in her skin, not useful items for this stranger.

"I'm leaving as soon as I can arrange it, so it will go to waste, but once again, I appreciate the gesture." Auden's doppelgänger smiled . . . and it made him want to shake her, force her to divulge what the fuck she'd done to Auden.

Because that practiced curve of the lips complete with eyes that warmed? It wasn't an inept grimace made by a Psy trying to interact with a changeling. No, this smile would've passed as normal to most people.

It was as psychopathic in its smoothness as Auden had been awkward.

Remi's growl threatened to escape his chest. "Shall I place it inside your doorway? I won't have to step into the cabin."

"There's no need. I'll take it."

"It's pretty light," he assured her as he handed it over.

She gasped and swayed the instant her fingers closed over the handle, the blue of her eyes eclipsed by a wave of black.

—WARMTH, laughter—

—satiation—

—green-gold eyes, small paws—

—impatience—

—a big male hand, a sense of home—

The imprints burned into Auden's senses, shoved through her veins, her synapses sparkling fire.

Pregnancy intensifies our ability to sense imprints.

The imprints pulsed in a living beat within her, her skin feeling as if it rippled with fur.

"Auden?"

Only then did she realize she wasn't alone. She stared uncomprehendingly at Remi. "When did you get here?" Her eyes caught on the arm she'd raised in a startled motion . . . and she realized that not only was she standing in sunlight, but that her dress was blue. The last thing she remembered wearing had been black.

The cooler slipped from her grip. "What—"

Her eyes clashed into those of feline yellow-green. She noticed with some distant part of her brain that he'd caught the cooler before it hit the ground, put it aside. But his attention was on her. "Do you know who I am?"

Auden's mouth went dry that he'd even ask that. "Why wouldn't I? Remington Denier, alpha of RainFire. Remi."

He watched her with unblinking focus. "Do you remember what we were talking about just before?"

Her shoulders grew tight, her hands clammy all at once. She tried to speak, but her tongue was too thick in her mouth. It had happened again, and this time outside of the Scott compound, where it could be hushed up and forgotten.

"Of course I do," she said, hoping she could bluff her way out of the blank spot in her mind.

"Liar." A single soft word that crashed her world to her feet.

Emotion rolled over her in a wave of terror held back far too long, and suddenly, to her absolute horror, she was crying. Huge gulping sobs that wracked her frame and had her searching her PsyNet shields with manic desperation to ensure they hadn't fallen.

Officially, Silence might no longer be the Psy way, but emotion remained verboten in her family. A single hint that she'd broken the line, and she'd lose the little freedom she'd carved for herself.

Across from her, Remi seemed to lock up that big body, his hands fisted at his side. Growling deep in his chest, the sound rough against her senses, he said, "Come here. If you can handle the contact, come here."

She shouldn't. It went against every rule of the world in which she'd been raised. It also exposed her to this changeling who was all but a stranger to her, and who now knew that something was very, *very* wrong with the ostensible scion of the Scott empire. But she stumbled forward anyway, her cheek ending up pressed to the hard warmth of his chest, and her hands gripping the sides of his T-shirt.

He burned hot, his scent of the forest wild.

And his arms, when they came around her, were so strong that panic fluttered at her.

"Just say the word when you want me to let go." His voice was a rumble-growl against her, a vibration that comforted despite the danger of the creature she heard in his voice. "Skin privileges are just that, a privilege not a right."

Skin privileges.

The words penetrated the sobs wracking her, but she was too distraught to understand them. She could've blamed it on the imprints on the handle of the cooler—so warm, so joyous, so of family and of *care*—but she knew the truth.

This was the result of months of fear, months of "waking" to find herself somewhere totally different from where she last remembered being. Months of Dr. Verhoeven telling her that it was a lingering symptom of her neural scarring. But if that were true, it should have improved as she became more and more herself.

It hadn't.

It was getting worse.

Never before, however, had she done an act this reckless—*flown* the jet-chopper from the compound to this remote cabin. A flight of which she had only vague memories. Of last night, after her arrival, she had *nothing*.

Dr. Verhoeven had suggested that she might be having "invisible" micro seizures that were wiping out her memory. Charisma had confirmed much bigger grand mal seizures after Auden came to herself with severe bruising on various parts of her body.

What if that had happened while she'd been in the air?

She could've killed her baby.

"Shh, little cat. You'll make yourself sick." A deep purr of a voice that vibrated into her bones. "Listen to my voice, focus on it." He kept on talking, telling her about the kinds of trees prevalent in this region, which birds called it home, which smaller creatures shared this land with his pack.

It was a glimpse into a wondrous world far beyond her experience.

She did what he said, *had* to do what he said because she didn't know how to get herself out of this on her own. Remi was all she had, even though she was painfully conscious that he wouldn't have chosen this.

Auden knew who and what she was—a Scott. Feared by some. Hated by others. Remington Denier was the alpha of a changeling pack. He wasn't helping her because he liked her. No one *liked* Auden.

They tolerated her, or found her useful, or saw her as a means to an end.

Jerking back, she wasn't surprised when he let her go. Of course he would if he was trying to win her trust, trying to show her that he wouldn't betray her. She couldn't trust him. She couldn't trust anyone.

Her father had taught her that lesson with the biggest betrayal of her life.

Her fingers drifted to her temple, the scar just under her hairline a ridged reminder of the price of trust.

Chapter 17

There is a point of terminal velocity, a moment beyond which the psychometric no longer has control of the inputs into their system. I didn't understand that prior to that day at the Johanssen farm, when I fell into the vortex of an evil so profound that the imprints have become a permanent part of my own memories.

I was institutionalized in the direct aftermath. Not because I was psychotic, but because I believed with every cell in my body that I had committed the atrocities for which I had such vivid memories both visual and emotional. I remembered not just the act of brutalization, but pleasure so violent it was obscene, and I was convinced that warped pleasure was mine.

—Excerpt from *Terminal Velocity: A Psychometric's Journey into Oblivion* by Crispin Nicholas (1973)

"I'M SORRY." AUDEN wiped her face on the sleeves of her loose sweater dress, an action which would've horrified her mother.

But Shoshanna Scott had been displeased by Auden from a young age. Why she'd made Auden her successor, even in name only, especially given Auden's injury, no one would ever know.

Auden *did*, however, know why Shoshanna had carried her in the womb, rather than using a surrogate. The vast majority of Psy believed that contact with the maternal carrier's mind influenced the child's mind—and psychic integrity was as important to the bloodline as genetic.

Her journey to birth had never bothered Auden. She hadn't even been wounded by her mother's disdain. To her, Shoshanna had just been her maternal donor, Henry the person who was her actual *parent*.

A good parent.

A good man.

A good *liar*.

"I'm sorry," she repeated through a throat that rasped, the need inside her an aching hurting thing that wanted to hide her face in his arms and pretend this was her life, her world. Safe. Warm. Full of the wild. "I don't know what happened."

"Pregnancy hormones?" Remi suggested, ducking his head in an effort to meet her gaze. "It's not a big deal," he said when she refused to cooperate. "I've held more than one crying pregnant woman in my time."

Auden tried to make sense of that, couldn't. "You have?"

"One of the lesser-known duties of an alpha. My chest is well used to being a landing pad for tears."

He was trying to ease her embarrassment, she thought, and wanted *so much* to take him at face value. To believe in someone enough to lower her guard even this much, it would be more than she'd known since the day her father sacrificed her to the altar of his ambition. "Thank you."

"Auden"—Remi's voice wasn't all human—"I don't want to push you after what you just experienced, but we have to talk."

Her muscles threatened to spasm, they'd gone so tight. "Yes." It came out a whisper as she thought frantically about how to explain what had happened without coming across as brain damaged. Her baby couldn't afford for Auden to be seen as weak, as prey. "I need to wash my face."

"I'll stay out here. Unless . . . how sensitive are you? To what you pick up, I mean? Will my presence inside leave strong impressions?"

"Imprints," she found herself saying—because no one in her life had ever been interested in her ability. "We call them imprints."

"Right, imprints." He nodded at the cooler. "You seemed to go into something like a seizure when you touched the handle. Rigid body, eyes shifting to black."

"It's better if you stay here," Auden said, rather than thinking about the image he'd sketched for her. It did sound like a seizure, a bad one. Maybe that was why she had no memory of their conversation, or even of accepting the cooler from him—the seizure had disrupted her neurons, wiped them clean.

Once inside her cabin, she made quick work of washing up. The eyes that looked back at her from the mirror remained that pale Shoshanna blue, so unexpected and striking against the rich dark of Auden's skin tone.

Shoshanna blue.

That was how she'd always thought of them, these eyes her mother's enduring stamp on Auden. She shouldn't have them—the genetic calculations done before her birth had put the probability of her inheriting her father's brown eyes at ninety-nine point eight percent.

Shoshanna, however, had never liked to lose.

So now when Auden looked at herself, she saw the same eyes that had always been cold and disinterested when deigning to look in Auden's direction, and icily calculating the rest of the time.

One last laugh on Shoshanna's part.

The rest of Auden's face was hollow, her skin pallid. Only her hair remained undisturbed and pristine in its tight bun at the back of her head, the strands sleeked over her head with a precision that she'd taught herself as a teenager.

As a preteen—when she'd finally been permitted to choose her own style—she'd worn a short, curly crop pushed back with combs. At least in her father's house. Outside and at Shoshanna's, she'd been expected to go to the hairdresser and get her hair put into a contained style that would be considered "professional" among the Psy.

Auden had never understood what her curls had to do with professionalism.

Pushing away from the sink, she dried off, then went to her small kitchen area and mixed up a nutrient drink. The last thing she felt like doing was eating, but her stomach was rumbling, which meant that her child had to be hungry, too. At least the liquid was a cold balm against the abused tissues of her throat.

She emerged to an empty clearing.

Disappointment was a lead weight in her gut, her abrupt loneliness hurting parts of her she hadn't known could hurt. But meshed with the hurt was a shaking sense of relief. Now, she wouldn't have to deal with his questions, wouldn't have to think of more lies.

It was hard to lie to someone who had held you while you cried, his big body a protective embrace.

Fingers trembling, she drank more of the nutrients, but was only halfway through the glass when the trees rustled and Remi emerged holding two slender metallic cases.

Her lungs expanded, the world back in Technicolor. "What are those?"

"We usually throw a couple of these folding chairs in the back of our vehicles." Opening one case, he quickly assembled it into a comfortable-appearing seat. "I'm likely to be the only one who's touched it for a while," he told her. "They don't get much use—it's pretty much only if we go down to the town to watch a game. A few of the juveniles have joined local leagues."

Auden went to the chair and reached out a single careful finger. One brush and—

—*excitement, Remi's excitement*—

—*fur, small hands, tiny paws, and a waving tail*—

—*sweet things, liquid spilled*—

—*family*—

—*worry, directed at* Auden—

The ache inside her spread, so deep that it threatened all she thought she knew of the world. "Yes," she whispered. "I can sit in this."

Sit in it and pretend that she was part of that happy family where children felt safe enough to clamber into an adult's lap, their trust a

sweet thread that resonated with her maternal heart . . . and where this
leopard alpha meant it when he seemed to care about her, his protectiveness embracing her as fiercely as it embraced his pack.

His imprint whispered that he *did* mean it, but that was a fleeting
kiss, a momentary burst of concern that might be directed at any pregnant woman alone in the forest.

It wasn't about Auden herself.

But for a few minutes, seated in this chair that he'd brought for her,
she could pretend.

The second chair ready, Remi rose to grab the cooler and put it in
front of them before he took a seat. "How are you feeling?"

Tears threatened again, a thick knot of them in her throat.

"Better," she said when she could speak, then felt compelled to add,
"You don't have to babysit me. I'm sure you're a busy man."

"Not too busy for this." He stretched out his legs, his gaze on the
trees beyond. "You mind if I ask what it feels like when you pick up an
imprint? I've never met a psychometric before."

Auden's first urge was to tell him everything. He sounded genuinely
interested. But aware of her current muddled state, she considered his
words, thought of how information could be used to cause harm not just
to her but to others like her, and hesitated.

"I know you sense emotion." Remi's eyes glinted at her. "Cat's out of
the bag there."

She exhaled, the decision easier now. "It's why Ps-Psy kept their
heads down during Silence," she said. "And why there are so few of us.
We were rare anyway, but while the Council didn't bother to crush us
as they did designation E—likely because we were too few in number
to make a ripple in the Net—the quiet pressure to select for less 'emotional' abilities had an effect."

"I did a bit of research after we first met," Remi said, "and saw some
pretty high salaries offered by universities and museums for psychometrics."

"We're prized in certain quarters now, but during the initial few decades of Silence we were considered one of the least desired of abilities. That generation took enough psychometric genes out of the pool that our numbers now are even smaller than they were prior to Silence. Small enough to command a premium at those facilities that need us."

Remi stayed silent, a big jungle cat who looked outwardly lazy but who she was certain could move at lethal speed without warning.

"Our low numbers," she added, "meant that even if we did breach Silence on a bad read, we didn't have a big enough presence to contaminate the Net with emotion." It had been a formless black back then, dotted with the cold and icy stars that were the minds of the Psy.

No empathic color, no desperate honeycomb to connect them to each other in an effort to stop the psychic network from crumbling. The latter terrified Auden, not for herself, but for her innocent baby, who would be born into a world with a PsyNet that was thick with holes and ragged with lost and broken pieces.

She felt sick when she stepped onto it these days, the thinness of the psychic fabric a stark warning.

"Makes sense," Remi said in that easy way of speaking, as if he had all the time in the world. "Why waste energy on such a small percentage of the population, especially when I'm guessing most of you tried to stay away from emotional reads?"

Auden nodded, feeling an odd expansion in her chest. This was the first time she'd spoken openly about her ability to anyone in real life. To someone who knew her as Auden Scott and not just anonymous user A9.

It felt so good that she broke her private rules, told him more. "Back in the old world, before Silence, psychometrics worked regularly with search and rescue and even Enforcement. They used to help catch serial killers.

"In one famous case, the Ps-Psy found a live victim because the victim had thrown her driver's license out the window of the car as it was traveling the highway, but she'd been reciting her abductor's registration number in her head at the time. Over and over again. Until it imprinted on the license."

Remi whistled. "Wow, that's seriously good tracking."

"It was also agonizing," she whispered. "I've read a copy of the book the psychometric published." It was passed around the forum like a holy relic, a forbidden thing from the time before Silence.

"The license was a clean item as imprints go, but Crispin Nicholas—the psychometric—later read the basement on the killer's farm, the place where he tortured and murdered his victims. Crispin wrote that it felt like fingers shoving into his skull while other fingers forced his eyes open and made him watch, made him see everything that had gone on in that place.

"He couldn't look away, couldn't make the images stop, was frozen in place until a human colleague figured out something had gone horrifically wrong and punched him unconscious before physically carrying him out—with no access to a strong telepath who could go in and disrupt the read, it was the only way to break him out of the loop."

Remi's agreement was quiet, his voice deep and low. "Be like picking up the scents at a murder scene a couple of days old. The fetid scent of decay."

"Yes, only a hundred times worse. Because scents fade after a short time when compared to imprints. And layered imprints, where the same action has occurred over and over and over, can be relentless."

—warmth, happiness, pride—

She realized she was stroking the arm of her chair, bathing in an imprint that didn't hurt but healed. How utterly lovely.

"The bad reads . . . they're chaos, nightmare pieces." Auden wanted so much for him to understand that she tried to think of a way to give better shape to the experience. "Like walking into a library to find all the books pulled off the shelves and thrown on the floor, only a few spines visible and all the pages ripped out and scattered out of order."

She found herself tracing Remi's profile with her gaze as he took the time to think over her words.

"That's why you only pick up snatches, images, or pieces."

It made her wonder all over again what she'd read on his comm device. "Yes." But then she told him more, because her defenses were down and any other motivations aside, he did care in at least an impersonal way.

"We *can* pick up more coherent things—that's what the academic psychometrics do, but it requires intense focus and energy. It's too difficult with emotion-touched objects. The resonance is too strong, starts to overwhelm the psychometric.

"Crispin called it terminal velocity in his book, the point at which the psychometric isn't able to turn back, get themselves out of the nightmare."

Remi's eyebrows drew together over his eyes. "Have you—"

"Only once—and I was so scared that I broke away before terminal velocity." It had left her a trembling, sweat-soaked wreck regardless. "A mistake in childhood. An object picked up off the ground at my small private school that had been dropped by a teacher who should never have been in charge of children."

Remi's growl made her nape prickle.

"My father was . . . not a good man," she said, speaking the words aloud for the first time. "But he did a good thing then. He believed me. And that teacher vanished." Swallowing, she met his gaze. "Do you judge me for not caring about what happened to him?"

"No. I'm changeling. If you're implying what I think you're implying about the teacher, then our sentence is death at the claws of the alpha. No mercy. No forgiveness. Not for violating the trust of the smallest and most vulnerable of us all."

Auden's shoulders softened.

His jaw yet a brutal line, Remi's eyes went to her empty glass. "How about it?" He nodded at the cooler. "You want to try the food I brought?"

Her stomach rumbled right on cue.

"I think your cub is saying yes." His grin creased his cheeks, eased up the grim line of his jaw.

Her stomach flipped.

She was still struggling with the reaction when he opened the lid to show her the goods within, his eyes bright with a feline wildness.

Right then, she understood what humans and changelings meant when they said a person's smile reached their eyes. It was a warmth that couldn't be faked, a sense that this being was glowing from the inside out.

"Auden?"

Flushing, she jerked her gaze away from his face and to the cooler.

Remi didn't rush her as she stared down at two items she recognized as muffins from seeing them on the comm, a swirling pastry that might've been a cinnamon roll, and what looked like a croissant. Then there was a sealed packet of cookies, a clear container of mixed berries, and a block of chocolate.

"I wasn't sure how into food you were, so I kept it simple. The cinnamon roll is probably the one with the strongest flavor."

Hungry in a way she hadn't ever been before her pregnancy, Auden felt as if she could devour it all, but limited herself to trying the croissant for now. It was still warm. What she'd assumed was a cooler, she realized, was actually a carrier designed to keep food at the temperature it was when put inside.

Having placed her empty glass on the ground, she now took a large bite of the croissant . . . and made a startled sound as flakes of pastry drifted down around her. It was no doubt all over her face, too.

But she didn't care.

"This is *delicious*." Forgetting every bit of manners she'd ever been taught, she took several more bites in quick succession . . . then looked sadly at her empty hand.

Instead of laughing at her, Remi creased his cheeks again with a smile she could almost believe held affection. "I'll bring more croissants next time."

Next time.

A galloping horse inside her chest, she decided to try the cinnamon roll despite his warning that it was the strongest tasting. A single bite and she moaned before licking up the frosting around her mouth.

"You should have some water to wash that down," Remi said, his voice sounding strangled.

She waved him toward her cabin.

He hesitated. "I'll have to touch your things."

"Glass is on the sink. Keep your shoes on. Tap is motion activated." Then she took another bite of the most delicious item she'd ever tasted. "And I like your imprint. It's like an enormous comforting purr that wraps around me." The words spilled out in a haze of sugar and cinnamon.

Chapter 18

Abstract: An argument in favor of why Psychometry should be moved in the Psy power charts to sit next to Foresight and the subcategory of Backsight. F-Psy see the future, while those with backsight see the past. Ps-Psy also see the past—the only difference is that their visions of the past are anchored to an object.

—*Psychometry and Its Placement on Psy Power Charts* by Faith NightStar and Tanique Gray, paper submitted to the Académie de la classification des Psi run under the aegis of the Ruling Coalition, June 2083

REMI FORCED HIMSELF to look away from the woman who was so lusciously enjoying food that *he'd* brought her—and who'd just murmured that he was like a "comforting purr."

Not the kind of thing he'd ever thought he'd want to hear from a beautiful woman, but yeah, it was a good feeling to know that she felt safe with him. Safe enough to tell him that, and to allow him into her haven.

Woman was food drugged so he should probably take the entire thing with a grain of salt, but damn if he didn't want to *actually* purr. She took another bite, moaned. His cock threatened to *react*. You'd have thought he was a wolf or a bear with the feral depth of his response. Courtship via food wasn't a cat thing.

Not that he was courting her.

First, Auden didn't need to be thinking about him putting the moves on her when she was in the final trimester of her pregnancy. Second, he still didn't know her motives or anything of who she was beyond being a pregnant psychometric.

Third—and most important—was her mental state and ability to consent.

His incipient arousal dying under the grim reminder of her personality shift and associated memory loss, he made sure to wipe off his boots on the mat outside the front door. It was obvious from the pristine shine of her wooden floor that she didn't wear outdoor shoes inside, and he felt bad doing so even though she'd given him the go-ahead.

Despite her statement that she liked his imprint, he took extreme care not to touch any other surface as he made his way to the sink. It wasn't hard to find—the place was all one bedroom, except for a closed-off area at the back that he assumed led to the toilet and shower.

Auden's home was almost militantly basic. She had a simple futon—*what the hell*—with white sheets and a white comforter. A single wonky chair and a narrow dresser sat beside the futon. The kitchen table was small and round, and had no chair.

There were no rugs on the floor, no cushions for her to shove behind her back when it began to ache.

As for entertainment, he saw a small mobile comm and a single organizer.

That was it. Nothing in here spoke of the woman whom he'd taught to shoot, or who was currently making little noises of pleasure that he could hear even through the cabin walls. Too bad she was in no state to play—even his cat understood that. As it understood that he couldn't allow her to keep avoiding the sobering subject.

Once back outside, he sat in his chair and waited until she'd taken a good long drink of the water before offering to hold the glass so she could finish her intense consumption of the cinnamon roll. He wished he'd brought more things for her now, wished he could sit her down and feed her delicious tidbit after delicious tidbit.

Only . . . this wasn't a simple playful date between a man and a woman.

Gut tight, he let her enjoy herself, finding a profound and primal joy in having given her that. Only after she'd finished the roll, licked her fingers, and emptied the glass of water did he talk. Or more accurately— growled. "Why the fuck are you on a futon?" Not even a proper one with a low base. A literal mattress on the floor. "Isn't it hard to get up and down?"

She nodded, her full lips turned down at the corners "Takes *hours*. Or that's what it feels like. But furniture has imprints and the bed, so close to my sleeping brain . . . the noise is unbearable."

Remi wanted to ask if she always slept on a futon, but that wasn't important. "We have a small mech facility—you know that. But we can do larger pieces. What if we printed a frame for you?"

"People still would have to handle it."

"I'll do it. Only me."

Auden stared at him, her motionlessness speaking of a creature wary and on edge. "Why?"

"Because you should not be sleeping on the floor!" He threw up his hands. "Will you try and see if it works?"

A slow nod.

Exhaling, he moved on to a far more problematic topic. "You know we have to talk about what happened this morning."

Her spine grew stiff, her features a plastic caricature of Silence. "You know I have mental problems," she said at last, her tone flat. "You saw that when you first met me."

"This was more than that." Remi could still taste the distasteful metallic layer to her scent even though it had vanished after she had her seizure. "You didn't know who I was, and you smelled wrong."

Frown marring her brow, cracking the plastic, she turned toward him. "What do you mean I *smelled* wrong?"

"Smells are powerful identifiers to changelings. I can recognize people from scent alone—it's like an ID. Each one unique." When he saw he had her full attention, he continued, "Your scent changed. It wasn't perfume or body lotion or anything surface level. It was your *base* scent, the scent that is you no matter what else might layer itself on top. You had two. This one and another."

AUDEN had no idea what Remi was talking about, and told him so. "I can't think of any reason for a shift in my scent, but I'm not changeling. I don't know what can alter a scent signature." She worried at her lower lip with her teeth. "Could it be the baby?"

"No. Babies don't develop their own scent until after birth. Until then, it's the mother's." Remi rubbed his face, his hand scraping against the beard shadow that darkened his jaw.

"But I don't know how Psy work well enough to guess why your scent might have changed." Shifting so that he faced her, his body on a right angle to hers, the warmth of him a near-physical touch, he said, "Even if we leave that aside, you were a whole different person—and you didn't remember any of our conversation afterward."

Auden struggled to think back, only to come up against the same black wall she'd already faced so many times after these incidents. "No one's ever reported a personality shift . . . but it's possible they didn't notice. I'm not this emotional at home." The words had escaped her mouth before she realized what she was admitting.

"I get that," Remi said. "I've heard that a lot of the older and more entrenched families prefer to continue on as if nothing's changed."

Auden gave a curt nod, her lips pursed.

"Do you want to know what you were like?"

No, Auden wanted to scream, no, she didn't want to know. Because the more she knew, the more she had to confront the fact that her mind was broken in ways that couldn't be fixed. She'd gotten lucky with what capacity she had now; this was never going to get any better.

But . . . She stroked her belly, a fist in her throat. This wasn't just about her. She needed to know so she could make decisions about her baby. So she swallowed the lump of fear in her gut and said, "Yes."

"Remote and cold enough to make me question if it was even you." Remi's words rumbled with the leopard's growl. "Silence so perfect it was unbreakable."

The hairs rose on the back of Auden's neck, her tongue going dry. She'd never come close to perfect Silence. Being a psychometric made that impossible. Even the best of the best among Ps-Psy only passed the Silence tests at around seventy-five percent—which was considered an acceptable score but one with plenty of room for improvement.

She'd barely scraped through with sixty-two percent.

Her father had put her in remedial school for Silence, and she wasn't sure he'd ever shared her results with her mother. As for the remedial school, their drills had pushed her scores up to seventy percent by the skin of her teeth, and that had been good enough for her to graduate to adulthood, leaving behind the lessons of Silence.

"Auden?"

Her hand clenched the chair arm. "I need to think about this." Needed to figure out if she'd gone beyond neural damage and into in-stability so bad that her personality had split in two.

Bile burned her throat.

She couldn't do that kind of life-altering thinking with Remi here, his presence so big and wild and dominant that it pushed against her senses in primal demand. "Please go. I need to be alone."

"I'm going to send patrols this way to check on you." His tone said she had no choice in the matter.

And since she'd had not one but two seizures in the past twelve hours, she had no will to argue. "Fine. They can look in the window if I'm not outside."

Expression dark with a scowl and eyes leopard, Remi nonetheless rose to his feet. "One more thing—thanks for sending the indi-mech deal our way. That was you, wasn't it?"

Her nod was jagged. "You were the best option. But the final decision will be based on your proposal." The words flowed off her tongue, as if she'd been running business operations for years.

A chill wind over her skin.

Some of what she'd been doing of late might be explained by things she'd observed in her years of blurred awareness, but not this, how her mind had begun to make calculations without thought in terms of business, how the right words just bloomed in her brain and took shape in her mouth.

"We get that." Remi glanced over at her cabin, then back at her. "Call me when you decide you've had enough aloneness, and we'll talk. I'll print you a bed in the interim."

TWO hours later, Auden got into her jet-chopper and flew herself home. Once she'd calmed down, she'd realized she had no choice. If she'd had a seizure bad enough that it had nearly wiped out all memory of her flight to the cabin, then her piloting the craft again was a huge risk, but it wasn't a deadly one.

She'd put on both biometers that Dr. Verhoeven had assigned her, then locked them into the onboard system. Any major fluctuation and she'd programmed the chopper to land at the heliport behind her family home—that heliport was equipped with emergency "homing beacons" that would guide the chopper safely down.

The same wasn't possible at the cabin, which meant she'd be stuck at the house until she could figure out another way to reach the freedom of this place of mountain and trees, morning mist and creatures wild.

She kept her eyes trained on the trees as she flew, searching for glimpses of gold and black, but jungle cats were masters of the hunt. All she saw were waves of fall foliage, the canopy so verdant that she couldn't even make a guess as to where RainFire made its home.

Her heart clenched when she cleared the final trees, their leaves a cascade of oranges and reds intermingled with lime green and the odd pop of a darker shade. It felt as if she was shutting the door behind herself, giving up on her quest of freedom for her baby. "No," she vowed. "This is just a roadblock. Even if I *am* irreparably damaged, my baby isn't. She's going to make it out."

Auden did everything in her power to keep that thought uppermost on her mind as she landed. Charisma was waiting for her, her organizer held at her side. "I thought you were planning to stay two days," she said once Auden had made it inside the house.

"I wanted to see Dr. Verhoeven," Auden said, and almost told Charisma about the seizures.

Usually, it wouldn't have mattered, because the doctor reported to Charisma anyway, doctor/patient confidentiality no proof against the other woman's power. But Auden was changing, becoming a woman far more able to manipulate and control. The idea made her a little sick— but that didn't mean she wouldn't use her new skills if those skills would keep her daughter safe. This time, the doctor wouldn't be spilling his guts to Charisma.

Auden would make sure of it.

"Oh?" Charisma's eyes sharpened. "Did you have a seizure?"

"That," Auden said with cold precision, "is none of your concern, Ris."

Never in all her existence, had Auden referred to Charisma as Ris. It had been her mother who'd done that, the two of them having worked together since Shoshanna's first company.

Charisma was also the only one who'd been permitted to shorten her mother's name to Shanna—though that had changed as Shoshanna grew in power, the informality strictly one-sided.

Charisma sucked in air, her pupils expanding. "Sir," she whispered, with the slightest bow of her head, and that whisper . . . it held a kind of awe that didn't make sense.

Gut twisting, Auden said nothing else, and kept her face emotionless— that, too, came easier than it should have. It wasn't that she was unused to wearing masks. She'd been wearing one from the moment she first became aware that as a psychometric, her Silence would never reach the level of her father's or mother's.

But this mask, it was different. Not just pretending true Silence, but having to use no effort to do so. As if this was her reality. So much so that she wasn't sure she could take the mask off. Her hand twitched, wanting to reach for the food carrier she'd left in the cabin, break the cycle of her thoughts with a violent surge of imprints brimming with emotion warm and happy.

"I'll leave you here, sir," Charisma said, once they reached the building that held their private medical facilities, her tone eerily subservient.

Auden gave a clipped nod that felt so natural it scared her.

When she walked into the doctor's office moments later, she felt zero surprise to find him watchful in a way he'd never before been. No doubt Charisma had telepathed him, warned him—about what, Auden wasn't sure. But he didn't give her any orders or just take her arm as he usually did.

Instead, he spoke with utmost politeness as he said, "If you'd follow me to the examination room and take a seat on the chair, we can collect your vitals. It's critical to keep an eye on all factors as you come closer to birthing the fetus."

"That's why I'm here," she said in a crisp tone as they walked into the examination room. "It's possible I had a seizure while in the air piloting the chopper."

"That's indeed a cause for serious concern." He set her up in the examination chair that had only ever been used for Auden, after being produced when she was a young teenager and being left fallow for years so any remaining imprints on it could fade.

Once she was in the chair that monitored far too many parameters of her body, the doctor examined the feed on his screens. "I'm seeing elevated levels of adrenaline, cortisol, and other indicators of stress."

"I'm concerned about the pregnancy," Auden said, shaping her words to echo the doctor's coldness.

"I assumed as much. Such physical responses are impossible to control no matter how good our Silence." He peered closer at the screen. "There are a few other minor fluctuations, but nothing important. We'll have to do a neural scan."

Chapter 19

None of Henry's biological material survived his death, and the other male members of his family are unsuitable for psychic reasons I've outlined below. I'm afraid we'll have to widen the search.

—Message from Charisma Wai to Shoshanna Scott (14 June 2082)

AUDEN HATED THIS. Doctors playing with her brain was how she'd ended up brain damaged. But for now, it appeared Dr. Verhoeven would do exactly as Auden decreed. "Nothing invasive," she ordered. "The pregnancy is too far along to take any kind of risk."

"Yes, of course. I would never put your well-being in jeopardy, sir." With that strange remark that focused on Auden and not the baby he'd been obsessed with to date, Dr. Verhoeven fitted a helmet of fine mesh over her head, then connected it to the scanner as well as the secondary scanner that would confirm his findings. "Shall I proceed?"

Hands curled lightly around the ends of the chair arms, and kept lax through sheer effort of will, Auden gave another one of those curt nods that were coming without effort. And though she believed the doctor would do as he'd said and not attempt an invasive procedure, she still had to clench her stomach when he began the scan.

From the outside, she knew it looked like blue-green fire dancing through the strands of the mesh, a strange beauty.

"Please recite the alphabet," the doctor said. "Then numerals from one to a hundred."

Auden was familiar with this part of the process—it was the way they'd calibrated the machines so that her readings could be judged against the same metric over time. The letters, then numbers emerged in a smooth progression.

"Excellent." The doctor looked about as excited as a man who'd spent seven decades in Silence could look, his florid face patchy and hot. "The increase in neural activity is remarkable. Almost ninety-five percent of the previously dead spots are once again active."

Dead spots.

Scars.

Put inside her by her parents.

If Auden had once known the graft's intended purpose, she'd lost access to that information during her blank years. She had, however, picked up hints since her mind began to work properly again. "Stretching" had been one term she'd heard the doctor mutter in relation to the procedure, and on its own, the word made no sense when related to the brain.

She could just demand the information . . . but she was currently balanced on a knife edge when it came to her autonomy—she couldn't afford to reveal any hint of weakness, even if only by making the doctor and Charisma consciously aware of her lack of knowledge. Both spoke to her on the assumption that she already knew.

As the doctor proved with his next statement.

"It's possible the seizure was triggered by the increase," the doctor mused. "As you're well aware, sir, this entire procedure is wholly new territory—we have no idea how or why the brain is recovering, though we believe it's linked to the fetus. But add in the other factor and things become more complicated."

The other factor.

What other factor? Auden wanted to demand, feeling as if she was playing a game to which everyone but her knew the rules. "I think it's time I had a good look through all my medical records, especially those that relate to my brain," she said at last, after calculating the risk of such a demand and deciding it was minimal; it fit the Auden the doctor knew in this time and place.

Perhaps she *could* finally gain answers to the mystery of what they'd done to her.

"I'll make sure you have access to them," the doctor said at once, "but I'm afraid most of the notes and scans are esoteric and will need a specialist eye to understand. I'm happy to go through them with you."

"I will look them over on my own first," Auden said in that cold voice that felt like a skin that had settled over her own. "You can explain the more rigorous sections to me."

"Yes, yes." The doctor's voice was absent as he stared at something on his screen.

"A problem?"

"No, well . . ." He spun the screen so she could see it. "This"—he pointed to a set of neural patterns—"is your brain as of the last scan." He touched the screen to pull up another file so the two were side by side. "This is from today."

Auden stared from one to the other. "I'm afraid you've lost me, Doctor."

"It's showing a mix of two patterns." The doctor spun the screen back toward him. "The secondary one is faded but interwoven into the primary. Fascinating."

Your scent changed. It wasn't perfume or body lotion or anything surface level. It was your base scent, the scent that is you no matter what else might layer itself on top. You had two.

Auden's heart galloped at the memory of Remi's disturbing words, but the doctor was too focused on her brain scans to notice. "I wish to get up."

"Oh, of course, sir!" He removed the helmet, leaving her free to rise from the chair.

Which she did at once. "What are the ramifications of the scan?" she asked, even as her skin stretched so tight across her body that she felt as if she'd explode.

"I can't say at this stage." He looked up at her from his bent-over position in front of the screen. "Are you experiencing any confusion, memory loss, or personality changes of which you're aware?"

Auden knew she should tell him the truth, but this doctor was the same man who'd helped her parents monitor her after the botched experiment that had left her with a broken brain. "No," she said with cold clarity. "I'm stable. More stable than I've ever been."

"I see that, sir," he said, but looked back at his screen. "It might be an artefact."

"An artefact?"

"A leftover piece of . . . code, if you will," he said at last. "It should fade as your own code settles into the system. But . . ." He went to another screen, brought up what looked like readings for another person altogether. "Hmm, I'm showing dual neural activity here, too. So you may be in a transitional phase."

Auden's face pulsed, her spine in knots. She might not know what was going on, but she understood instinctively that it couldn't be anything good for her. "I see. Send me those records, too, for completeness."

The doctor tapped the screen. "Sent to a secure device I have here. I'll authorize you as the only user. I'm not sure what monitoring software is on your current devices or if Hayward has access."

So many questions crowded Auden's brain, panic beating at her underneath the strange ice of her skin, but she knew one thing: she had to keep Dr. Verhoeven onside now that he seemed to believe she was back to full capacity. "I won't forget your loyalty or forward thinking."

The doctor straightened, a slight flush under his skin. "I have always been loyal to the family, and you *are* the family, sir."

The sick feeling persisted in Auden's gut even as her brain fired again. "Are there any implants yet in my body?" she asked. "I do not wish to be tracked." The existence of those tiny devices had penetrated her mind at some point during the years she'd been in limbo.

"We removed everything after the pregnancy was confirmed," the doctor said, and once again, it was a procedure of which Auden had no memory and for which she'd given no consent. "We had no idea how the transmitters might interact with the development of the fetus, so took the safer option."

At least now they couldn't track her like an animal. "Excellent." She wanted to push for more information, but the risk of rousing his suspicions was too high.

There was also no chance he'd leave her alone in here to properly read the devices he'd touched. Even if there had been, she wouldn't have taken the opportunity—not when she had no idea of what she might face.

If it had been just her, she'd have risked it. But not with her baby. A bad read could lead to a catastrophic psychic reaction. All else aside, the last thing she needed was to be vulnerable in front of this man who'd treated her as a lab subject without agency or will.

She needed someone she could trust by her side.

A flash of green-gold eyes in the privacy of her mind, the feel of a wide chest and strong arms holding her safe, the memory of a rumbling voice asking if she was all right.

Trust him, whispered the part of her that was coming to the bleak realization that she could not do this alone, not if her brain was starting to fracture again. *One last risk, Auden. For your child. So she'll grow up free.*

"The fetus is fine." The doctor's voice was a scratch that disrupted the desperate stream of her thoughts. "All readings normal."

"Excellent."

"I'll keep digging deep into the neural scans," the doctor said as he showed her out of the examination room. "This is a once-in-a-lifetime project for any physician."

Too bad Auden had no idea of the project's aims. There were too many sentences spoken that had another layer of meaning, too much knowledge assumed by those working with a woman who had documented neural deficits, and too much attention on a baby who shouldn't have been part of Auden's life for many years yet.

"I assume you'd prefer to handle it yourself?" the doctor said after leading her to a small cupboard in his office and opening it to reveal what appeared to be a brand-new organizer. "My assistant touched it for a short period when she set it up, but otherwise it would've just been the manufacturers."

"Do you have a disposable glove?" Auden's voice was losing its ice, she realized, becoming softer. Driven by her protective instinct toward her child, she dug hard and deep to find it again. "I'd prefer not to chance a read."

"A good precaution." Dr. Verhoeven nodded. "Especially at your Gradient level. My assistant's Silence is flawless, but you never know what she might have thought of when handling it. The dispenser is behind you. If you'll let me—" He touched the pad that would extrude a glove. "There you go."

The sterile glove itself was like most of its brethren. It had no imprint to speak of—created by machines before being packed into slabs of gloves by machines, which were then fed into a box by a machine, there wasn't much chance of handling. Even putting them into the dispenser didn't require contact—just pick up a slab, slot it in. The machines were designed to "eat" the plas wrap of the slab, storing the rubbish in a small section that could be emptied when full.

After retrieving the organizer with her gloved hand, she allowed the doctor to use voice activation to transfer ownership to her, with her voice and retinal scans the new passcodes. "Thank you, Doctor," she said in a crisp tone. "You have far exceeded my expectations of you— and they were high to begin with." Again, words with too much meaning, words she hadn't thought about saying until they were out of her mouth.

"It is my greatest honor to assist you in this extraordinary endeavor."

Heat rose in a scalding wave over Auden's body, a burning warning from deep in her psyche. She was thankful her skin tone made it impossible for the doctor to pick up her involuntary reaction. Not saying another word, she left the medical suite to emerge into dazzling sunshine that was a welcome contrast to the swirling darkness inside her mind.

The warmth made her want to linger, drink it in, but Scotts didn't do things like that, so she turned to head toward the house. Only to see her uncle striding toward her, his face a hard blank. "Auden," Hayward Scott said when he met her. "Charisma tells me that you are now at full mental capacity and thus in charge as Shoshanna's official heir."

Well, that was fast.

"It is my legal and biological right," she said, the words rote memory. Her parents had spoken them often enough.

"I would never argue with that." Hayward inclined his head. "As Devlin no longer needs to learn operations, he'll be moving out of the main house and into my residence in the compound."

Auden went to say that was fine, but the words that emerged were, "I think it's better that you and my cousin return to your estate in Surrey. We do not wish to foster any confusion in or out of the family about the line of succession."

The tiniest tic at Hayward's temple, a quiet sign that he'd had more ambitions for his son than he'd ever had for himself. "Surely that's a farfetched concern?"

"That's interesting phrasing on your part." She found herself wondering how many other times he'd tried to subtly convince her that she was crazy; because Uncle Hayward was, after all, a Scott. "But no, it's not farfetched. I will become far more visible once the child is born and I need to be known as the *only* viable heir to Shoshanna Scott. Devlin will be a distraction."

He took a small step back. "Is that a threat?"

Auden belatedly realized it could be taken as that . . . and this was a game of power for her unborn child's life. "Of course not, Uncle." She held his gaze as she spoke in a voice so without emotion it chilled her from the inside out. "I am simply stating facts."

"I must say I didn't expect this of you, Auden, but well done." His shoulders were stiff. "You learned well at Shoshanna's knee. Devlin and I will be gone within the week."

"A wise decision."

Auden kept up her front until she reached her bedroom. But right when she would've collapsed, she remembered how Charisma had run into her room two months earlier, after Auden stumbled and fell onto her hands and knees.

The walls were watching Auden.

A scream built up inside her.

She turned it into rage as cold as the heart of midnight and said, "Charisma, I want a clean room. *Now.*" Maybe she was crazy and talking to the empty air, but she didn't think so.

Charisma appeared at her door three minutes later, a flush on her cheeks and her chest heaving. "I apologize, sir. I didn't think. Security will be here momentarily."

A short man with round cheeks and a clean-shaven head ran down the hallway just then, his eyes flared so wide it was obvious he was terrified. Too terrified to hold up the pretense of Silence. Not meeting Auden's eyes, he ducked into the room after Charisma gave him a nod, and—after pulling on gloves—began to remove listening devices dotted throughout the room.

The only visual recorder was by the vanity mirror.

"Slight overkill don't you think, Ris," Auden said in a tone of voice that she'd heard from her mother when she was in a more relaxed frame of mind.

Charisma's expression was wary. "The neural deficits were significant enough that I judged there was high risk of inadvertent harm to you or the child." A pause. "You did have that one fall where your balance was off . . ."

Auden left her hanging, her eyes on the short man. He ducked into the bathroom. When Auden looked at Charisma, the other woman quickly said, "Only two biomonitors. To ensure we'd know if you had a fall or a faint. You had multiple small seizures after the first attempt."

Attempt.

Another word with a meaning behind it that Auden didn't under-stand. "Acceptable," she said at last. "The last thing I'd want is to crack my skull and bleed to death at this point in the process."

The security man emerged from the bathroom on the heels of her words. "All clear."

"Show me."

His hands shook as he tried to pass over his organizer.

Grabbing the device, Charisma spun it around to show Auden. On it was a design that displayed the exact location where each device had been embedded. Every single one now bore a red cross over it. "I will be displeased in the extreme if I find even a single errant monitoring device left behind," she said, and she wasn't looking at the security man.

It was Charisma she had in her sights.

"I oversaw the installation," the other woman said. "The room is now clean, sir. You know, I would never lie to you."

Despite the aide's vow, Auden didn't lower her guard even after the other two had left—and even though maintaining this mask washed exhaustion over her in deep waves that made her want to sway on her feet.

To save her child, she had to play this game to the end.

Chapter 20

She made another attempt despite the fact the fetus isn't yet ready. A test because the situation is so dire, but it seems to have been a complete failure.

—Dr. Nils Verhoeven to Charisma Wai (3 October 2083)

CHARISMA CUT OFF Jitan when he would've spoken, and only spoke herself once they were out of the house. "You did as requested," she said. "Your task is done."

"It's not just my head on the line!" he said, his voice coming out through gritted teeth. The man's Silence had fallen as fast as *he'd* fallen for sexual contact and gambling highs, but unfortunately, he remained the best in the business at this kind of covert surveillance manufacture and installation. "If she finds out we left one in there—"

"She won't find out. I can remove it without her ever being aware it was present." Before she did that, however, Charisma had to be a hundred percent sure. Because while she wanted to believe, she didn't.

Not yet.

Auden's gaze seemed to flicker at times, her expression to soften. That could be a glitch in the transfer process, but it could also be a sign that either Auden was playing them or something had gone very wrong.

The latter was far more likely—Auden had been too brain damaged for too long a period to have learned to play such games with expert dexterity.

"I can't believe I let you talk me into this." Jitan used a rag from his pocket to mop up the sweat that had broken out over his face. "I should—"

"Think about betraying me," she said, her tone brutal, "and I'll stop paying those debts of yours." Debts he'd taken out with the worst of the worst in the Net.

Face going white, he nodded. "Your head's on the line, though. If she finds out, I'll rat you out in a heartbeat. What she'd do to me would be far worse than the loan sharks."

Charisma waved him off, unworried. The man's vices made controlling him child's play, which was part of the reason she had him on the payroll. But she kept an eye on him and his activities and proclivities for the same reason; there would come a time when the vices would make him a liability.

Suddenly sensing that she was being watched, Charisma looked up . . . to see Auden at her window, her eyes on Charisma. It was too far for it to be possible, but Charisma could swear she felt the vicious blue of those eyes drill right into her brain.

She swallowed hard and raised a hand in greeting.

Auden didn't wave back.

Chapter 21

Severe tear above Bavaria. Repair in progress. Casualties stand at fourteen.

—Report to the Ruling Coalition from PsyNet Response
Unit Foxtrot (21 October 2083)

"THERE WILL BE no third attempt," Kaleb said to the Ruling Coalition as they met in their secure PsyNet vault—which was holding for the time being. "There are no other sensible iterations of this experiment for us to set in motion."

"I agree with Kaleb," Payal said. "It's possible a small group—five or six—would hold, but at that level of fragmentation, we'd destroy the PsyNet anyway. We may as well advise that as the final in-case-of-emergency measure."

Ivy Jane's mind was the most dazzling in the vault, a cascade of colors in it that marked her as an E. "The Honeycomb can maintain for the time being—I've pulled all my Es off any non-urgent tasks so they can focus on shoring it up. It might buy us a little more time."

"It may be time to consider a physical contraction linked to a psychic one." Anthony's clear voice, his mind a stable presence with a cool silver center. "It would involve the physical migration of millions, so I don't say this flippantly. But we appear to have no other choices."

"The problem," Aden said, his presence Arrow black and martial, his shields present even here, "is that a contraction won't work with this level of damage. We'd just be delaying the inevitable and not by much. There are too many thin patches, too many holes in the fabric of the network—the tear above Bavaria is the largest in that region yet."

"At least the Scarab activity has died down." Nikita's mind was as hard and ruthless as the woman. "Though I'm concerned at their silence."

So was Kaleb; he'd rather know the locations and activities of the unstable Psy who were grenades just waiting to go off. "I have my bots watching for emergent activity."

"What are our other options?" Payal said. "Has there been any word from the Human Alliance?"

"Yes," Nikita said. "As well as the changeling groups in the Trinity Accord. All have agreed to assist in whatever way they can, but they can't offer us a silver bullet. They aren't Psy, don't have our need for biofeedback."

"Is that it, then?" Ivy Jane whispered. "We're out of options?"

On the physical plane, Kaleb's back grew stiff as he leaned his hands on the deck railing. He hadn't cared if the PsyNet lived or died once, but then Sahara had asked him to save it.

He'd made a promise.

Kaleb did not break his promises to Sahara.

Chapter 22

Status: Ten percent increase in neural decay.

—Notes on Patient X by Dr. Nils Verhoeven (17 October 2083)

MORE THAN A week after her return to the compound and Auden knew she'd snap if she didn't get to the cabin soon, to the one place she knew was safe. She was so paranoid about being monitored in her room that she'd even risked a read of the walls and other objects to see if she could find the device she was certain was hidden within.

But Charisma knew this was the room of a Gradient 9.4 Ps-Psy, had no doubt taken precautions. All Auden sensed were random echoes from those who'd stayed in the room while at the compound for training. None had stayed long enough to create a true imprint. Transient—as Auden felt transient. Because this place wasn't home, would never be home.

Trapped as she felt, she shut Charisma down the instant the other woman suggested she not attend next morning's meeting with Rain-Fire. "I need to do this negotiation," she said with Silent precision. "Once it becomes known, it will add to my reputation."

Charisma parted her lips to argue, but Auden held up a hand before the other woman could speak. "I am getting the impression you don't trust me, Ris."

"I apologize, sir. I've had to care for you for a significant period of time and it's hard to break the habit."

"Do it anyway," Auden ordered. "You're useless to me if you're second-guessing my every move." She rose to her feet, cutting off Charisma's repeated apologies with a harsh look. "I need you to function as my aide, my eyes and ears. Figure out if you can in this new reality."

Charisma's eyes flared, a rare physical sign of her emotions. "I will," she said, that unnerving awe back in her tone. "I am the only one who has always been loyal to you, sir."

While Auden nodded in the moment, she was still chewing over Charisma's words the next day when she took a seat at the conference table situated in an office building in the nearest town. Her family had purchased it as a local business base after relocating her to this area, in order to keep up the facade of her being the new Scott CEO.

The table was an expanse of black glass, the executive chairs around it glossy leather that proved unexpectedly comfortable. Exhaling, she tried to see through the frosted glass of the wall that looked out into the reception area. Charisma was waiting out there with the nondisclosure agreement. Only once that was signed would she allow RainFire inside.

Her heart stuttered, even though she knew that was foolishness.

Then the door opened.

Charisma walked in first. "NDA signed." She slid a copy of the phys-ical contract over to Auden. That was a quirk of changelings—they wanted things in physical form.

Auden ran her eyes over it, but saw nothing, her attention on the leopards who waited outside. "Good," she said out loud. "Let's get this meeting underway."

Her skin prickled before *he* prowled into the room. The predator she'd decided to trust because there was no other choice . . . and because he'd never yet caused her harm. She couldn't say the same for any other person in her immediate circle.

"Ms. Scott," he said, with an incline of his head, while she fought not to let her mouth fall open.

Remi Denier was wearing a suit. A cool gray one he'd paired with a white shirt and a tie in a darker gray. His hair was neatly brushed back, his jaw shaved. You'd have taken him for one *very* good-looking CEO . . . but for the wildness that prowled beneath his skin and lived in his eyes for a heartbeat in a glimmer of yellow-green.

Relieved beyond belief at seeing that he was still the same wild creature, even in this corporate skin, she said, "Mr. Denier. I apologize for not rising to greet you." She'd now passed the eight-month mark, and her body felt like it was all belly.

"Call me Remi," he drawled, following her lead without a hitch. "And I'd have been insulted if you rose. This is Mliss Phan, my chief operating officer. She'll be your people's first point of contact should you accept our proposal. Though, of course, you will always have a direct line to me."

"Ms. Phan." She greeted the other woman before waving to the seats. "Please."

"Ms. Scott," Mliss Phan responded with a smile. "And please, call me Mliss."

Tall, with a stylish haircut and a light layer of cosmetics applied with a skilled hand, Remi's chief operating officer wore a black pantsuit paired with a simple silk shell of dark green. Look at her corporate appearance, her complete civility of expression and you'd never, not for a second, guess that this woman was a changeling, much less a leopard.

"You've met Charisma Wai," she said to Remi. "Mliss, Charisma will be the primary contact person from our end."

"I think we'll work well together," Mliss said with a smile. "From our correspondence thus far, Ms. Wai is efficient and thorough, and I prize nothing more in business."

Charisma, her seat beside Auden's, leaned forward to brace her forearms against the table. "I must say the same. I was pleasantly surprised by our interaction. Forgive me if this is ignorant, but we've heard rumors of less than businesslike dealings with changelings."

That was a ringing endorsement coming from Charisma.

"Bit players." Mliss sighed. "I'm sure you have them among the Psy, too. RainFire takes its business operations as seriously as the DarkRiver leopards in San Francisco. In fact, we based our business model on theirs—no point in messing with success."

"I see." Charisma's telepathic voice in Auden's mind. *This is excellent. While DarkRiver has been problematic in many ways politically speaking, their business reputation is stellar. The only complaints come from the usual quarter.*

Those who wish to find loopholes in contracts and throw a tantrum when they can't, Auden answered. The lack of emotion in Silent Psy had never stopped behavior that Psy like her mother and father found excruciating.

To them, cheating your partner in business was fine—*if* you could do it in a way that no one ever caught on and there was no risk to your reputation. That they'd both thought that an acceptable way of doing business—and had taught their minor child the same—was an accurate assessment of their morals and values.

The worst of it was that they'd done it to her: made her believe in a truth except for the one right before her eyes. Henry more so than Shoshanna—but even Shoshanna had convinced Auden she had value to her: as a genetic legacy if nothing else.

"So"—a deep voice, clear eyes of topaz brown rimmed with yellow-green, drawing her back from the past—"you've seen the proposal and since we're here, you must like it. Shall we talk contracts?"

"That's highly presumptuous of you," she said, playing the game because it was expected, even though she was exhausted from maintaining her front for four endless days. "Your proposal is passable, but we need to negotiate more than a few matters."

Remi's eyes narrowed, his gaze skimming her face as if he could read her tiredness. His response when it came, however, was even. "Where do you want to start?"

An hour of vigorous debate later and they had a satisfactory-to-both-sides breakdown of contract terms. "Charisma," she said, "please take charge of drafting this up and sending it to our future partners for review." She winced. "I apologize. Ris, would you be able to get me a glass of nutrients?"

Remi looked like he was about to offer to rise, but she met his eyes with a silent no. He frowned. "Is everything all right?"

"Yes," she said, as Charisma got up. "I just need an infusion of energy. Happens at times with my current status."

The instant the other woman was out of the room, she turned the contract terms toward herself, went to an empty page of the physical pad on which they'd been working, and made a note. "I have an idea about point seven," she said. "It's minor, but it could prove profitable on both sides."

Remi read the note before throwing back his head in a laugh that was a caress over her parched skin. "It would only be profitable for you," he said, then ripped out the page and scrunched it up into a ball in his hand. "We're new, Ms. Scott, but we're not green."

Though her pulse was racing, Auden lifted a shoulder in a mild shrug. "It was worth the attempt. You may have been more gullible than it appeared."

She was conscious of Mliss Phan watching with an intense quiet, but the other woman didn't interrupt, and they sat in silence the short time until Charisma's return. "Here you go, sir."

"Thank you." Taking the drink, Auden lifted it to her lips and only then realized she *was* truly hungry.

Her mouth watered at the memory of the cinnamon roll and the croissant . . . and of Remi's creased cheeks and brilliant eyes as he said, *Next time.*

The nutrients tasted like dust.

Remi spoke after she put down the glass. "We do have one more point to discuss," he said. "We'd like you to tour our manufacturing facility, get agreement on the ground floor in terms of the processes used. I don't want a costly disagreement down the road where you're expecting handwork on a piece we consider better made via machine."

He glanced at Charisma. "We can clear out the place so it's only me and Mliss, and you and Ms. Scott. We can even do it at night if you prefer, so there's less chance of her being seen—and you can drive a vehicle straight into our internal goods bay. Nothing to see from the outside."

"That's an excellent idea," Auden said, telepathing Charisma at the same time. *I should do it as soon as possible, well before I get to full term.*

Are you sure you want to come? I can do it on my own.

Charisma.

A slight flicker in the other woman's eyes at the chilly reminder of the promise she'd made not to second-guess Auden. *Yes, sir.*

Auden didn't interrupt while Charisma worked out the details with Mliss Phan; her attention was on Remi.

His gaze met hers, the leopard bright in them. A shiver rippled over her.

"That's settled, then," Mliss said. "We'll see you at the facility in two days' time."

REMI'S leopard, its growl a low rumble only Mliss would pick up, paced inside his human skin as he left Auden behind in a situation that was clearly dangerous for her.

"What was all that about?" Mliss asked him once they were in their car and pulling out of the parking lot. "We don't need them to tour the facility. I could've shown them the entire place onscreen."

Reaching into his pocket after he'd turned the car to the left, Remi passed Mliss the note Auden had given to him under the guise of negotiation: *Need to talk in unmonitored location.*

"I see." Folding the note up into neat quarters, she placed it back into the hand Remi had outstretched.

He put it safely back in his pocket.

"You know what's going on?"

"No," Remi admitted, his hands clenching on the steering wheel as his claws sliced out. "But your job on the day of the tour is to distract Charisma so I can talk to her."

"Consider it done." A pause. "She still just a business associate, Remi?"

He and Mliss, they weren't friends the way he was friends with Angel or Aden, but he respected and trusted her. And she'd be his partner on this. So he told the truth. "That's all she can be for now. She's too vulnerable for anything else."

"The hard-nosed negotiator we just met didn't strike me as vulnerable." It wasn't a criticism—Mliss was as hard-nosed.

But he heard the question she was asking.

"I've thought hard on this, Liss, and I keep coming back to one fact: no heavily pregnant woman would leave her home for an isolated cabin in the Smokies if she felt safe in that home." An instinctive truth he'd fought against because of the visceral draw he felt toward Auden.

"*She's* the one at risk in that scenario. We could knock her out, take her captive, keep her under so she couldn't call out for help on the psychic plane—there is no point at which a lone civilian Psy in her last trimester is the threat against a pack of predatory changelings."

"Well, shit." A stir of sound that indicated Mliss's claws were out, too.

Remi growled. "Yes. Exactly." Whatever was going on with Auden, it had nothing to do with business.

Chapter 23

Those in favor of it say that this protocol of "Silence" will fix our problems, but it seeks to do that by erasing part of our very *nature*. More than that, don't people understand that empaths and psychometrics, even those of designation M won't fit under the proposed regime?

Where will they go? Will they be erased, too? What will be the end result of all this erasure? For surely a closed system like the PsyNet cannot maintain if it suffers amputation after amputation?

—Letter to the editor by JJ Balakrishnan, *PsyNet Beacon* (17 March 1974)

THE NIGHT BEFORE the tour of the RainFire facility, Auden dreamed of webs of translucent blue, floating streamers delicate and light that spread out into an infinite darkness.

Such a strange, lovely sight that had her waking with a soft sigh.

But the sense of wonder didn't last under the weight of the decision she was planning to carry out, and her mouth was dry and her back in knots as she got out of the car inside the closed RainFire loading bay. Remi, who'd opened her door, watched as she began to lever herself out. His jaw worked, tension stiff across his shoulders.

"Is it a breach of Psy protocols if I offer you a hand?" A gritty question.

Auden wanted nothing more than to accept, but she was conscious of Charisma's watchful gaze on the other side of the vehicle. "No, an offer is fine, but I'd rather do it on my own."

Hand gripping the top of the door, she maneuvered her body out with effort, her belly leading.

Charisma seemed about to come over, but Mliss Phan engaged her in conversation then began to lead her into the building.

Sir?

Go ahead. Our guards have secured the area. She'd had no problem authorizing those guards, since she knew Remi would ensure the facility passed any and all security inspections. *I may as well talk to the alpha one to one, ensure he understands that I am the one with the final say.*

Charisma's hesitation was slight, but Auden noted it. Her aide still didn't quite trust in her ability to lead.

Yes, sir.

"Thank you," she said to Remi after he shut the car door behind her.

He gave a small nod, then made eye contact with the driver, who was also a guard. "I have two people watching the front of the premises and two on the inside." He lifted a hand and two changelings in leopard form materialized out of literally nowhere.

Even as her own pulse jumped, Auden saw the driver's eyes flicker at the realization that maybe he wasn't the most dangerous creature in the area. His partner on the other side of the car was no doubt coming to the same realization.

"I also have two people at the back," Remi said, his voice polite and unthreatening. "Please don't engage with my pack unless necessary to sound an alert. They're working and need to be left alone."

It would, Auden realized, also stop any aggression from either side.

The driver looked at her and, at her nod, said, "Understood. We'll watch the bay gate from here. It's secured?"

"Yes."

The two of them began to walk toward the huge roller door that led into the facility proper, Charisma and Mliss already some distance ahead. "I need help," she said the instant she was out of hearing range of the guards, even as she fought the urge to get closer to Remi, draw in the scent of the wild that he carried in his skin. "There is something disturbing going on in my family home."

The brutal truth behind her decision to trust Remi was that she couldn't protect her baby on her own. She needed help. And of one thing she was certain: whatever this big, deadly leopard alpha thought of her, he wouldn't hurt her "cub." Trusting him was still the biggest gamble she'd ever taken.

Remi's chest rumbled. "Danger level?"

"High, but I can't figure out why or even what's going on." She exhaled, fighting the urge to rub at her belly as she would've done if alone. "They're monitoring the baby. Too much. I'm also under constant surveillance."

He pointed at something as they entered the main floor of the facility, as if he was telling her about the machinery. "Is your pregnancy high-risk?"

The warehouse roof rose high overhead, the open space crisscrossed with walkable girders that made no sense to her . . . until Remi glanced at her with eyes gone leopard, and she realized she was in a place built for and by changelings.

Her breath caught, the idea of seeing him prowling up there a fascination.

"Auden?"

Jerking her attention away from the girders, she thought back to his question about her pregnancy. "It might've been high-risk when I wasn't mentally competent," she said, because to lie about this could endanger her child. "But while I'm now fully cognizant of my surroundings and my physical state, they continue to hover."

She took a deep breath. "I do still suffer seizures, which is their explanation for the surveillance." Skin cold, she didn't look at him, not wanting to remember that morning at the cabin and the blank wall in her mind.

"But you don't believe them."

"No, because, most times, while they do a standard neural scan on me, they do *multiple* scans on my child. The tests they've run on her are extreme from a diagnostic angle—including full brain imaging."

No matter how well Dr. Verhoeven treated her, he seemed to be following a plan her mother had set when it came to her baby. "The doctor in charge of me has also informed me of the full psychic sweep to be done on my baby after her birth."

She pressed a hand flat against her lower back, arched it.

Remi's shoulders stiffened as he went to raise his own hand.

She knew what he was about to do, craved to know what it would feel like. "*Don't.*" Too many eyes. Too many watchers.

His fingers curled into a fist at his side. "What's the purpose of a psychic sweep? Will it hurt the cub?"

"No, it's more a fact-finding mission, same as the diagnostic imaging—but I've never heard it being used for babies. It's most often done during Gradient level tests. Part of the system to determine power levels. Babies are too young, their brains too unformed. There is *no reason* to do this to an infant."

Remi's anger was in the slight growl of his voice as he stopped by a piece of machinery and put his hand on it, as if he was explaining an important factor. Up ahead, Charisma had stopped and was looking at them while Mliss spoke, but she was still too far to hear their conversation.

"There's more," Auden said past the rock in her gut. "I had a seizure twenty-four hours ago." Fear closed its clammy hands around her throat and squeezed. "I haven't had one since my return from the cabin." And as with the others, she had no recall of the seizure itself. "I woke with a memory blank of *eight* full hours."

Remi's expression shifted, the corporate mask slipping to reveal the predator at his core. "You told me once you had a brain injury. Was that true?"

"Yes." Panic beat at Auden for how much she was revealing, but she had no other choice if he was to have the knowledge to protect her child. "It was significant. I still have lesions on my brain as a result."

"Could they be acting up?"

"It's possible," she admitted. "I have to rely on Dr. Verhoeven's reports, and I don't know if I can trust them." Sensing Charisma's gaze, she made a questioning face as she pointed to a machine. "But . . . and this could be paranoia caused by the same lesions, but I feel . . . *wrong* after a blackout. As if I've been doing things—or having things done to me—of which I'm unaware."

She couldn't stop her hand from curling into a tight fist. "I feel dirty and used, as if I have a film of *stuff* on me I can't get off, no matter how hard I scrub."

REMI'S blood boiled at the idea of such a violation. "Medical tests?"

"Possible." She rubbed the crook of her arm. "I'm sure I was injected here once, but that was back when my mind was still fuzzy. This time around . . . I went to sleep as myself, and I woke up in front of my computer, and when I looked through the computer's history, it had been wiped."

Her lips tightened. "Even worse, I was given access to an organizer with my medical records on it. The information was dense and complex—I was going through it with painstaking focus, looking up medical terms line by line, and hadn't gotten very far—but now that device is empty, too. Wiped using my own authorization codes."

"Why would you wipe your own computer's history, or erase your own medical files?"

"I don't know." Mingled rage and fear in those extraordinary eyes. "I don't understand any of this—what I do know is that I need to get out of that house."

Her cadence grew faster, more urgent. "It *only* ever happens at the house. I've never had an onset *at* the cabin, or when I was at a private medical facility at a different family home during the early stages of my pregnancy. But . . ." A hard swallow. "I do have brain damage. There is a minor chance that none of my information is reliable."

Remi's gut clenched, his mind flashing with images of another woman who'd lost piece after piece of herself as disease ate away at her. His mother's slow decline had devastated Remi. And she'd never lost any of her sharpness, her mind acute till the end.

"You need to be in a controlled environment to test it," he said through the heavy weight on his chest. "Somewhere safe, and away from your home."

"It's not my home," was the pointed response. "It's my mother's house. There's a difference."

No home. No safe place to land.

Remi understood that in a way few changelings ever would. After his alpha kicked him out, he'd had not a chance in hell of stopping his mother from joining him in exile. She was the one who'd found them a new home in the pack associated with her own lost mama—but by then, Remi had been too wounded in the heart to trust any alpha.

However, he'd *always* had his mother, always had one person who was home, who was trust, who was comfort and loyalty and strength when he might've been faltering.

Quite unlike Auden . . . but this same woman who didn't feel safe in her own mother's house was fighting like a leopardess for her cub. His pride at her courage and ferocity both was a growl within.

"I've barred myself from flying until I can be certain I won't have a seizure," she said now. "I can't get to the cabin on my own."

"Does teleporting affect pregnant women?" Remi knew the Arrows would do him this favor—not for Auden, but for the child growing in her womb. All the adult Arrows had been abused children once upon a time, and if they had a trigger point for rage, it was harm to a child.

"I don't know." Auden bit down on her lower lip. "I don't want to risk it, regardless, not now I have a choice. I've already almost lost my baby twice." Her hand threatened to creep to her belly. "Even a tiny fluctuation during teleportation could cause a stillbirth."

It took everything Remi had not to haul her close, just cuddle the worry and tension out of her. "I can fly a chopper." He'd learned to do so during his days as a race car driver—just another beautiful machine to control, as he couldn't control so many fucking things in his life.

Auden sucked in a breath. "After we sign the deal," she said. "Then I can swing your offer to fly me as a way to stay in our good graces. Stress," she murmured under her breath, "that's not good for the baby— and I can make sure something stresses me out enough that I need calm surroundings."

"Auden. Stop pandering to these people. You're the CEO." Remi hated the idea of her being controlled and made smaller. "You're also tougher than they'll ever be."

"You don't see," she said, low and quiet and potent. "I'm not playing their game. I'm playing *mine*." A glint in her eye that was almost feral. "I'll do anything to protect my baby, and if that means lulling them into a false sense of security by appearing weak, then so be it."

His leopard's fur brushed the insides of his skin; the more he learned about Auden Scott, the more he wanted to have her to himself, know all of her . . . even if the idea of watching her lose pieces of herself until all that remained was a hollow shell was a howling terror in the back of his brain.

Never again, he'd promised himself after he buried his mother.

But how could the nineteen-year-old he'd been have predicted Auden? A woman he'd never even touched but whose existence had become a visceral part of his.

"Faking being lame to ease their suspicions while you prepare to rip out their fucking jugular?" he said, wishing he could brush his thumb over her lower lip, rub his jaw against her skin. "I approve." It came out a rumble heavy with the leopard's approbation.

Auden's pupils dilated, her breath catching. But the scent that made his nostrils flare wasn't fear. It was richer, tarter, more delicious.

"And you, Auden Scott, approve of the animal inside me," he said, using the word animal on purpose because that was part of him and he was proud of it.

She stilled, their eyes locked in contact intimate and naked.

"Sir!" Charisma's voice cut through the air. "Have you been told about this advanced new method?"

The spell broken, their time alone at an end, Remi let Auden take the lead in this dangerous game. All the while, the clock in his mind ticked down to when he could issue the invitation to fly her up to the cabin. Where they could be alone. Where they could talk without boundaries. Where they could plot to break Auden out of her fucking jail cell.

But when she sent him an assessing look not long after, he felt the hairs rise on the back of his nape. That look . . . it was of the woman who'd stood on the doorstep and looked at him as if he was a stranger. His Auden wasn't in there.

A blink and the impression was gone, Auden's the mind behind the gaze once more.

The chill inside him lingered.

Chapter 24

I've reviewed the schematics you sent. As designed, this biograft would remove a major neural safeguard when it comes to psychic overloads. It cannot ever be placed in a Psy brain—not without risking a psychic burn severe enough to cause brain damage.

—Message from Dr. Ilma Wang to Councilor
Shoshanna Scott (1 January 2075)

AUDEN MADE IT through the next two days with gritted teeth—and little sleep. She was afraid if she closed her eyes, she wouldn't wake to herself again, her mind a total blank. She survived with catnaps that were never long or deep enough to put her brain into a state where things happened. Where she lost herself.

That kind of sleep wasn't enough for a woman in her eighth month of pregnancy.

"You're displaying signs of significant sleep deprivation," Dr. Verhoeven said at her next check-up. "We may need to bring in a sleep specialist empath."

That he was even considering bringing in an outsider indicated the depth of his worry.

Auden rubbed at her forehead, and suddenly, she was speaking without conscious premeditation. "I find it difficult to sleep in this house knowing how long my uncle and cousin had access to it. Uncle Hayward spoke a good game, but he'd become used to the taste of being so close to power—and he's not as meek and mild as everyone believes."

That much, at least, was true.

"You shouldn't worry," Dr. Verhoeven said. "Charisma has no doubt run a comprehensive security sweep."

"Yes, but my uncle is weak, not stupid," Auden said, the words coming faster than she could process them. "He could've thought to plant an object in the house that might send me into shock if I come into unexpected contact with it. It could be as simple as a pen purchased from the estate of a serial murderer. Do any of us ever really think about it before picking up a pen to make a quick note?"

Stunned by the idea that might be an actual credible threat she'd never before considered because *she just didn't think in such a mercenary way*, she leaned her head back on the examination chair. Her pulse felt erratic, but she didn't fight it—let Dr. Verhoeven note that down, add it to his list of problematic factors.

"All I need is a location neither he nor my cousin has ever accessed."

"Perhaps you should go to the cabin," the doctor mused. "It's secure, and the leopards are no threat now that you have a major deal with them—they might even provide protection as part of their attempt to build a relationship. The biomonitors let me keep an eye on you, and we have a teleporter on standby if I need to get to you."

Auden couldn't believe he'd given her the cabin on a silver platter, had to struggle not to jump on the offer with betraying eagerness. "I'm unable to fly, teleportation is out for me, and you know the problem with having a different individual in my chopper."

"Hmm, yes."

"Though . . ." She paused. "I accidentally touched a few surfaces the changeling alpha touched during our recent tour of their manufacturing facilities, and while I picked up multiple changeling echoes from those who work there, I had no negative reaction."

"Interesting." The doctor sounded like he meant that. "A result of their natural shields do you think?"

"Makes logical sense to me," Auden agreed. "Perhaps if I continue to have trouble sleeping, I'll hire a changeling pilot to get me to the cabin so I can rest without concern about what Uncle Hayward or my cousin may have left behind for me."

"I really do recommend a period of significant rest." The doctor made a few notes. "You know how important it is that you stay in top shape. There's no knowing how long this brain will function at the level you need it to function."

The hairs on Auden's nape quivered.

There was something *extremely* wrong with the way the doctor had phrased that—but she couldn't exactly question him without betraying herself. So she responded with a cool, "Exactly so." She got off the ex-amination chair by swinging her legs to the side, then pushing up on the arm.

The M-Psy offered her a hand, such contact having been permitted even in Silence when another Psy was in a physical state that made move-ment difficult, but she shook her head—both to maintain her image of being in control and powerful, and because she didn't want that man touching her.

Auden was no touch telepath, as some of the Justice Psy were said to become after years of their grim work, but this man had talked about her *brain* as if it were an interchangeable tool. She did not want him near her, much less touching her.

"I'll see what I can organize in terms of acceptable transportation," she said, her hand lifting to her temple without conscious volition.

But it was the right move, because Dr. Verhoeven reiterated the need for her to take a break, adding the words, "The child is critical. Early signs are that its neural structure is developing as required."

Auden was going to throw up.

Swallowing back the bile with effort, she gave a curt nod, then made her way out of the infirmary suite. She wasn't surprised to find Charisma waiting for her in the reception area. And after the creepiness of Dr. Verhoeven's words, she'd had enough. She channeled Shoshanna. "Do you wish to be demoted?" Her voice was ice coated in frost. "Because I can make that happen today."

Clever, Auden, whispered an internal voice as cold as the one that had come out of her mouth. *You didn't threaten to fire her. She knows you'd never do that, not with all the information she holds in her head. But a demotion? Yes, that she might believe. Especially as she has witnessed such "demotions" before, all of which involved the telepathic scraping of a mind.*

The bile returned. Who was she that she could have such emotionless thoughts?

"I had no desire to overstep." Charisma bent her head. "I came to discuss a personal matter with Dr. Verhoeven."

Auden believed neither the sudden submissiveness, nor the excuse for her presence. "Then do go in, Ris." She waved a hand . . . and felt her lips curve into a smile that she'd seen on her mother's face as she grew from child to adult.

Charisma visibly drew back, sucking in a breath at the same time. "Sir." A shaky tone.

Auden left without waiting for anything further. She didn't know how she made it to her bedroom, or how she kept it together until she was behind the closed door of her bathroom suite. She had to believe this room wasn't monitored—and even if it was, all they'd hear was a pregnant woman throwing up.

After it was done, she cleaned up, brushed her teeth, and made herself think of the doctor's words. Why "this brain"? What had he meant by that? It wasn't as if a person could switch brains—not even Psy could do that.

Staring in the mirror, she reached up to her hairline, to that faint scar hidden beneath the fine hairs there. "What did you put in me?" she whispered so quietly it was inaudible to her own ears, her question directed at her dead parents.

She'd gone into surgery, for what her mother had told her was a corrective procedure to fix a blocked artery that could one day lead to a stroke, and come out fine. It had lasted one week. Then had come the burning storm in her brain that had altered the trajectory of her life.

Anything else she knew, she'd learned from Shoshanna. Her mother used to sit beside her bed and speak to her after she took over primary custody. Auden only remembered pieces of it.

"Unfortunate that the updated variant of the graft had the same flaw." Her mother rising from the seat. "Not much of a loss in the grand scheme of things. Despite Henry's delusions, a Ps was never going to run his family or mine."

A graft. A foreign part. Inside Auden's brain.

Whatever it was Shoshanna and Henry had been attempting to do, there was more wrong with Auden than she'd realized. She might be able to function again, but her thoughts weren't always her own . . . and neither were her actions.

Her stomach rumbled.

Heart gentling, she rubbed at her belly. *I'll go get us food*, she telepathed her baby. *Sorry about the disruption to the peace just before.*

The baby kicked, safe and content inside her womb where none of the horrors of the world could touch her. And where she couldn't understand the horrific implications of an M-Psy talking about her brain developing as "required."

Required for what?

For another experiment as had been done to Auden?

She squeezed the edge of the sink, rage filling her to the brim at the idea of them butchering her child like they'd butchered her. *No one* was getting their hands on her baby. No matter what she had to do . . . or whom she had to kill.

That last thought? It was hers. *All* hers.

That rage gave her the impetus to push away from the sink and stride

down to the kitchen area, where the member of staff on duty was preparing a tray of high-nutrient food.

"Sir." The staff member bowed her head. "Dr. Verhoeven sent through
an order to be delivered to you."

"Good. I'll take the drink now." She picked it up. "Please bring the
rest to my office." Her politeness was natural, but it was also one of the
rules of the Scott household. Shoshanna had been unfailingly polite to
her staff.

"They are cogs in the machine," her mother had told Auden on one
of the infrequent occasions when she'd had charge of her minor child.
"Cogs function better with a little grease, and the grease here is the
appearance that I care for their psychological well-being—and it's not
a lie. If they are unwell, they can't perform their duties."

Shoshanna had never been a caricature of evil. That was what made
her so dangerous. People respected her, trusted her, even believed she
cared. The truth was that Shoshanna had cared only for herself.

Her staff and Auden had mattered to her in the same pragmatic way.
Cogs in the machine.

Once at her desk, she finished the drink before pulling up files on a
number of business projects. Not simply as cover, but because information was power.

Both Henry and Shoshanna had drummed that into her.

When the staff member came in with the tray, Auden only acknowledged her with a nod. Another small act designed to make the entire
household believe that she wasn't only back, but that she was back as her
mother's daughter.

She completed the work she wanted to do in record time—even
compared to her work before the brain damage. She seemed to know
exactly where certain files were located, or how to retrieve documents
she'd never before seen.

Including videos of her interacting with others in a way that
should've been impossible with her brain injury. Complex, detailed in-

teractions that couldn't be faked with a nod here and there while Charisma did the talking.

Auden was the one doing the talking.

Parched, she grabbed the glass of water that had come on the tray, emptied it. Her lips remained dry in the aftermath, her heart pumping. Because . . . *she shouldn't be able to access this material.* It was stored in a system that had been well above her security clearance when she'd been "normal"—she'd been too young then to have access to this depth of business information.

More than that . . .

Passwords.

A number of the documents she'd just pulled up had been password protected, and she'd breezed past the security as if it didn't exist, her fingers typing in the necessary codes without hesitation.

Not only that, but when she checked some of the more obscure financial records, she saw that the last access had been by Shoshanna. Which meant these were documents even Charisma couldn't access— she hadn't been given the override by her mother before Shoshanna's untimely death.

Her heart hitched.

There had to be an explanation. Perhaps she'd had other periods of lucidity while her mother was alive, and Shoshanna had decided to pass on the information. That must be it. Because what other possibility—

Chest tight, she touched the scar at her temple again.

What if her mother had done something else to her? She would've seen Auden as already damaged, so it would've been easy for her to justify. Whatever it was, Dr. Verhoeven had to know, as did Charisma.

That was when it hit her: the codes to the system, the thing that allowed Charisma to hold the reins.

Face hot, she pulled up the deceptively simple login page and stared. Nothing. Her mind a blank.

She swiped out her arm, crashing her empty glass to the soft carpet.

Her vision wavered, her brain hitching, a murmur inside her skull that rebuked her for the loss of control in a voice that *wasn't her own*.

AN impatient and quietly angry Remi turned into the road that led to the Scott compound after nightfall. The past three days, as he waited for the contract to be finalized, had ground his patience down to the bone. All he could think of was Auden, so fierce and protective, trapped in a house that wasn't a home while her brain misfired on her.

"You look like you want to murder someone," Mliss murmured from the passenger seat. "Rein it in, Remi, or you'll give away the game."

He'd picked his COO up from her apartment along the way because RainFire couldn't afford to sacrifice a vehicle, and there was no way he'd leave it in enemy territory for the duration.

"I have it," he muttered, clenching his teeth even as his leopard settled in a quiet that was deadly. "Now?"

"It'll do."

"Remi Denier," he told the guard on duty at the gate. "Here for Ms. Scott."

The man—who'd also accompanied Auden to the mech facility—said, "You're the only one cleared. I can call up about Ms. Phan."

Good man, Remi thought. He'd made note of Mliss's name and face despite having never interacted with her. "No, that's fine. Mliss's my ride." Getting out, he waited until she was in the driver's seat before he said, "Drive safe."

Mliss's gaze gleamed leopard gold at him. He could almost hear her voice in his head: *I'm not the one walking through the gates of the Scott compound.*

He waited until she'd turned the all-terrain vehicle around and was on her way before allowing the guard to lead him inside. The compound was spacious but not huge. One main dual-level building painted a crisp white with dark gray trim, multiple other single-level houses, all with decorative touches like scrollwork on the eaves that clearly came from another era; overall, it gave the impression of being a refined old estate.

Underneath that first impression, however, was intense modern security. The guards with their visible earpieces were just the start—and given that more subtle earpieces were standard for security work, these had been picked on purpose, to warn off anyone thinking to infiltrate the estate.

Then there were the wrought iron fences Remi had clocked were wired with motion sensors, the generator somewhere on the property that was a mild but distinctive hum to his acute hearing, the internal alarm systems he couldn't see but had no doubt existed, and external motion sensor lights designed to appear a natural part of the house.

Those lights weren't needed tonight as the pathway through the compound was well illuminated with tall standing lamps that matched the iron fences in their design. As he'd expected, he had no chance to look inside the house itself, because the guard took him around the building and to the very back—where Auden stood with Charisma beside a chopper on a launching pad.

Charisma Wai's face was stiff with disapproval, but she was polite enough to Remi. "Thank you for acceding to Auden's request. You have an unusual work and skill history for a changeling alpha."

No surprise that Wai had looked him up. "Misspent youth," he said casually, then turned to Auden. "Are you ready to go, Ms. Scott?"

"Yes." She got into the chopper's passenger seat with help from a step that had already been placed beside it. The seat, he saw when he went around, had been pushed all the way back.

It was still a tight fit for her belly.

Frowning, he took his own seat, wanting her out of this machine and more comfortable as fast as possible. Small as the chopper was, his shoulder brushed hers as he took the controls after putting on his headset.

A shiver from his passenger before she settled, and maybe it was his imagination, but it felt as if she was leaning into the contact rather than away from it.

Happy to have her in his care, he began takeoff procedures, and when the bird lifted, saw Charisma Wai staring after them with a grim look in her eye.

Chapter 25

Remi Denier: Alpha of the RainFire leopards.

Never say we don't keep you in the loop, our dear wild women. Because it appears our friends in RainFire have been hoarding this gorgeous feline specimen all to themselves. But our intrepid journalists go where even bears fear to tread in order to keep you informed.

Eyes of a pale brown shot with gold and filled with light, a charming smile that makes us want to rip off our panties, and hair so many shades of brown that it's a leopard's fur in human form, Mr. Denier is a tall bite of gorgeous hunk.

Rawr.

And yes, ladies, the man is single. Not only that, but he's got serious claws if he's set up a pack and held it against all comers—including multiple other predatory changeling packs in the region. Surely he needs a mate to keep him warm on those cold mountain nights.

Who here is ready to volunteer for this onerous, *onerous* task?

—From the "Scary but Sexy" column in the September 2083 issue of *Wild Woman* magazine: "Skin Privileges, Style & Primal Sophistication"

REMI'S PRESENCE WAS a primal pressure against Auden's skin, a prowling heat that discomforted and comforted at the same time. She could've shifted to break contact, but she did the opposite . . . and he didn't appear to mind from the small smile he shot her after they were aloft.

She wanted to drink in the sunshine of his attention, was greedy for more of it, but she had to warn him. "What was Charisma referring to, regarding your history?" Formal tone, cool intonation.

From the way Remi's jaw tightened, he understood her warning: this vehicle wasn't safe, might be bugged. Auden wasn't, however, worried about visual surveillance. Too difficult to pull that off in such a tight area with so few controls.

"I drove race cars from roughly twenty to twenty-five," Remi said, his voice that rumble, familiar and deep. "Fell into it, really—changeling speed and reflexes are a good fit for that career."

"Is it a difficult field to join?" Auden asked, as any other Psy might ask about the dangerous sport—but *she* was compelled by Remi, wanted to know all of what had shaped him into the man he'd become.

"Yes, but I stumbled into a back-end spot with a small outfit, and they let me try out for a novice position when they realized I had excellent reflexes. Turned out I was a natural on the track—took us to a championship trophy in my fifth year as a driver."

"You retired while at the top?"

"It was time," he said, his voice firm. "Look down."

When she did, she saw a ribbon of light in the moon-washed silver of the world. Wonder in her veins. "What is that?"

"Park path. Town lights it up at night. Some of the pack like to go down there on romantic dates."

Auden bit down hard on her lower lip, wondering what it would be like to walk hand in hand with Remi along a softly lit path. Her baby kicked right then, as if reminding her that she had other priorities.

Looking down, she stroked her belly. *I never forget you, my baby.*

The sensation that came back to Auden was of happiness . . . and comfort. Safe. Her baby felt safe and warm and content.

It made her throat tight.

"Cub doing all right?"

Her heart did that freefall thing again at the open concern in his tone. "Yes. It's just a little uncomfortable being in this seat in my current shape." She met his eyes, told him without speaking that there was so much more she wanted to tell him.

"Won't be long now."

They didn't speak again the rest of the trip, all the words they couldn't say building in the small space until they became a pressure as inexorable as the feel of Remi's shoulder against hers.

Auden didn't move. Didn't want to move.

She wanted to sit in this cockpit together forever, and imagine that he was hers . . . and that she could trust him without question, without hesitation. Inside her mind, a sensation bloomed—but it wasn't the one that felt wrong, outside of herself.

This was a flutter, an innocent touch.

Reaching out to Remi.

Auden blinked rapidly, her eyes burning. Even her baby was attempting to touch Remi.

REMI brought the chopper to land with an inward grunt of satisfaction. Soon as it was down and locked in position, blades slowing to a stop, he jumped out and ran around to the other side to help Auden out.

Neither one of them spoke, but she didn't wave off his help this time and he all but lifted her out. Even so pregnant, she weighed nothing to his changeling strength. After shutting the door to the chopper behind her, he took her lead as she ignored the cabin's back door to walk around the side.

When she rubbed at her back, he realized she had to be stiff. "Let me," he said, his voice rough, but didn't touch her.

Not until she met his gaze . . . and dropped her own hand, the air a shiver between them.

Auden is off-limits, he reminded himself. *You protect, you don't take. Not her. Not until she's in a space where her consent means something.*

But not about to allow her to hurt when he could help, he rubbed with firm downward strokes as they continued to walk in the glow of the heavy silver moon. "It was time for me to build a pack," he said, finishing the conversation he'd cut short in the cockpit because these words weren't for any ears but hers. "That's why I stopped racing. I only ever did it in the first place because I figured I'd be a shit alpha."

Auden halted. "But why?" Her features scrunched up into an expression so confused it was adorable. "I knew from a single touch of that chair you gave me that you're beloved as an alpha."

He shrugged even as his leopard rubbed against his skin, wanting her petting words to turn into a petting touch. "My father abandoned me when I was five, and that kind of desertion is all but unheard of among changelings."

Most changeling species didn't become fertile except when mated or in a long-term relationship. With leopards, that rule was an absolute. As a result, every cub was seen as a gift, a treasure.

Or that was how it was supposed to be.

But Remi's father had decided he didn't want to live up to the commitment he'd made to Remi's mother and their son. "Then my alpha kicked me out when I was only seventeen." No one had stood up for him because Rhett Farley had surrounded himself with the weak. "I was a messed-up kid who had no idea what to do with all the dominance inside me. If I hadn't had my mother, I'd have been fucked up to all hell."

"She sounds like an amazing woman."

"She was." Remi's chest squeezed hard enough to hurt. "Biggest heart of us all—and the irony of it is that it was her heart that killed her. A rare genetic mutation that stole the light from her eyes in the prime of her life."

Auden touched his arm with a tentative hand. "I'm sorry. I . . ." She hesitated, lines forming between her eyebrows. "I want to say she loved you to the end with a fierce maternal devotion. I *know* that."

Remi spoke past the thickness in his throat. "First time we met, you read her imprint on a gift she gave me." He tucked back a fine flyaway curl behind her ear. "I'll let you read it again one day. So you'll get to know her, see her." His mother might never be able to meet her, but Auden could meet the strong, powerful leopard named Gina Delphine Denier who'd raised him.

Auden's eyes burned. "I would love that. And Remi?" She shook her head. "I hope you don't worry now—about yourself as an alpha. Your pack is so *happy*." Her eyes shimmered. "RainFire might be small and young, but it's joyous in a way I've never been my entire life."

He cupped her cheek because he couldn't not touch her when she'd just torn her heart bare to make him feel good. "You will be happy," he promised roughly. "No matter what we have to do, we'll figure out a way."

Auden's lower lip trembled before she pressed her lips together and took a deep, shuddering breath. "I want my baby—my little girl—to feel like the cub who sat in your lap in that chair. No fear. No concern. Trust absolute."

"She will. She has you for a mama." And of one thing Remi was certain: Auden Scott loved her baby as much as any leopardess.

A hard swallow. "Thank you."

Forcing himself to let go of her, he walked again with her under the moonlight, and he thought of a future where he might walk with a miniature version of Auden, curious and wild. Holding her little hands from above as she found her feet, as she giggled and looked up at him.

Neither man nor leopard was ready for the emotion that punched through him.

"What is that?" Auden was staring at what sat at her front door, a food carrier . . . and a single extra-large package.

"Bed frame." Remi was damn glad to be distracted by the practical. "I dropped it off this morning before I headed into town, and our healer delivered the food about the time we lifted off. I figured he'd be the best person as far as imprints go?"

Auden nodded, the movement a touch jagged. "Empaths don't affect us badly, so I'm guessing a healer won't, either." She reached into her pocket to pull out a slimline black device that looked like a remote. "Before anything, sweep the cabin with this."

Recognizing it as a detector, Remi took it from her and went to the cabin to run the scan immediately. Only once he was certain the cabin was clean of any bugs did he come back outside and return the device. "I didn't pick up any other scent except for yours inside, either," he said. "No one's been here since you left."

Her shoulders eased.

Shoving up the sleeves of his gray sweatshirt, Remi went to the carrier. "You hungry?"

"I feel like I'm constantly starving," Auden admitted with a little groan.

Remi's gaze took her in with an intensity that felt like a touch. His eyes gleamed in the silver light of the moon and she knew she stood with a wild creature.

A flutter against her mind, a reminder that it wasn't just the two of them in this clearing. "The baby's . . . excited to see you again." A pause. "Her brain isn't formed enough to give me much, but I sense her emotions. She knows you."

"From the outside, psychometrics and empaths have a lot in common." He passed over a cinnamon roll. "I can put together the bed while you devour this." A slow grin.

Her stomach tumbled, leaving her breathless. Unable to speak, she just nodded.

Then she watched him move with feline grace as he opened the package to take the pieces inside. His every move held a wild power and for this moonlit fragment of time, she allowed herself to believe that he was her man.

Her Remi.

Looking after her not out of obligation because she was pregnant and in need, but because he wanted to.

A silly fantasy but no one had to know.

"Futon needs to be moved out of the way," he said. "You want to use your feet to do that in case my imprint does make the frame unusable? I don't want you without a place to sleep."

Auden nodded and, after finishing the cinnamon roll, went over to nudge the futon to the far wall using her socked feet. Remi was in socks, too, having told her he'd worn two pairs to insulate his imprint from the floor.

Auden wasn't so sure she didn't want his imprint everywhere. He filled up the space, big and warm and wild.

"Here." He'd put together a chair in the time she'd been moving the futon. "Try this. Easy test—and you need a proper chair."

Auden touched her pinky to one surface first, got no real feedback. So she placed her whole hand on it . . . and got a faint but distinct wash of protectiveness . . . and annoyance.

Cheeks hot, she said, "Why are you annoyed?"

He raised an eyebrow. "I didn't know you could do that."

"It's because it's fresh. Psychometrics can usually only pick up embedded imprints, but direct contact within minutes can occasionally open the doorway."

"I'm annoyed because you're tired and pregnant and standing when you should be resting. *Sit.*"

Auden wasn't one to take orders, but because her back ached, she sat. "You don't have to be rude about it," she muttered, even as she reached back to undo the tight knot of her hair and finally relax the pressure on her scalp.

Growling, Remi grabbed the food carrier, placed it next to her, then picked out a flat, bread-like creation with tomatoes and cheese on it to put in her hand. A bottle of nutrient-enriched water was placed beside her chair. "Now, behave."

Remi knew he was acting like an uncivilized bear, but she was so small and had huge shadows under her eyes, and it was infuriating. Despite his growling, she didn't seem mad, or—even worse—cowed or scared. Her hair was longer than he'd thought—past her shoulders, with big and loose curls that bounced the instant they were set free, her eyes bright as she watched him work while she nibbled at the pizza bread with obvious pleasure.

His fucking heart melted.

That had not been in the program. Even if Auden was in any state to play with him woman to man, Remi was shit in relationships. He could commit to being an alpha, would die for his pack, but when it came to women? He was a fun bed partner, and then he was gone.

"You're not your father, Remington." His mother's slender fingers against his cheek, her face so frail that final month before he'd lost her. "Your heart is a huge and powerful thing, your love a storm force. Why won't you let yourself love and be loved like you deserve?"

The thing was, intellectually, Remi got it. He wasn't his shithead of a father. He didn't abandon people. He was still friends with kids he'd known as a cub, even though they'd scattered across states and continents; the Arrows considered him a rock-solid friend and ally; and not a single member of RainFire would give a second thought to picking up the comm and calling him if they needed their alpha.

Each and every one knew Remi would come, that Remi kept his promises.

But emotions weren't that easy. Because tangled around his worry about what he'd be like with the woman he loved was grief old and deep. Losing the only person who'd stuck by him from childhood, it had wrecked him. He'd had no pack to fall back on, no family who'd embrace him. Only Angel, a friend new, the bond between them in the process of forming.

His mother's death had left him hollow and adrift, a leopard without a home, a changeling without a pack—because he wasn't going to take advantage of their foster pack's kindness by saddling them with a dangerous dominant who had no loyalty to them, and who was, quite frankly, angry and messed up. A part of him had broken the day they put Gina Denier into the earth, the fracture a permanent part of his psyche.

His leopard had learned that love on a personal, private level equaled pain so deep it was beyond blood and bone. And now he was falling for a woman who might cease to exist, her brain injury eroding her sense of self until only the cold darkness remained.

"You're thinking too far ahead," he muttered to himself. "Focus on the bed."

"Did you say something?" Auden licked a bit of cheese off her finger.

His groin tightened, the most primitive part of him in no doubt about what he felt for this woman with the eyes of luminous blue who'd walked into his life without warning. "Just figuring out the join," he said, and put his head down to work. "How did you escape Ms. Wai's iron grip?"

"I didn't tell her until you were almost there. I also let her know the doctor diagnosed me with stress." She swallowed a bite. "I don't know how long she'll stay away. The attention on my baby"—her free hand cradling her bump—"it's intensified even further since we spoke at the factory. I can't think of any good reason why they'd want her so badly, but they do."

"What about the father?" Remi asked, his leopard annoyed at the idea of anyone else having even a vague claim on Auden and the cub. "I know Psy do business deals to create children, but is it possible he has some special ability they believe the cub might inherit?"

But Auden shook her head. "I had the same idea, but he's a pure telepath. Extremely high-Gradient—9.7—but that's not rare in terms of the donors my mother earmarked for me. Not a single unusual thing about him. All his medical and psychic records are on our system and will be updated until my baby is of age. Part of the fertilization agreement."

Remi shook his head. "It's much more fun making cubs the old-fashioned way."

A whisper of scent from Auden that made his entire body tighten. Strangling the desire that crept over his skin, he said, "Bed's done. Come test the frame so I can put the futon on it, and then you can tell me what you think might be going on, and we'll come up with a plan to help you and your child." Because Remi was in this to the end.

For Auden. For her cub.

And for the whispered promise of a future that clawed at his heart.

Chapter 26

Eastern Europe is too thin to hold. Failure imminent.

I'm forcing an emergency psychic migration to the nearest safe zones by utilizing my own power to move people—but it's a stopgap measure. They can't remain in a different part of the psychic network than their physical location for too long.

Kaleb, Nikita, I need your assistance.

Payal, watch the Substrate. Ivy, we need the Honeycomb to move with these people.

Anthony, it might be time for you to consult your foreseers as you offered. Perhaps they can see something that'll help us.

—Emergency alert from Aden Kai to the
Ruling Coalition (10 November 2083)

THIRTY SECONDS AFTER Auden pronounced the bed frame safe for her, he had the futon on it, along with her pillow and blanket. Ten seconds after that, she was lying on the bed with a sigh of satisfaction.

Her feet did a happy little wiggle.

Half a minute later, while he was checking every seal and join a third time over, she curled over onto her side and her eyes fluttered shut. He figured she was testing the bed by really sinking into her ability—but by the time he finished his final check and came around to face her, it was to see that her eyes were still closed, her breathing deep and even.

She'd fallen asleep.

Protective warmth spread through him as he picked up the blanket at the foot of the bed and spread it out over her. Making a little murmuring sound in her sleep, she snuggled deeper into the bed.

Didn't look like she was having trouble with his imprint.

His entire body tightened with a raw possessiveness.

But much as he wanted to, he couldn't stay and watch over her sleep. He'd been away from the den for most of the day, needed to go and deal with multiple small matters. It was early enough that a juvenile who needed to be disciplined would still be up—and Remi would never leave the boy hanging overnight—and all the adults would be available for various discussions.

More than that, his young pack needed to know their alpha slept close by. It wasn't that he could never be away from them at night, but this proximate to all the nights he'd spent away because of business commitments? It was necessary. His presence while they slept would calm their animals, allow them to rest in truth. The cubs, especially, reacted to Remi being in the vicinity.

But leaving Auden alone wasn't an option.

Stepping outside, he closed the door behind himself, then made a call. Angel didn't answer; his best friend was probably running in tiger form. Remi was considering who else might have availability when a tiger prowled out of the trees.

Of course Angel had figured out that Remi might need backup tonight. That was why he was RainFire's second-in-command. "Keep an eye on her?" Remi crouched down, put his hand on Angel's back.

Because Angel was a tiger—tigers were far more reclusive than leopards when it came to changelings—their bond wasn't the same as the alpha-sentinel one he had with Lark, Theo, and Rina. It was that of equals, especially given their history together. Angel would always be Remi's friend first, his sentinel second.

Tonight, the tiger nodded to show he'd accept the charge.

"Shouldn't be any problems," Remi said, "but I'll leave my phone here in case you need to call for an assist." He'd have access to his main comm at the den, and Angel could always call one of the other senior people directly, who'd then contact Remi.

Angel waited with feline patience as Remi walked into the shadow of the trees.

Stripping, he left his phone on the pile of his clothes, then shifted. His body disintegrated into endless pieces of light in an ecstasy of pain, only to become again a heartbeat later.

His leopard stretched, flexing its back, before padding out to meet Angel in the clearing. They brushed past each other in silent greeting, then Remi took one last look at the cabin before turning toward the forest and breaking out into the leopard's ground-devouring lope.

FINE streamers of blue in Auden's dreams, so thin they were spidersilk against a night sky brilliant with starlight. Breath a soft gasp, she reached out a hand to tangle her fingers around the silk and felt her baby giggle in delight. It saw the web, too, was as intrigued by it as Auden.

Her eyes opened.

The first thing of which she was aware was warmth and softness. She was cocooned snugly in bed, surrounded by an imprint that felt like a purr to her senses. Shivering, she began to snuggle back down.

Only for her bladder to protest.

Groaning, she threw off the blanket and made her way to the facilities. Afterward, she glanced at the window and it seemed to her that the world held the barest edge of light, a sheen of dark gray to it.

One glance at the clock showed her it was about an hour till true dawn.

She'd gotten lucky her body hadn't woken her up earlier.

Feeling as if she'd slept the sleep of the dead, heavy and deep, she decided to stretch a little by walking off the stiffness from having been in much the same position most of the night. It had been the best sleep she'd had for months . . . because of him. The man who'd built her the bed while being annoyed with her because he thought she wasn't taking care of herself.

Strange how that annoyance translated into a warm embrace in his imprint. As if he was cuddling her close even though he was irritated by her. Never would she have thought that would feel so good.

Part of her hoped he'd be outside when she opened the door, but it was a tiger that prowled out of the forest to look at her with unblinking eyes of shining gold. Her hand clenched on the doorjamb. "Change-ling?" It came out tense, wary.

A slow nod, the tiger keeping its distance—no doubt because it could sense her fear.

When it tilted its head slightly upward, she understood the question. "Just needing to walk a bit."

Not responding, the tiger melted back into the trees with such stealth that she didn't even see it go. Had to be one of Remi's people, even if he was the wrong species of cat.

It made her wonder what other species made up RainFire.

So many questions she had about the man who had . . . looked after her. No one had done that for her since the day of her father's betrayal. And that betrayal had tainted anything Henry had done prior to it.

Cheeks chilled, and heart achy from missing a man to whom she was an obligation of kindness, she stepped back inside the cabin. Hunger was nipping at her, and the one thing Auden would never do was starve her precious baby.

"Let Mama put something together," she said to the child in her womb whose mind was already a delicate brightness. "Then I'll sit down and read more of the parenting and infant care books I downloaded onto my organizer."

She knew what Charisma and Dr. Verhoeven had planned, that they intended to take the baby and have professional nannies assume her care, but Auden wasn't about to permit that to happen. She'd chosen who she intended to trust with her child, a man wild and protective, and that man wouldn't ever try to keep her from Auden.

A scratching sound on the door some time later startled her out of her concentration on the text. Cocking her head, she listened . . . and heard it again. A deliberate sound.

Heart thumping, she shifted to get out of bed.

Nothing scratched again the entire time it took her to get to the door, and she suddenly felt foolish. Remi no doubt had a thousand calls on his time. He wasn't out there at her door. It might even be a danger-ous wild animal.

Opening the window to the right hand side of the door, she looked out.

A leopard sat by her door, its tail waving lazily. Rising when it spot-ted her, it let out a rumbling growl that didn't seem like a threat but a greeting.

"Remi?" she whispered. "Is that you?"

The air shimmered around the huge jungle cat in incandescent golden sparks, and where it had stood now crouched a muscled man with tou-sled hair of endless shades of brown and eyes that were still cat. His skin gleamed in the dawn light, his body devoid of clothing.

Beautiful. He was beautiful.

"Hi," he said. "Angel said you were awake."

Angel must be the tiger, she thought. "Hold on, I'll open the door."

"I'll shift back," he said, those eyes gleaming at her primal and po-tent. "Save your eyes from my birthday suit."

Flushing as she realized he'd be fully visible to her if he rose from his crouch, she couldn't help but watch the transition again. His body breaking apart into a million pieces of light before forming once again into the powerful shape of the leopard that was his other half. Her fingers curled into her palm, the urge to touch almost overwhelming.

He looked over.

"Just a second," she said, and closed the window before walking over to unlock the door. "Come in."

The leopard on the doorstep hesitated.

"Oh," she said, her eyes flaring. "I've never knowingly touched a new changeling imprint when a changeling is in their other form. I don't know the impact."

Raising one deadly-looking paw, his claws out, Remi just brushed the side of the doorway. Auden went to touch it, test her senses—and hit an immediate snag. "I can't bend that far."

They stared at each other, her halfway down, him looking up. And suddenly, she felt a snort of laughter leave her lips, followed by another and another, until she was laughing so hard that she had to brace her hand against the door to keep herself upright. The leopard's eyes gleamed, as if he was laughing along with her.

It was the first time in her life she could remember feeling untrammeled joy.

After she recovered enough to think, she said, "Can you touch anything higher?"

The leopard padded back and back, before bunching up its body into a pounding run toward her door. Her eyes widened as it went airborne. A bang from above as the cat landed on her roof.

She was staring upward in shock when the leopard curled its paws over the top of the doorway, and peered down at her. So close, she could see all the striations in the yellow-green of its irises, sense how the eyes held both an intense wildness and something that wasn't animal at all, but the human part of his self.

"Beautiful," she whispered, her hand rising before she was aware of it.

The leopard didn't attempt to escape her touch, and she found her fingers brushing the soft fur below its jaw. It grumbled and made a movement as if it tickled, but still let her touch. He was warmth and power and patience, and he compelled her.

When he growled again with more intent, she finally dropped her hand. But he wasn't mad, was just patting at the bit of the doorjamb he'd touched.

"Right," she said, and took a deep breath before brushing her fingers over the spot.

Wildness. Warmth. Remi. Red leaves shaped like stars under paws. Moon-bathing. The scent of ozone before a rolling storm. Hunting, slowly stalking prey. The satisfaction of a hunt completed. Blood so hot and fresh.

"It's so different," she whispered. "I can sense you, but mostly, I sense the part of you that's the leopard." Because the leopard was in charge right now, she thought, understanding now that when a changeling shifted, they truly *shifted*. They weren't human in a cat's skin. They were a cat with a human part deep within.

No imprint this half of Remi left in her home would cause her hurt. Because even though the leopard had hunted, it hadn't killed for the joy of it. While she'd picked up its satisfaction, it was a satisfaction without cruelty—a simple pragmatic thing that she would've never been able to understand without touching this imprint.

"You can come inside," she said, and moved back from the doorway.

The leopard's face and paws vanished, only for his body to land in front of her not long afterward. She gasped, having no idea how such a muscular creature could land so lightly. Tail flicking, Remi prowled in and did what felt like a perimeter check to her. After which, he walked to the kitchen and looked back at her in a pointed way.

"I've eaten," she told him. "Baby here was hungry." She patted her belly, then winced.

When the leopard rumbled a question, she said, "Backache. I'm controlling it using my usual methods, but it's persistent."

Rising, the leopard prowled around, managing to open cupboards and poke its head inside as it did so. She watched, utterly fascinated by this beautiful, wild beast inside her home. She wanted to touch him again, feel the living warmth of him.

When he finally returned after his exploration, he stared at her again until she threw up her hands. "I don't need to lie down! I need to move and stretch it out."

A shimmer around the cat.

Her breath caught.

She knew she should shut her eyes to give him privacy, but she couldn't have torn away her gaze if her life depended on it—so she was looking right at him when a tall and muscular man appeared where the cat had been a heartbeat ago.

This time, he didn't remain in a crouch.

From shoulder to flank to calf and everything in between, he was all liquid muscle and gleaming healthy skin. And wicked smile. "Hey, my face is up here," he said, the leopard there in the growl in his tone.

Her eyes jerked up, her cheeks blazing.

Eyes of leopard yellow-gold gleamed at her. "How about a back massage?"

Breath a roar in her ears, and skin so hot it was a wonder it wasn't melting off her body, Auden said, "Um." She knew words. She knew lots of words. They were just unfortunately missing from her brain right now.

"No pressure." A purring rumble that seemed designed to soothe. "I know I'd still be a naked man in your bed."

A naked man.

In her bed.

Those words somehow computed themselves into meaning. And her mouth opened. "Maybe a towel?"

"I'm teasing you, Auden." A smile in his voice. "I left my clothes outside. Give me a minute."

Disappointment curled into the pit of her stomach when he vanished out the door, even though she knew she'd been rude in how she'd stared. Except . . . he hadn't seemed to mind.

She turned toward the bed, not knowing what to do . . . and felt a stir at her back.

The movement had her turning—to look straight at an upper body that rippled with muscle, his chest lightly dusted with dark hair, and his shoulders broad. Big, she realized, he was a big man. She'd never appreciated exactly how big until this instant, when he was naked but for jeans hitched low around his hips.

"My sweatshirt is a bit damp from the morning dew." He held it up. "I'll hang it over your chair to dry. So, you comfortable with me giving you that massage?"

She jerked up her eyes again when they wanted to wander south, trace the path of the hair that narrowed down toward his groin. "How should I . . . ?"

"Hmm." He rubbed his jaw, a frown creasing his forehead. "How about lying on your side? Is that fairly comfortable?"

Nodding, Auden got into bed, and positioned herself the way he'd suggested. The loose pajama pants and soft sweater in deep green that she'd changed into after waking covered her more than well enough, but she still felt exposed with her back to him.

Then the bed moved, and the wave of heat that hit her was very much a primal thing.

"Okay?" Another one of those rumbling purrs that felt as if he was stroking her with his voice. "I won't touch if it's making you tense. I can run down and get a heat pack."

"No, it's okay." She forced herself to exhale. "I've just never . . . Tactile intimacy isn't common in my race."

"Yeah, I heard." The bed moved again, as he situated himself. She'd expected him to lie behind her, but instead, from what she saw in her peripheral vision, he was kneeling in a position that allowed him to see her back.

"I think I can get better leverage this way," he said. "But you tell me how it feels."

She nodded.

"Auden?" This time it *was* mostly a purr.

Her toes curled. "Yes?" she whispered.

"I need you to tell me if it hurts or if you don't like it or even if my

touch is too much for you. Don't let me hurt you without meaning to."
Gentle words that held a demand—the first hint this morning of the
dominant alpha that lived under Remi's skin.

She shivered, responding to that in a way that confused her. Control
was critical for her. She didn't want anyone else to have it over her. And
yet there was a wild pleasure in knowing that if she yielded it to him,
he'd know exactly what to do—and the one thing he wouldn't do was
hurt her.

"I'll tell you," she promised, because even in her confusion, she knew
this was important.

"Good girl."

She wasn't a girl. But her toes curled even harder at the praise, her
teeth sinking into her lower lip.

Chapter 27

"WE'LL START EASY," he said, the purr back—and louder, until it vibrated through her bones. "You have any oil, even moisturizer I can use?"

"Yes. In the bathroom." Dr. Verhoeven had given it to her to help prevent stretch marks, and she'd followed the regime mostly because she enjoyed having the chance to stroke her baby. That the oil had worked as advertised was a bonus.

Remi's weight vanished from the bed, only to return moments later.

"Got it. I'm going to push up your sweatshirt so I can touch skin, all right?"

Auden somehow managed a jerky nod.

His fingertips on her lower back creating the gentlest pressure.

The shock of contact was so intense that it took her at least a minute to think through the roar of sensation. "Harder," she whispered at last. "That's too gentle."

"That's it," he praised again. "Tell me exactly what you need." He dug his fingers in, and the pressure was so intense and so painfully pleasurable that she cried out.

He halted.

"It's good," she gasped. "Please."

A chuckle, before he began working the muscles of her back. Then he began that purring sound in his chest again, and it *did* vibrate right through his hands and into her back and oh, *oh*. Every part of her resonated on the same wavelength, her entire body relaxing muscle by muscle as his purr entered her very bones to melt her from the inside out.

REMI'S cock was rigid, but he didn't do anything other than keep up the massage. Seeing Auden's tension melt away, hearing the little sounds she was making without realizing it, it was the best aphrodisiac on the planet. As was the fact that she'd sneakily scooted close to him.

He rumbled in his chest, his leopard very close to his human skin right now, felt her shiver . . . and the excited beat of a second heartbeat from inside Auden.

He smiled. Yes, the cub knew him, too.

"How does she know you?" Auden whispered just then, the curve of her butt pushing into his knee because she kept on backing up to him.

"All cubs know their alpha's voice."

A sucked in breath, a pause, before Auden said, "Remi, I need to ask you something."

His fingers stilled. "What, little cat?"

Shifting, she tried to sit up. He helped her until she was leaning against the headboard. And even though he'd just spent pleasurable minutes kneading the tension from her, she was stiff, lines of strain around her eyes and mouth.

When she spoke, her words had his claws slicing out. "I'm going to ask you the biggest favor of my life." Those haunted moonstone eyes held his, potent in their pain. "Do you think RainFire can give my baby sanctuary?"

"Yes," Remi said without hesitation.

"It'll be dangerous for your pack," she said. "But I have money. My father left me an enormous trust fund, and no one in the Scott family seems to know about it. It can buy you help, protection."

Remi sliced out a hand. "You don't have to worry, Auden. One of my best friends is an Arrow. No one will touch your baby or my pack."

Remi and RainFire were very careful never to take advantage of the squad, their relationship built on a foundation of mutual respect and trust. But for a cub? Remi would ask and the entire squad would say yes. Because none of them would *ever* abandon a child at risk.

Auden's eyes flared wide, and he could all but see the flames of her curiosity. But she seemed to shove that curiosity aside with a conscious hand to say, "I have to make a plan, because I might not be able to do it later, and my baby needs to be protected from whatever it is my mother set in motion before her death. Because there is something very, very wrong with me."

Remi wanted to argue with her, but he knew they had to face the cold, hard facts. Rising off the bed, he paced around the room. "The scent and personality changes."

Auden's nod was hard, her breathing erratic. "Memory issues, too. Periods of lost time." She exhaled. "All I know of what was done to my brain is that it involved a biograft that malfunctioned. Sometimes, I dream of fire engulfing my brain."

Her fingers lifting to her temple. "The lesions are still there—my brain has apparently learned to work around them, but they didn't just vanish. And there's external evidence of things I did at points where I *had* to be lucid, and yet I recall nothing. Not just me managing to pretend for a couple of minutes on my better days. I pulled off a meeting with *Kaleb Krychek*, for one."

Remi didn't interrupt, a low-level rumble deep in his chest. The same instinct that made him a good alpha told him that what she was saying was important, and that she needed him to *listen*.

"I also have no memory of signing a fertilization agreement with another Psy family. But there's a recording of me having a full contractual interaction with the other family." She spread her fingers over her belly. "I'm speaking in a crisp and clear manner, negotiating the fee, and watching as the donor signs away all rights to the resulting child."

Remi knew Psy did things that way, though his changeling mind struggled to accept it. He also knew that the woman in front of him was a creature of emotion. "You think like that, Auden?"

"*No*. I never have. That was my mother's problem with me." Her throat moving, her eyes shining. "My father didn't mind that I was a psychometric and what that entailed, but I was never Silent enough for Shoshanna—except that I *was* on that video."

Remi was caught by something else she'd said. "Why are you with your mother's family if you were closer to Henry?"

Shadows across her face. "My father didn't want me after I was damaged. The terrifying thing is that Shoshanna shouldn't have, either. She kept me alive for a reason—because per her worldview, I should've stopped existing when I stopped having value to the family and became a drain on their resources instead.

"It wouldn't have been hard for her to pull off. She was a Councilor at the time, and she had Dr. Verhoeven's unconditional loyalty. A single injection and I'd have been gone, the death labeled as natural. But she didn't do that. That is the scariest thing in all this—*what did my mother want with me that she kept me alive?*"

Rage scalded Remi's veins at the idea of Auden's light being snuffed out with such callousness.

"I hero-worshipped him, you know," Auden added softly before he could respond. "My father. I thought he was such a good man for a long, long time. He was kind to me, often personally gave me the lessons I needed as his heir-in-training."

Her voice faded on her next words. "I was fourteen when I got the freedom to explore the PsyNet without babysitters—though I'm guessing those babysitters were still there, just well hidden. I started to hear things about my father, started to learn things. And still I wanted to believe in him. Then . . ."

Her fingers lifted to her temple. "He let Shoshanna do this to me."

"You sure he was aware what she intended?" Remi said, not because he thought Henry Scott anything less than a psychopath, but because he couldn't quite see a father who had a happy, bright child he was raising as his heir agreeing to an experiment that would cause her harm.

"Maybe not." Auden shrugged. "But, you see, it doesn't matter—because he chose to give me up after the brain damage." Her face twisted. "I read the document. It's all spelled out. I was created as the heir to the Jackson empire, but the Scotts didn't have to compensate them for taking me because I was 'of negative value' to the Jacksons by then."

Remi released his growl. Walking over, he sat on the side of the bed and twisted so that his hands were on either side of Auden's head on the headboard he'd put together for her. "They didn't break you," he growled, eye to eye with her. "You're still standing."

"That's just it," she whispered in a husky tone, "I'm not sure I'm still standing." One small, cold hand against his chest. "I'm acting in ways that aren't me. I have knowledge that isn't mine. I know passwords I never learned."

A chill passed over Remi's skin. "Auden," he began.

But Auden spoke over him, needing to get this out. "I'm starting to believe that my mind has split into two or even more fragments." It was a truth she'd been avoiding since the day on the doorstep to this cabin when he'd said she didn't know him.

"No one can fix that. It's one of the worst mental afflictions a Psy can have—a psyche so broken that it literally becomes more than one person. Only a partial fragment inhabiting the body at any one time."

Remi's frown was dark.

She kept on speaking before he could say anything. "It's called dissociative identity disorder and it exists in all the races, but for Psy, there's an added layer. Our personalities don't fully splinter, you see. All Psy are telepaths—it's necessary to be one to attach to the PsyNet."

His frown grew heavier. "I never picked that up from my friends."

"I suppose we don't talk about it because it's a given. Like the fact you can shift is a given—an indelible part of being changeling." Her fingers curled into the muscled heat of his chest. "From what I remember of my elementary school lessons, I'm pretty sure Gradient 1 telepathy is the prerequisite. Any lower than that and you might *have* psychic abilities, but you aren't considered Psy on a neurological level."

Remi's eyes shifted to human in front of her, but his arms still bracketed her, the warmth and scent of him a haven. "How does the telepathy impact the splintering?"

"Bleedover." A rapid inhale, a sharp exhale. "I think in the other races, the separation is much more significant. One personality won't know what the other is doing, that kind of thing. I don't either . . . but there *is* bleedover. That's the only way I can have all this knowledge. One part of me was told or taught it."

Remi's body was rigid with tension around her, in front of her. "Could there be any other explanation? Someone trying to mind control you?"

Auden flinched, her fingers wanting to touch the scar at her temple again. "There's no one with that kind of power in our family home. My mother was the most powerful telepath I've ever known and even she had difficulty maintaining mind control without technological assistance."

Only when she rubbed her scar did she realize she hadn't been able to fight the compulsion to worry at it.

Taking her hand, Remi brushed away the baby hairs from that spot. "The biograft?"

"Yes. Removed after the failure of the experiment, but the scars remain—inside and out." Auden found herself stroking the hair-roughened skin of his chest. "Will—" A violent wrenching pain in her abdomen, a sudden wet heat on her pants, her baby's mind screaming in distress. "*No.*"

Remi's nostrils flared in front of her. "You're bleeding."

Panic shrieked warnings in Auden's brain. Her baby was coming too early! "They'll find me! They'll take her!"

"No one's taking anything." Remi's gritted-out voice, his hands cupping her face as he made her look into his eyes. "Breathe, little cat, *breathe.*"

"My baby," she sobbed, her emotions huge and violent. "I can't let them know!"

"Can you hold on to your shields?"

"No," she admitted, the surge of emotions inside her so intense that she'd never felt the like. "They'll fall in minutes."

"I'll get you help." He moved away from her with a speed that felt impossible to her Psy vision, was out the door before she realized he had left.

He'd come back with help. Auden believed that with everything in her.

"A little longer," she begged her body. "Please hold her inside a little longer."

The first contraction hit. Not a big one. Small. But dangerous. "No, no, no."

Remi ran back inside, a phone to his ear, and sat back down on the bed. She gripped his hand, panic a drumbeat in her skull.

Through the roar inside her head, she caught only snatches of what he was saying. ". . . shield . . . help . . . premature baby . . . pick up Finn. Anything he should know for a Psy birth? What? I'll send you the image now."

A snapshot being taken with the phone, Auden's brain too full to process why until the air shimmered at the end of the bed moments later.

A petite woman dressed in the stark black combat uniform of the Arrow squad, her hair short and feathered, stood with a tall man with sandy hair and eyes of leaf green. He wore a checked red shirt, and his face . . . it held a gentleness innate.

The Arrow vanished a heartbeat later, but the man snapped into action.

Putting down his small case, he came over to take her hand. "I've got you, sweetheart. Finn. RainFire healer. Remi briefed me on your ability—all the medical tools I've brought, only I or my nurses will have handled."

Auden squeezed his hand, sobs tearing at her chest. "*My baby.*"

"I know, sweetheart. Let's see what's happening—and don't you worry." He thrust a thumb in Remi's direction. "You want him here or out?"

Even in her panic, Auden knew this procedure was too intimate to ask Remi to stay . . . and yet she still met his eyes and said, "Please stay."

"You couldn't make me leave," he growled out, then shifted so that he faced her fully, while giving Finn his back—and her some privacy as Finn quickly cut off the clothes on her lower body. "Finn," he said out loud, "I have Dr. Bashir on the phone. He's spoken to an obstetrician colleague since your last conversation and can confirm the process is the same physically. It's the psychic that's different."

"Got it. I've delivered many a cub in my time, so this'll be child's play." Words warm and calm that gave Auden confidence. "I'll put this sheet over your thighs. There, that's better, isn't it?"

Auden appreciated this kind, gentle man so much. Tears hot in her eyes, she nodded.

Remi's gaze held hers after he hung up on the doctor he'd mentioned. "You know what to do?"

Auden made herself breathe, think. "Yes. I have to calm the child on the psychic level."

Which was when it hit her—her shields had become a formless and unbreakable black. "My shields. Who?" Who would she owe after this was all over?

"That friend of mine I mentioned," Remi said, even as he made a second call and asked whoever it was to be on standby. "No one will get through that shield, little cat, so just worry about your baby."

Auden knew favors were a currency and those in debt were always the losers, but today, all she cared about was her child. Sweat beaded on her brow, her abdomen rippling as another contraction hit on a wetness of rich iron. "I'm bleeding too much," she whispered. "My baby is weak. Her mind is fighting but she's so small, not yet ready to leave the womb."

"Don't think about that." Finn's voice was firm and comforting, something about him inspiring trust even though he was a stranger. "You just do your job, mama, and let me worry about the rest. Your cub's had over eight months inside you. She'll be fine. Now, I need you to push."

So she did, her hand locked with Remi's and her mind surrounded by a shield so deadly she should've been terrified. But her terror was reserved for her child's fragile mind, so young, *too* young. Shoving aside her fear, Auden concentrated on enfolding the baby's mind in psychic arms, comforting and calm.

The baby's mind hiccuped, settled.

Shh, Auden whispered to her child, *I have you. I'll never let anyone hurt you.*

Filaments of blue spidersilk swirled between them, her baby's mind reaching for a filament even as pain wracked Auden's physical body. *Pretty, so pretty*, she said, her focus absolute. *There's nothing to fear. I have you. Mama has you.*

A wrenching in her womb that was pure agony.

Auden couldn't keep her baby inside anymore, her body ejecting her precious child when all Auden wanted to do was hold her inside, where she could protect her.

It was no use, the violent contractions of her body not in her control.

"Promise you'll keep her safe if I can't?" Her words came out in a sob, her nails cutting into Remi's skin as well as her own.

She tried to stop the spasm, ease her grip, couldn't.

"I promise," he said without hesitation. "Don't you worry about that, Auden. Your cub is one of mine now."

Their mingled blood seemed to glow to her panicked brain.

She gave birth on a piercing scream, the agony of it nothing compared to hearing her child's mind stutter. She enfolded her in love, in calm, her own screams nothing but stifled echoes in the background.

Stay, my baby. Mama has you. Stay.

The spidersilk escaped her dreams to float outside her mind, the fine blue filaments hitting the black shields that protected her from exposure. Right as she felt her child leave her body on another gush of blood.

Auden's mind faded, her hand going limp in Remi's.

Chapter 28

Emergency teleport request received from RainFire. Nerida handled first 'port, but they need two teleporters for the second transport.

—Message to Vasic Zen, second-in-command of the Arrow Squad (11 November 2083)

REMI YELLED, "GO!" into the open line as soon as Finn had the child in his arms, and suddenly, there were two Arrow teleporters in the room.

Remi had already grabbed Auden's bloody body, the sheet Finn had placed over her thighs crumpled between her limbs and his arm.

A pulse of disorientation later, and they all stood inside Finn's infirmary. The healer raced to place the child in an incubator designed to protect its fragile life, while his nurses, Hugo and Saskia, as well as the Psy doctor—Dr. Edgard Bashir—whom Nerida had brought in after she dropped Finn off, worked to save Auden's life.

She'd lost blood, far too much of it.

Remi made himself release her hand, give the medical staff room to move. The teleporters had already left, but a tired Vasic reappeared soon afterward with an equally tired-looking Aden, the three of them meeting in the hallway outside the large infirmary suite that was the biggest of the three cubes.

"Is she safe on the PsyNet?" he asked one of the deadliest men in the PsyNet.

Aden nodded, the slick and straight black of his hair gleaming in the artificial lighting; he wore it short, no fuss. "Her shields are airtight. No one knows she's given birth. Zaira handled the initial response and I took over when I finished up in Europe. I added a secondary shield to protect her privacy from me, too."

Remi knew a lot of fucked up shit was going on in the PsyNet, could see that both men were worn to the bone. And still they—all of the squad—had responded to his call for help. "Thank you."

"No thanks between us, Remi, you know that." His friend's dark eyes held Remi's gaze, the olive tone of his skin too pale—as if he hadn't had much chance to get out into the sunlight. "I didn't even know Auden Scott was pregnant."

"Not security related." Remi kept his tone even, because these men didn't deserve his anger. "None of anyone's damn business."

"Agreed," Aden said without hesitation, and that was when Remi remembered that his friend had trained as a medic. Not only that, but Aden wasn't just an Arrow—he was a good man, a good mate to Zaira, a good friend.

"Status?" Aden asked.

"Critical. Both of them." Remi had to fight every instinct in his body not to push back into the room. "Does Dr. Bashir have any idea why she began to hemorrhage?" He knew they had to be in telepathic communication with the man.

"No, not yet. But he's a neurosurgeon who's also trained in trauma-related injuries because of the squad, not an obstetric specialist—we'd have to go outside the squad to get you one of those, and we haven't yet zeroed in on a trustworthy candidate," Aden said. "Do you want to take the risk?"

Remi thought rapidly, and came up against an unexpected solution: *Tamsyn Ryder.*

DarkRiver's healer had assisted with Psy births. He had the feeling she had more training than any other changeling healer when it came to the Psy—and he knew she had infinitely more experience with women and childbirth than Dr. Bashir.

"I'll make a call," he said to the Arrows, then walked away to do so.

"I need Tamsyn," he said the instant Lucas answered. "Don't ask me how, but I have a Psy with me who's just given birth and she's hemorrhaging. Finn can't work on her and the cub both—though he's trying—and the Psy doctor we have has no experience with births."

"I'll organize it," Lucas said, offering him the respect of not asking questions that'd delay things. "One of your Arrow friends available for teleport?"

"Vasic."

It was arranged in a matter of minutes, tall and elegant Tamsyn "Tammy" Ryder soon in the infirmary with Bashir and Finn—who yelled out a heartfelt, "I thought you'd never get here, Tams!"

Then, as the medical people worked, Aden and Remi spoke in the hallway, with Vasic teleporting out to handle "a glitch in Eastern Europe."

Remi frowned. "You need to go back, too, Aden? I know it's hell on the Net right now."

"No, I'm close to flameout. Kaleb's taken over, with two other cardinals assisting—add Vasic to that, and that situation is under control."

Undoing his jacket, Aden put his hands on his hips above the waistline of his black combat pants. "I understand why you had to bring her here," Aden said, nodding toward the closed door that held Auden and her child. "But you know the room is compromised the instant she wakes and gets an image she could give to a teleporter?"

Folding his arms, Remi set his feet apart. "She'd never betray us." He'd stake his life on that. "She'd die for that cub of hers."

"Scotts are masters of deception." Aden's voice was even, his eyes unflinching.

"I *know* her." Remi thumped a fist against his bare chest. "All she cares about is her baby." He held Aden's eyes. "I know the same way I knew you and Zaira wouldn't hurt us." Even as he spoke, he remembered the *other* Auden, the one who repelled his leopard and who had cold-bloodedly negotiated with the man who was the baby's biological father.

That woman he didn't know or trust.

Splinters.

Multiple personalities.

Bleedover.

"Be careful, Remi." Aden's voice was quiet with warning. "The Scott family . . . they're a lineage of power, but power gained through a kind of ruthlessness that's extreme even for the Psy."

"She's worried about them taking her cub. How high is the possibility she's right?"

"High," Aden said at once. "The big families are militant about controlling their bloodlines." He looked to the closed door. "The child is innocent. We can hide her in the Valley, inside our shields. No one will ever find her."

Remi's heart expanded—because he hadn't even had to ask the question before the offer was made; RainFire and the Arrows, their friendship was a thing of blood and loyalty. "I might have to take you up on that if the shit hits the fan. It won't be permanent—cub is one of mine now." Born into RainFire under Remi's rule, she was under his protection, and in his heart just like Jojo and Asher and all the others.

Aden nodded. "Even if you're right and Auden Scott isn't a threat, she could still betray you without meaning to."

"Are you saying her own family would rape her mind, just take the information?" He knew the answer even as he asked the question, his fingers tingling with the tactile echo of that small, telling scar on her temple.

"The Scotts don't have any lines they won't cross."

"Fuck." Remi locked his fingers behind his head and looked up at the ceiling. "Right, what can we do to protect the pack while also protecting Auden and her cub?" Because he'd made two promises and he'd damn well keep both of them.

Dropping his hands to his hips, he got ready to listen.

"Keep her isolated to the infirmary—which shouldn't be difficult given her current state." Aden held up a hand when Remi would've spoken. "Right now, her mind is safe because I'm protecting it—when I need to pull my energy, Zaira will take over. No one will ever be able to get to her.

"But PsyNet shields are different from the ones she has against telepathic powers—which means she'll be vulnerable once she returns to her household."

It's not my home. It's my mother's house.

Auden's words vibrated inside Remi's mind.

"The instant she leaves," the Arrow leader continued, "you need to alter the room in a way that no one can use it as a teleport lock. Easiest way would be to clear the equipment or cover it, and splash the room with a different color paint.

"A messy solution, but in combination with the shifting of equipment, it'll distort the teleport lock—unless she has an image point that's hyper-specific, unique, and can't be changed. A chipped tile in a distinctive pattern, for example."

"No, the room is all but new. Smooth lines, clean walls, only necessary equipment in there."

"Good. That'll help." Aden's eyes went to the room where the healers fought for the lives of a woman and a child who deserved to feel safe, feel protected. "I know you hate the idea of caging anyone, but every other part of your aerie community is unique in many ways. Teleporters who can lock onto faces are rare, but a specific enough location lock ameliorates that—the enemy could teleport into the center of the pack with ill intent."

"I understand." His alpha's heart pulsed at the idea of any such harm coming to RainFire—and it raged against trapping Auden and her cub.

She'd already been wounded over and over again by the people who were supposed to care for her—and now he was being backed into a corner, forced to stifle what little freedom she'd managed to claw for herself.

Never before had he so totally hated himself for the decision he had to make.

Chapter 29

The Mother found you. She was angry you weren't hers. I heard. I told the others. I said we should ask you. If you could say no to her, you must be strong. Will you be our Father now?

—PsyNet message from unknown sender to
Pax Marshall (circa September 2083)

PAX MARSHALL, HEAD of the Marshall Group, stood on the balcony of his San Francisco apartment, the setting sun's rays a dance of gold and orange on the silvery waters of the bay.

Father. Father. Father.

It was a constant murmur in the back of his brain now, the whisper of his Scarabs. Because they *were* his. Who else was going to look after their tormented souls? He was the most powerful one, and he was the lucky one.

Because he had his twin.

The far better half of their pairing.

And a big part of the reason he was sane while other Scarabs had lost their grip on reality.

His sister wouldn't understand his choice, would tell him to take the Scarabs to a treatment facility. But that was just it. Pax knew the options, knew that there just weren't enough specialist empaths to help all the Scarabs.

The Es were burning themselves out trying, but they couldn't force abilities that weren't there—because it was only a subset *of* a subset of Es who could stabilize Scarabs. The rest . . . could put on Band-Aids. Short-term fixes that dulled the mind and the heart in the quest for sanity.

A soft cage.

How could Pax lead all these broken people to that? They hadn't done anything wrong. All of them—Pax included—had simply been unlucky enough to be born with a mind that was never designed to process the amount of power that now rushed through their system.

Silence had hidden that flaw their entire lifetimes. Its fall had opened floodgates that could never be closed, their power driving them to madness as it filled them to overflowing with delusions endless.

The others in the PsyNet had little sympathy for them these days, even knowing they were victims of their own minds. Because the erratic Scarab energy was a large part of the reason the PsyNet was on the brink of collapse. It had been heading that way prior to the rise of the Scarabs, but Pax's kind had sped up the disintegration to critical.

Major tears in the psychic fabric, casualty after casualty, were a daily occurrence now. The PsyNet couldn't be saved. His sister, his twin, his heart, would be fine. When the time came, she'd be wrenched into the changeling network inhabited by her bear mate.

As for Pax and his Scarabs . . . if they were to die anyway, wouldn't it be better that they die alive and dazzling in their manic brilliance?

One final incandescent flame before the lights went out forever.

Chapter 30

I see a spider . . . filaments of blue. Death. Light. Anarchy. Order. Screams. Peace. I can't untangle it. Two different timelines melded into one. It doesn't make any sense.

—Faith NightStar (Cardinal F-Psy, DarkRiver) to Anthony Kyriakus of the PsyClan NightStar (12 November 2083)

AUDEN WOKE WITH her brain fuzzy. Panic stuttered in the back of her mind. Was she regressing? Going back to who she'd been before the pregnancy? Had she lost more time? Who had she been—

My baby!

A deluge of memory, of pain, visceral and stabbing, that had turned into rolling waves of agony. Her child's fear, the scent of blood in the air, a leopard's gold-green eyes looking into hers as he growled at her that she had this, that her cub would be just fine.

She couldn't feel her baby inside her anymore, and when she managed to move her hand to her abdomen, it didn't feel right. Too small. Not hard enough.

A delicate psychic light, a bond unbreakable.

Her child was alive, but where? Had her family taken her? Please. *Please.*

Her breath coming in pants, she struggled to open her eyes.

"You're all right, sweetheart." The touch of a hand on hers that *felt* gentle.

An empath?

"There you go, your vital signs are stabilizing. Don't force it, just let yourself come out of it naturally. You didn't put yourself under so whatever you feel when you come out of that, this'll be different. You lost a lot of blood—your body shut down."

She'd understood all those words, she realized, and she wasn't fading into a heavier fuzziness but coming out into clarity. Her eyes opened on that thought—and she found herself looking into the face of a man with smile lines at the corners of his eyes and sandy hair that fell over his forehead.

"My baby." It came out a rasp at the same time that she remembered the man's name: *Finn.* His name was Finn, and he was one of Remi's people.

Remi, who'd promised her that no one would steal her baby.

"In the incubator," Finn said with a smile. "I'll wheel it over so you can see her. She's tiny but perfect. Strong little lungs, too. Just needs a bit of extra help keeping her body temperature stable—you can still give her cuddles, but we'll have to time it."

He vanished on that, but she soon heard the sound of wheels on a hard floor. Turning in that direction, she watched as the clear box of what appeared to be a state-of-the-art incubator neared her bed.

Her eyes teared up. Her little girl was so small, so fragile. "Is she—"

"Totally fine," the healer assured her. "Enough weeks on her that she was out of the danger zone as soon as I got her over the shock of the birth."

After locking the incubator's wheels, he helped Auden struggle up into a seated position, then—with infinite care—removed her baby from the incubator—and from the wires that went out from her tiny body. "Skin-to-skin contact is the best, especially as you won't be able to hold her for long until she graduates from the incubator."

Not caring about her modesty, only about her baby, she undid the strings of her loose hospital smock from around her neck, and lowered it off her arms and down her chest. Finn kept his eyes gently averted as he handed Auden her precious baby.

So small and fragile, her eyes closed and her skin delicate beyond bearing, her baby nonetheless curled her hands against her heart and Auden heard a whispered sigh in her mind. "I have you. I'm so sorry it took this long, my baby." Tears streaked down Auden's face. "I won't let anyone hurt you."

She was barely aware of Finn throwing a soft blanket or shawl around her shoulders that she tugged to wrap around herself and her child. "Mama will never ever let you go." She pressed the softest of kisses on her baby's head, which was covered in a tiny knitted cap. Under her hand, she wore a diaper of the same tiny proportions.

Auden didn't know what color her eyes were. Might be blue like her own, or brown like those of the male genetic donor. Her skin was far paler than Auden's, which wasn't a huge surprise. The paternal donor's skin had been on the other end of the spectrum to Auden's. But . . . She frowned, checked her baby's body, and saw not a single hint of the level of melanin in her own skin.

Her baby's skin was the color Auden's mother's had been—a creamy white.

Odd genetics, she told herself, thinking of an article she'd seen once where a set of twins had come out divided when it came to skin tones, one with skin of ebony, the other with skin of white. As if each parent's genes had chosen a child in the womb.

None of it mattered, Auden's love for her child a fierce beat in her soul.

She wanted to see if her girl had tiny black curls or if she'd been born with mere wisps, but she didn't want her head to get cold, so she left it for now. Something to discover another day.

Today, she just inhaled the sweet, innocent smell of this child she had no memory of conceiving and who she loved beyond compare, and she hugged her close and she listened to her near-imperceptible breathing—

and her murmurings inside Auden's mind. Even so young, her voice was crystalline.

Her baby was a strong, very strong, telepath.

And she loved being cuddled by her mama.

Auden could feel that deep within.

Finn didn't disturb her as she rocked her baby, wishing she could keep her close always. But time passed all too soon, that tiny body and mind too young to be out of the womb, and she didn't argue when Finn came to put her back in the incubator.

"We can do another session later in the day," he told her, as she fixed up her smock. "I don't know about Psy, but changelings believe skin-to-skin contact to be critical for newborns."

Auden nodded. "Yes, even under Silence, physical contact with babies was deemed necessary." Apparently, her race had tried it the other way, and ended up with psychologically damaged children.

"See here." Finn pointed out a circular section on the clear case of the incubator, then pushed in. His hand went through. "It's so you can continue to stroke her while she's in there. It won't affect the warmth."

"Oh, I'm so glad. I don't want her to feel lonely." She used the backs of her hands to wipe her face. "Was she alone while—"

"No, sweetheart." A reassuring smile as he finished hooking her baby back to the tubes and wires and closed the door of the incubator. "Tammy—another healer—and I took turns placing her against your skin so she could feel your heartbeat. And I hope you don't mind, but we let Remi hold her a few times. Cub seems to calm when he's around— alphas often have that effect."

"No, I don't mind." Remi was the reason her baby was alive. "Thank you for everything, Finn." Her heart overflowed with emotion for this kind, gentle man who was very much a healer to the core. Not once in his presence had she felt embarrassed or ashamed or anything but cared for.

"Just doing my job," he said. "Talking of which, we stopped the bleeding and fixed the problem that was causing it. Unexpected but positive end result is that you're in far better shape than most women after childbirth—thanks to an injection of medical nanos. You might feel a little weak, but the actual physical damage from the birth is ninety percent fixed. A couple more days and the process will be complete."

Auden had been wondering about the lack of pain. But more importantly—"Medical nanotech is hard to acquire and extremely expensive." And RainFire was a young pack with limited resources; it was clear they had connections who could gain them access to the nanos, but the purchase must've blown their entire medical budget.

It also meant that whatever had happened to her body, it must've been close to catastrophic. Medical nanotech—the new-generation kind at least, the type that could achieve this level of healing—wasn't broken out for anything less. Nanos of this complexity also had to be *programmed* for the specific patient and injury, and med-nano programmers weren't exactly thick on the ground.

A soft shake of the head. "Don't worry about that, Auden. Just worry about regaining your strength."

Auden dropped the subject, but while there was no way she could repay RainFire for the precious gift of saving her child, she *would* ensure their medical supplies and budget were topped back up. No member of RainFire would suffer because the pack had a heart huge enough to help a stranger. "You're a miracle worker."

"Hardly." He laughed, eyes crinkling. "Had a whole team in here—including a Psy surgeon with an ego the size of Mars. Surgeons, right? I've got literal decades more experience in obstetrics, and he kept on poking in his nose with advice, but man did pass on a bit of cutting-edge knowledge and help source the nanos, so I can't complain too much."

Auden had so many questions—about the surgeon, about the teleporters, about how a tiny pack in the middle of nowhere had such powerful friends, but her heart was too awash in wonder that she'd birthed this baby so tiny and beautiful to ask any of them.

"Your milk hasn't come in yet," Finn continued. "Might take a few days to kick in—happens that way with premature births at times. If you'd prefer she use the bottle throughout, we're all set up for that, too. Whatever it takes to keep her healthy and happy."

Auden's heart filled and overflowed with hope and joy at the idea of nourishing her child in such a profound way. "It wasn't allowed under Silence," she whispered. "Too intimate, too high a chance of an emotional bond. In my family, mothers don't feed their children at all, regardless of how—that task is delegated to professional carers."

While other races had created drugs to help women who wished to breastfeed their baby but couldn't, the Psy had created a drug to stop the flow of milk. Dr. Verhoeven had told Auden about it, said it would be part of her post-natal care.

"No one here will force your choice either way," Finn said in that calm voice of his that was as peaceful as water lapping on a placid lake. "But don't be hard on yourself if you decide to breastfeed and your milk takes a while, or if your baby doesn't latch at once—every woman and every baby is different."

Auden nodded, the move jagged. "I'm just happy she's all right. If I get to experience that with her, it'd be wonderful, but I'm so full of joy right now that I can't imagine how I could want more."

Finn smiled. "Someone wants to see you. You feeling up to it?"

Her heart stuttered in a way it had no business doing. "Yes." Only after the healer had gone to the door did she realize her face was a wet mess.

It didn't matter.

Because her child was alive, and she slept with a tiny baby smile on her face right next to Auden's bed.

REMI wanted to strangle Finn when the other man finally opened the door and waved him in. At the same time, he wanted to hug Finn and never let go. Because keeping Remi out? That had been the act of a healer who put his patient first, above everything.

"She'll need time alone with her cub," he'd said in a stern tone when he'd alerted Remi that Auden's readings were looking like she might wake today. "Don't come lumbering in like you're a bear and not a cat. Give her that moment she didn't get at birth. Give her the privacy to just be with her child."

That was why Finn was such a damn good healer: when it came to his patients, he had zero fucks to give as to the opinions and desires of others—even when that other was his alpha. "How is she?" Remi asked, his leopard clawing at his skin.

"Good. Told you she was strong." Finn's expression was grim. "I haven't spoken to her about the other thing yet."

Remi clenched his beard-shadowed jaw. Finn had been caught between a rock and a hard place when he'd discovered something about Auden and her child during the scans after he stabilized her. Not all the scans and panels he'd run had been standard, but given the complex birth and Auden's history, Finn had decided it was better to go for overkill than not do enough.

He'd been stunned at what he'd discovered—and worried about the possible implications. In a changeling pack, the alpha was always told of any such situations, but Auden wasn't changeling, wasn't part of their pack. In a normal situation, Finn would've held her confidence and spoken to the person who had the authority to make medical decisions on her behalf.

But Auden didn't trust anyone in her family, her doctor, or Charisma Wai.

Which had left Finn only one choice: to default to Remi, as Auden fell under his protection while in RainFire territory.

"We wait," Remi said. "Let her have some time with her cub before we tell her."

Finn gave a nod, then stood aside so Remi could walk into the room.

Auden was sitting with her legs over the side of the bed, her hair a tumble of glossy curls down her shoulders. Saskia had asked a packmate who had similar curls what to do for her patient's hair to make sure she felt good when she emerged from her unconscious state, but Remi didn't think Auden had even noticed.

Her eyes were huge with happiness as she watched her baby, her hand inside the incubator through the little circle built for that, her finger gentle as she stroked her baby's fist. The cub flexed a tiny hand and closed it over Auden's finger—to her gasp.

"Did you see that?" she whispered, looking at him with a tearstained face that was painfully young and sweet.

It kicked him again, just how *young* Auden was in comparison to the women in the pack who'd given birth. Aden and Zaira had both mentioned that, per Psy cultural norms, she was nowhere near the age where fertilization and conception agreements were even considered much less authorized—especially in a family like the Scotts.

What did my mother want with me that she kept me alive?

Remi's hand threatened to go clawed.

"Yeah," he managed to say past his fury, "the kitten's got a strong grip."

That tiny hand had wrapped around his own finger when he'd held her, her fingers so fragile that it incited every protective instinct in his alpha heart. It seemed impossible that anything could be so small and fragile.

He'd reminded himself that he'd held a premature Jojo at birth, too—the first cub born into the pack had decided to arrive over a month before her due date, a wrinkled little bean who'd cried the thinnest cry Remi had ever heard, her little fists shaking in fury at being deprived of the warm haven of her mother's body.

He'd fallen in love at first sight, his leopard purring in welcome. It had purred for Auden's baby, too. Claiming it with the same possessiveness he'd claimed Jojo.

"Also, no patience," he muttered, growling in his chest over the incubator. "Had to rush to be born, didn't you, kitten?"

The indicator lights on the panel flickered.

"What does that mean?" Auden's voice was quick, her inhale rapid.

"That's what she does when Remi's around," a passing Finn said with a grin. "It's all good stuff, don't worry. She likes our growly leader for some reason."

Auden looked at Remi, then at her baby. "You're the reason she's alive." Her voice was choked up. "Thank you for getting me, getting *us* help."

Remi waved that off; he didn't want gratitude from Auden.

But she wasn't done. "I feel so stupid. I really didn't think I was putting her in danger . . . I wanted her out of it, was buying time to ask you to give her sanctuary."

Withdrawing her hand from the incubator as if she didn't dare risk her child feeling her anguish, she hugged her arms around herself. "All scans prior to my trip said the pregnancy was stable."

"It was," Remi answered, since Finn had just stepped outside. "Finn can give you the technical breakdown, but he and Tammy did a bit of research on Psy births after Dr. Bashir managed to get them into a Psy medical database, and it looks like you had a rare complication. Unpredictable. No way for you to have known."

She bit down on her lower lip, her arms still around her body.

Unable to stand it, he went over and pulled her into his embrace, nuzzling his chin on her hair. She was motionless for a moment before melting into him. "What's wrong with me?" A whisper. "I'm stronger than this. I *have* to be stronger than this for her sake."

He petted her with long strokes of her arm, his chin on the soft springiness of her curls. "You just gave birth two days ago. Cut yourself some slack." Physical healing was one thing—the shock of it all quite another.

"Two days!" She jerked out of his hold. "Did Charisma try to contact me?" She shook her head. "Oh, how would you know?"

"We hacked your phone," he said without compunction. "I remembered seeing it in the cabin, went back and grabbed it. It's over there, on Finn's desk.

"After we hacked it, we forged a message from you that said you didn't wish to be disturbed as you were practicing 'meditative pain management' prior to the birth. A Psy contact told us the words to use. Charisma Wai replied in acknowledgment."

"Your contact was smart," she murmured. "Even Dr. Verhoeven recommended that to me—and I have been working on it. You know Psy don't react well to most narcotics and the like?"

"Yes." He ran his hand down her back and was gratified when she cuddled close to his chest again, one hand at his waist, the other on his chest. "As for Ms. Wai, I have a feeling she won't stay out of contact much longer."

"I'll be ready." Pulling back, Auden reached up to touch her hair, frowned. "It feels so soft." Grabbing a hank, she brought it to her nose. "And it smells beautiful."

Remi told her about Saskia. "Redhead," he said. "Her hair is her crowning glory and she believes all her patients should wake up looking salon ready." Actual words Sass had said to him once.

"Oh." Auden smelled her hair again. "That's a nice thing for her to do." She sounded like she didn't know how to take that.

Dropping her hair, she said, "I need to prepare to look more like myself—Charisma might call without notice."

"I like seeing your curls." His cat wanted to bat at them, play with them.

Hearing a tiny snuffle before he could give in to the feline urge, he reached over to place his hand flat on the top of the incubator, growling in his chest at the same time.

The monitoring lights danced.

"She's happy." Auden's voice was a whisper. "I feel her here." A soft punch to the heart. "No wonder my race has—had—all these rules around pregnancy.

"I don't understand how any Psy who carried a child to birth, who *felt* that child's mind come awake when it reached that stage of development, who sensed its emotions, could ever treat that child with anything but tenderness and joy and love."

Her bewilderment made his leopard growl in affectionate agreement. The cub's monitoring lights lit up.

Auden smiled, startled and happy—and beautiful in a way it was difficult to describe. Happiness suited Remi's Auden.

"She really likes you."

"Cub knows charm when she hears it."

Her lips twitched, the woman in front of him as far from the Auden he'd first met as it was possible to get . . . and nothing at all like the cold and *different* creature he'd seen that one morning at the cabin.

A stone hand squeezed his heart at the reminder of the sword hanging over Auden's head.

Chapter 31

Remi, we've got a serious problem with the cub's DNA panel. I've run it three times. Same result.

—Dr. Finn St. James to Remi Denier (12 hours ago)

AUDEN TUCKED HER hair behind her ears. "Will you keep the baby company while I fix myself up in case Charisma loses patience quicker than we think she might?"

"Me and the cublet have plenty of conversation to keep us busy." Remi offered Auden his arm. "Have you been on your feet yet?"

"No." She gripped his forearm hard as she settled her weight on her feet, but though she wobbled, she was able to stand.

He heard a demanding little rumble at the same time, felt his lips curve. "I'll organize food for you."

"I should be embarrassed at that, but I'm too hungry." Releasing his arm, she looked around.

He pointed to the door to the back and left. "Shower and toilet through there. If I know Hugo and Sass, both will be fully stocked with what you need."

It took her time to make it to the door, and he kept his eye on her throughout, ready to race over and catch her if he thought she might fall. Finn had told him that her weakness might linger for twenty-four to forty-eight hours. Knowing the facilities had sensors that monitored a patient's vital functions and would send out an alert if anything went astray, he didn't worry once she was inside with the door shut behind her.

"Your mama's as strong as you are," he said to the littlest member of his pack—because Remi and RainFire had taken Auden's request for sanctuary seriously. He'd already discussed it with his senior team, and not a single person had been anything but infuriated that this helpless infant might be used as a pawn by Auden's family.

That they'd protect her was a given.

Reaching inside, he stroked the baby's arm with his finger, his protectiveness in overdrive.

His leopard rumbled again, and the cub seemed to smile in her sleep.

He could swear he felt her inside him, same way he could feel every other member of his pack. He'd asked Lucas once, if that changed as the pack grew, if the bond became weaker. The alpha's answer had always stuck with him: "An alpha's heart is big enough to encompass every single member of his pack, Remi. So long as he lets that heart grow and grow until the love inside hurts—and he never flinches from that hurt."

Remi could do that. He *wanted* to do that.

What he did next, however, wasn't the act of an alpha, but of a man looking after a woman who was far more to him than he could permit her to guess while she was so vulnerable. Taking out his phone one-handed, he called their chef. "Fabien, can you put together a plate for Auden? She's partial to your pastries. Don't forget to use gloves and the 3D-printed serveware I made for her."

"I've got all her items in a separate spot," Fabien assured him in his French-accented English. "I'll add a glass of the nutrients we keep for the squad. Arrows say those are still the best to give Psy a jolt of energy after a big drain, and I think our new *maman* could use it, *non?*"

"Good thinking." Tamsyn had also mentioned that Psy brains required energy of a kind the nutrients were designed to provide in a far more efficient fashion than ordinary food. "Send a couple of extra sachets that she can mix up at will."

"Will do. How is our cublet?"

Of course every single member of his pack wanted to cuddle and hold Auden's baby, but they understood why they couldn't. Little Jojo had nodded solemnly when he'd described it to her in terms a child could grasp. "I got it, Remi. The cub got borned out of her mama's belly before it was a full baby. So that's how come it's gotta stay in the 'firmary."

He'd grinned and tapped her on the nose, while Jojo snuggled in for a cuddle. "Exactly right."

Finn walked back through the door at that moment, his eyes immediately going to the empty bed. When he raised an eyebrow, Remi nudged his head toward the back. "I think she's ready for that tough conversation," he said, his gut tense as anger beat a rapid tattoo at his temple. "She's worried Wai won't wait to contact her, and I think we need to know what we're dealing with before then."

Finn rubbed a jaw as bristled as Remi's; neither of them had been in any frame of mind to think about grooming for the past two days. "She's in better mental shape than I expected, so I can't see any reason to hold back."

After checking the readings on the incubator, the healer said, "Adorable, isn't she?" He placed his hand against the plas, his own leopard rumbling.

The lights flickered in a different pattern from when it was Remi.

"Already have a favorite, do you?" Finn grumbled. "And after all I did for you. That's gratitude for you." Gruff words, but his tone held nothing but affection.

The baby, Remi knew, was soaking it all in. No, he didn't have scientific proof, but he was an alpha. He *knew*. He felt her happiness, her sense of contentment . . . and when Auden was near, a calm absolute and unbroken. "How long will she need to be in the incubator?"

"I'd say a couple of weeks," Finn said, moving to strip Auden's bed as he spoke. "Some cubs need longer, some shorter, but her lungs are well-formed, so she might graduate out of it faster."

A stir of sound as the door opened on the other side of the room, the scent of soap and body lotion hitting Remi's nose, but below all that was the scent of Auden. Just Auden. Warm, strong, enigmatic Auden.

She swayed on her feet. "Whoa."

Remi was by her side before she could topple over. "Lean on me." He supported her all the way back to the bed—which Finn had fitted with a crisp new sheet at the speed of light.

Once at the bed, he just lifted her onto it.

"How do you *do* that?" she muttered, while Finn settled her with a pillow behind her back.

Remi was about to stroke his hand over her cheek when he caught the scent of food. Going to the door, he took the tray from the juvenile—who was wearing gloves Fabien must've given him. "Thanks, JD."

Jojo's brother made a sign with three of his fingers that was the newest rage among his age group. "Cub awake?" His leopard in his eyes, eager and bright.

This one, Remi thought, was going to grow up to be a soldier, one of the protectors of the pack. "Cubs that small just sleep and sleep and sleep some more."

"Wow, and Mom says I'm bad." He raised a hand. "I gotta buzz. School. When can I go into full soldier training?"

"When you've graduated and decided on your other specialty." That was another thing he'd picked up from DarkRiver: to increase the pack's intellectual capacity by ensuring that each and every packmate studied a skill, trade, or profession.

Lucas, for example, had an architect, multiple engineers, builders, an accountant, and more in his pack—all of which fed directly into the pack's success when it came to their construction arm. Then there were the teachers, chefs, and even a budding chemist. And that wasn't anywhere near the full extent of the pack's basket of trades and professions.

Tamsyn was a qualified doctor as well as a healer, a path Finn had also taken. Remi hadn't made an exception for himself, either—in his final year as a driver, when the ache to set up his own pack had become overwhelming, he'd put his nose to the grindstone to do an intensive course in business management. Because being a good alpha meant learning to deal with every weapon—even the political and business ones—so that no one could take advantage of his pack.

"I'm gonna be soooooo old," Jayden groaned before limping off in an exaggerated fashion, his back bowed, and one hand pressed to his spine. "See, this is how *ancient* I'll be. Oh my bones! Where's my cane? Get off my lawn, you feral cubs!"

Leopard huffing at the juvenile's dramatics, he carried the tray over to Auden. She'd drunk half a glass of nutrients and had a croissant in her hand in under a minute. She ate one-handed, her other hand inside the incubator, stroking her baby.

Remi glanced at the mobile comm that Auden had told him his mother had bought specifically for him. The knowledge made him warm inside, the memory of his mother's love a bigger force than his grief. "I've got to go handle a bit of pack business. Back in twenty so we can talk." He met Finn's eyes.

The healer gave a subtle nod, while Auden continued to alternately coo at her baby and make sounds of orgasmic delight at the food that went straight to parts of his body that he needed to put the brakes on.

He almost ran out of the infirmary.

Just as well that the business he had to deal with was a comm call with a hard-ass human who thought he could underbid for RainFire's services as security specialists just because they were newer on the block. "Your loss," Remi said laconically, leaning back against the wall opposite the comm screen. "I'm sure the cut-rate guards will put their bodies in the line of fire for you just fine."

The man blustered for another few minutes before agreeing to their rates, and Remi told him the contract would be coming through. Angel, who'd been standing out of visual range of the potential client, groaned. "He's going to be a nightmare of a client."

"I know—but man is connected." It was the only reason Remi hadn't already booted him. "Just think of all the work that'll flow our way when people start to notice that his guards are top-tier and discreet."

While their mech arm was part of their long-term business strategy, RainFire had had to come up with *something* with which to quickly generate income the first couple of years of their existence as a pack. Because a pack that couldn't look after its people was doing those people a disservice. Better for it to dissolve and for everyone to go their own way.

They'd had a packwide meeting that included every single adult in the group, figured out the skills at their disposal—and realized they had a significant number of people with experience in security.

Angel had *run* security for a major racetrack.

"He also has close associates in the indi-mech industry," Remi added when Angel continued to look dubious. "Try not to strangle him."

"No promises," Angel muttered as the two of them left Remi's aerie.

Angel then took the tree road to go meet with his security team, while Remi jumped down to the forest floor, his goal the infirmary.

He heard Auden's voice before he entered the part of the structure that held her and her baby. She was touching and talking to her child, but shot him a smile. He hated that she'd smoothed her hair back into a tight knot that took all the energy out of it, but if that was what made her feel safe, that was what made her feel safe.

Her clothing was simple enough—a white shirt, below that sweatpants. Hugo and the other maternals had done a good job with the spare clothing they'd put together for her. The shirt would pass muster in any comm conference, and no one was going to see the sweatpants except for those in the infirmary.

Not wanting to wipe the soft joy off her face, he nonetheless knew it was time. "Auden, we need to discuss something."

. . .

AUDEN'S heart squeezed into a knot small and agonizing. Removing her hand from her baby's skin after one last touch, she faced Remi. "I know. I'm a security risk, aren't I?"

But he frowned and shook his head. "Not if you stay in this cube. I don't want to cage you, but—"

"Telepathic images for teleport locks," she interrupted. "I get that. It's smart. And with what's going on with my memory blanks and personality changes, I can't be sure about my ability to protect your pack." Never would she want to bring any harm to Remi and his pack, people who had protected her and her baby even though most of them had never even met her.

She spread her hand over the clear plas top of the incubator. "I don't want to go anywhere anyway. I want to be with her every second. I'm so *afraid* that I'll lose myself, that I won't know she's my baby, that I'll forget how to love her." A painful thickness in her throat, she looked at where Finn sat at the other end of the room in front of a small but impressive computer station. "Did Remi tell you?"

The healer nodded. "Yes. I'm sorry we—"

"No, you had to know." Auden kept finding herself interrupting them—because if this wasn't about security, then it had to be about her brain. She didn't want to know, didn't want to hear, a child clapping her hands over her ears.

"I could've come out of the birth in an altered state, could've hurt my baby while not myself . . . but I suppose any personality I inhabit *is* me, which means the ugliness that comes out is me, too." It was an awful thing to accept about herself.

Finn rolled his chair over from across the room, his expression solemn in a way it hadn't been since she woke. "There's another thing, Auden. The graft you said went into your head?"

Mouth dry, Auden nodded. There was nowhere left to go, nothing left to say to stave off the inevitable.

"It's still there. Encased in scar tissue, but present. I'm guessing they couldn't get it out without destroying part of your brain."

Auden blinked. She'd expected to hear of new neural damage, not old scar tissue. "Frankly I'm surprised that stopped them," she said on a roar of relief. "Do you think there's any danger of it going active?"

"In a stroke of luck, the Arrow doctor we had with us is a neuro-surgeon who's worked with experimental tech, and I was troubled enough to show him the scan—don't worry, he might have an ego, but he takes medical confidentiality seriously, so he won't talk about it."

Auden nodded, her faith in Remi and this healer a thing unshak-able. If they said she could trust the Arrow doctor, then she could trust the Arrow doctor.

"He says all signs are that it's dead, effectively burned out," Finn added. "And the way your brain's scarred around it, it won't migrate and cause further damage."

Auden's chest rose and fell in a deep inhale and exhale. "So, that's good news." Warmth began to flow through her blood . . . until she felt Remi's hand on her lower back, his eyes leopard when they looked into hers.

Heart thunder, she found herself breathing fast and shallow. "What is it?"

Remi's voice was a rumble against her. "Finn did the standard birth DNA panel on your cub to check for genetic diseases."

"It's so we can handle anything treatable straightaway," Finn said.

Auden hadn't realized she'd turned into Remi until her hand clenched hard on his T-shirt. "Did you find—"

"No." The healer held up a hand. "She's got a clean bill of health. But the thing is . . . she wasn't created from your egg."

Auden's mind vanished in a white haze that blurred all light and sound. She was conscious of Remi speaking, of the growl in his chest, of the way he held her close to his warmth, but she felt distant, removed from it.

Then came a flutter inside her mind, and with it a roar back to the bright colors and even brighter emotions of reality. "I don't care," she said, her voice hard. "She's *my* baby. I love her until I can't breathe. No one is ever going to take her away from me."

"What did I tell you?" Remi's chin on her hair, his fingers massaging the stiff tendons of her neck.

Finn rolled his eyes, his lips kicking up at the corners now that he'd delivered the news that had clearly been weighing him down. "That Auden would tear off the head of anyone who tried to say this cub wasn't hers."

Auden's chest filled with air again. She hadn't known how much she craved Remi's approval of her as a mother until she got it. Because he was changeling, a creature of family and loyalty. More, he'd had a mother he loved. He understood what it meant to be a good mother, a mother who protected and shielded.

That he saw that in her? It made her feel bigger, stronger, worthy of her child.

"No argument from us on the cub being yours." Remi's hand continued to massage the tension out of her nape, the act so luxurious that it felt decadent to indulge in it in front of Finn, but she couldn't make herself move away. "Your love for her fucking shines, Auden."

Chapter 32

My mother is dead, Mr. Krychek. A result of a genetic flaw that was unfortunately never picked up. She died of sudden neurological failure and her body was cremated soon after the authorities signed off on her death. I am now in charge of Scott family operations.

—Auden Scott to Kaleb Krychek (20 August 2083)

AUDEN SHUDDERED, HER hand flexing open on the soft fabric of Remi's T-shirt—but she stayed cuddled to the wild heat of him, her body and mind craving his touch. "You both know I have mental issues," she said, her eyes on her precious girl. "But they're not genetic. I don't understand why the family wouldn't just use my own eggs. Is it possible they were having trouble fertilizing my egg?"

Finn's eyes met Remi's.

And she knew. Twisted and an unimaginable violation though it would be, it was the only thing that made sense in that house, in that family. "Whose egg?" Ice in her blood, in her veins. "Just tell me."

Though Finn was the healer, she looked at Remi.

He didn't make her wait. "You're half-siblings. You share maternal DNA."

The cold inside her continued to spread. "My mother's egg?" she said, to be certain.

"I triple-checked." Finn's voice. "There's no mistake. My system kept flagging her DNA as a sibling match to you, and I thought it was a glitch. It isn't." A rough exhale. "We managed to get hold of Shoshanna's DNA profile, compared it against both you and the cub to be certain beyond any doubt."

One day, Auden thought, she'd ask Remi how RainFire and the Arrows had become such friends—because no one else could've gained the pack access to a former Councilor's DNA profile—but today, her mind had no room for anything but the cold reality of the decisions made for her when she'd been unable to protest or even understand what was going on.

"Shoshanna must've frozen her eggs at some point," she said, her mind an ice sheet unbroken. "It could've even been a requirement of the family when she was younger." The Scotts, after all, were all about bloodlines.

She nodded, working it through; the cold inside her made it easier to think. "My mother must've hoped to produce a child with more active abilities than mine. Continuing the primary bloodline rather than defaulting to my cousin. I was a convenient incubator."

That didn't matter.

This child had grown in her womb. Auden had felt her mind wake, and even now the baby murmured baby ramblings that were a sweet whisper inside her. "I don't care about her DNA," she reiterated, stepping away from Remi to touch her child once more. "I won't ever hide the truth from her, but I won't treat her as anything but my precious baby, either."

Neither man challenged her, though she knew the psychological impact of what her family had done would hit her hard at some point. She just had to make sure it never hit her baby. She'd make it sound like she'd chosen to be the surrogate to ensure her sibling had the best in utero care, tell her baby that she wouldn't permit anyone else to carry her.

"Will it hurt her?" she asked Finn, this healer who understood emotion. "When she's older?"

"Not if you tell her the truth from the start," Finn said. "Make it a naturalized part of her life. Surrogates are common enough, and though carrying your own half-sibling is unusual, children are adaptable. If you tell her the truth in an age-appropriate way, she'll probably simply accept it and only ask questions at an older age, when you can discuss it with her with the help of a healer or an empath."

Rage simmered in Auden, washing away the ice and leaving embers dark and violent in its wake. "They hurt her before she was even born," she bit out. "Created her because they decided my mother's genes mattered more than her psychological well-being." At least now she understood why this baby was so important, why her family would do anything to keep her. "What about the paternal DNA?"

"No match on any system I could access," Finn said, "so whatever you were told might be the truth."

"A high-Gradient telepath with zero signs of any other minor abilities," Auden murmured. "Yes, that makes sense if they were determined to produce another high-Gradient Tp." It also made sense that they'd left Henry out of the equation. It might've been as simple as the fact that his genetic material hadn't been saved. But she had the feeling it was more because that match had produced a psychometric.

Better not to risk the same a second time around.

So Shoshanna had chosen a family of telepaths so pure that—per Auden's memory—they hadn't had a non-Tp in the line for at least two generations. Pair that with Shoshanna's genetic profile, and whoever had done the calculations had been right: Auden's baby was going to grow up to be one hell of a powerful telepath.

"Do you know why I started to improve, neurologically speaking?" she asked Finn, very conscious of Remi's prowling presence as he walked around to the other side of the incubator. "Any indication on the scans?" Because Auden needed to know if she would regress—and how much time she had to make sure *no one* would ever have a chance to harm her child . . . or the alpha who had enfolded that innocent life into his heart.

She'd hurt anyone who dared touch him.

"No, but it might be related to fetal stem cells released by your baby," Finn muttered, wheeling back to grab his organizer. "All the decades of research and there's still not a ton we know about them. If it was that, then the effect should be permanent—they would've physically healed the damaged parts of your brain."

Auden wanted to believe him. Dr. Verhoeven had theorized the same thing . . . but her baby was Psy. A Psy with a mind so piercing at such a young age that she had to be on the verge of being a cardinal. 9.8 or 9.9. It was as likely that the effect was a psychic one, and that it would fade now that her child was no longer somehow compensating for her mother's neural damage.

A small beep sounded on Finn's wrist unit, the screen flashing yellow. The healer rose to his feet. "Non-emergency injury, but I'll go take a look and see what's happened."

Finn's eyes met Remi's on the way out, and Remi saw the anger in them. Finn was fucking pissed at what had been done to Auden by medical staff who should've *done no harm.*

Removing her hand from the incubator after the healer had left, Auden turned to him. "Remi?"

"Yeah?" It came out rough, his need to pull her into his arms a storm.

"What I said, about the need for a successor?" The blue of her eyes was a turbulent storm against the lush dark of her skin. "It makes sense, but the doctor said something to me on my last checkup that I can't forget. He said that I couldn't know how long 'this brain' would function."

"What?" Remi scowled. "Like you can replace it like a tire on a car?"

A nod from Auden. "That was my thought process. It's an entirely strange way to discuss my possible neurological decline now that my baby isn't assisting me in staying functional."

Remi said fuck it and hauled her against his chest. She needed to be held and he was going to do the holding.

Her arms came around him, gripping tight.

"You'll be fine," he said, and they both knew it was more hope than true knowledge. "Finn and Dr. Bashir found absolutely nothing, no signs of any new damage."

Auden's reply avoided answering him. "The brain discussion, there's something behind it. Because it's not just that. All the scans I remember having? They weren't only tech-based. I had psychic scans, too. I have only vague memories of those, but what reason would there be for a psychic scan of my brain when the damage was physical?"

Her fingers clenched at his back. "Charisma might be paying lip service to my supposed status as CEO, but I'm an ignorant pawn on the chessboard." Heat in her voice now, nothing even close to defeat. "I won't let them win."

Shifting back without letting go of him, she met his gaze. "I need to be certain my baby is safe before I fragment again into that other Auden . . . or Audens. I don't know how many pieces of me exist, how many different Audens there are. Right now, I'm holding on to *me*, and I need to utilize that limited window of time."

Remi growled. "Your family will get to your cub over my fucking dead body. RainFire might not be a power, but we're leopards. We can take her and disappear into the wild and no one will ever find her."

Auden's pupils flared. "But what kind of life would that be for her, for you, for your pack?"

"The Arrows have also offered to take her, protect her." It would tear out Remi's heart to let go of this child who'd been placed in his care, but he'd do it if it would protect both her and the children of the pack.

Fisting her hands, Auden shook her head. "So much kindness," she said, her voice rough. "So many strangers helping us." A tremor. "No one ever warned me that the outside world could be so *good*."

A sheen in her eyes, she said, "But I don't want a life in hiding for my baby. I want freedom for her. I want her to be able to live *life* unfettered." Protective fury in every word. "To do that, I have to unlock the box of secrets my mother left behind."

"We," Remi corrected, cradling her face. "If you think I'm letting you walk into that snake pit alone, then you have no idea who I am, Cupcake."

"Cupcake?" Her lower lip quivered.

He rubbed the pad of his thumb over the fullness of it. "Cinnamon roll didn't have the same ring."

"Cupcakes are sweet and pretty."

"And delicious and bitable."

She flushed before her hands closed over his wrists, her fingers long and slender and her eyes stark and brilliant. "I have a vague memory of overhearing a conversation—I didn't have to lurk or eavesdrop. Most of the time, I was standing right there, spaced-out, but . . . the odd thing got through.

"Charisma and Dr. Verhoeven were arguing, with Charisma saying I was in no state to carry a pregnancy, while the doctor was saying it had to be me, that I was the only viable candidate and that . . ."

Remi's leopard prowled against his skin. "What?"

"How they said I was the only viable carrier." She frowned. "It's factually wrong. Members of our family *have* used professional surrogates. Strong telepaths, of course, but not blood related to the Scotts. It's not the preferred option, is in fact heavily discouraged—*unless* it's the only viable option. That exception should've applied if their other choice was a woman with brain damage who might do something to cause harm to the child."

Remi wondered how she didn't see it—probably because she was too close. "Has to be psychic stuff. A psychic mother must affect the child's development in a way they couldn't be certain they could replicate in a surrogate."

Auden made a face. "As far as psychic powers go, I'm the weakest of the weak according to my family's way of measuring such things. I could be a cardinal but as a psychometric, I'd still be at the bottom rung of the ladder." She worried the edge of her shirt sleeve with her other hand, but her eyes were unfocused, her thoughts inward.

"I also had neural deficits at the time, deficits that were believed to be permanent," she said. "They could've locked me up in a med ward, but even so, a scared and mentally distraught mother would've nullified any psychic gain."

Remi gave a slow nod. "Which leaves you with the same question with which you started. What's so special about your brain that makes you and your daughter so valuable to them?"

Auden swallowed. "I have strange dreams," she said, the words a near-whisper. "Even when I was unconscious, I feel like I dreamed. Of a web created of glittering blue spidersilk against a night sky. I'm not scared in the dream. I feel wonder."

"A link to your ability?"

"It's possible it's an echo of an imprint I don't remember, but . . ." Shivering, she rubbed her hands up and down her upper arms. "It's as eerie as it's lovely but at times, it feels like it's coming from the outside in." She stroked the top of the incubator. "As if it's from another Auden."

His leopard rumbled in rage at being unable to fight this for her—because this battle was inside her brain, far from his claws and his anger. "You're planning to go back into the Scott home."

"Yes. Only me. Never her." Her jaw tightened.

Arms folded, Remi worked through the possible options. "Chances they'll guess she's here?"

"Nil. It just wouldn't come up as a possibility in their thoughts—perhaps it would if you were that big leopard pack out in California with prior Psy contacts, but right now—"

"—right now we're a barely noticeable blip on their radar," Remi completed. "You also have access to funds that mean you could've hired a teleporter to send her someplace far away."

"Yes. A fact I'll make clear." Auden's face was grim. "I don't know if Charisma was ever aware of my trust fund—Henry signed it over to me at fifteen, an irrevocable transfer his family likely has no idea was done, it was so many years ago." A hitch in her breath. "He loved me once, I think. As much as my father could love anyone."

Remi knew all about asshole fathers, understood her ambivalence about Henry. "My father got in touch with me about seven months after my mother's death."

"What did you do?" Auden asked softly with the understanding of a woman who knew the dueling desires of a child abandoned or abused.

"I'd always thought I'd punch him in the face, but when it came to it, I felt nothing." Remi could still remember staring at the man who had eyes the same color as Remi's and seeing nothing but a waste of space. "Part of it was probably grief over my mother's death, but to this day, I don't regret telling him I had nothing to say to him. Some choices, once made, you don't get to walk back."

Auden spread her hand over the top of the incubator. "Have you ever felt the need to seek him out again?"

Remi didn't have to think of his answer. "No. I learned how to love, how to be loyal, how to be a good son, a good man, without him. He had nothing I wanted, just a hollowness of the soul that repelled me." He closed his hand over Auden's on the incubator. "You love your baby with the fierceness of a leopardess. You outpaced and outgrew Henry and Shoshanna one hell of a long time ago."

Tears in the blue, her voice husky as she said, "Do you think your mother would've liked me?" A question so quiet it was almost inaudible.

His throat grew thick. "She would've *adored* you." Gina would've seen the same courage and heart in Auden that had tangled Remi in ropes so strong that he knew he'd be indelibly scarred if she splintered into another Auden, his Auden forever lost. "You're planning to fight for your cub like she fought for hers. If she was alive, she'd be right by your side, claws out."

He wove their fingers together. "She might not be here, but that cub of hers is going to walk with you into that house, and find the truth."

Auden's pupil's expanded, obsidian in the blue. "I don't know how to get you in. I'm planning to use my baby as collateral for my safety—they touch me physically or psychically, and they never see her again." A twist of her lips. "They'll never see her anyway, but it might buy me time to unearth the truth."

Remi's claws sliced out of his skin, but he made sure he didn't cut her. When the cub made a complaining sound, he rumbled deep and low in his chest to calm her back down. Only once she was snuffling away did he ask his question. "Can they tear open your mind to get to her?"

"No. Infants are tied to their mothers. A mental assault on my mind would murder her, too—especially as she's premature." Auden looked down at the baby. "I'm just pretending, baby. I'd never give you to them, no matter what."

Remi narrowed his eyes. "Hire us."

"What?" Auden stared.

"Hire our security arm," he repeated grimly. "I don't actually expect you to pay us, but set it up like a business deal."

Auden's mouth opened, closed again. "Yes," she said after a long pause. "They'd see me hiring you as a convenient option since we already have another deal, and you've built trust by flying me in the chopper."

A look at her baby. "But not in a million years would they consider that I'd leave her with you—because whatever is wrong with me, they still believe I think like a Scott."

"And Scotts believe they're better than others, and infinitely better than any changeling," Remi guessed.

Auden's gaze turned unfocused, and he could almost see her thinking it through in every minute detail. "Does your pack have any kind of a security presence? It has to look real."

"RainFire Security has a strong reputation in our region. Even have Psy clients who won't trust anyone else—I'm sure they'll cooperate if your people reach out to ask for a reference."

He tapped the side of his head. "Changeling shields. Changeling speed. Changeling strength—and crucially, changeling senses. We make damn good bodyguards against physical threats, and can hold up much longer than humans against a psychic assault. Now that Silence has fallen, there's no taboo against Psy hiring changeling bodyguards."

She stared off into space for several seconds. "They could attempt to cut off access to my trust fund once they become aware of it. It'll be harder to sell a transactional relationship if I don't have the funds to pay you."

"I have a hacker in the pack." Why hide it when it was part of the toolkit of every smart alpha? Psy liked to put things in computers and Psy also liked to attack changeling systems—it was just good sense to have both defensive and offensive capabilities on that front. "If you trust me with the details of your account, we can secure it."

"Give me an organizer and I'll load the access details onto it," Auden said without hesitation. "The requirements include a live retinal scan, so your hacker will need to come here. Or you'll need to be the one to take that scan, since it's better if you keep your packmates from my memory."

Her face went bleak. "I'm going to fight my hardest, but I'm a Ps-Psy. I can't keep them from my mind if they decide to rape it in order to get to my baby. It might take them a few weeks to get to that point—or they might wait a couple of months until they're near certain the baby would survive."

Remi's chest rumbled. He found himself curving one hand around her nape, his claws scraping her pulse. "Make me a promise, Auden."

She waited, fierce will and unshakable courage.

"It would kill me to be unable to protect you against that kind of assault. So the first hint of something happening, you tell me—and then you tell me who it is."

"You won't be able to get to them on the psychic plane," Auden said, anguish in her tone. For him.

"No, but I can shoot them in the head."

Auden stared at Remi, the blunt violence of his answer a cold shock . . . but a good one. Because he *could* stop a psychic assault if she could get him to the right target. "People can attack on the PsyNet it-self," she said, "and that can be done from a distance, but I think with the baby's life on the line, it'll be up close so they can stabilize me after they take control. I'll tell you. I promise."

The warmth of his hand squeezing her nape felt good. Too good.

She had no right to it, or to the warm, happy, sweet feeling of being called "Cupcake" in that deep voice, but she held on to it all the same.

Her phone began to beep, the sound distinctive. When Remi looked at her, she nodded, and he grabbed it for her from where it sat on Finn's workspace.

She glanced at the screen. "It's Charisma. I'll answer in the bath-room. There's a faux-wooden wall that looks similar to the walls of my cabin. A white background will make her suspicious."

And it was time Auden began to not only play this game—but lead it.

Chapter 33

Humans have no reason to trust the Psy, but this is a crisis of unimaginable size, with millions of lives on the line—and I am prouder than you can imagine to see how our people have reacted in the face of that terrible truth.

We have given all we can to assist the Psy in staving off the collapse of their PsyNet, including creating places where friendship could blossom between our two races, because a bond of emotion is the only way to infuse the PsyNet with human energy. So many of you have held out a hand to a Psy, and the Psy Ruling Coalition tells us that a number of bonds *have* formed, that the PsyNet does now have a sprinkling of human energy.

However, to get such bonds back to pre-Silence levels will likely take decades, perhaps a century or more. And the PsyNet does not appear to have that much time left.

As such, I have spoken to the Coalition on the safety of those humans already linked into the psychic network. They have assured me that, should the worst occur, human minds will simply be cut free, and will experience no backlash. Only the rare human will even feel the disconnect.

The individuals most at risk will be those who have infants who are half-Psy and are linked into the PsyNet—or who are, at the time, pregnant with a child conceived with a Psy. Given the recent nature of renewed contact between our two races, your numbers are low enough that you should already have received a visit from a dual Psy/human team to go over your options. If not, please reach out to me directly.

It is a matter of unfathomable sadness that those same options are not available to the far larger numbers of Psy infants. It is simply a matter of scale. But we haven't given up, and will continue to search for ways to save every life we can.

Even as they do the same, the Ruling Coalition has also handed over all research done by their scientists on an effective way to shield human minds from Psy intrusion.

The Psy have kept their part of the bargain between us—so now I ask you to hold on as long as you can. And if there are Psy you could call friends, open your heart to them earlier rather than later.

The time left is now measured in a matter of months.

—Giovanni Somme, official head of the Human
Alliance, to its membership (1 October 2083)

TAKING A DEEP breath once inside the bathroom, Auden thought back to her mother. Shoshanna had simply never had a maternal gene—Auden didn't blame her for that. What she *did* blame Shoshanna for was her choosing to have a child for the simple reason that she could use that child to control Henry.

Yet both of them were monsters of equal ugliness.

Now her mother's sycophants had created another child who carried Shoshanna's genes—but come what may, Auden's baby would have a far different life than Auden.

"Charisma," she said, cold and remote when she answered. "What is the emergency? I assume it must be an emergency for you to so flagrantly contravene my order not to disturb me."

The other woman had frozen for a moment, but regrouped quickly. "I am used to caring for you," she said with every appearance of sincerity. "Dr. Verhoeven's diagnosis of stress has me worried for the pregnancy."

Auden wanted to snap back an even colder response, almost stopped herself. But then she remembered that Charisma had worked by her mother's side. "That is no longer your concern," she found herself saying, even though the words weren't ones that made any kind of sense to her. "I am now in charge—or can you not see that?"

"Your mind is currently blanketed in a black shield," Charisma said instead of responding directly. "We can't get through . . . and to be frank, it appears to be an Arrow shield. Are you in trouble? Is the operation in jeopardy?"

What operation?

As for the shield, Auden kicked herself for not preparing for this. Of course Charisma had an eye on her mind in the PsyNet. Even as she thought that, her lips parted and words spilled out. "I have friends in many places, Ris." She held the eye contact until it was aggressive. "Do you not understand that even now?"

Charisma seemed to flush, as if Auden had flustered her enough to beat her Silence. "Of course, sir. But you must forgive me for being wary—it has been a long time."

Auden stayed silent, the words she'd just spoken an oily film on her mind that felt alien. Not herself.

Frost in the air, a shimmering blue web in her vision.

Another Auden in charge.

"So you're feeling fine, medically speaking?" Charisma's voice tore through the web. "Your pregnancy is stable? I can send a medic to do a checkup if needed. The biomonitors don't seem to be functioning."

"The monitors are functioning fine. I just didn't wish to use them during my meditation," Auden said. "I'll reinstate them today." Surely RainFire's hacker could work it so that it appeared Auden remained

pregnant. "I'll be back home in four days regardless." It was the longest
she could expect Charisma and the doctor to stay patient. "I'm getting
too close to full-term to remain in such a remote region."

Charisma's shoulders relaxed. "I'll see you soon, sir."

Auden's heart thumped after she hung up, but she had no time to
stress, no time to worry. Walking out as fast as she could, she met Remi's
gaze. "I have another request for your hacker."

Remi gave a curt nod. "Just one question before I get him to work.
What're you going to name this gorgeous cub of yours?"

Auden replied at once. "Liberty. Liberty RainFire." A name built of
hope and heart. "Is that all right? To ask for her to carry the name of
your pack until this is all over? Whatever happens, I don't want her to
be a Scott."

Remi's eyes gleamed yellow-green. "It's more than okay, little cat.
Liberty will always have a home in the heart of her pack."

AFTER getting the hack of Auden's own account and biomonitors
underway, Remi turned to the specifics of Auden's security detail. It
would have to be at least two people—Remi could catnap with the best
of them, but he wouldn't be at full strength if he wasn't getting good
chunks of sleep.

At first, he considered that his partner should be male—leopard
females could be deadly opponents, but Psy could be stupid about changelings. And this was about making a big visual impact from the start.

Then again . . . Auden's mother had been the alpha half of the Scott
pair. Auden hadn't said that to him, but he had eyes—and even though
he hadn't been too interested in Psy politics before becoming an alpha
himself, he'd seen enough news reports over the years to come to his
own conclusions.

Shoshanna had been smart and vicious—behind a veneer of ele-
gance. A slender brunette, she also hadn't been imposing on a physical

level. So yeah, maybe he could play on that. It was with that thought in mind that he called a meeting of his sentinels after Lark had had time to get a few hours of sleep.

It wasn't that the pack kept putting her on night shift—it was that she *loved* the night shift and requested it more than any other person in RainFire.

"Why be born a leopard if I can't slink about like a shadow?" she'd whispered while wiggling her fingers as if casting a magic spell. "Try to spot me in the dark. I dare you."

Remi could of course spot her—but he was her alpha. She truly was a ghost to most people, even most cats, had made an art form out of using her leopard coloring to meld into the shadows. Now, she walked into their meeting in his aerie bright-eyed and freshly showered—and dressed in an adult version of Jojo's purple overalls paired with a sparkly pink T-shirt.

"Hello, people!" She threw out her arms. "Alpha man, I need food."

He groaned and threw her a croissant. "I told you I'd strip your fur if you called me that one more time. Also, where did you even get that outfit?"

Unrepentant, she blew him a kiss and slumped down in one of the large cushions on the floor that comprised most of his furniture in this section of his open-plan aerie. He did, however, have a small sofa for anyone who didn't feel like doing the leopard sprawl.

"Online bargain—Jojo likes me best now." She smirked, striking out her hand and making clutching motions. "We did a twinsies photo-shoot."

Her hand motions should've been nonsensical, but he'd known her too long. He put the mug of coffee he'd already doctored to her require-ments in her hand. "Here you go, Madame Purple Queen."

A wicked grin and a salute just as Theo flowed into the aerie in leop-ard form. The biggest leopard in RainFire was light on his feet when he wanted to be. He brushed his body against Remi's before wandering off

into the bathroom where Remi had already put a change of clothes for
him after the sentinel mentioned he was going for a run in leopard form
before their meeting.

Changelings weren't shy about nudity, but neither were they exhibi-
tionists, and every one of them had a different comfort level. Theo could
be as pragmatic about wearing his skin as the rest of them—but he
didn't like getting naked in front of Lark when he could as well change
out of sight.

"Too weird, since she's basically like my sister," he'd said of his cousin.

Meanwhile, other changelings were never more comfortable in just
their human skin than with family.

When Theo walked out after shifting, he wore jeans and a black
sweatshirt, his feet bare. "Are you being a brat again?" he said to Lark
after grabbing coffee and a sandwich for himself.

"I am *beloved*, never a brat." She chomped down on her croissant.

Used to their sibling-like bickering that never amounted to anything—
touch one and the other would gut you—he nodded at the tiger in human form who'd just jumped onto the balcony from above. Eyes of deep
ultramarine met his, the color reflected in the short-sleeve shirt that had
been a gift to Angel from Finn.

That Angel actually wore it was a testament to Finn's ability to read
his packmates.

"Thanks," the tiger said when Remi handed him a black coffee, before serving himself from the tray of food.

"Um, I could do with a sandwich." Lark batted her lashes at the tiger, her croissant long gone.

Angel, as quiet as Lark was not, rolled his eyes at her, but his lips
twitched as he passed her the sandwich with her preferred filling.

Lark beamed. "You're my favorite, Stripes."

Twitching lips curving into a rare deep smile, Angel just shook his
head before he went to sit in the window seat, long legs sprawled out in
front of him. "How was it last night?" he asked, his voice a quiet rumble.
"Any surprises?"

"Nope. Borders were quiet. Auden's cabin, too, with no new scents anywhere in the vicinity." Lark paused. "Though I suppose they could've teleported inside . . ."

Remi considered that. "Not a big risk. We can sniff it out if Auden needs to go in there for any reason."

A sound on the balcony, then in walked Rina.

The blond sentinel grinned at seeing how Lark reclined on her cushion, Theo on the one next to her. Her nod at Angel was more muted, but that didn't mean anything when it came to their work together. On the whole, Rina had melded into RainFire as if she'd been part of their pack from the beginning.

She'd almost brought a senior soldier with her—a man named Barker. Remi had had the feeling the two were linked romantically, but in the end, Barker had chosen to remain behind in DarkRiver, and as far as anyone was aware, Rina was single.

Remi didn't know the whys of it, but there didn't seem to be any bad blood.

After all four sentinels had settled in with coffee and a snack, Remi leaned his shoulder against the wall and said, "Auden is going to hire us when she goes back in."

Surprise from everyone but Rina. "Makes sense," she said from her position on the sofa. "I learned how the big Psy families operate from Sascha—and I wouldn't be taking my newborn cub into that situation unguarded, either."

"Oh, her cub's staying with us."

That set them alight, questions flying every which way. He told them what they needed to know to protect Auden—but he didn't tell them that her pregnancy had been done without her consent, or that the baby was technically her half-sibling. That was for Auden to share if and when she wished.

"I'll be going with her," he said—and raised an eyebrow when no one argued.

Theo shrugged. "You're growly protective of her. We got the memo."

A grin that was a masculine echo of Lark's. "Sooo, anything to share on that front?"

"She just gave birth, you big dumbo." Lark pretend-slapped him on the back of the head. "Give her space before thinking of amorous feline intentions."

"Amorous feline intentions?" Angel shook his head.

"Who're you taking as your partner?" Lark asked after scrunching up her nose at Angel. "I won't work. Psy don't take me seriously because I'm small." Matter-of-fact words. "I could claw off a few snooty faces to make my point, but I figure you don't want a bloody scene."

"No." Remi turned to Angel. "I need you to stay here. We can't both be gone."

Angel nodded in silent agreement.

"That leaves me and Theo or a senior soldier," Rina said. "Theo's big and can be scary looking, but you're going into Shoshanna Scott's domain. I say take a woman."

Yes, RainFire had lucked out in getting Rina.

"And," the sentinel continued after a sip of her coffee, "I say take me and not one of the senior soldiers because, quite frankly, nobody in this pack knows as much about how Psy work as I do. I might be able to figure out vulnerabilities that wouldn't occur to the rest of you."

"Hey," Theo protested, twisting his head to meet Rina's gaze. "We're not total country bumpkins."

Rina smiled at him—it was obvious she had a huge soft spot for the big sentinel. "No, you're just in the middle of nowhere with not a single Psy packmate. While I was, until recently, part of a pack with not only Psy packmates, but in a city that thousands of Psy call home."

"Rina's right." Angel's voice. "It should be her."

Remi nodded in agreement. "We won't have much prep time—four days. After that, RainFire takes official custody and protection of little Liberty—"

"Liberty?" Lark's face lit up. "Is that the kitten's name?"

When Remi nodded, she sighed. "I love it. It's so meaningful and pretty."

"What about the cub's psychic needs?" Angel asked.

It was Rina who answered. "I think Auden can take care of that from a distance." She frowned. "When Sascha had her and Lucas's cub, she mentioned that the cub was inside her own shields. It's like how we keep our cubs close before they get smart enough to avoid dangers and obstacles."

"That sounds right," Remi said. "But I'll ask Auden for clarification. I'll also do everything I can to make sure she can come back and see her cub as much as possible."

"Good." Angel's quiet but firm agreement, a slight growl in his words. "Cubs need that contact."

Remi understood as the others wouldn't, Angel a closed book to most people when it came to his emotions. But he and Remi had taken on the world together as youths, a lone tiger, remote and quiet, and a leopard with too much anger and confusion inside him to stay put.

Angel had vanished for weeks at a time during that initial period. But he'd always come back; and in the end, he'd stayed. He'd even picked up his first security gigs so he could travel with Remi to his races. And he'd trusted Remi with his story, a story of a cub lost and in pain whose psyche had been forever damaged one dark winter's night.

"We'll talk to Auden together, get a full briefing on the compound," Remi told Rina, to her nod. "Any other pack business before we break?"

"We need a school of our own for the littlest cubs," Lark said, her acute intelligence a clear light in her eyes. "We've gotten away with computronic teaching so far, but with the new families who've joined us, we've got enough to start up our own small school.

"We could still have the computronic aids to deal with the needs of the different ages, but we need a teacher to ensure they stay on track—and all the other stuff kids do together at school. Projects and art and music."

Remi considered that. "Given the numbers, we'll need two teachers—one for kindergarten, the other for elementary school."

Lark made a face. "How are we going to lure two teachers out here? I love our pack, but we're small and can't pay anything like what they're worth, and it would mean a move for anyone outside the region."

"There's something to be said for being at the ground floor of setting up a pack," Angel offered. "Not many people ever get to experience that."

"Angel's right." Rina leaned forward, her long ponytail sliding over her shoulder. "DarkRiver will always own a piece of my heart, but everything was set up by the time I came of age.

"Here, everything's raw, unfinished in a way that means I can help shape the foundations of the pack. A certain kind of person will find that enticing." She smiled. "Kit's loving seeing the pack literally build and grow before his eyes."

Lark was already on her phone, taking notes. "That's it. I'm going to pitch it as a once-in-a-lifetime opportunity to help start a pack. I mean, it's not like that happens every day."

She frowned, looked up. "*Wild Woman* is one of the best places for an ad—we all know *everyone* reads that, even those people who pretend not to." A speaking glance at Theo, who feigned a searching glance around the room.

"But it's expensive." Lark read out the rates with a wince.

"Do it," Remi said. "This is a critical need, and we currently have a buffer thanks to that bulk security job."

"Or," Theo murmured, "maybe you can pitch it as an article?" Arms folded behind his head, he frowned. "I mean, we just talked about how setting up a new pack isn't something that happens on the regular. People might be interested in reading about that, and you can sneak in how we're in the market for teachers."

Rina was nodding. "It'll probably gain more attention than a straight ad, too."

"Worth a shot." Lark shrugged. "I'll figure out how to pitch an article and report back. Who's gonna write it, though? I'm not a writer."

"Vessie," Angel suggested, naming a packmate who'd been a journalist before she retired.

Theo gave an enthusiastic thumbs-up to that. "I know she said she's all about her grandcubs now, but have you heard that woman take down smartass juveniles with nothing but her tongue? I bet you she'd enjoy the challenge of getting us into *Wild Woman*."

All five of them were in a good mood when they closed the meeting, but Remi wasn't done. Once his sentinels had left, he made another call, asked another favor.

Aden replied after a short pause. "Zaira says yes."

Then he added, "Remi, we don't have any intel on the Scott compound—it's locked up tight, and we haven't prioritized it as the Scotts have been keeping their heads down since Shoshanna's death, but one thing I can tell you is that it's crawling with Scott loyalists. Watch your back."

"I will." More importantly, he'd be watching Auden's back.

He'd tear out the throat of anyone who tried to lay so much as a finger on her.

Chapter 34

The tests are definitive: none of the drugs in the trial offer long-term amelioration of the problem. As psychic remedies have already been ruled out, only one option remains.

—Classified Report to the Psy Council by PsyMed: Pharmaceutical Development & Testing. Project Manager: Councilor Neiza Adelaja Defoe (circa 2016)

AUDEN WOKE FROM a deep sleep to find Liberty lying skin-to-skin with her, both of them covered with a blanket. She smiled, cuddling her baby to her with one hand. Liberty's pulse was a faint butterfly against Auden, her skin fragile. "Finn?"

"Over here," he said softly from his workstation on the other side of the room.

After kissing and cuddling her baby, she said, "Why am I not scared of you? Why do I not care that you touched me while I was asleep?" She would've expected to wake at even the gentlest contact.

The sound of wheels on tile, as Finn rolled over his office chair. "It's because I'm a healer—same effect as empaths as far as we can figure. Must be our pheromones or something. Pretty noticeable effect from childhood—future healers tend to help people calm down even without trying."

That made sense to her. "How else could you work with growly leopards."

Chuckling, he took out a scanner to check on Liberty. "You got it."

She watched him as he worked, took in the kindness and compassion. "You're a brilliant healer," she said, needing to vocalize it. "Not only in your skills, but in how you treat your patients. I feel privileged that you're Liberty's primary medical carer."

A flush on Finn's cheekbones, his smile a touch lopsided. "She's a sweetheart, and her mama's a fighter." Leaf green eyes on hers. "Never forget that, Auden. Your baby is safe here because you made sure she would be safe. Don't ever allow any other voices to make you forget."

Auden swallowed. "I'm so afraid," she whispered to this healer who had renewed her faith in the medical profession after Dr. Verhoeven had annihilated it. "That the voice that makes me forget will be my own." A sharp, cold splinter who thought with manipulative pragmatism.

Finn's frown was deep. "Bashir got me into multiple PsyMed databases. I'm digging deep to find you answers and a solution. Don't you dare give up on me."

Auden knew his hope was genuine, his intent pure, so she said, "Never." But she also knew that a fragmented personality couldn't be welded back together. Prior to Silence, people like her had either stumbled through a short life—or, if one personality was a violent one—were locked up in institutions.

After Silence, the affliction had "vanished."

Auden wondered what this good doctor, this good healer, would say if she told him that her race had eliminated the problem by executing those with it. Should anyone look up individual names, all they'd find in the records was the unremarkable. Death by misadventure or by natural causes.

No acknowledgment of psychological illness.

Not even a hint of murder mandated.

And nothing to challenge the Council's position of Silence being a resounding success.

The door opened on her dark thoughts, Remi walking in. And her entire being felt as if it had lit up from within. Her baby made a tiny movement at the same time. "She knows you're here," she said to Remi, as Finn rolled his chair back to his workstation.

Remi stroked the baby's fisted hand.

Liberty's fingers opened and she gripped at his finger. When he chuckled, the sound was a reverberation through Auden's bones.

"Can I hold her?"

After Auden surrendered Liberty to his careful hold, they just adored her together until Finn said it was time to put "the kitten" back in the incubator. After that, Remi chatted to Finn while Auden got herself refreshed and into proper day clothes.

The healer was gone when she returned.

"I have a proposition for you," Remi said, brushing his knuckles over her cheek in a gesture that melted the coldness inside. "But first, food."

Only then did she notice the tray sitting on Finn's desk, loaded with pastries and a hot nutrient drink. She sat down in Finn's chair, knowing he wouldn't mind, and took a sip of the drink before gorging herself on the pastries. "I think I'm going to get fat," she said around a mouthful. "I never had to worry about weight before—Psy nutrition regimes are calibrated for exact nutritional needs. But I can't stop eating these."

Grinning, Remi leaned against the wall to one side. "Cupcake, you'll be even more gorgeous in your cuddlier form."

Her cheeks heated, her toes curling inside the fluffy hand-knitted socks that a member of the pack had made for her. It delighted her that they were a sunshine yellow. "Finn's really good at getting people to talk. He doesn't even do anything and it comes out."

A scowl on Remi's face. "Healers are like the fucking truth serum on steroids." Gruff words, but the love, the affection beneath them, it was potent. "What did he make you spill?"

Auden stared at the pastry in her hand. "Fear," she admitted. "It gnaws at me, the idea that one part of me might betray the other part—betray *Liberty*." Swallowing hard, she met Remi's gaze. "I couldn't ask this of him, because he's a healer. He couldn't do it."

Remi's face went motionless, his eyes switching to those of his leopard.

"Liberty comes first," Auden said. "If I become *any* kind of threat to her, you take me out of the equation." Dropping the unfinished pastry to the plate, she gripped his hand. "Please, Remi. I'm asking this as her mother, as the woman who loves her beyond breath, beyond life. If another part of me does anything to hurt her, it won't matter if I come back. I'll have died already."

Remi's fingers tightened on hers almost to the point of pain. "I promise." A harsh statement.

All the air rushed out of her. "Thank you for not arguing with me." Because she'd never change her mind on this.

"No point." He cupped her cheek. "And no reason to—because you know what? I'm betting on this Auden. The one who has so far outsmarted the entire fucking Scott family to keep her child safe. This Auden, *my* Auden, is going to win. I'll never have to act on my promise."

His faith was a lightning bolt in her blood, electrifying her senses and making her believe, too. Because she *had* outsmarted her family, outsmarted Charisma. She'd won this round—the most important round. Liberty was safe.

"I'll win," she vowed, and picked up her pastry. "Not only will I win, I will crush them under my fluffy yellow foot."

His grin was a primal thing. "That's my girl."

"What did you want to talk to me about?" she demanded after swallowing a bite, her blood yet hot.

"Your telepathic shields." No humor now, nothing but protective intensity. "You want some expert training to make them stronger?"

"Yes. Charisma's an 8.3 telepath and she trained under my mother. I'll take any help I can get to keep her out."

"Good. I'll tell Zaira you're ready to see her."

Auden almost choked on the bite she'd just taken, had to gulp nutrient liquid to wash it down. "Are you talking about Zaira, the Arrow who almost took out a would-be-assassin's eye with a knife on a public street?" she squeaked out afterward, her hot blood tempered by sheer amazement.

"That's her. Don't worry. She only murders people who try to hurt her own—and she likes cubs." A slow smile that made her understand why humans spoke about butterflies in the abdomen. "So you're safe."

AUDEN thought she was prepared for Zaira Neve, but the petite Arrow was not someone for whom you could prepare. Power contained in a small and deadly body, her eyes an impenetrable darkness and her expression conveying nothing.

Utter remote nothingness, that was Zaira's expression as she looked at Auden, and Auden had the sense of being sized up by the most dangerous person she'd ever met. Perhaps she should've thought that about Remi, with his claws and his power . . . but Auden knew Remi would never hurt her.

Zaira on the other hand . . .

Heart racing hard and fast, Auden shifted so that she was in front of the incubator.

The Arrow took off her uniform jacket and threw it on the end of the bed. "I like you, Auden Scott."

Auden didn't move. "Why?" she asked warily.

"Because you just got in between a trained killer and your child." A shift in her expression. "I wasn't sure who I'd meet today. It wasn't a woman with Shoshanna Scott's eyes melded with the protectiveness of an Arrow mother."

Auden's emotions were all over the place, but she realized that if Zaira had wanted to do her harm, she could've done it the instant she came through the door. Arrows were Arrows for a reason; she had no idea of Zaira's specialty, but that didn't matter—*all* Arrows were lethal.

Taking a deep breath, she shifted aside. "Would you like to meet Liberty?"

Zaira came over to look into the incubator, her shoulder-length black hair sliding against her neck as she glanced down. Her expression gentled. "I like that name," she said afterward.

"It's a promise to her," Auden found herself saying. "Of a life lived in freedom."

Zaira Neve's dark eyes locked with hers again, words unspoken within. "Telepathic shields," she said at last. "I need to examine yours to make them better. I'll get a couple of chairs from outside so we can sit facing each other."

Auden knew she had no real choice with the required trust. And even if she didn't know or have any reason to trust Zaira, her faith in Remi was a thing unbreakable. And it was Remi who'd brought Zaira to her. "I'll use Finn's chair," she said. "Healer imprints seem to be like empathic imprints; my senses don't react."

"Of course."

After they were in position on the chairs, she gave the Arrow the necessary access. Zaira's eyes went black as she expended psychic power, but her mental touch was so subtle that Auden didn't even feel it. That told her the deadly truth: Zaira was a combat telepath.

Her father's voice filled her mind.

Most combat telepaths are experts at shield destruction and war on the psychic front, but the really good ones can slip past defenses without a whisper. You'll never know one has infiltrated you until they've melted your brain from the inside out.

She sucked in a breath.

Zaira spoke at the same instant. "Apologies. I wasn't intending on picking up that thought, but it was too strong to avoid. I'm not planning on melting your brain. If I did, Remi would try to kill me, we'd fight and both be badly hurt, and then everyone would be mad at me, including Jojo."

"Who's Jojo?" Auden choked out.

"A young friend," Zaira murmured, the black retreating from her eyes. "Hmm, that was interesting. I've never been inside the mind of a psychometric before."

Auden closed her fingers into her palm. "Is it different from other Psy minds?"

"Yes," Zaira said, to her surprise. "Your shields have a layer of complication I've never previously encountered, but it makes sense if you're getting data through tactile contact." She glanced at Auden's hands. "No gloves?"

"I gave up on them after they did nothing to protect me during pregnancy," Auden said. "Finn's already ordered me a couple of new sets now that my sensitivity's settled back down to normal levels. The thin layer generally blunts the impact of unknown imprints."

"I've never thought myself ignorant on Psy abilities," Zaira said, "but I realize I know next to nothing about psychometrics."

"Not many people do. Can you show me what you saw in my mind?"

Zaira nodded. "I'll project the information."

The images were crystalline. "Your telepathy is beautiful," Auden whispered, astonished. "Even Shoshanna didn't send with such clarity."

"Let's not bring up your parents." Zaira's voice held ice for the first time.

Auden's entire being went still. "I'm sorry." For all that her family had done, the atrocities they'd helped commit.

"Nothing for you to be sorry about." Zaira shoved a hand through her soft curls. "I apologize for snapping at you. You had nothing to do with their actions."

Auden wasn't sure quite how to take that.

Zaira held her gaze. "We, all of us Arrows, are learning to believe that we are not how we were brought up, that now we have a choice, we can *choose* to be better. So for me to accuse you of evil simply because of your parents goes against our very ethos. I was wrong. Simple as that."

No one had ever apologized to Auden. Not that way. Not so real and honest.

"I accept the apology," she said past the lump in her throat. "Thank you for giving me those words."

Zaira kept on looking at her with eyes that were too incisive. "Did you grow up like us?"

"I don't know what growing up as an Arrow is like," Auden said, "but no, I don't think so. My father wanted me, you see. He didn't even care that I had a passive ability. He treated me well."

Zaira's expression held a quiet intensity. "I'm learning subtlety and nuance," she said. "And how people can have different faces. I suppose I never expected Councilor Henry Scott to ever wear the face of a doting father." The Arrow waved a hand in a slicing motion. "But that's not why I'm here."

Auden was glad to move past the topic of her parents. "How bad are my shields?"

"Not bad at all," Zaira told her, to her surprise. "Who taught you shield construction?"

"My father."

"I thought as much. He was good. But you have an erratic crack through your psychic pattern at the foundation—it's destabilized things at the very start so that the error runs outward."

Auden could've made excuses, hidden the truth, but if she was going to do that, she might as well end this session now. "I was implanted with an experimental biograft. It did permanent damage."

Zaira's eyes had gone gleaming obsidian at Auden's first words. "So," she said after a pregnant pause, "you were brought up like us after all."

"No," Auden said, "I had sixteen years of a life where I felt safe and protected."

Though Zaira didn't push the point, Auden could follow the line of her thoughts: that Auden didn't want to believe she'd suffered because to do that would be to destroy everything she'd believed about her childhood.

"I wasn't raised as a sacrificial lamb," she whispered, wondering who she was trying to convince. "Until the brain damage, I was meant to be his genetic legacy. I'm almost certain Shoshanna was the one who decided to implant me."

"All those things can be true," Zaira said and the words weren't harsh, just straightforward. "That your father cherished you in whatever way a Councilor born in Silence could cherish a child, and that he saw you as a tool that, once broken, was no longer worthy of his attention."

Except the latter cancels out the former, Auden thought, but didn't say aloud. "Can I fix the crack?" she asked instead, her voice rough with all the emotions she couldn't release, all the things she couldn't say.

"Yes," Zaira said, "but we'll have to rebuild from scratch. That means a purposeful destruction of your current shield. I realize that's asking a lot. You don't know me and it'll leave you vulnerable, but it is the best possible option to ensure we don't leave the error behind at some level of the psychic code."

"Remi trusts you," Auden said without hesitation. "And I trust him." She took a deep breath, exhaled. "Please make sure my baby is protected from any psychic shock waves."

Zaira nodded. "You know she's a strong telepath?"

"The squad can't have her."

Zaira's lips kicked up. "I wouldn't dare make that claim with such a mother—and with Remi in the mix. I was just going to say that she'll need to learn psychic discipline earlier than most. Bring her to me when she starts cracking your maternal shields and I'll teach her."

The Arrow gave a curt nod after that extraordinary offer. "Shield destruction in three seconds. Three, two . . . one."

Chapter 35

Miane, it's a go on our idea to blood-bond the half-human children to you.

The theory is that given the strong ties of family and friendship between BlackSea and the Alliance, the children should be pulled into the BlackSea changeling network the instant after their minds separate from the PsyNet, but EmNet has assigned a team to psychically force the transfer if necessary.

The infants could also end up pulling their Psy parent into the network, due to the parent-child bond.

The scientists are certain that, with no PsyNet to return to, the children will cling to the new network out of instinct, even with no adult Psy to hold them in place.

—Bowen Knight, security chief of the Human Alliance, to
Miane Levèque, alpha of BlackSea (2 November 2083)

IT WAS FULL dark and dinner was over by the time Zaira left Auden.

"I'll be back tomorrow," the Arrow told Remi when he met her outside, the tree canopy above them a sprawling darkness against the starlit sky. "This isn't a task that can be completed in a day—especially not when she's weak from childbirth."

"Can you get her to a point where she'll be safe inside the Scott household?"

Zaira nodded. "From everyone but a telepath of Shoshanna's strength and skill—and Auden says they have no one like that in the family."

"Thanks, Zaira." He reached into a pocket. "Before I forget—I don't know how Jojo figured out you were here, but she made you this."

Zaira smiled at the painstakingly drawn image of a leopard, its coat purple with sparkly silver dots. At the top it said, "For Zai," the wobbly words nonetheless legible. "Give her a hug from me, and tell her I love it and that I'll be back for a proper visit with her soon."

With that, the Arrow faded off into the darkness, from which Remi had picked up a familiar—yet unknown—scent. Zaira's teleport assist was most often the same Arrow: Alejandro. Yet Remi had never laid eyes on the man—Alejandro preferred to stay in the shadows, for reasons neither Aden nor Zaira had ever vocalized, but Remi figured plenty of Arrows had scars.

Aden thought Alejandro was safe to permit knowledge of RainFire.

That was good enough for Remi.

Turning on his heel after Zaira vanished into the night, he went toward the infirmary and caught sight of Finn heading toward him. "Both asleep," the healer said. "Auden barely managed to stay awake long enough to cuddle Liberty even after all the nutrient drinks Zaira pumped into her through the day—the shield stuff must be heavy-duty mental lifting."

Remi grumbled. "I wanted to say good night."

Rolling his eyes, Finn yawned. "Go. You won't wake Auden, and Liberty falls asleep as fast as she wakes at the moment, so you're safe to pet her a little."

"You need sleep, too," Remi said with a scowl, and shook his head when Finn went to argue. "Go to sleep. That's an order from your alpha. Who else is on medical watch?"

"Sass." Another jaw-cracking yawn.

"Then we'll be fine—I'll help her keep an eye on the patients, and we'll wake you the instant anything goes wrong." He squeezed the other man's shoulder. "Shut-eye before you fall asleep mid-operation."

"As if I'd ever," was the grumpy response before Finn walked over to his home—the aerie closest to the infirmary.

Once inside the cubes, Remi told Saskia what was up—to the shake of her head, the rich scarlet of her hair in a neat French braid. "Hugo told him that before he went off shift, and I told him that two hours ago, but would the stubborn man listen to us?"

"Healers," they said in unison, and laughed.

Remi cupped her face afterward, her skin the hue of cream, and said, "And you, Sass? You doing okay?" She and Hugo were both so efficient that it would've been easy to forget that they, too, needed their alpha's attention—except not forgetting was Remi's job.

"I'm wishing Rina's little brother was a few years older so I could lure him to my aerie without guilt," Saskia said with a wicked glint in her eye. "Then again, he might be into older women."

Chuckling, Remi touched his lips to hers in a kiss that had nothing to do with romance and everything to do with affection, his protective instincts toward the healers in the pack a thing unbound. "I have no comment on that," he said after cuddling her close. "Just remember that Rina knows where you sleep."

Saskia's shoulders shook in his embrace. "Excellent point."

After a couple more minutes speaking to the nurse, he went to check in on Auden and Liberty. Their cube was quiet and dark, the only lights coming from Liberty's incubator, and the soft night lights built into the skirting of the walls.

Auden was frowning and tossing in her sleep, her curls tied up in what appeared to be a silk scarf that looked like something Saskia would choose for herself. Since he'd briefed all the medical staff on Auden's needs as a psychometric, it had to be brand-new and machine-made—Sass wouldn't have risked giving Auden a used one. He had good people in his pack—and they appreciated a mother who fought for the happiness of her cub.

"Shh," he murmured with a brush of his palm over her cheek, rumbling deep in his chest in the way he'd noticed she liked. "I'm here. I'll watch over her."

A sigh, her body turning into his.

He stroked her back until she was in a deep sleep, then turned to Liberty. He'd kept an ear out for the cub from the start, but she hadn't woken. Now he touched her through the little circle in the incubator, and felt her in his heart. Strange, but it was almost as if she was blood-bonded to him, same as Finn and his sentinels.

A memory of the rich scent of blood, of a child born while her mother clutched at Remi's hand and begged him to protect her baby. Of Remi's claiming of the baby as one of his. Of a tiny life Remi could feel as he could feel every member of his pack.

"You're mine, aren't you, little one?" he said, certain beyond any doubt that Liberty was linked into the PsyNet through her mother and into RainFire through him. No one had to tell him if it was possible— he knew.

It was a long time later that the baby whimpered.

Aware by now how long she needed to spend in the incubator, Remi knew it was safe to take her out for a cuddle. "Hey, now," he rumbled as he picked her up after tugging off his T-shirt so she'd have skin-to-skin contact. "What's this, hmm?"

She settled the instant she was against his chest, her little hiccups adorable. Smiling, he nuzzled at her, felt her smile in his heart. And for a fragment of a heartbeat, he saw a glittering blue spiderweb in his mind, a creation lovely and eerie . . . and so real that he knew he hadn't imagined it.

AUDEN lifted her eyelashes and smiled. A half-naked Remi was purring deep in his chest while he rocked Liberty, and her heart, it couldn't bear it. Then she noticed the light, so blue and clear, and looked up to see the web floating above their heads.

Wonder filled her veins, spilled over her hands . . . and spread in a web across the infirmary floor in a slow sweep that made Auden frown. She was forgetting something important.

But the thought slipped out of her grasp as quickly as sleep swept her back under. And when she woke to the morning dew, she wondered at the surreal clarity of her dream. She might've been concerned about why she was dreaming of webs, but what was there to fear from a thing so lovely?

"Is it you?" she whispered to Liberty with a smile when she rose. "My little telepath dreaming big dreams?"

The baby slept on, her rest that of the innocent.

THE four-day window over, Auden stood beside the incubator dressed in a black shift dress with sharp lines that nonetheless allowed room for her body to recover at its own pace. To her joy, her milk had come in and she'd been able to feed Liberty four precious times. Today, she'd pumped what she could, then Finn had injected her with a medication that would stop her milk supply for the next eighteen hours.

She could do this five times in a row before the effect became permanent. Which meant she had to play this game to the end before then. She'd had too much taken from her—she wouldn't allow her family to take this joy from her, too.

Auden touched her baby one last time.

Her eyes swam wet when she turned to a suit-clad Remi. He was big and handsome and when he closed his arms around her, she felt more safe than she had in her entire lifetime before him.

Hand on his chest, she pulled back only enough to look into his eyes. "I've heard Psy can survive in changeling networks," she said. "From what I've picked up since waking, the PsyNet situation is getting more dire by the day. If the worst happens—"

Remi squeezed her nape. "You don't have to ask, Auden. I'll make sure Libby is safe." He touched a fisted hand to his heart. "She's bonded by blood to me, is one of mine, part of RainFire. No matter what, she'll fall into the arms of her pack." He gripped her chin. "And I expect you to follow. It won't be difficult, not for you. Not when you're mine, too."

Auden's heart hitched but she didn't—couldn't—give a direct answer until she knew who or what she had inside her. "Let's go, or I won't be able to leave."

Rina, who'd been chatting to Finn, walked over at Remi's signal. Her suit was identical to Remi's in color—a crisp black paired with a white shirt—and cut to her body. Unlike Remi, she wasn't wearing a tie, but both had tiny dot microphones on their collars that were all but invisible, paired with equally subtle earpieces, and Rina carried a sleek briefcase over her shoulder that held their security gear.

Mliss would be dropping off spare clothing for them at the gate.

The Arrow named Vasic appeared next to Auden a heartbeat later. He wasn't, however, wearing the squad's uniform. Instead, he wore jeans and a sweatshirt, the hood of which he now flipped over his head. The deep cowl of it effectively hid his features, but he'd further helped that along by wearing sunglasses.

Unlike when they'd been introduced, he wore a prosthetic arm that filled out the left sleeve of his sweatshirt. The hand was so realistic that she did a double take. From a distance and in the split second that he might be caught on camera if Auden was wrong about that particular part of the house not being under surveillance, no one would ever pick him as the only known true teleporter in the world. Especially after he eased his body into a relaxed slouch no Arrow would ever consider proper posture.

Remi whistled at the transformation. "Who taught you that? Juvenile?"

"Yes. It appears that contented young men have no actual bones."

Laughing, Remi touched the top of Liberty's incubator. "Finn and the pack will look after you while we're gone, kitten. Be good."

The last thing Auden felt before the world tilted and blurred for a slight second prior to coming back into clear focus was her baby's happiness at hearing Remi's voice. Then Vasic was gone and the three of them stood in the shadows of an alcove at the far end of a corridor.

Auden's mind shifted, her maternal instincts transforming into a weapon razored and without mercy. To these people, her child was nothing but a pawn to use as they wished. Over her fucking dead body. "Let's do this," she said, and strode out, with Remi and Rina a step back and on either side of her.

On a real protective detail, they'd have been in front of and behind her, on alert for threats from any side, but she'd wanted to make an entrance—and Remi understood the importance of taking power by demanding it.

Auden knew that didn't mean he and Rina weren't both on high alert, their senses attuned to every scent, every sound, every possible threat. No doubt they'd spotted the three cameras they'd passed, as well as picking up any scents in the vicinity.

"Charisma." Remi's voice giving her quiet warning at least ten seconds before her mother's aide appeared from around the corner.

The other woman froze, her eyes going immediately to Auden's no longer distended belly.

Remi came to a halt the instant Auden did, then he and Rina stepped out to put their backs to the wall on either side. Neither made any attempt to hide their constant scans of the area.

Charisma found her voice at last. "Was there a medical emergency?"

"It was dealt with," Auden said, without elaborating.

"The child?"

"Is receiving excellent care." Not allowing the aide time to respond, Auden said, "I'd like to advise you that I've hired two members of Rain-Fire as my personal security. You'll recognize Alpha Denier."

Charisma's face twisted into the cold facsimile of a smile that she'd learned from Shoshanna. "You have no need of personal security here. You are the head of this household."

"Don't be foolish, Charisma." Auden's voice was so frigid and cutting that Remi wouldn't have believed it was her if he hadn't been able to see her. "We both know Auden has been nothing but a puppet for a long time."

His hackles rose. Why was she talking about herself in the third person? And what the hell had just happened with her scent? It wasn't as bad as before, but the metallic edge was back. He caught the flare of Rina's nostrils, knew the sentinel had picked up the impossibility of it, too.

People's true scents did not change between one breath and the next.

"It's time I ended that state of affairs once and for all," Auden added. "I'm ready to reclaim my position."

Charisma's thin shoulders squared underneath her black turtleneck, a flat hardness to her expression. "You realize you'll have to go through a test to confirm your competency."

"No, I won't," Auden replied, the smile on her face as cold as a cobra's. "Because this family made sure Auden was never legally declared incompetent in the first place."

Charisma's face went white. "Sir, you said . . ." She shook her head. "This isn't what was agreed."

"I *make* the agreements." Ice-cold words. "I am now your boss, and my first order is that you go and make sure my suite is clear of any and all surveillance devices. Both my guards are experts at detecting them through scent alone, so if you value your job, you'd better ensure you don't accidentally 'forget' one as you did before."

The temperature dropped another ten degrees. "Did you think I didn't notice, Ris?" A silkiness to her voice that made Remi's leopard snarl. "As if that pathetic weasel of a man wasn't leaving his sweaty imprints everywhere, even through the gloves. At least the hypersensitivity in pregnancy had a benefit there. I also want you to assign the suite next door to my guards. Make sure it's clear."

Charisma's face had frozen into that horrible smile at first, but her expression was almost hopeful when she next spoke. "Sir, you can't blame me for my caution."

"Honestly, Ris." Auden held out her hand. "Give me your organizer."

Once she had it, she input something, then handed it back. "Will you stop hovering now and act as my aide?"

Charisma's breathing turned unsteady as she stared at the screen. "Of course, sir." Eyes so bright and shiny that Remi would've called it adoration had this not been a Psy who continued to cling to Silence. "Your guards will have to be assigned house armbands so they're not stopped."

"No, Ris. It's your job to tell everyone that they are mine. Anyone who so much as touches either one will answer to me."

"Yes, sir. I'll take care of the suite now," the aide said, almost bowing before she walked away on rapidly clicking high heels.

None of them spoke in the aftermath, conscious the public areas were monitored. The silence gave Remi's thoughts too much space to grow: the Auden he'd just seen . . . she was a vicious creature wholly different from the one who'd cuddled Liberty and eaten pastries with gusto.

He wanted to shake her, make her return to the Auden he knew . . . and not this *other* who had taken her over like a cold storm with no empathy or mercy in her.

"This is my office," Auden said, leading them into a meticulously neat room with no papers on the desk of black glass and no art on the black walls. Not even a fake wall of books for decorative purposes.

"Clinical" was the word that came to mind.

"Security sweep." Auden's voice was an order that ruffled his leopard's fur the wrong way—but not because it was an order. Because it had been given by this alternate version of Auden.

Rina closed and locked the door behind them before they both took out scanners they'd purchased through a contact of the squad. They were the highest spec on the market, and so far had never failed to detect any covert surveillance devices. Because while Auden hadn't been lying about their senses being able to pick up things that didn't belong, such small devices rarely had a scent strong enough to make a difference.

Still, he wasn't against helping strengthen the legend of changeling abilities.

Auden stood motionless and watchful by the door as they worked, but her eyes had gone obsidian in a sweeping tide and he realized she'd taken off her thin black glove and was touching the door handle, checking for imprints.

He and Rina found ten devices between them, depositing the components in a neat pile on the glass desk. "Clear," Rina said after a secondary scan.

Remi then did a third. "Clear," he confirmed.

Eyes of haunting obsidian stared off into nothing for another long second before Auden said, "Clear." Staggering forward in the aftermath, she placed her hand smack on the glass of the desk.

A hiss of sound.

Chapter 36

Bo, the blood-bonding is now complete.

After discussion with Sahara Kyriakus and Ivy Jane Zen, we also bonded in as many fully Psy children as they calculated the clan's changeling network could handle, and it's possible the little ones may make it—my innate urge to protect means they live in my heart now, so there is an emotional tie. I only wish we could take so many more.

As for full-blooded adult Psy who aren't linked to us by emotion—no change on the needle there. Still, we've laid the groundwork with multiple empaths because the children will need psychic oversight, and Es seem to be the best bet. Let us hope that we're all wrong and that we won't have to stand by and watch the loss of life on a scale incalculable.

—Miane Levèque, alpha of BlackSea, to Bowen Knight, security
chief of the Human Alliance (4 November 2083)

"PROBLEM?" RINA ASKED from where she kept watch by the door, even as Remi growled deep in his chest and went to Auden.

She shook her head when he would've touched her, her gaze pleading with him to keep his distance. Those eyes, that expression, it was the Auden he knew—but a faint whisper of the metal remained tangled in her scent.

He halted, man and leopard both fighting the urge to shake her and hold her close at the same time.

"No, this desk is cold." A pause. "In the psychometric sense. That's why so many of my designation go for hyper-modern furnishings. Less chance of embedded history. But this particular desk is cold in the sense that I don't think anyone's touched it since I was gone."

"What did you do at it?" Remi asked, unable to imagine his Auden in this space.

"Prior to this past month, nothing much." She rubbed her chest, her face flinching.

"Auden." A growl and this time, he gripped her jaw, held the moonstone blue of her gaze.

"It's me with a piece of another," she whispered, low enough to reach him alone.

He scented the truth of that in her body.

"I need her," she added with a hard swallow. "She knew the code to *Charisma's* private files. I don't understand why I would've ever had that."

He understood what she was asking of him, but that didn't mean he had to like it. "You're in control," he told her, and this time, he pitched his voice so Rina could hear as well—Auden had asked Remi to brief her on the possibility of a hostile personality. "I can scent it." He released her jaw. "Yours is ascendant."

"I scent the same," Rina said, her eyes narrowed. "Whatever is going on, that metallic part of you is only a thread."

Auden took a deep breath, then looked from Remi to Rina and back. Her spine grew straighter. "Can you make it so we'll know immediately if anyone enters after today?"

"That won't be a problem. We'll do scent sweeps on a regular basis."

"Good." She shifted so that she could see both him and Rina, her expression set in unmoving lines. "Let's do this. For her." Love in her scent itself, Liberty's scent tangled with Auden's on an indelible level—and that part of her scent, Remi realized on a roar of satisfaction, had never altered.

The other Auden could no longer get past his Auden's love for her child. It was a thing enormous, and the Auden he loved—because yeah, why the fuck fight that when it was a blazing star deep within—was stronger, tougher, harder to break because of the power of her heart.

"I," she added, "want to blow the secrets of this house wide open."

"That's my girl." A rumbling purr in his chest, his leopard's claws pushing at his skin. "First thing is for you to give us a tour of the compound, so we can assess any obvious threats."

"I'll show you from upstairs."

Professional mask back on, Remi fell into a walk behind her as Rina took the lead. He'd have liked to enjoy the view of Auden's curvy form, but that pleasure would have to wait. Right now, his every sense was on alert for any sign of danger, even as he made note of possible entry and exit routes, as well as any cameras or other indicators of surveillance.

"This is the most private part of the property," Auden said, after walking them upstairs. "The family bedrooms are all up here. Right now, I occupy the one center right, with Charisma across from me but one down to the left, nearest the stairs. The other three bedrooms are unoccupied."

Leading them into her room, she took them past the bed made with pale gray sheets that seemed to float in the spartan space. The only other piece of furniture was an armchair with a high back, its cushions a deep green, that sat by the main windows.

He would've expected the walls to be a formless white, but they'd been wallpapered with a fine gray pattern against white. His eyes narrowed at the unnecessary detail. Better, he thought, to hide listening devices.

He tapped his ear to indicate the need for silence, then got out his scanner. Rina was already at work with hers.

The room was clear.

"Look here," Remi said afterward, indicating a fine tear in the wallpaper. "Rush job pulling it out."

"That's the one the installer left behind the first time around." Auden's jaw was a hard line. "I didn't know it but *she* did, the other part of me."

"Good. Keep on using her. You are the alpha," he reiterated, because this could well be the fight for Auden's life. "You know why? Because your heart is bigger than hers could ever be."

Her pupils expanded, her breath catching. "An alpha must have a huge heart," she said, and it wasn't a question, rather a wondering statement. "All this time, I thought the key ingredient was dominance, but it's not, is it?"

"It is and it isn't," he corrected. "*Both* must exist for a changeling to be an alpha. An alpha without a heart would be a dictator, and an alpha without dominance couldn't hold his pack together."

Auden nodded slowly. "Balance." A murmur almost to herself before she shook it off. "Come, I want you to see the view from the window. You can get an overview of the rest of the compound from there."

Three other buildings dominated, one on either side and one to the front. All were smaller than the main residence, but were painted in the same white color palette, with touches of dark gray. Elegant and unobtrusive against the crisp and clean lines of the landscaping.

"The building to the left houses other staff who work in or close to the house, while the building to the right is the infirmary. Dr. Verhoeven's apartment is in back of it."

"Why is the guard station so big?" Rina asked, pointing to the building out front.

"The guards have barracks inside. Fences are all wired for motion detection, but the guards do live patrols at regular intervals." A wince. "I never bothered to work out the intervals."

Remi curled his fingers over her hand below the line of the window; her skin was cool, as if this place had stolen all her warmth. "We know the intervals." When she shot him a questioning look, he allowed himself a faint smile, his cat pleased with itself. "Soon as we knew we'd be coming here, Rina and her brother, Kit, came down to spy."

"Cats are excellent spies," Rina said, her own leopard in her voice. "And Kit can still climb better than me, which is annoying in the extreme. But it meant he was able to set up a hide a short distance from here in a tree, and watch the goings-on through binoculars, while I used my night vision to prowl around a bit closer."

Auden's skin prickled with a pride as wild as the two changelings who stood with her. "Charisma and the other Auden have no idea what they're up against."

"Damn straight," Rina said with a grin before she stepped out to go check the neighboring room.

Remi nudged Auden away from the window at the same time, one big hand warm on her lower back. "Windows offer clear lines of sight. Try to avoid being immobile in front of one."

Auden could feel the heat of his palm against her even after he broke contact. It burned, a silent brand. She wanted so much more, *craved* it even knowing that it was the wrong time, the wrong place . . . because panic beat in the back of her brain, warning her that time was running out. She intended to fight to the death to win this war, but she never forgot that the enemy lived *inside her mind*. Victory was in no way guaranteed.

"Remi," she whispered.

His eyes glowed in a way that wasn't human, wasn't Psy. "Not in this house." It came out a growl that held no menace, his chest rumbling against her as he wrapped her up in his arms.

She held on tight, the muscled heat of him making her shiver.

A nip to her ear that made her jump. "You're not ready, either." He nuzzled her. "Finn would have my head if I did what I wanted to do."

But Auden had found her voice now and she wasn't about to give it up. Especially not when it came to this man who walked in her dreams and whose scent was her compass. "You taught me what it is to crave touch. You can't just stop now that I'm an addict," she argued on a wave of that simmering inner panic. "You've cleared this room, too."

She shifted, held his gaze. "As for not being ready . . . I had time in the infirmary. I did a little research." Sure that the erotic searches were emblazoned on her forehead, she'd hidden her organizer under the sheets each time Finn or the nurses walked into the room.

Remi had retrieved her organizer and her clothes from the cabin, and she'd known the device—unlinked to the Scott system—was free of any bugs. So she'd shed her inhibitions and typed in searches that had given her an erotic education that made her squirm.

"I watched videos late at night," she admitted, even though it made her cheeks burn from the inside. "I saw all the things lovers can do to each other."

Groaning, he pressed a kiss to her throat, then another. The shiver that ran through her this time was a thing electric. Her already sensitive breasts felt engorged, her nipples tight buds. She pressed herself to the hardness of his chest, her body hot and wanting.

"Enough." Another kiss to her throat. "I want time, and I want privacy—and I want you to be sure." He drew back, held her gaze with those of alpha yellow-green. "No mental disruption, no other Auden. Just you and me."

She wanted to argue with him that that might never happen, but she also knew that this wasn't just about her. Remi was a man of honor, and he'd never forgive himself if he thought he'd taken advantage of her.

But after swallowing to wet a dry throat, she said, "Can we do things like this, though? When my scent is mine? Not the complete sexual act, but . . . touching like this?" She *knew* it was all too soon, her mind still reeling after the birth even if her body was physically healed thanks to Finn's use of the nanos, but the wild desperation in her wasn't listening to reason.

What if, whispered that desperate part of her, *what if she lost the battle without ever experiencing this piercing intimacy with Remi?*

A scowl. "That's definitely my stubborn Auden." His hand cupping her jaw, his lips taking hers in an intimacy so sweet and sensual at the same time that she couldn't breathe.

She gasped when he broke the kiss, her fingers rising to her lips. "I never . . ." Another rough inhale. "Kisses. I never understood why people would want to do that. Until now." His breath in her mouth, his fingers so firm and warm on her face, it was the newest addition to her list of cravings when it came to Remi Denier.

His own breathing not exactly steady, Remi ran the back of his hand over her cheek. "It's okay, Cupcake." Infinite tenderness in his voice. "We'll have time. No one is going to stand in our way."

She should've been ashamed that he'd so quickly glimpsed her panic, but all she felt was a sobbing relief. Remi *saw* her, complete with her ability to love and her faults and her fear. "We'll finish our kiss?"

"And more," he promised. "In our own time, at our own pace. No rush, no driving force but our own desire." He rubbed his thumb over her cheekbone before pressing a gentle kiss to her forehead. "I didn't bruise your lips, but you want to check your makeup to make sure it'll pass muster?"

Nodding, Auden walked into the bathroom on legs that held a faint quiver.

Remi stood in the open doorway while she touched up minor details that wouldn't escape Charisma's eagle eye.

"So," he said, leaning one wide shoulder against the doorjamb. "Did your mother favor this house? Is that why Ms. Wai chose the place for the duration of your pregnancy?"

Auden shook her head. "In the last year of her life, Shoshanna didn't stay in one place for too long."

"Do you know where she was when she died?"

"Charisma told me it was her residence in Nevada, but who knows." Auden sleeked back a fine curl that had escaped its bun. "Her body was cremated, the ashes disposed of before I even truly understood that she was dead."

Turning, she met Remi's eyes. "I think that's why I feel her presence like a malevolent shadow at times—because I never saw her dead. It feels like this house is still hers, and I *know* the people are all still hers, each and every one following a blueprint she put down that has to do with me and Liberty."

Remi straightened. "By the time we're done here, the only name that'll matter to anyone in the outside world is that of Auden Scott." His vow held the power of an alpha leopard—and his gaze held the promise of the protective man who'd sung a lullaby to Liberty while holding her in his arms late one dark night.

A flicker of memory.

Blue spiderwebs of haunting loveliness.

Then Remi ran his hand down her back, his body a solid shield behind her, pure power and warmth, and the faint remembrance whispered out of her mind.

Chapter 37

"What does it feel like, Sophie? Does it talk to you?"

"It used to. But, it's so tired now, Max. Most of the time, it sleeps and it dreams the most astonishing dreams. I catch pieces of the dreams now and then, and they make me feel insignificant against the vast span of its knowledge and existence. Yet . . . it's also a child. A dying child."

—Conversation between Sophia Russo and Max Shannon (date unknown)

KALEB WAS EXHAUSTED on the psychic level. A thing most people wouldn't believe was possible for a dual cardinal, but at this point, he was holding a large section of the PsyNet together by feeding it with his own energy.

He knew he couldn't keep that up.

Which was why he'd come to this sliver of the PsyNet that was healthy and calm. A small island of peace hidden in the noise of the chaos around it . . . around the mind of Nikita Duncan's aide, Sophia Russo. He didn't think Sophia ever noticed his presence when he visited, but he made sure to cloak himself regardless.

Because he had no desire for or intention of scaring the J-Psy, or of alerting Nikita to his presence. He came for two simple reasons. *Are you awake?* he asked the NetMind and DarkMind, the twin neosentience that had once been the librarian and guardian of the PsyNet. The vast majority of his race thought the entities dead, murdered by the disintegration of the PsyNet, and Kaleb had never disabused them of that notion.

In truth, the twins *had* almost died. But as long as the PsyNet existed, some fragment of them would exist. In the final hours, when he'd seen the light going out of both of them, he'd given them an order. They were young, the NetMind and DarkMind, and they understood that he was a power. More, they understood that he cared for them in a way that no one else could duplicate.

Not even Sophia.

The J-Psy with a mind that was in perfect balance between dark and light, and thus provided the perfect home for both the NetMind and DarkMind. *Go to her,* he'd said. *Hide. Protect yourself.*

He'd known Sophia wouldn't eject her psychic visitors. He knew that because *they* knew it. So they'd gone, and curled up in the deepest recesses of her mind, inactive and conserving their energies as their beloved PsyNet crumbled in ways that hurt them, but that they couldn't stop.

They'd shared with Kaleb that Sophia believed them mere pieces of the bigger whole, and Kaleb had told them to allow her to continue with that belief. Sophia already worried about the twin neosentience—how much more pressure would she put on herself if she knew that she protected the last precious flickers of what had once been two vast and growing neosentient entities?

No answer today.

He wasn't worried. It often took them several minutes to wake from their dormant state.

Flowers blossoming in his mind, blooms of white with rivers of black, and blooms of black with rivers of white.

His shoulders lost their tension on the physical plane, his body in the water of the pool he'd built for Sahara, and his arms braced on the tiled edge. She leaned against the edge with him, her hair a water-slick black rain down her back as she waited for him to return from his task.

"Still there," he murmured out loud for her.

But even as he spoke, he realized that the presence who'd come to him was singular. *Where is the other?* He shaped his question in images of twin streams: one white, one black.

The answer was an interwoven thread, black and white that had begun to meld in places to a luminescent steel gray.

The sight woke the scarred, twisted boy deep within his psyche, the child's joy holding an intimate understanding of what it was to be hurt over and over again until you broke. "They're merging back into one sentience."

The NetMind had always been one, until Silence fragmented it, creating the DarkMind out of all the pieces of themselves the Psy refused to accept. It had been angry, violent, the unwanted child who only wanted to hurt others in turn.

Kaleb responded with fireworks, a symbol the NetMind understood as joy.

The fireworks were returned to him multiplied.

After the joy came the sorrow, image after image of crumbling edifices, cliff faces sheering away, land falling into sinkholes.

Yes, Kaleb said. *The PsyNet is dying. I came to ask you if there's anything I've forgotten, anything that can be done that isn't already being done?* Because though the neosentience was young, it was vast beyond any comprehension. It knew every corner of the PsyNet.

No answer . . . but then, it showed him a secretive spark of intermingled white and black traveling through the PsyNet at such speed that the world was a blur. It stopped at a mind within which nestled another, much, much smaller mind. The spark whispered inside the two minds, heading for the small one, but leaving a trail behind in the bigger.

When the spark reemerged, it was devoid of energy, and had no light to it. It limped back to Sophia's mind at such a slow and pained pace that Kaleb wanted to gather it up in his hands and take it to safety. *What did you do?*

The NetMind showed him a cascade of images:

A spider bloated sitting in a web.

A spider screaming as it fell from the web that burned with silver fire.

A spider curling up and hiding in a dark room.

A spider weaving a new web of razored, bloody sharpness.

Kaleb's gut clenched on a violent wave of understanding. Before he could vocalize any of it to Sahara, however, the series of images altered without warning.

A mirror flipping from the rusted and black underside to the smooth unbroken reflective side.

A glass vase with a severe crack through it.

Glue being applied to the vase . . . glue of intermingled and glittering black and white.

Flowers in the vase. Such small flowers.

Of a shimmering blue . . . with a heart of luminous steel.

Hope had once been a foreign emotion to Kaleb, but now he felt it stretch his skin. But the NetMind wasn't yet done.

Clawed hands around the vase and the flowers. Holding. Protecting.

Blood, so much blood.

The clawed hands cut and shredded by the spider's razored threads.

Chapter 38

Councilor Scott was very clear in her instructions: we *must* run the listed battery of scans, and have her answer the questions the Councilor left behind.

However, I'm not certain we can do that without first incapacitating Auden—and the two feral guards she's brought into the residence. It's the latter that makes me question the success of the procedure.

—Charisma Wai to Dr. Verhoeven (now)

AUDEN SHOWED THE two of them the entirety of the house, including all entry and exit routes. They also stepped outside to take in the external area.

Cloudy gray light bathed Remi's face.

He shrugged his shoulders, settling his skin back into place. Being trapped inside that house hadn't been his favorite thing in the world. There was a reason he lived in the forest, in an aerie. But he knew this reprieve was temporary. "Does this place have an attic or a basement?"

"A small basement," Auden said. "It's used for storage."

"We should look at it regardless." If her family was hiding a secret, it was possible some component of it was physical.

Nodding, Auden led them to a door that came off the kitchen—which wasn't like any kitchen he'd ever seen. "No one cooks here?" he asked, motioning at the gleaming counters and lack of anything resembling a device to actually cook food.

"Until recently, we stuck to the regime of nutrient drinks prescribed during Silence," Auden told him. "We're branching out now, but only in limited ways." Nothing in her face or voice gave away the memory that throbbed between them of her devouring the pastries he'd brought her.

Next time, he promised himself, he'd feed her the damn pastries—while she sat naked in his lap.

The idea was so enticing that his cock threatened to react, but private fantasies aside, this place was dangerous for her, and both parts of Remi knew it wasn't playtime. When Auden went to open the door to the basement, he shook his head, then took over. There was no lock or code, and the handle turned easily in his hand.

Beyond was a set of simple plascrete steps bathed in a clean white light that had come on automatically when the door opened.

"Stay up here," he told Rina. "Watch our backs."

She gave a curt nod and took a neutral stance with her back to the door.

Walking down, very conscious of Auden behind him, Remi found himself in a space used for storage. Everything was stacked neatly on metal shelving, each bin or storage box labeled with a black marker. Boxes of nutrient packets, flat packs of furniture, items used for household maintenance; there was nothing unusual about the goods.

And yet . . .

The hairs on his nape prickled, his leopard at the surface of his mind as he used all of the animal's senses to try and understand his reaction. Slowly walking the perimeter of the room, he checked the walls, but sensed no hollows, and the basement area was the right size for the footprint of the house.

Under his feet, the plascrete was smooth and unmarred.

Frowning, he wondered if he was just on edge and did another intensive search. Still nothing. "Let's head back up," he said at last, because doing the same ineffectual thing over and over again wouldn't give him any new intel to explain the nagging sensation in his gut.

Auden, who'd stayed halfway down the stairs, didn't ask him any questions. He didn't know if that was because she had no questions, or if she was holding her tongue in case of spyware.

What a nightmare of a place to live, where she couldn't even speak in freedom.

Claws pricking at his skin and those hairs on his nape yet prickling, he stopped close to the top of the stairs and scanned the area one final time. The shadows fell differently when looked at from that position, and his eyesight wasn't that of a human or a Psy.

His hand tightened on the banister.

"Is everything satisfactory?" Auden's voice grated on his nerves—because that wasn't *her* voice, not the voice of the Auden he knew.

Her scent, he told himself, focus on her scent. The metal was the finest of threads, Auden using it to bolster her mask to anyone who might be listening. Hundred percent chance the place was bugged, especially given what he'd just discovered.

"Yes," he said, tone calm and professional. "I'd also like to walk outside, check for possible ingress and egress points."

"If you don't need me, I'd like to do a walk-through the house in leopard form," Rina said.

Remi smiled, and knew it held teeth. "Excellent idea." Let this Psy house feel fear at the presence of a predator unlike any they'd ever before seen up close and personal. "We'll meet up afterward." He had no need to tell Rina to take care; the sentinel knew about threats unique to Psy opponents, and she was no green soldier.

"Sir," Rina said, and turned to head upstairs to get out of her clothes before she shifted.

Neither he nor Auden said a word until they were outside and far enough from the house that they had no chance of being overheard.

Auden exhaled. "What is it? What did you see?"

His hackles flattened at once. Because this was her. His Auden. Even the thread of metal was gone. "You do one hell of a good cold face," he said.

"I always had trouble before." A painful tightness to her jaw, she turned and stared down the trees that lined the drive like stiff-backed soldiers. "There's a risk of the bleedover becoming a permanent part of my psyche."

Remi's claws threatened to shove out of his fingertips, but he forced himself to look at the facts with hard-eyed clarity. "How much do you love Liberty?"

"I'd burn down the world for her." No hesitation, no avoidance.

Man and leopard both settled. "If the bleedover elements make you tougher to defeat, more dangerous to this family? Use them."

"You're not afraid it'll change me on a fundamental level?"

"No," he said. "You might gain new aspects, but as far as I can tell, my Auden is still standing—not only that, she's in control. You're taking pieces from the second Auden, not the other way around."

Silence for a long minute. "I never thought about it that way. She's colder, harder, more dangerous—I can sense that through the bleedover, like the blurry outline of a person I'll never see. I also sense evil . . . it's a malevolent taste in the back of my throat, a hovering darkness."

She folded her arms. "But I'm not evil. And I *am* in control. I haven't had any blank spots in my memory since before Liberty's birth."

He wanted to kiss her fierce, beautiful mouth.

A nod from her, as if she'd come to a decision. "What did you find in the basement?"

"It's the floor," he said, adding another fantasy to his collection of what he planned to do with Auden—this one involved her lush mouth and a kiss while she was riding him. "Beautifully constructed, but they couldn't quite get rid of a *very* slight shadow along the lines of what I'm sure is an access hatch."

He looked back toward the house. "If there's a cavity below the basement, it has no obvious external access unless we're talking tunnels."

"Or teleport-capable Tks," Auden pointed out, a vein at her temple pulsing. "We have one bonded into the family—literally contracted for life on a high income, with the unspoken caveat that any disloyalty will mean death."

"How powerful?" Remi asked.

"Gradient 5.7," Auden said. "My parents had access to stronger ones, of course, due to their positions, but even they couldn't get away with bonding anyone stronger. The teleporters just wouldn't do it—they know their value. And neither the Jackson nor Scott line is known for Tks, so there's no internal supply."

"So most access is probably through the hatch, with teleports only used when absolutely necessary. You wouldn't want to burn out a Tk with such basic work when there was another way to get to the same spot."

Auden nodded. "It's most probably the actual security center for all the covert monitoring. The one I showed you in the house isn't that big."

Remi glanced around, making eye contact with the two guards on the fence line who were attempting to keep unobtrusive watch on them. Both gave small nods before continuing on their way.

His leopard smiled.

"Makes sense," he said in response to Auden's suggestion. "Easy to keep a subterranean area temperature controlled. Especially if the people working down there barely come in and out."

"We find out tonight." Auden's voice was even, but a fine tremor ran through her body. "If it's not important, we strike it off the list and carry on."

Remi didn't have to ask to know the reason for her rush. Her pain was a scent in the air, her love for her daughter altering the chemistry of her body. "Tonight," he promised. "We're not going to drag this out any longer than necessary."

"It's as if a part of me has been cut off, and I'm bleeding out in the open." She looked at her family home. "How can they not see? How can they not know?"

"Because they have no idea what it is to love like you do. Their fucking loss." He wished he could touch her, pet her, comfort her with skin privileges that had nothing to do with sex.

Then, and though she knew all this already, he told her again—because right now, Auden needed to hear it. "Finn will have set up a rotation of carers the instant we left. The cubs will also be allowed to come in and talk to her because Finn says cubs react happily to other cubs."

He could already imagine Jojo regaling Liberty with stories of her day, convinced that the baby could understand her even if Liberty couldn't talk yet. "The bigger ones will probably tell Liberty all about how Liberty got 'borned' early and that's how come she can't come outside to play yet."

No softening in her expression, but her eyes, those stunning, expressive eyes that no longer reminded him of anyone but Auden, went fuzzy with love. And his heart, it kicked with brutal force.

Auden Scott was it for Remi Denier.

Even if the metal never left her scent, even if she absorbed that colder aspect into her nature.

What if it goes the other way? A chilling whisper from the most primal part of his psyche, the one from times primeval when monsters stalked the dark. *What if this is a false dawn, and the other Auden is waiting in the wings to launch a final assault . . . an assault so deadly it forever erases your Auden?*

Chapter 39

H: Judd thinks he and Sienna and the others can save a few people through sheer psychic brute force, but they're hitting the same problem as always—changeling networks aren't designed to host Psy with whom we have no emotional link.

I've still gone ahead and blood-bonded as many children as I can from the region, and damn if the pups aren't in my heart now.

L: I've done the same and I've heard that pretty much all the other packs have signed on to attempt the same. But fuck, Hawke, even if it works, it's not going to be enough. We're going to lose tens of thousands of lives in San Francisco alone.

—Messages between Hawke Snow, alpha of the SnowDancer wolves, and Lucas Hunter, alpha of the DarkRiver leopards (today)

BACK UPSTAIRS, THE three of them checked Auden's bedroom again to ensure it remained clear of computronic spies. Rina also once again cleared the neighboring room, though she planned to sleep in leopard form high up in a tree on the property when it was her turn to rest.

"No one can attack me if they can't see me," the sentinel said as Auden slipped into the bathroom. "And trust me, they won't see me."

"I'll stay in Auden's room overnight." Remi touched the control to lower the blackout blinds before activating the lights. "I don't want her alone even though I know you'll be right outside the door."

"Normally," Rina muttered, her hands on her hips, "I'd tease you about just wanting to snuggle up to her, but after being in this house today . . ." She shuddered. "Something is *not* right. I didn't see anything I can pinpoint, but the way that doctor and Ms. Wai look at Auden? Creepy as fuck."

Never had Remi agreed more with a statement. "Did you bring the surveillance blocker with you?"

"It's in the kit," Rina confirmed, nodding at the corner of the room where she'd placed the case that could only be unlocked using a retinal scan alongside a complex code.

Remi shifted to unlock it—they never kept it locked when one of them was within reach and might need something from it.

"But you know it has a short radius," Rina reminded him. "Plus the blocking causes a literal blackout, so if someone is watching the feed, it'll be obvious."

"We'll be moving," he told her. "Feed will recover itself after a blip as we pass out of range. Just a glitch."

Rina raised an eyebrow. "Where are you planning on going?"

He told her about the basement and the possible trapdoor. "When it's time, you stay here, guard this room, while we sneak down. I want you to be a big gold and black distraction, make anyone who's watching think Auden is in the room."

Rina scowled. "How are you going to sneak her down? Even putting aside how recently she gave birth, she's not a cat, can't just climb out the window and jump."

"I've worked out a route that'll skirt most of the surveillance, and we can use the blocker on the few spots that remain. I'll scent anyone coming close regardless."

Retrieving the blocker, he rose to check the settings were as he needed them. "The real problem will be when we open that hatch—no way to know what's on the other side."

Auden, who'd returned from the bathroom having changed into loose pants and a sweatshirt, said, "I can do a telepathic scan. My telepathy isn't strong, but it exists. Enough for me to figure out if there are people on the other side of the trapdoor."

"Good girl," Remi murmured after walking close to her—and he used those words because he knew they did something to her.

Her breath caught now, her pupils flaring.

But they had no time to play, so he left it at that and waved Rina over. Then the three of them went through the plan step-by-step. Rina would have her phone beside her even when she was in leopard form, could respond to an SOS in under a minute. They also had to build in contingencies to deal with the situation if Remi and Auden found themselves without phone coverage once inside.

"Your Arrow friends won't be able to help." Auden's voice was heavy. "A member of the staff just sent out a household-wide telepathic alert about another major PsyNet collapse not far from here. So many people are dying." A shaking hand pressed to her mouth. "My baby is in that same Net."

Remi curved his hand around her nape, squeezed. "One problem at a time, Cupcake," he rumbled. "Libby is also blood-bonded to me, and we know Psy can survive in changeling packs even if cut off from the PsyNet."

Auden gave a jagged nod.

"We can handle tonight without the squad," Rina said after touching her hand to Auden's in silent comfort. "We've got four senior soldiers a bare five-minute run away—and oh, my baby brother, too. Because he's a cat who likes to poke his nose into everyone's business."

Auden frowned. "What?"

"Last-minute addition to the plan." Remi didn't mention that Kit had been cuddling Liberty while it was discussed. She didn't need the reminder of her baby, not when she'd almost been in tears when the medication wore off early and milk began to engorge her breasts.

She'd just given herself another dose—and from the redness in her eyes, she'd given in to the tears, too. He'd told her he could do it, press the injector to her skin, but she'd insisted on privacy and handling it herself.

"Time for you to get some rest, Rina," he said, both because it was the truth—and because he wanted to hold Auden. "I'll need you back on shift in a few hours, while I'm down."

Rina nodded. "I'll stay next door today. Wake me when you're heading to sleep."

After the sentinel left, he didn't hesitate to cuddle Auden into his arms.

But she flinched, her body as stiff as a board. "How can you want to touch me?" A raw statement. "I feel broken, tainted—and worse, I feel a failure because I'm not there for my child."

"You are none of those things," he said on a growl. "You are a warrior fighting for your child's future using all the tools at your disposal. You might not have claws, Auden, but you have a mind that's brilliant and a determination that's fucking unbreakable. No one and nothing will stand in your way when it comes to your cub."

Cupping the back of her head when she remained mute and rigid, he nipped her ear. She jolted . . . then seemed to crumple. "In the bathroom, it struck me that this is all illusionary." Her fingers gripping at his jacket. "A phase where I'm ascendant and the other Auden isn't. What if it flips in another week?"

Pushing out of his arms, she paced around the room. "There are no guarantees, Remi. Not even if we figure out why they want Liberty so much!" She tapped the side of her head. "Scars don't just vanish. Not scars like this." Her chest heaved, her breathing erratic. "How can I go back to my baby when I don't know who I am?"

Remi snarled. "*I* know. All you have to do is trust me—I'll lock you the fuck up if you turn into the other Auden. I can scent her, remember?" He gripped her jaw. "Because, little cat? I'm not letting you go."

"You made me a promise." A harsh rasp, Auden toe-to-toe with him.

She was fucking incredible.

"I promised to take you out if you become a threat to Liberty." Remi ran the pad of his thumb over her lower lip. "You can't become that if I rip you the hell away from her the instant your scent changes."

"You can't be there all the time!"

He smiled, and knew it was a thing wild, without boundaries. "You'll be living in a pack, Auden. I can make it so you're never alone with Liberty if that's what it takes to make you feel safe. Any member of the pack will grab her and run if you start to turn."

"What if I become that other Auden forever?" Auden knew she shouldn't have asked the question, that there was no good answer, but she pushed at the wound, wanting him to strike out, throw her away.

Remi's words, when they came, were quiet—and slammed into her like bullets. "You might lose all your memories of us, Cupcake, but I'll still have them. And however long you have with our tiny kitten, she'll have them." Claws brushing her cheek. "No matter what, your name will be carved onto our hearts for all eternity."

She crumpled against his chest again, sinking into the protective warmth of his embrace, this man who saw all of her, and still wanted her. Why was she fighting with him? Because she was angry at herself? At her parents? At fate?

She didn't know. What she did know was that the idea of losing her memories of Remi was as horrifying a thought as losing her memories of Liberty. Because this alpha leopard had become as much a part of her as her child, his growl, his arms, his beard-shadowed jaw safety to her.

"I'm going to write her letters," she whispered against his chest. "While I'm still me, I'll write her letters that I need you to keep for her if nothing we do works and I turn into the other me."

Remi's body went rock-hard, a block cold and jagged, but he didn't interrupt.

"I want her to know I loved her. So much." Her throat grew thick, her eyes burning. "I want my baby to grow up knowing she was the best thing that ever happened to me."

Remi's chest rumbled, his hand warm and protective as he cradled the back of her head. "She'll know. No matter what, she'll know."

Sobs rocking her, Auden cried. But she only gave herself so much time, no more. Because she couldn't break down. She had to use the time she had as herself. "While we wait for the house to settle," she said, wiping her face on the backs of her forearms, "I'll see what I can dig up on the system. Rina said she put my organizer with your kit."

Remi didn't argue—he probably saw how close she was to the edge, how much she needed to do something for her baby. "Yes."

After retrieving it for her, he said, "I'll duck into the bathroom and change out of this suit. Mliss handed our stuff over to Rina at the gate, so no one in your house has had a chance to embed anything in them."

"Change here," Auden whispered from where she sat on the bed, because the idea of seeing all that masculine beauty made her skin stretch, dulled the pain until it no longer throbbed like blades in the skin.

"You can scent me." She used his own words against him because it had struck her all over again that her life—as *Auden*—could end without ever experiencing intimate touch at Remi's hands. And this time, it wasn't a realization she could fight, wasn't a panic she could think away. It was too deep, too vicious. "Please be with me while I'm me. While I know you."

"*Auden*. We've already talked about this. Anything we do, we do on our own timeline."

"I know . . . but I've realized . . . I need that time to be now. I need something good to balance out the ugliness of this house, of my family, of my *entire life*." She swallowed her tears, fisting her hands in the sheet. "I need you, Remi."

"You've just given birth." It came out a growl.

"I'm healed, thanks to the insane amount of money your pack blew on me." She tried to smile at the words she'd meant to be light. "My hormones *are* all over the place, my emotions a huge storm, but they're not affecting my ability to think—and while I might still be trembling from the shock of the birth, it was the most beautiful shock of my life.

If I'm shaken, it's in joy. If I'm lost, it's only because I'm a new mother. There's nothing bad in it."

The tears burned her irises now. "And you. You're the most extraordinary, wonderful shock I could've ever imagined—and I don't want to miss out on knowing you in this way that's integral to your nature. Each time I close my eyes, I'm afraid I won't wake up as me. *Please*, Remi. Give me this piece of you to fight the nightmares."

A growl before he reached up to undo his tie. "I'm going to spank you later for disrupting all my plans," he threatened . . . only it wasn't a threat at all.

His voice was thick, leopard eyes awash in emotion.

The alpha heart of him, it wrapped her in its embrace, holding her close to his primal warmth.

"You're making me break all the rules." Tie off, he looked at it for a long moment before hanging it carefully over the end of the headboard. His jacket he threw over the armchair after prowling over to that side of the bed.

Then, eyes of green-gold locked with hers, he began to undo his shirt. "Only for you," he murmured in that rough, deep voice. "You understand that, Auden? I don't let go of what's mine."

Her tears retreated under a wave of languorous warmth that made her toes curl. "Yes," she whispered. "I understand."

Her breath was no longer in any way steady, her breasts so tight that she was afraid the medication had worn off again, but when she touched one taut mound, it felt different. Hot, wanting.

Remi's gaze followed her hand as he continued to open button after button to reveal a strip of golden skin faintly dusted with dark hair. "Take off your sweatshirt and touch yourself just that way." It was an order.

The part of Auden that had been fighting for her freedom all her life thought she should rebel, couldn't understand why she didn't want to.

"It's a game, little cat." Piercing tenderness in Remi's deep purr. "Played only between us. Because it makes you wet and me hard."

The blunt carnal statement twined with raw affection had a whimper escaping her mouth and any thoughts of clinging to control slipping out of her grasp. As he pulled his shirt out of his pants to finish unbuttoning it, she reached for the bottom of her sweatshirt and pulled it over her head in a single move.

Remi hissed out a breath at her exposed body, her breasts bare because they'd ached too much for her to put her bra back on when the medication first wore off. "Fucking beautiful." A petting growl that felt like a touch. "Do it. Hands on those gorgeous tits."

The words he used, so rough and unpolished, they only made her . . . wetter. So wet that she saw his nostrils flare.

"Good girl," he purred again. "That's how I like you, so wet your musk sticks to my throat and makes me want to lick you up." A narrowed gaze. "But we can't do that yet—and we definitely can't give my cock what it wants—because that'd be going straight to a hundred from a standing start. So we'll do something else."

He flicked a look at her unmoving hands. "*Do what I said, Auden*"— his voice dropping an octave—"*or you'll be punished*."

A game, she remembered. This was a game he was playing with her. Because cats liked to play games . . . and her lover was a cat.

A big, gorgeous, prowling predator.

He was also brutally protective. Never would he hurt her—or allow her to hurt herself.

She raised her hands to her breasts. She didn't know what to do at first, just cupped them . . . and felt sensation shoot through her. Especially when he growled his approval and ripped off his shirt to throw it atop his jacket.

His hands dropped to his belt and so did her eyes . . . the belt, and the rigid bulge underneath. Her hands tightened on her breasts of their own volition, but she eased up when her nipples protested with a sharp twinge of pain. "They're too sensitive," she found herself saying in a whisper, as if in apology.

"See, my sweet, delicious Auden, you know how to play this game."

Sliding out his belt on that silken statement of approval, he folded it in half, then prowled over to run the strip of leather up her leg, over her abdomen, and up to tap against one heavy breast. "Because that's what a good girl does. She tells her lover what feels hot, what doesn't, and every single one of the naughtiest fantasies inside her beautiful head."

A kiss, the belt thrown aside as he knelt on the bed and circled her throat with his hand while pressing her lips open with his own lips and tongue. There was nothing tentative or exploratory about this kiss—it held the stamp of ownership, as did the hand around her throat that tightened the merest fraction just then.

She shuddered and clutched at him with her hands.

Breaking the kiss, he smiled again, those wild eyes so inhuman that she felt it: she was in bed with a predator. Claws and teeth . . . and a cock that wanted to mount her. Her cheeks flushed at her own thoughts.

"So, my Auden likes this." He ran the pad of his thumb over the skitter of the pulse in her throat. "Maybe I'll get you a necklace with a little lock pendant on it. A reminder of who you call lover—the *only* man you'll ever call lover." A kiss proprietary and raw, his hand stroking her throat as he made love to her mouth in ways she hadn't known were possible.

Then he kissed his way across her cheek and whispered in her ear. "The necklace would be for when you're in public. In private, I might just put a collar on you and have you wear that and nothing else."

Auden's entire being felt as if it was liquid. She ached, but she didn't know for what.

"Shh." Another kiss, his hand cupping her breast—but being careful not to brush her nipple. "Does this hurt?"

"N-no," she gasped out. "But my . . . nipple. I think it's too tender." There was no awkwardness in admitting that, in referring obliquely to the reason why her breasts ached and her nipple was unbearably tender. Because it was Remi. Her Remi.

"There you go, being my good girl again." A nuzzle, a stroke of her hip that was so affectionate her eyes burned. "I know what you need."

Removing the rough warmth of his hand from her breast and throat, he said, "Offer your breast to me."

Desperate to have him come back, she cupped her breasts as she'd done before, and said, "Please."

His pupils expanded and then he was dipping his head and all that dark hair was brushing over her sensitized skin as he gently—*so gently*—suckled a wet kiss to the underside of her hypersensitive breast. The heat, the wet, it was everything and it was too much.

She cried out.

Just as Remi inserted his hand into her pants and nudged up with his knuckles.

Her thighs clamped around his hand, her hands tight in his hair, her body and mind flying apart in a surge of pleasure as primal as the man who'd given it to her.

The last thing she remembered hearing before she lost her senses was Remi's growl in her ear. "Oh, you're going to be one hell of a playmate. I can't wait to have my mouth on your pussy . . . and your pretty, pretty mouth on my cock."

Auden's brain exploded.

Chapter 40

Henry will one day understand that I did him a favor. Auden was never suitable to take over his position as head of the Jackson family. Had the biograft succeeded, he'd have ended up with a child with an active ability; the graft was designed to expand her neural pathways and trigger a large-scale psychic expansion *outside* of her passive main ability.

I had hoped for a significant Gradient increase in her already-existing basic Tp. It seemed to me that "stretching" Auden's mind to make her more powerful had a higher chance of success than attempting to trigger a wholly new ability. That the endeavor failed has cost Henry nothing— Auden was already a useless part of his genetic legacy. He can no doubt create another child soon enough.

—Shoshanna Scott's private notes (20 February 2076)

AUDEN SWAM TO consciousness with the awareness that someone was stroking her breast to hip and back again with a lazily feline touch. Shivering, she opened her eyes to look into those so wild, she'd never mistake them for human.

"There you are." A purr of sound before Remi brushed his lips over hers.

She was so, so glad that the Arrow who was protecting her mind had created a second layer of shielding so that nothing of her emotions got through to them. Because she'd lost control at the end there, become nothing but a creature of flesh and pleasure.

"I didn't get to see all of you," she complained, her voice coming out rough.

Had she screamed at the end? Had he kissed her to capture the sound? It was hazy, her brain blurred with the sensations erotic and more extraordinary than she could've ever imagined. Because, unlike the videos she'd watched to teach herself about the intricacies of sexual intimacy, it hadn't been about just the body. She hadn't understood that until he touched her with such care, until he *took* such care with her.

Remi Denier had ruined her. She'd crave him to the end of her days.

"I wanted to see you," she said, turning into him, greedy and needy and unashamed about it—because it was him.

Taking her hand, he brought it to his body. "Oh, that was only the first act."

She gasped as her hand met the hard, warm ridge of his arousal. He was naked.

Heat rolling over her in a luxuriant wave, she glanced down. Her hand looked small and fine against the veined thickness of him, and she found herself thinking about what he'd said at the end. About her mouth.

Her stomach clenched. She'd never even considered she might want to do the act he'd described, but now . . .

She looked up at him. "Can I? What you said. With my mouth."

Claws against her skin as he stroked her back. "Zero to a hundred," he said, his purr more of a growl now—but intermingled within was laughter affectionate and intimate.

She nuzzled his throat as he'd done her, felt him smile.

"You know your limits, Cupcake?" That clawed hand curling around her throat. "Hmm?"

"No," she admitted, that pet name making her all warm and silly and happy inside. "That's why I have to trust you to stop me if I push it too far."

He kissed her, hard and deep and with such possessiveness that her inner muscles clenched again. They felt a little bruised, but in a good way. A delicious hurt. And that without him ever being inside her. She didn't know what would happen to her when he pushed his thickness inside her.

The idea made her squeeze her thighs together, the pressure exquisite.

"You are such a sexy bite of woman." He nipped at her lower lip. "And I do want to see this luscious mouth of yours on me. But I want to lick you to pleasure first. And even if it's physically safe, you're not ready."

Auden trusted his judgment—and given how hard she'd orgasmed after what they'd just done, she wasn't sure she'd survive the intimacy of his mouth on her most private flesh.

"Please," she begged, stroking her hand over him. "I really want to try." Her mouth watered, her breasts aching. "*Remi*."

A groan before he put his hand on her shoulder and pushed gently down. But before she could move, he reached behind her to release her hair from its bun. "I need something to hold," he said on a growl. "So I can show you how to move your pretty mouth on me."

Her heart was a drum, her entire body electrified.

This time, he didn't stop her . . . but he did have his hand in her hair. He didn't push her when she just looked at him, stroking him with one hand. His thigh muscles had gone rock-hard, however, his breathing jagged.

It did things to her that she could affect him as much as he affected her.

He was so hot and hard in her hand that she felt like she could stroke him forever, but she got a tug on her hair now, a sign that her wild lover didn't have endless patience.

It made her even wetter, hotter.

Dipping her head, she closed her mouth over the tip of him. His hand fisted in her hair, his body rigid. "*Fuck*." A low growl.

Confidence in her blood now, she drew him deeper and sucked a little. She knew she had zero technique, and no idea what she was doing, but he did what he'd said—he directed her. And she loved it.

Hands on his thighs, she found herself coaxed into a stroking motion with her mouth. Still shallow, nothing forceful, letting her get used to him. And oh, she liked it. Loved being able to give him intimate pleasure, loved the scent of him, the feel of him.

"Fuck," he gritted out again, his hand tight in her hair. "I'm going to come. In your mouth or on your breasts, those are your choices."

Auden's brain hazed again.

Lifting her mouth, she said, "Breasts," even though she wasn't conscious of making a decision.

Wet heat on her flesh, the intimacy of it searing.

Even more intimate was what came after. Remi carrying her to the shower, stripping her, then stepping into the cubicle with her and soaping her all over. He wouldn't let her do it in return however. "I need to prepare for the op," he said, kissing her neck from behind as he stroked the flare of her hips. "I will not be able to do that, beautiful, if you keep putting your hands on me."

Auden loved how he said those things to her . . . how he meant them. Even though her body wasn't taut and trim as she'd seen on changelings. She'd just had a baby, but even before those changes, she'd always been more curves than muscle.

But it turned out that Remi did love her "cuddlier" form.

She saw that in the wickedness of his grin when he toweled her dry, and felt it in the playfulness of his kiss and the little slap he gave her bottom. He enjoyed her body. She'd never known how good such a simple thing could feel.

The happiness buzzed through her even after she'd gotten into some comfortable clothes and sat down in bed with the organizer she'd abandoned earlier. Remi, dressed only in sweatpants, lounged beside her on one arm, his eyes on the screen. "Where are you going to look?"

"First, I have to link into the house system, but that shouldn't be too hard since I'm on-site." It only took her a minute, her mind clear on the process. "I was able to get into some secure files before, so I'll try there first. Might be a clue in old documents they forgot to move to a vault."

But after touching the screen to bring up the necessary access page, she found herself entering code after code in an unbroken chain. Shimmering, the screen went blank for a moment before clearing to reveal a stark dual S symbol in solid black against a starlit background. Black on black, the symbol erasing the stars beyond.

Auden gasped and peered closer.

"What is it?" Remi's previously languid form was predator-ready.

"My mother's private mainframe—remote access to it, anyway." Auden's heart was thunder in her chest. "I have no idea where it's actually located, but I know it exists. My father mentioned it to me at some point."

"Auden?" Remi's big body sitting up next to her now, his arm braced behind her.

Making a listening sound, she frantically scanned the files that were opening out in front of her in a rapid-fire cascade. She was half-afraid they'd vanish as fast as they'd appeared.

"Are you sure you don't know the physical location?"

She started to ask how would she, when she realized what she'd just done. Face going ice-cold then red-hot, she slumped back against his arm. "How do I know? How could any part of *me* know?"

She jolted forward a heartbeat later. "The answers might be in here. This is the heart of all her operations."

"Could she have told you the access codes while you were impaired?"

"No," Auden said at once. "This was *her* private archive. She'd rather have let it crumble to dust than allow anyone else inside."

Her fingers moved on the screen, pulling out data, drilling through files. "What's this? 'Architect.'" She frowned. "It's a sizeable subsection of the files."

Remi whistled, the air of it brushing her cheek as his naked upper body curved slightly around her. "The Architect," he said. "Arrows told me about that. Individual behind terrorism designed to destabilize the world and fracture the Trinity Accord."

"Hmm." Auden scanned the files before putting them aside.

"No surprise she was the Architect?"

"My mother loved power more than anything else in the world. Manipulation like that sounds right up her alley." A sharp stab of pain in her temple, agony so visceral that it burst blood vessels in her eyes.

REMI smelled blood before he saw the first drop fall from Auden's nose to the screen of the organizer.

Her face was frozen, gone blank, the metal in her scent beginning to deepen.

In transition.

Not permitting himself to second-guess his plans, he moved at leopard speed to the kit. Inside was his ace in the hole.

He was shoving it into her hand in a matter of a second or two.

Auden's fingers spasmed to clench around the tiny knit cap.

Her body jerked an instant after that. "My *baby*." A whisper. "I can feel her. So unformed, her thoughts more sensation than anything else. I feel Finn, too. Affection, care. Another person, the person who made this. Concentration. Cramped hands. Happiness. And I feel you. Wild protectiveness. A feral love."

Remi's heart squeezed. "You're bleeding. I'm going to grab tissues from the bathroom." He did so even as he spoke. "Here."

She dabbed at her nose with her free hand, her other holding on to the knit cap so hard that a vein on the back of her hand throbbed. After she finally stopped bleeding, she went into the bathroom to clean up.

The woman who walked out of the bathroom was cool, calm, collected . . . and held that knit cap as if it was the most precious diamond in all the world. After lifting it to her mouth, she pressed a kiss to it, then held it out to him. "Just in case."

He took it and knew he was breaking her heart in doing so, even if she had asked. "I'll keep it safe."

"I know." Her trust was a punch to the heart, bringing him to his knees.

"What happened, little cat?"

"Rage formed of Silence," she murmured. "An overwhelming sensation of cold beneath the rage, and I could swear it was directed at me for being inside the private archive." Her eyes narrowed. "But I don't care if the other me doesn't want me looking."

She sat down again, her face grim. "Let's find out what I'm not meant to see."

But though she spent hours in there, there was too much material to wade through to find anything—even when she tried using her own name as a search term. The only thing she was able to confirm was that Henry hadn't known about the biograft. That didn't alter what he'd done in giving her up, and she'd already accepted that the father she'd once loved had never existed.

She finally gave up at eleven, her eyes gritty, knowing she had to be up in four hours to access the basement.

THEY made their move at three in the morning, long after everything had gone quiet. Rina had already prowled the corridors in leopard form, and Auden could well imagine the reaction of anyone who ran across her during her patrol, those nightglow eyes a warning to the hindbrain.

The sentinel had told Remi that the staff had left the premises, with only Charisma Wai in the house. Last Rina had seen—ten minutes ago—the aide had been alone in her office. "Dr. Verhoeven's still up, too—I did a quick sortie outside, spotted him inside his lab. But," the sentinel had added, "I did just hear the back door open and close, so either Wai's gone out or someone else has entered. Interval between open and close was too short for more than one person to come in or go out. You want me to do another sweep, make sure?"

"No," Remi had said. "A single extra person shouldn't cause us any problems."

Rina had further confirmed that the lighting through the hallways was on muted night settings, and any lights set to activate to motion—such as in the kitchen—had also switched over to the night settings.

Now Auden fixed a black knit cap over her head, having already pulled her hair back in a tight bun to create a sleeker fit. Remi had scowled at her action, and she'd blushed, thinking of how he'd fisted his hand in her curls, and how later, when she'd put it up for the shower, he'd purred to her about how much he loved her hair.

She'd learn to do the same, she decided then and there, to give him frank words of appreciation and affection. She'd tell him she loved the breadth of his shoulders, was fascinated by how he had a hundred colors in his hair, that his thigh muscles made her mouth water, and his smile caused the butterflies in her stomach to take flight.

She adored everything about Remi.

Cap on, she smoothed her hands down her black sweater. It was the same shade as the cap and the tights on her legs. She'd even pulled on the gloves she used to dull her psychometric sensitivity in day-to-day life.

"You look like a cat burglar." The stroke of a big hand down the curve of her spine.

Her skin shimmered beneath her clothing, attuned to his touch as she'd never before been attuned to anyone. She hadn't even thought this was possible for her.

Then had come a leopard alpha who'd taught her to shoot, fed her delicious pastries, and made her laugh . . . and in the doing, prowled right into her heart.

Unable to not touch him when he was near, she ran her hand down his black T-shirt, his lower body clad in cargo pants the same color. His boots were dark and heavy and she had no idea how he managed to move with graceful silence in them. She'd gone for simple trainers because Remi had told her socked feet were too much of a risk, given that they had no idea what surfaces they'd face under the trapdoor if it proved to not be a hidden security suite.

"I'll try to be as quiet as possible." She knew she had nowhere near his stealth, but she wasn't about to let him fight her battles, take all the risks.

A quick kiss that made her warm inside before they set off.

Auden had already seen Rina in leopard form when the other woman entered the bedroom to give her report earlier. Despite their previous encounter, however, she sucked in a soundless breath at seeing the leopard who sat against the wall opposite the bedroom door, its tail curled on the polished wood of the floor.

Never, she thought, would she become used to the wonder of it.

The jungle cat rose to walk over to Remi, allow him to run his fingers over the top of her head. "Two hours max," Remi murmured. "Any longer without contact and you send in the troops."

Rina rumbled low in her chest in acknowledgment, the sound more vibration than actual audible noise. Her tail brushed against Auden's leg at the same instant that she turned to situate herself against their bedroom door, and Remi indicated for Auden to follow him.

It was time to unearth the secrets of Shoshanna's house.

Chapter 41

I need the strike team ready and waiting to move on my mark.

—Charisma Wai to the head of Scott household security (five hours ago)

REMI HATED THE feel of this house. It ruffled his leopard's fur the wrong way and made him want to tear it down, start again. Place was elegant on the outside, but so damaged by decades of loneliness and ice and secrets that it couldn't be renovated to a better state.

The cold was in the walls itself.

He'd wondered how Auden could bear to touch it, had asked her earlier without pressing on the wound. "What about all the contact points in this house?" he'd said, after he'd stroked her to bone-melting softness before they fell asleep. "I've seen you touch things without any impact."

A yawn before she'd answered. "Seems to happen with psychometrics and their long-term residences. Might be a survival instinct. We stop sensing the space and things attached to it unless we make a conscious effort. I only had trouble during my pregnancy but I had trouble with *everything* then so was hyper-conscious of any direct contact."

Another yawn, her eyes closing. "I do pick up imprints from any new object placed in the house, which is why I usually avoid new things until they're at least a year old—there's a scientist in the psychometric group I belong to online, and his theory is that our brains connect a new object to our residence after a period of time, at which point they become safe."

Her voice had turned into a near-mumble. "An artefact of evolution, he says. Only those psychometrics who had this ability to nullify their domestic environment surviv . . ."

She'd fallen asleep in his arms, her hair wrapped up in a silk scarf of a simple gray, and her face soft in rest, but—and despite the pleasure they'd shared—the shadows under her eyes no less deep. He'd known she'd dream of Liberty, would wake with worry for her child's future heavy on her heart.

He'd held her as he slept himself, confident that Rina would alert him to any threat—and confident, too, in his own instincts. Remi's leopard would never allow an intruder to get close.

Now he held up a hand, then pointed ahead at a spot in the wall that held a surveillance device. When he made a downward motion, he heard Auden go flat on the ground. They'd discussed this after they'd woken, with Remi having already mapped out their entire route.

It infuriated him that she had to sneak around her own fucking house, but he was willing to play this game to find out why Charisma Wai and her pet doctor wanted a tiny, vulnerable infant enough to impregnate Auden. She hadn't spelled that out to him, but she hadn't needed to—he'd figured it out given all the other pieces of information.

These people had stolen even her consent.

They crawled five meters before he gave the signal for Auden to rise, but neither one of them had made a move to get up when he caught the sound of a voice. He held up his hand again, signaling Auden to stay down.

Less noise that way, less chance of attracting attention.

Cocking his head, he tried to pinpoint the source of the sound . . . and realized it was coming from the partially open door of the room three doors up to the left. No light showed through, and he couldn't quite hear what was being said, but it appeared Charisma Wai remained where Rina had last spotted her—in her office.

He made a quick decision.

Rising in a smooth motion, he turned and all but lifted Auden up onto her feet, to lessen the chance of extraneous noise. He put a finger to his lips afterward and had her follow him to the other side of the hall and nearer to the door. He could hear parts of the conversation already, but aware that Auden's hearing was less acute than his, he took them to right beside the door.

A careful glance inside told him why he couldn't see any light—Charisma Wai was sitting in a chair at her desk, with the desk lamp illuminating only the immediate area.

She wasn't alone.

Though Remi could only see the back of her companion's head, it wasn't hard to identify him from the conversation: the doctor who'd violated Auden. Verhoeven was the person Rina had heard open and close the back door.

". . . neurological recovery is remarkable," he was saying, "and something I'd write a paper on in other circumstances."

"Will the drug you've suggested risk her brain?" Charisma Wai asked.

"No. I'd never permit that. It would nullify the point of the entire project."

"This brain isn't the important one," Charisma said, her tone off-handed. "We need the infant."

"Have your hunters had any luck locating it? I did look on the PsyNet, but Auden's entire mind is surrounded by an impenetrable shield, and the child will be within that."

"No," Charisma gritted out. "We should've embedded a tracker in the infant in utero, as I suggested."

Remi met Auden's gaze, saw the rage within, and shook his head. These two would pay, but they couldn't risk tipping their hand just yet.

Auden squeezed her eyes shut, but stayed in place.

"The risk was too high," Verhoeven said. "But regardless, we must confirm if the temporary transfer is complete. Have you worked out how we can get Auden to the infirmary for the necessary tests without her bodyguards?"

"No point in subtlety. A strike team is assembling to move in within the hour. Changelings are fast, but bullets and lasers are faster."

Remi's claws pricked at his skin, but he shook his head at Auden again when she bared her teeth in a snarl. Not yet. Let the assholes talk.

"Is that wise?" Verhoeven asked. "The death of an alpha changeling will cause political ripples."

"He's acting as a bodyguard. He got in the way of an assassination attempt. And it isn't as if his pack is powerful enough to take on this family." Charisma's voice was unconcerned. "As for Auden, I don't know. She has knowledge she shouldn't have, but she also responds in ways that aren't *quite* right."

"A partial integration?" the doctor said. "In all honesty, I'm finding it increasingly hard to connect on the other end so I can't confirm. The psychic fragmentation has picked up speed. If the integration has failed with Auden, we need the child as soon as possible."

A tapping sound, nails against a wooden desk. "She should've never attempted Auden's mind again. It was always meant to be the infant. Undamaged. A pristine canvas."

"Unfortunately, we are not the ones making the choice."

The scrape of a chair. "We need to rest, be ready to move after the strike team has done its job."

Remi nudged at a trembling-with-anger Auden to move down the hall. He followed her in a stealth of shadows, blending in with the dark like the cat under his skin. He could feel her desperation to talk to him, discuss what they'd just heard, but fury or not, she held to their plan and maintained complete silence all the way to the basement storage area.

Once there, he put his lips to her ear. "Liberty is safe. Whatever happens, these bastards will never get their hands on her. My pack will rip out their throats before that and Zaira will join in."

"Yes." Then she turned, took his face in her hands. "And *I* will shoot them dead before they ever get a bead on you or Rina." Fury in the kiss she laid on him, a depth of protectiveness that was rarely directed toward Remi.

He was the alpha. He was the protector.

Except, it seemed, to his mate. Because of course that's what she was to him. Some part of him had known that since the start; that was why he'd allowed her touch that first day, and why his leopard had reacted so badly to her apparent inability to be the partner he needed.

"No more." Auden's whisper was rough and low but potent. "We find out tonight, even if that means we hold Charisma and the doctor down and inject them with their own fucking drugs!"

He growled in agreement before pulling out his phone to send Rina a text alerting her to the incoming strike team: Prep our people, but don't move until the last possible minute. We need them to believe we're exactly where they think we are for as long as possible.

Not expecting an answer given her current form, he slid away the phone, then hunkered down to begin searching for an access point.

Auden's hand on his shoulder, her leg pressing into his side. "Switch is on the wall to the left, behind the shelf that holds the long-life protein bars." Her voice was ice, the hand on his shoulder warm. "There is no threat immediately underneath the hatch."

The hairs on his nape rising, he looked up into those eyes of moonstone blue, and saw a woman of frigid control looking back at him . . . but beyond the control burned the rage of her need to protect those she had claimed.

Bleedover.

With Auden in control. Because his fucking mate wasn't about to allow *anyone*, even another part of her psyche, to get in the way of her protecting her people. That metal in her scent? It had returned, but as such a fine thread that it had no chance of overpowering her.

Rising, he crouched down by the shelf she'd indicated, removed the two boxes of protein bars . . . and there it was. A slight depression in the wall that would be invisible if you weren't looking for it.

Heart thumping, he pressed his thumb to it.

Nothing.

"It's DNA encoded." Coming down beside him, Auden put her thumb to the depression.

The hatch slid back with soundless precision.

Looking at it, Auden's eyes narrowed. "Let's go find out who the fuck is trying to hurt my child and my man."

Remi's leopard rumbled in his chest, furious with pride, his own anger claws against his fingertips.

After squeezing her nape, he went ahead.

The hatch had exposed a well-made set of stairs. Nothing rickety. These were gleaming clean plascrete. Despite Auden's ability to open the entrance, he scanned the stairs using the same device he and Rina had used to clear the rooms. Security was about taking the extra step, looking behind each door twice.

"Clean," he said.

"Because only people with the right DNA can get in," Auden said, the ice now a mere element of her voice rather than all of it. "Why DNA encode access for a woman who had brain damage?"

Remi had no answers for her, but—"We find out tonight."

Auden's jaw grew hard. "Yes." She put a hand on his arm when he would've entered the hatch. "I go first. There may be a secondary DNA confirmation on entry—the way these systems work, I should be able to take an unknown individual with me if I go first."

Every one of Remi's instincts struggled against allowing her to go first into possible danger, but he knew the kind of high-end system she was talking about—if anyone might have one in the house, it would be the Scott family. "Go," he said, muscles bunched in readiness to haul her out at the first sign of danger.

Auden didn't hesitate, and took three steps down. "Now."

Remi stepped in after her.

Nothing happened until they were at the bottom of the short flight. At which point, Auden reached to her left and pressed her thumb against another small depression, and the hatch slid shut above them.

The lights brightened at the same time, to reveal that they stood in a small room in front of the heavy steel cage of an elevator. The doors gleamed at them, their mirror images grim-faced.

Auden stepped forward and touched another depression, while Remi did a second scan.

"Still clean," he said, slipping the device into his back pocket.

"We can talk," Auden confirmed. "No one would dare monitor me in such a way." Once again, her voice had shifted to a far icier version of the one he knew, but the fire in her gaze was his Auden, the way she stared at the doors to the elevator pure rage.

"What's happening, Cupcake?" He deliberately used his private little name for her, wanting to touch that part of her that got all soft and happy when she heard it.

"I don't know. But I'm me. The me that would die for Liberty—and kill for her."

The last came out as grim as the cold dark of midnight. It didn't bother him. He'd kill for little Liberty, too, would kill for any of the cubs in his pack.

He let his claws slice out as he brushed her cheek. "Let's go find the fuckers."

Her smile was deadly.

The lift doors opened at that moment.

Remi was already in position to attack should they find a threat, but the woman in the cage wore white scrubs with the Scott logo on the pocket and was holding an organizer. She was blond, about five feet four, her build stocky. And Remi hadn't seen or scented her in the house even once since their arrival.

Her pupils expanded as she stared at Auden. Her gaze flicked to Auden's belly, then back up.

"The plans have changed," Auden said, the words clipped and remote and coming from the part of her that wasn't her . . . but that had become infected with her love for her child. "The infant didn't survive. We have to complete a permanent transfer to this brain."

"Oh no." The nurse or doctor shifted back, so Auden and Remi could step inside the lift with her. "Did Dr. Verhoeven authorize it?" A hesitant question as the lift doors closed. "You know he has significant concerns about this brain even though you prepared the telepathic interlock over many years."

An ugly truth emerging in the recesses of her mind, Auden looked at the other woman without speaking until the blonde dropped her gaze. A pulse jumped in her neck, faint perspiration breaking out over her upper lip.

"*I* am making the decisions now," Auden said, sick to her gut. "You would do well to remember that, Nurse Lomax." The name fell from her lips as if she'd always known it.

"Yes, of course, sir." The woman tapped at her organizer. "I was actually on my way to consult with the doctor. Your brain patterns are destabilizing even further."

"How bad?" she asked, as the other part of her retreated without warning, but Auden didn't need her anymore.

The monstrous truth was taking darker and darker shape inside her mind.

"A fifty percent decline in a matter of hours." The nurse dared meet her gaze. "We might lose the pattern altogether if we don't finalize the integration tonight."

"Just as well I'm here then," Auden said.

—*how long this brain will function*—

—*integration*—

—*a pristine canvas*—

—*telepathic interlock*—

—*destabilizing*—

Her gaze met Remi's, and in the feral green-gold of his eyes, she saw the same realization as her own.

The doors opened in front of them.

When Auden stepped out, the nurse hesitated. "Should I fetch the doctor? He's the only one you taught to oversee the mechanics of the integration—and he needs to be on standby in case of heart failure, as happened the first time you attempted a full transfer to this brain as a stopgap measure."

Heart failure. And they wanted to do the same thing to her tiny, fragile, cherished baby?

Auden would murder each and every one.

The other part of her surged to the surface before she gave in to maternal rage—because that part had merged with her core nature, *was* her now. And that part loved Liberty, but could keep a cool head at the same time even in its murderous rage.

"Verhoeven can do nothing," she said, frigid contempt in her tone. "His job was to maintain the pattern and the fetus—both tasks at which he has failed." Her tone of voice made it clear that the doctor would not appreciate the cost of failure.

The nurse went pale.

Silent or not, everyone valued their skin.

"Yes, sir." The nurse stepped out. "Should I come . . . ?"

"Yes," Auden said, as the other part of her faded out, a wave surging in and out. "You may as well give me a full update while we walk. I haven't had a chance to read the latest report."

She was aware of Remi falling into step behind them.

When the nurse glanced back and hesitated, Auden said, "He's mine," and the words felt right in the purest sense, with no connection to power or control. He was hers . . . as she was his. And Liberty was theirs. A symbiosis of love. "You can speak freely."

"Yes, sir," the nurse said with compliant obedience, and led her into a long and scrupulously clean tunnel before beginning a rundown using complex medical terminology that went right over Auden's head.

But one thing was clear: the nurse was talking about a person.

A person whose brain patterns had begun to falter.

A person who needed a *new brain.*

A person who everyone in this household was doing everything they could to assist in what was, quite frankly, an insane endeavor. Because even the most powerful Psy in the world couldn't just move their consciousness into another brain.

She felt no surprise at all when they emerged into a large chamber with white walls, two hospital beds, and masses of complex medical machinery to see the emaciated form of her dead mother.

Chapter 42

Auden will never be my first choice for transference, but her brain injury provided me with perfect access to test my idea of telepathic mesh. She was a malleable doll as far as her mind was concerned—and though attempts at psychic control failed as they always do because of the energy requirements, I was able to overlay a mesh over her mind that permits me to hook into it. Into *her.*

It's nowhere near as smooth a transition as with my Scarabs, but those transitions are temporary *and* any such transition wouldn't give me access to my web. It would also leave me stuck in the mind of a being without power, without wealth, just another weak pawn on the chessboard.

It's possible Auden has a dormant ability to web that I can uncover. But I'm not relying on that. Neither do I have any intention of being stuck in a damaged brain. I will *create* the brain I need for the next phase of my evolution, and this time, I'll begin to build the mesh from the moment of my host's birth.

—Private journal of Shoshanna Scott (personal archive, address unknown)

"THE BODY HAS degraded even further than I recalled," Auden said with clinical detachment, and this time, it wasn't the other part of her. It was anger so profound that it was a sheet of glass over her emotions.

Because if she let it go, if she cracked the glass, she would be a thing out of control, a mother who *loved*, a mother who would beat in the brains of the *thing* on the hospital bed.

What had once been Shoshanna Scott was a much-too-small lump of a torso with a head. No arms. No legs. Not even a full torso. "Alive" only because she was hooked up to so many machines that she had become some science fiction writer's macabre creation—a human brain at the heart of a network.

"Yes, I'm afraid even with the amputations, the Councilor took too much energy from her body and organs in her valiant effort to keep her brain alive." A glance at Auden, back at the bed. "I don't know what to call you and her, sir."

"Stick with the usual," Auden said. "It'll make it easier for both of us, and it'll ensure you don't slip up in the future."

"Yes, of course," the nurse said, and Auden wondered if she had any idea of her likely fate if Shoshanna *had* come back in Auden's body.

The nurse would have had to die.

As would the doctor.

The chance of a leak would otherwise be too great. Charisma alone would have survived—because Charisma had already kept countless other secrets for Shoshanna.

"Wait at the monitoring station," she ordered the nurse.

"Yes, sir." Lomax moved to the far left of the room, from which she'd never get past Remi to escape and send up an alarm, should she be so inclined. It was possible that she'd already voiced a telepathic alarm, though she appeared to believe the story Auden had told her . . . but that made no difference now.

Auden knew what she had to do.

"Auden." Remi's rumble of a voice, quiet enough that the nurse would never hear it.

She looked up, the anger inside her a storm of violence born of years of abuse dressed up as medical experiments. "It's time to finish this."

He came with her as she walked closer to the body that was an abomination of what a living being should be—what remained of her mother's body had all but mummified, her mutilated torso shrunken in. Her once glossy black hair was brittle straw, her face parchment over bone, but her eyes moved rapidly under her eyelids.

"She's alive." If this could be called life. "I haven't felt her in the PsyNet since her supposed death, but that's not a surprise. We didn't have much of a bond." Shoshanna could've been hiding in plain sight, and Auden would've never spotted her.

More likely, someone else—one of the faithful—had been shielding her mind from the world.

"What do you want to do?" Remi asked, the leopard in his voice.

Auden wondered what it made her that she didn't hesitate. "I want her dead, this time for real. She's done enough damage—I *will not* permit her to harm Liberty as she did me."

Foolish girl, came a voice emotionless and arrogant inside her head, *do you really believe you're in control? I've had you in my power since the first day.*

Auden's breath caught, her eyes flashing to Remi. "She's telepathing me."

He went to move, as if to tear Shoshanna's head off her body, but Auden stopped him with a hand on his arm.

Because her mother was still speaking. *I think ten steps ahead. That's why you were pregnant long before the unfortunate incident that caused my current state.*

She was right; Auden had been impregnated while Shoshanna still lived. Liberty, Auden realized, had been created to hold Shoshanna's mind *no matter when* Shoshanna died. Her mother had intended to mess with her baby's sweet, emerging consciousness from the moment of birth.

We are connected, you and I. It was so easy to overlay my mind on yours for short bursts well before the incident that took my body from me. I negotiated the fertilization and conception agreement. I made the world see you as whole when it suited me.

Telepathic mind control, Auden thought. A difficult but not un-known thing among their race. Especially when it came to a telepath as powerful as Shoshanna who'd had unhindered access to her daughter's damaged brain for years.

The thought sickened Auden.

But the transfer glitched when I attempted to take permanent charge after the incident, leaving part of me in you. If I die, the psychic shock will kill you, too.

Auden's breath raced, her hand squeezing Remi's forearm as she quickly relayed what Shoshanna had said, then turned back to her mother. "Why did you attempt a transfer into me in the first place?" she asked aloud and on the telepathic level at the same time. "You created a child for your transfer—a perfect, unbroken brain with specific genet-ics designed to ensure she'd be a high-Gradient telepath."

I— A hesitation, a sense of white noise. *I— The fetus. I wanted to enter the fetus as soon as possible. Better to embed while she was still forming and influence her development.*

Auden frowned, because that didn't make sense. "My brain is scarred. You had no guarantees you wouldn't degrade once inside me."

Holding facility. Better than this one. Brain . . . failing . . .

The hesitation was more obvious now, Shoshanna's voice fading in and out, a touch of confusion in her tone. "She's not all there," Auden said to Remi, not sure if her mother could hear her or know what was in her head, but none of that mattered. Because the choice was clear. "As long as she lives, our cub is at risk."

Remi's jaw worked, a growl in his tone. "What about the threat to you?"

Auden's eyes were pools of melted glacier ice, pristine and clear, with not a ripple in their resolve. "You know the answer, my Remi. You'd make the same choice." She touched her fingers to his. "I'm only sorry"—tight words, pain in the fury now—"that I never got to know all of what it could be with us."

Rage was a leopard's snarl in Remi's throat, but he knew there was no convincing her otherwise. Because he *would* have made the same choice. To lay down his life for a cub? It wasn't even a question.

But he wasn't about to just give Auden up to evil.

He gripped her hand, his claws on her skin. "Open to me, Auden. If I reach for you, you *open*."

But she shook her head. "No. She's still a Gradient 9.5 telepath and her brain has enough function that she was able to somehow transfer a piece of herself into me. I don't know how—I'm guessing through sheer brute force because the idea of it is unadulterated insanity. If she somehow manages to get into your head via me, she'll use you as a weapon, use your entire pack."

Remi wanted to tell her that changeling shields were too strong, but that didn't apply here. Because if she allowed the mating bond, they'd be linked on a level so deep that it was beyond shields or walls. "Fuck!" It came out a roar.

She tangled her fingers with his. "Whatever happens, know that I regret nothing." Her gaze shone at him. "Make sure Liberty knows that my love for her *made* me. She is my heartbeat and my soul and she is the reason I understand love." Fingers touching his jaw. "I love you, Remi Denier. Until when I look into eternity, I see you in every frame."

Remi couldn't speak, his chest thick. "Is she still in your head?"

Auden stared at her mother. "Fragmented thoughts. Telling me that we're linked, that it's too late to separate." A pause. "I think she's right. *She's* the other Auden. I didn't splinter. I didn't fragment. She stamped herself onto part of me."

"But in the end, you won." He hugged her roughly to his body, his voice shaking. "Your love for Liberty won."

Auden let him hold her for a long second before she drew back. "Remi, my Remi." A single tear streaking down her face before she turned toward the bed.

Remi growled, his cat wanting to rend that shriveled body to a hundred pieces, his rage an ineffective shield against his pain.

"Good-bye, Mother." Auden pulled the plug on the machine that powered her mother's heart, then unhooked the breathing tube . . . just as all hell broke loose.

Pounding feet in the tunnel, yells, every alarm on the machines around Shoshanna going off. But Remi didn't give a shit about that.

Because Auden was convulsing, the sclera of her eyes streaked red when she looked at him. Grabbing her before she could collapse, he was only peripherally aware of the scream of the machines as Shoshanna's heart flatlined.

Charisma Wai entered the chamber with a weapon a heartbeat later, the doctor at her heels. Remi figured the nurse had called them even before she yelled that they'd disconnected the "lifelines." The doctor was bleeding from claw marks to his cheek, while Wai's loose sleep pants were torn at the knee.

Rina and the others. Fighting against that strike team Wai must've activated early. Now, his people were keeping the same team busy because Rina knew that Remi could easily take care of one slender Psy woman and an out-of-shape doctor who was huffing from his run.

Wai couldn't shoot or hit him with a psychic assault before he could separate her head from her body.

But that wouldn't save Auden. "Councilor Scott completed the transfer," he said in a growl of a voice.

Charisma's eyes widened. "What?"

"Her body was about to fail. She made the executive decision, but there's been a physiological issue," he said, as Auden's body went rigid in his arms. "Deal with it!"

The weapon trembled in Charisma's hand. "How do you—?"

"Did you think it was a coincidence that Auden found me?" he yelled. "The Councilor and I have an agreement. She comes back, and we get a payment big enough to take my pack into the future. Now *move!*"

Wai shook her head. "No, why would she do that?" But her hand wavered. "Your people attacked us."

He snarled. "Some don't agree with my decision. I'll handle them— that's my job. You can do *your* job now or you can let the Councilor die!"

Dropping the weapon, Wai urged the doctor forward. "Go!"

"That body is dead," Remi snapped when the doctor would've gone to the emaciated frame on the bed. "If it worked, she's inside this body." And if that was so, then he'd keep his promise to Auden and end her.

The action would haunt him all his life, but to take any other course would be to spit on her courage and love for her daughter.

He stood, Auden's now limp body in his arms, and headed for the second bed.

Two beds. One for Shoshanna. And one for the baby meant to be hooked up to her by methods unimaginable so she could rape that tiny and vulnerable mind.

"Right, right." Dr. Verhoeven followed him.

Though Auden was limp, her eyes moved rapidly under her eyelids. The echo of Shoshanna's dying body sent ice through his veins, but her scent . . . it was still Auden.

Until it wasn't.

Back again.

Lost.

Back.

Fighting, he realized, she was fighting a battle to hold on to her own mind, her own sense of self. "You can make it," he said, not caring if the doctor heard—the other man would no doubt believe he was talking to Shoshanna Scott. "Think of the future." *Think of Liberty.*

Removing the tiny knit cap from his pocket while everyone else was distracted, he placed it in her flexed open hand.

It clenched instinctively around it.

AUDEN was no combat telepath. She wasn't a powerful telepath at all. She didn't have the weapons to battle the psychic tendrils her mother had shot and somehow *hooked* into her mind in her dying agonies. She had no blades to cut her off, no acid to burn them aside. And fuck if she'd ever reach for her baby's nascent powers.

Never would *anyone* use her little girl.

She leaned on what she did have—a ferocious love and a vicious anger—and the awareness that they made her stronger than her weakened mother. Instead of fighting Shoshanna's blows, she blanketed Shoshanna in her rage, a rage with a near-viscous quality that was a thick net stifling Shoshanna's strikes.

Auden hadn't known her mind could do that, but she was a psychometric. She *touched* emotion every time she felt an imprint. It made sense that the same emotions could come out of her in this strange and almost tactile way.

Her friends on the forum would be happy. She could tell them that there *were* such things as killer psychometrics. Auden intended to be one.

Stop this! You know you've lost!

Ignoring Shoshanna's order, Auden continued to pump out rage. She could've used love, too, but she wasn't about to waste that precious emotion on this woman who had never been a mother to her except in biological terms.

At the same time, she made a strategic shift that meant her power would encircle Shoshanna's, creating a suffocating trap. A chill in her heart. This kind of strategy wasn't in her bailiwick. This was part of her mother's skills.

Bleedover.

Auden steeled her heart. She couldn't panic, couldn't rail against what had already happened. And whatever her mother had left in her during the earlier attempted transfers, that part was no longer Shoshanna. Because if it had been, it would've been trying to derail Auden.

Instead, every part of Auden—even the cold and strategic element introduced into her by Shoshanna—was fighting to protect Liberty . . . and get back to Remi, this man who had taught her what it was to trust.

He'd kept every promise, never let her down, was fighting for her even now.

A ferocious kind of power waited on the periphery of her mind, ready for her to open the door so it could prowl in.

Remi.

She couldn't open that door. Not when there remained the merest drop of a chance that her mother would find a way to slip through, infect with her frothing insanity the wonderful group of people who had kept Auden safe—and who were now ready to uproot their entire pack for her baby's life.

You are weak! You stand no chance! Stop this foolish game. It is annoying. Sharp telepathic blows against Auden's shields . . . but the blows snagged on the tactile thickness of emotion inside her mind, and what got through were dull thuds at best.

You sound desperate, Mother, she said. *The lovely nurse did let me know your brain is going critical. How much longer can you last?* She deliberately channeled the piece of Shoshanna that was now part of her, the part that could think with cold clarity and the part, she now realized, that could be used to defend as well as attack.

Shoshanna had used her will and her ability to think with crisp clarity to hurt people. Auden could do the opposite with the same tool. Because that was all it was, a tool, and one that would stand her in good stead in the years to come as she protected all those who were her own. Liberty. Remi. And the pack that had enclosed her baby in its arms.

No one would ever get to RainFire as long as Auden lived.

Changelings! A shocked cry from Shoshanna. *You are consorting with changelings!*

That answered one more question. *Strange that you didn't know already, if you transferred your consciousness to mine. Seems like I'm tough enough to keep my memories and experiences safe from you.* The relief she felt at that confirmation was a roar through her veins that gave her even more power. *You are dead, Mother. You died that day you collapsed. What you are now is an abomination, a fragmented shadow that is half-insane.*

A screech of sound that hurt her mental ear—and removed any doubts about her conclusion. The Shoshanna she'd known would've never lost control that way. Auden had never, not *once,* seen her mother display any emotion.

But even half-mad, her brain functions nowhere near optimal, she was still a 9.5 telepath with razor-sharp offensive capabilities.

No. Auden frowned. Shoshanna now had access to the same brain machinery as Auden—which meant all she had was psychometry and the most basic telepathy. This was Shoshanna using her knowledge of strategy and telepathic combat to confuse and distract in an endless barrage that stole from Auden's own power.

Auden shoved back with every violent tactile memory she had—and knew it wasn't enough. Even with the piece of Shoshanna inside her, she didn't have enough offensive knowledge to outsmart a woman who'd once been a Councilor. Even with only the brain of a psychometric in her arsenal, Shoshanna was winning.

Auden felt herself bleeding on the physical plane. Blood vessels bursting in her eyes from the pressure and tiny hemorrhages appearing on the skin of her body as her mind tried to redirect the violence. *I will never give up! I'd rather die than let you live!*

That was Auden's line in the sand: Shoshanna ended here, her evil stopped before it could continue on.

Because Auden knew she wouldn't be the last if this infernal "transfer" and "integration" actually worked and Shoshanna maintained even a semblance of thought. She'd find another victim, might even track down Liberty.

You can't stop me. Chilling confidence, Shoshanna's control returning as a clawed telepathic hand gripped at Auden's mind, every ounce of her own telepathic power concentrated in a way she'd never known could be done. But Auden had one final ace up her sleeve that she'd prepared long before she'd stepped foot back in this house.

One last act of love from a mother to her child.

Chapter 43

Henry is showing signs of mental degradation. A lingering effect from the implants we decided to utilize precipitously? It seems the most logical answer, given his previous stability. It is pure luck that I have not been similarly afflicted.

—Private journal of Shoshanna Scott (personal archive, address unknown)

AUDEN COULD STILL see and feel her direct link to the PsyNet. The Arrow shield didn't affect that. Nothing could affect that. It was so deep inside a Psy mind that it was a thing primal.

Cutting that link with no attempt to lock into another network would be a death sentence. Psy brains couldn't survive without the biofeedback provided by a psychic network. It was a necessity akin to air.

A piercing beeping on the physical plane that seeped into her consciousness.

Bye, my baby, she whispered to Liberty, *I love you.* Because her baby would survive. The Arrow watching over her would notice the shock wave, move to protect the child. She trusted in that unknown Arrow because she trusted in Remi.

I love you, Remi, she said, even though he couldn't hear her.

Such a huge emotion she had inside her when it came to the alpha who'd prowled into her life and shown her happiness, pleasure, laughter. It was so different from her love for Liberty, had so many more jagged edges and harsh demands, and it was as beautiful.

I wish I could say bye to you. I wish I could tell you all you are to me. I wish we could've had forever.

But her time was over; she'd held the line until she knew she was hemorrhaging internally—but death of the body wouldn't end Shoshanna unless Auden ensured a psychic death at the same time.

The only way to take Shoshanna down was for Auden to go down.

Auden sent out one last pulse of rage in an attempt to distract Shoshanna while she cut the link . . . but that rage burned with a feral anger so hot that it singed her insides. It had claws and teeth, was a thing of muscle and strength of enormous size. As if it was the rage of tens . . . a hundred . . . more . . . people fired up in battle against the monster that was Shoshanna.

Auden roared with them, as feral and as ferocious, her psychic claws digging into the bed and her eyes shifting form.

That was when she knew.

Remi had come into battle with her. He'd brought with him the wild fury of every single member of his pack. She didn't know how, but she knew it was a one-way street. Shoshanna couldn't get to him— because even Auden had no idea how he was there.

So she surrendered to the primal storm without fear for RainFire, and that storm was far more violent a foe than Shoshanna had ever faced. Her mother withdrew in an effort to regroup, retracting her hooks from inside Auden as she did so.

But the hunters on her tail continued to chase after her, the pack's rage coalescing into a black mass that suffocated Shoshanna until she whimpered and screamed in a tiny corner of Auden's mind.

Good-bye, Mother, Auden said.

Because Remi's storm? It was waiting for her to make the choice, a crouched leopard that quivered with bloodlust.

Only one choice would protect not just Liberty, but all the Libertys to come.

Auden ended her mother with a fine blade of rage that slammed into Shoshanna's psychic core, causing it to implode. The rage that was Auden and Remi and RainFire didn't permit the pieces of Shoshanna to escape. Instead, they watched like the cats they were, until she disintegrated into nothing, no trace remaining of the woman who'd once been Councilor Shoshanna Scott.

Auden's mother was dead. This time, forever.

REMI snarled when the doctor tried to put some kind of net on Auden's skull. "Get that the fuck away unless you want your arm ripped off!"

The doctor halted, hovered. "I've done what I can for the body, but she needs this to stabilize the transfer. She was very clear about that!"

Remi saw Charisma Wai reach toward her lower back at the same instant. The aide was on the other side of the bed and quite a distance away—but Remi was an alpha leopard. He vaulted over the bed and slammed Charisma to the wall before she ever touched the weapon, much less attempted to fire it.

Her head hit the wall so hard that it left behind a streak of blood as she slumped to the floor. The weapon clunked uselessly to the hospital-grade plascrete.

He turned to the doctor, claws out. "The instructions have changed."

"Yes, of course." The doctor babbled, right as alarms began to shriek throughout the facility. "I didn't realize. I'll do whatever the Councilor wishes, of course."

Remi had never wanted this man anywhere near Auden, had only permitted him to work on her because she would've otherwise died. "You are no longer her physician. Don't touch her unless you want to end up like Ms. Wai."

"She's hemorrhaging badly—I've only temporarily stabilized her." Dr. Verhoeven hovered over Auden. "I can—"

But Remi had already scooped her up in his arms and was racing out at a speed no Psy could ever match. He wasn't surprised to find Rina running toward him in leopard form. The sentinel would've felt it when he leaned so heavily into the pack the instant he'd felt he could get to Auden through a bond strange and oddly *young*.

He'd known then that his team were fine. None of them had leaned on him in turn, had just given and given.

"Teleport!" he yelled at her—and hoped the Arrows would have the capacity to help them. Because if they didn't, then he *would* have to trust Auden to the same doctor who'd caused her harm after harm. "Dr. Bashir!"

Changing direction, Rina raced back up.

The hatch was open when he reached it; Wai or the doctor must've left it open in their rush, giving Rina an easy entry. Lift must not be DNA encoded. Whoever had installed the security system had probably considered it overkill when entry was so difficult.

He took the final stairs three at a time.

It wasn't an Arrow who waited for him in the basement—alongside Rina who'd shifted back into leopard form after making the call for the teleporter's assistance.

Remi hadn't even known she had this particular number.

Kaleb Krychek didn't speak, and didn't wait for Remi to reach him. Remi was mid-run when he emerged into the center of a high-tech treatment facility, Krychek and Rina at the same distance from him that they'd been in the basement.

Fuck.

He got it, what people meant when they called Krychek a power.

Shoving that realization aside, he put Auden on the stretcher Dr. Bashir himself was pushing into the room. The surgeon might not know much about obstetrics, but he'd had plenty of training in trauma injuries thanks to his links to the Arrows, and he got to work on Auden at once.

Remi refused to leave the room, but shuddered back against the wall while the medical staff worked.

Krychek's starlit obsidian eyes stared at Auden with an intensity that had Remi snarling.

The cardinal turned to him. "It's not her," he said almost to himself. "Then why?"

"That's Auden," Remi said, wondering if Krychek had responded to save Shoshanna.

His claws pricked his skin.

But Krychek said, "I know." Then he was gone.

"I forgot how . . . intense he can be," Rina said, her chest heaving now that she'd shifted into human form. "I didn't call him. He arrived before I could even get to a phone."

Remi had no fucking idea what was going on, and he didn't care. All he knew was that Auden was alive. "The others?" he asked, his alpha heart unable to rest until he knew.

"Safe. Scott team had no idea how to fight against trained change-lings. They thought they'd be fighting dumb animals and ended up facing a tactical team better organized and more skilled than them. Lark is holding the house with the others and will clean up whatever is in the basement."

Remi nodded, his eyes on the medical team, and—his heart no longer torn in two now that he knew his people were safe—slid down to the floor, back braced against the wall.

Stars in his peripheral vision as Rina shifted back into her feline form, so she could lean her body against his chest. As if she'd sensed he needed the comfort of pack in a way she could better provide in this form.

"I got to her," he rasped, his packmate's fur a thick gold and black under his hand, and the warmth of her body a caress of family. "Like I can get to you or Angel or the others when you need pack energy."

Zaira thought it was a type of psychic ability Psy didn't understand. Remi didn't think about what it was, just that it worked. An alpha's heart reaching for his people when they were wounded and in pain . . . but it could work in reverse, too.

"We're not mated," he said. "She wouldn't allow it. Said her mother might be able to use the bond to get through to me, then RainFire." The hollow inside him where Auden was meant to be ached. "But I still got to her. You felt it."

The leopard nodded, a question in that wild gaze.

"It felt so young, the bond, somehow unfinished and fuzzy." He smiled, his aching heart roaring in pride. "*Libby.* Sweet, ferocious cub as tough as her mother. Bonded to me through blood." Others could take charge of figuring out how a child could be blood-bonded to a changeling alpha, and still be linked to the PsyNet, but he had no doubts about the bond after today.

Liberty wasn't old enough to have made a conscious choice in reaching for Remi. No, like any cub in the pack, she'd run to her alpha when she was scared—and her alpha had held her safe in his clawed embrace as he fought off the monsters.

Only . . . he didn't know if he'd been fast enough, strong enough.

Because Bashir was still yelling out commands, asking for more blood, more drugs, and Auden remained motionless on the hospital bed, the sheet stained with streaks of red. Remi couldn't reach her anymore, could no longer feel the tempest of love and rage that drove her.

Liberty was only an infant. She'd fallen asleep once the storm broke.

Knowing what Auden would ask of him in this instant, he rose to his feet while indicating that Rina should stay, keep watch on the dying, bleeding woman who was Remi's mate.

Once outside the chaos of the hospital room, he made a call. "Finn, how is Libby?"

"Vital signs spiked just before I suddenly had Zaira and an Arrow I've never before seen in the room. I think he's the teleporter she talks about—Alejandro. A minute later and the cub's snoozing away, all stats stable. No fear in her scent. Wait, I'll put you on speaker so you can talk to Zaira."

"I was the one holding Auden's shields today," Zaira told him. "Whatever took place destroyed the secondary shield over her mind, alerting me to a psychic blast that might impact Liberty. I was ready to shield her, but wasn't needed in the end." A question in her voice.

Finn came on the line again before Remi could respond. "Remi, Liberty's in distress again." His tone changed. "Hey, now, little one. I have you. Shh." A fine, thin cry reached Remi through the line. "Something's wrong."

Remi growled loud enough that the cub would hear, then purred low in his chest until the cries trickled off into sobs. He kept it up until Finn whispered that she was asleep.

"She's scared because she can't reach her mother," Remi said, his voice rough. "Auden's hurt bad. She must've done something to block the baby. She would never want Libby to—" Remi's entire chest threatened to collapse in on itself. He couldn't say it, couldn't refer to the possible backlash from Auden's death.

"Understood." Zaira's tone was softer than the harsh word implied. "I'll maintain a close watch so I can cocoon the child against psychic shock."

"You're protecting Auden's heart, Zaira. I'll never forget this."

"You protected mine once, Remi," was the curt Zaira-like reminder. "No ledger between us. Ever."

"I've taken you off speaker." Finn's voice. "What happened? Did someone assault Auden?"

Remi told the healer about Shoshanna's psychotic attempt to transfer her consciousness by an unknown process. "She and Auden fought—inside their minds. I don't know the details, just that Auden won."

Because if Auden had lost, then Liberty wouldn't be blocked from her mother—and Finn wouldn't be concerned only about fear in Liberty's scent; the infant's scent would've been drenched in unmistakable cold metal as Shoshanna attempted to use her in her horrific quest to live forever.

"I was able to pass on pack energy to her through Liberty, but the damage done prior to that . . ." Hand fisting against the wall, he pushed off. "She gave *everything* she had."

"Can you—"

"No," Remi interrupted, well aware what his friend was suggesting. "She's blocked me, too." One last act of honor and courage from the only woman who'd made her way into Remi's heart. "I've tried to get through."

He'd never have pushed for the mating bond if she hadn't been bleeding out in front of him. It was meant to be a choice. *Her* choice. But with the mating bond would come a direct link to him and his pack—and the energy of a changeling pack was a thing primitive and potent.

But Auden wouldn't even let him try.

Protecting him from the unending grief of losing his mate. As if it wasn't already too late, Remi's heart forever tattooed with the name Auden Scott.

Chapter 44

My section of the PsyNet will most likely survive intact. I don't know why but it's the most stable piece in the entire state—and we have a disproportionate number of high-Gradient Psy inside it, thanks to its proximity to my HQ.

According to the experiments run on creating PsyNet islands, the Gradient load is skewed enough that we should be able to hold it, even if it'll take everything we have.

There is room for refugees, and I suggest we prioritize empaths. This all began when Psy decided to erase emotion from our lives—and murder designation E along with it. It seems fitting that we should begin the war of survival by making the opposite choice.

—Nikita Duncan to the Ruling Coalition (18 November 2083)

KALEB DIDN'T ATTEMPT to get in touch with the NetMind.

The neosentience had been faded and weak when it sent its desperate request. The image of a leopard. A keening impression of help needed.

He'd locked onto that image without hesitation, though he hadn't understood why the NetMind was sending it to him.

That leopard had stared at him in shock, too.

Mere heartbeats later and he'd seen Auden Scott in the arms of a man with clawed hands and shaggy hair myriad shades of brown, his eyes green and gold. It had made sense then. Of course it would be Shoshanna Scott's daughter who had the rare ability to create a PsyNet island. A small gift, not enough to save the Net, but enough to save hundreds or—if she was strong enough—perhaps even thousands.

Then the NetMind had whispered to him once more, with a heavy sense of the negative.

Not her. But still important enough for the NetMind to spend its precious energy to save. Could she have a child? Surely, that was impossible. Auden was only twenty-four, and Kaleb had heard no rumors of a pregnancy.

Kaleb!

He responded to Vasic's call at once. Another huge section of the PsyNet was collapsing.

All thoughts of Auden Scott left his mind, his attention only on saving as many lives as he could, even though he felt he was only plugging an unstoppable dam with a single finger.

Days. Only days.

That was all the PsyNet had before terminal failure.

Chapter 45

I bequeath all my worldly goods and assets, tangible and intangible, to my sole biological offspring, Auden Scott (previously Auden Jackson). See Appendix A for complete list of bequeathed items.

—The Last Will and Testament of Shoshanna Scott

FORTY-EIGHT HOURS AFTER the events in the basement, and Auden lay clean and dressed in a crisp blue hospital gown, her hair a soft halo around her head because Remi had released it from that punishing bun in which she'd put it before they walked into Shoshanna's bunker. Her body was connected by wires and fine tubes to multiple machines that monitored her or provided nutrients and drugs.

Her face was soft, none of that Auden energy to it, and per Dr. Bashir's latest scans, her brain activity was sluggish. "I spoke to your pack's physician," the exhausted doctor had told Remi an hour ago, before he left to catch a few hours' sleep.

"He advised further me of the older injuries to Ms. Scott's brain. They weren't clear on the latest scans, because, unfortunately, there's been more damage. We'll have no idea of the repercussions of that damage until—*if*—she wakes."

Remi clenched his hand around Auden's, furious at fate for hurting this extraordinary woman over and over. And yet . . . "I know you'd do it all again if you had to."

A knock on the door.

Having already scented his best friend, Remi rose and allowed the other man to draw him into a crushing hug. Angel might not like to get close to people, but when he did, he went all in.

"Did you bring everything?" Remi asked when he could speak past the lump in his throat.

"Yeah." Angel handed him a small daypack. "The cub's stuff is in a bag inside." The tiger glanced at Auden. "Any change?"

Remi shook his head. "Nurse Evans—gray curls, short, brown eyes—can you grab her from the nurses station? Don't let anyone else inside."

Angel vanished with feline silence, and the senior nurse to whom Remi had spoken in advance was soon in the room. While Angel stood guard outside, Evans disconnected the medical lines, and Remi quickly changed Auden out of the hospital gown and into one of Remi's large T-shirts. Evans then connected the lines back up. "I hope this works, Remi," said the woman with the rational face of Silence . . . and the kind heart of a healer.

Remi's nod was jagged, his attention on Auden. He wouldn't have done this if she hadn't already allowed him skin privileges. Worn for so many years that his scent was embedded into the fibers, the T-shirt was beyond soft—and surely awash in his imprint.

The door clicked as the nurse left.

Having settled Auden back under the blanket, he now lifted her head to gently place the scarf Sass had given her under her hair. He'd asked Auden why she wrapped up her curls to sleep that one beautiful night they'd had together, and she'd told him certain fibers helped safeguard the strands from tangling and breakage.

Remi would do anything to protect his mate.

Her hair safe against the silk, he put one of Liberty's knit caps on Auden's palm.

He'd tell the medical staff to cut his T-shirt down the middle if they needed to for access, but he was hoping his imprint and Liberty's would call Auden back from wherever she'd gone in her mind.

Another knock some minutes later. "Safe to come in?" Angel asked. "Yeah."

The tiger held up a disposable cup of coffee that he'd fetched from somewhere. "Drink. I brought in food, too, since I wasn't sure this place wouldn't just have nutrient bars." He ducked outside to grab another daypack.

Remi wanted nothing less than food, but he didn't argue when Angel handed him a heavily stuffed sandwich. An alpha couldn't fall into grief and shut out the world. "You can update me on the pack at the same time," he said instead.

As Angel spoke, Remi took bites of the sandwich with grim deliberation, tasting nothing.

Auden, he thought, would be so disappointed in him for not appreciating the food.

"The indi-mech deal's been canceled from the Scott end," Angel said after he'd updated Remi on more personal pack matters. "Not put on hold. Just flat out canceled, with no cancellation fee paid. Termination notice said they don't wish to be associated with, and I quote, the 'violent mercenaries hired by Auden Scott in her attempt to stage a familial coup d'état.'"

Remi's rage was a black wave. He didn't give a fuck about the money, but he did very much give a fuck that they were trying to erase Auden while Auden lived and breathed and still had the fucking *majority controlling interest* in Scott companies.

She'd told him that the night they'd shared intimate skin privileges.

"A lot of families work with the ownership vesting in the family as a group and there's a board that makes major decisions," she'd said, "but that was too egalitarian for my mother's taste even though, in practice, no one would have ever gone against her decisions. She built her own private empire to the extent that the Scott Group companies are a minor part of the family's overall operations."

She'd shrugged then. "I have no idea why, but she gave it all to me in her will."

Because Shoshanna had intended to take control of her own assets through Auden's child.

The insanity of Shoshanna's plans aside, the blunt fact was that one couldn't simply erase that inheritance—not when it had been put together by a team of legal sharks working under former Councilor Shoshanna Scott. And while it might've been intended to be a masterstroke in manipulation, it had failed. Because Auden had fought and won.

The fucking Scotts didn't get to just *steal* her legacy for her child.

Remi crumpled the empty coffee cup in his hand. "No one gets to make those calls until we know about Auden."

"Cancellation letter was signed by Hayward Scott, with the notation that he has power of attorney over Auden since she is medically indisposed. I looked him up—he's Shoshanna's younger brother. Auden's uncle."

Remi snorted. "Auden's more likely to have given power of attorney to a random person on the street." His leopard prowled against his skin. "I think it's time the Scotts learned that she isn't alone anymore. And that her friends know the family doesn't have the codes to the system with Charisma dead. Fuckers have to be panicking."

Turned out Remi had snapped Ms. Wai's neck when he'd thrown her against that wall. He felt fine about that. There wouldn't be any consequences, either, not with Lomax and Verhoeven having undergone judicially mandated telepathic scans that confirmed Remi had acted in self-defense against an armed Wai.

The Scotts had also disavowed any knowledge of the medical staff and their "unauthorized" medical experimentation on their former CEO, and they were, at present, confined to a prison holding facility designed for Psy.

Everyone else at the compound at the time of the incident had also fared much the same. The Scotts cleaning up their mess by claiming ignorance of the entire operation; he'd heard they were pinning it all on Charisma Wai, not that they had any idea of the entirety of what had taken place.

It amazed him the games the assholes continued to play while their lives hung in the balance. An exhausted Aden had visited him here, told him the crippled status of the PsyNet as they sat side by side on hard plas chairs in the hallway. "It's going to fail any day now," he'd said. "Liberty will survive—she'll be pulled into the RainFire changeling network through your bond with her."

"The squad?" he'd asked the man who was an alpha with the attendant heart; it'd crush him to be unable to protect his pack, all these wounded Arrows who looked to him for hope.

"We have a statistically unbalanced number of high-Gradients. We'll survive in a small private network, as will others. None of us have given up on finding a solution, but the clock is close to midnight now.

"If the worst does happen, even with the highest possible number of projected survivors, including the stable island held by Ivan Mercant, it'll only equal a single-digit percentage of our current population."

"What can RainFire do? Just tell us, and we'll do it."

"You're already doing everything you can for a population of your small size—you can't take any further load," Aden had explained. "My people have bonded with yours. The emotional ties will further strengthen our local network. We may end up having to move closer to you and ask for you to initiate blood bonds to help with the integrity of it. It might be uncomfortable, but it shouldn't hurt your pack."

"Consider it done," Remi had said without hesitation.

The leader of the squad had stared at the floor, his shoulders slumped and his hands hanging between his knees. "And your home territory, it's far from where millions of Psy will die in a matter of days. Our children deserve not to grow up in a graveyard."

Too bad his brave, loving, little cat's family was full of cockroaches who'd probably survive the biggest loss of life the world had ever seen. The horror of it was something Remi's brain struggled to comprehend.

So for today, for this minute, he focused on a wrong he could put right, a piece of the world he could fix.

"Where is this Hayward Scott?" he asked Angel.

"Moved into the compound with his people a couple of hours ago, soon as the authorities cleared it."

Those authorities hadn't been from Enforcement but from an arm of the Ruling Coalition set up to deal with the crimes of the powerful. Each member of the team was both strong on the psychic plane and—crucially—underwent regular sessions with empaths to ensure they remained uncorrupted and devoted to their task of justice.

But the team had to follow its own ethical rules.

The Scotts were about to learn that Remi's ethics were those of a predator who understood honor as well as it understood violence.

HAVING something concrete to do gave him focus and energy. He left Rina with Auden when he went on the op with Angel.

Just the two of them, because this was about stealth.

He could've initiated legal proceedings, but that would take too long, and he wanted the Scotts to be *afraid*. From how they were acting, given the oncoming collapse of the PsyNet, they clearly thought they had an exit strategy figured. No need for fear.

That was about to change.

The Scotts were about to gain a close, private understanding of the emotion. He especially wanted them to be afraid of Auden so they'd stop treating her as a commodity they could use and discard.

Most of all, he wanted to punish them for making her afraid for so long.

Auden could make the final call about what she wanted to do when she woke, but he wasn't about to let them steal that choice from her as they'd already stolen so many others. "Ready?" he said to Angel in the depths of the night.

He could only see his friend because of his night vision—they stood a significant distance from the security lights around the compound. While Remi was dressed in black, complete with a mask that covered all of his face but for his eyes, Angel wore the stripes of a tiger.

Now he rumbled a growl of acknowledgment, and they moved.

He and Angel, they'd pulled off plenty of ops when they'd been out on their own, barely needed to communicate to understand what the other wanted in the heat of a fight. But this, they'd discussed down to the minutest detail, because Angel wouldn't otherwise be familiar with the layout of the compound.

As Remi watched, his best friend streaked into the lights, deliberately allowing himself to be seen by the guards who monitored the external feeds. He moved so fast that it appeared multiple tigers were prowling the compound.

Auden's changelings on the attack.

The guards boiled out of the house, shouting orders and reaching for weapons.

He counted. Idiots. They were all outside. He knew that because Angel had organized a surveillance crew to keep an eye on the place since Auden was hurt. All of them understood that the Scotts were snakes, and snakes had to be watched.

For all her psychopathic faults, Charisma Wai would not have hired imbeciles like this.

As a result of their incompetence, Remi was able to run straight through to the house while every single guard was distracted hunting the tigers that appeared and vanished before they could get off a single shot. Angel growled several times right as Remi ran, once again capturing all their attention.

A heartbeat later and Remi was climbing up the outside of the house. Psy just didn't think about changelings when they built. This house had so many hand- and footholds—and so many shadows of which a cat could take advantage.

All the security lights pointed outward, leaving the walls of the house itself dark.

Having aimed himself at the floor that held the family's rooms, he now hauled himself in through an open window. He'd been prepared to break one if needed, would've just waited for the next burst of noise from the guards as Angel ran them ragged. But once again, the Psy sense of arrogance came to his rescue. They didn't expect entry from such a high point.

He landed on the carpet with feline stealth before making his way down a hallway swathed in shadows. In his hand was a blocker that hid his progress from the cameras, because—if the Psy staved off their oncoming apocalypse—Remi wasn't going to play into the desire of certain Psy families to start an interspecies war.

No one would ever have any proof of his presence here tonight.

Less than thirty seconds after he'd entered, he knocked on Hayward Scott's door, the rap a firm one. "Sir."

Rustling, as the man inside moved to unlock his door. "What is going—"

His words ended in a gasp as he came face-to-face with Remi—and the fast-acting sedative in the auto-injector in Remi's hand. Psy didn't do well with drugs, but he'd checked with Dr. Bashir about sedatives. The doctor, believing Remi was thinking about Auden's possible future need for them, had given him a short list of fast-acting agents that would knock a Psy out almost at once.

"The problem will be at the other end," Dr. Bashir had said. "When the patient wakes. Their psychic senses will be tangled, take time to unravel. However, with the ones I've listed, there's no chance of a permanent injury."

Dr. Bashir hadn't been overselling how rapidly this stuff worked.

Hayward Scott slumped forward, unconscious almost before Remi had pulled the injector away from his neck. Remi was confident it had all happened too fast for him to scream for help on the telepathic plane. Throwing the older man over his shoulder in a fireman's carry, he walked down the stairs, sticking to areas in a surveillance shadow because there was no point in being arrogant and relying only on the blocker.

The house was more active now—he could hear movement, see lights at several corners. But it was a big house, and the entire group in residence was focused on the area Angel had turned into a circus. Remi heard a scream at that instant, knew his friend had taken one of them down to ensure they saw him as a continued and deadly threat.

Smile cold, Remi slipped out of the house right under the noses of the guards. Even if they spotted him in the external lights, none of them could match his speed. On their cameras, all they'd see was a human form racing away with one of their own.

As for Angel . . . well, there was no tiger pack in the country. Only friends and packmates were aware that Angel was a tiger, not a leopard. Remi could deny sending an assault force of "tigers" with a straight face.

He'd sent only a *single* highly intelligent tiger.

Who joined him at their vehicle ten minutes later, jumping into the back seat beside their package before Remi drove out. No one sought to stop them. If Remi had to guess, the guards were still hunting ghost tigers.

A shimmer of light in back.

"That was fun," Angel said with a rare grin Remi saw in the rearview mirror. "I got four of them. Left them alive, but nicely mauled."

Remi's own grin was vicious. "We have to keep this asshole drugged until the Scotts decide to toe the line."

"We could send the family his pinky finger in a lined box as further incentive."

"You're terrifying sometimes, my angelic friend." Because he knew Angel—protective and fiercely loyal Angel—had meant that.

A shrug he heard in the rustle of the clothing Angel was pulling on. "Sometimes, you have to play with bastards on their own level."

It was at times like this that Remi wondered about the lost years of Angel's childhood, the ones about which he refused to talk even to Remi. "Scotts are about bloodlines, and they have no one else suitable of age if Hayward vanishes."

Remi felt no pity for the unconscious man; he'd decided to take advantage of Remi's wounded mate. Now he was paying the price.

"The family will do what we tell them to do." Or more of them would meet with a leopard's claws one dark night.

Remi didn't play when it came to his mate and child.

Chapter 46

PsyNet status: Critical. Total collapse predicted in thirty-six hours. Mass casualties are to be expected.

Cooperation from the Human Alliance and all major changeling groups has been fed into the survival projection, but the possible success or failure of those attempts to merge with changeling networks, and/or to incorporate humans into small Psy networks as an emergency measure will not be known until Net failure.

The ShadowNet is also ready and waiting to accept refugees, but experiments to date suggest that direct links are not possible and must be made through an emotional tie to an individual already in the ShadowNet.

Current projection: 92% loss of Psy life.

—Report to Ruling Coalition and EmNet from PsyNet
Research Group Alpha (21 November 2083)

SILVER MERCANT, DIRECTOR of the Emergency Response Network and mate to the alpha of the StoneWater bears, stared at the report that had just popped up on her organizer. She'd known. They'd all known. But to see it laid out in black and white . . .

Shoulders locked to rigidity, she pushed away from her desk to look below it—where a small polar bear cub sat playing with wooden blocks. "Dima?" she said, holding out her arms to the child she was babysitting while his mother ran errands.

Sleepy and lazy because it was close to his naptime, he came happily to cuddle with her, and she held him close as her eyes burned and her heart reached for her mate. Valentin was the reason she would survive the collapse—and he was the reason her family would survive.

She and her brother had both mated into the bear clan, and between them, they were near certain they could wrench the rest of the family into the clan.

Because Ena had built a family linked by bonds of love and loyalty unbreakable.

But near certain wasn't complete certainty. And the Mercant family's lives weren't the only ones at stake. Snuggling a half-asleep Dima to her, she thought of all the people with whom she worked on a day-to-day basis, all the good, honorable people who might have no way out.

And the children . . .

Silver squeezed Dima tight enough that he grumbled little bear grumbles in his sleep. Softening her embrace at once, she kissed his head. If she could, she'd hold all the children of the PsyNet in her arms, give up her life for theirs. Her bear mate, with his huge heart, would do the same. But that wasn't how it worked, no exchange of lives on the table.

The entire world had stepped up to the plate in the past weeks, when the collapse of the PsyNet had gone from a slow erosion to a sudden oncoming crash. Changelings, humans, the Forgotten, they'd offered to assist in any way possible, but the reason the PsyNet existed in the first place was that it *needed* to exist.

Even if every one of the contingencies—even the most unlikely—worked as intended, they'd be left with a shortfall of millions.

Millions of lives. Millions of hearts. Millions of deaths.

Hiding her face in Dima's soft fur, Silver Mercant, ice queen to many and beloved mate to Valentin, cried tears silent and hot.

Chapter 47

Jaya, sweetheart, I have a patient for you. Coma as a result of bodily trauma and insult to the brain. I know things are difficult right now, but if you have even a couple of minutes, I think you could help her as I can't.

—Message from Sascha Duncan to Jaya Laila Storm (21 November 2083)

"I'M GOING TO put our cub in her carrier for a little bit so she can warm up." A deep rumble of a voice familiar and beloved. "Libby doesn't need the incubator anymore, but Finn wants me to use this carrier in short bursts during her visits with you."

Auden felt the loss of skin-to-skin contact like a limb being cut off, the small warmth on her chest suddenly gone . . . but the loss was so deep because her joy had been even deeper. Remi had brought her baby to her. She knew it had been him even before she'd heard the rumble of a purr against senses dulled and wrapped in cotton wool.

Our cub.

He'd claimed Libby, would protect her with his life. Libby would never know loneliness, would never be treated as disposable, would never wonder why she wasn't good enough. She'd grow up loved—by an entire pack, but most of all, by the man who owned Auden's heart.

At times, she could feel claws against her shields, his leopard wanting to enter. She wasn't holding him back, didn't have the power. Her mind was just broken, the shields that held him out the final desperate act of a psychometric bent on survival. Thick, almost tactile shields that had gone up the instant she began to slip into unconsciousness.

The thought started to whisper out of her grasp almost before it had formed, another wave of exhaustion rolling over her. Driven by a sense of vital urgency, she'd struggled against the waves at the start, only to find it tired her out and led her to sink even deeper into the dark, into a place where she could sense nothing.

Now she let the waves sweep her along, and she slept.

She had no idea for how long, but she knew Remi was there when she surfaced. His voice vibrated in her bones and made her want to curl up against his body so the sense of him could cover her all over. And then . . . *Oh, my baby.* Love poured out of her, rising through the dark to encompass the child Remi had placed against her chest.

Liberty's tiny hands flexed against the shield, but that shield wouldn't open even for her.

Auden cried inside, wanting to hold her baby close, but knowing her mind wasn't a safe place for Liberty. Too many shattered and sharp edges, too many tangled threads. *I love you so, my baby.*

A brush of a rough hand on her cheek, cupping her face with protective warmth.

Her chest swelled with love as ferocious as the leopard who was hers.

She knew he was speaking to her, but couldn't make out the words through the thickness of cotton inside her mind. And that mind, it was fading again even as the urgency pounding at her got louder and louder.

A faint voice that wasn't a voice—not her own, not her mother's ghost—was pleading with her to wake. It didn't have words, didn't speak, but she understood that it was dying and it needed her to wake. Auden tried but her bruised and battered mind couldn't hold on, not even when the entity that spoke to her tried to offer her its very life in exchange for the unknown thing it needed from her.

The next time she "woke" it was to the awareness of a stranger nearby. An odd stranger. One who didn't trigger any of Auden's defenses when she inserted a thread into Auden's locked-down mind. A touch that—how extraordinary—didn't feel invasive but warm and considerate and wanted only the best for her.

On the structural level, the probe reminded her of her own ability. A psychometric? No, it couldn't be. Psychometrics didn't work with living beings.

Empaths do, murmured an undamaged corner of her mind. *Psychometrics are the physical mirror to empaths.*

When the probe began to withdraw, Auden halted it by wrapping a tendril of emotion around it. A hello. As quickly, she released her tendril to set the empath free. She'd never cage another creature, no matter how lonely she was inside the shell of her mind.

The empath halted . . . and then she began to drop sparks of emotion in a starlit highway. Auden looked at the lovely construct and, with urgency a thrumming beat in her blood, took a step forward, picked up a star.

Primal fury, raging anger, and pain. Oh, *such pain.*

Auden's protective instincts surged. Who was hurting Remi? She'd kill them. And she realized she was running, gathering star after star in her arms. Sensing her baby's confusion and grief at missing her mama alongside Remi's pain, and Finn was there, too. He was so sad. Oh, and Rina, Rina had cried for her.

The stars overflowed her arms, but she kept on picking them up, until at last there were no more, and when she looked back, she saw that she'd run right through the survival shield her mind had thrown up to protect her. It fell away in front of her eyes, a parting curtain that revealed a mind riddled with a glittering blue spiderweb.

Oh.

A growl.

She turned, looked forward, laughed, and ran straight toward the crouched leopard who was snarling furiously at her for making him wait so long. She smashed into him with unstoppable force and he was primal heat in her mind, devotion unending, and loyalty boundless.

Remi, my Remi.

Her mate had a heart bigger than the sun, his love for her and her child—*their* child—a thing enormous, and his love for his pack a vastness no one but an alpha or an alpha's mate could ever understand.

She fell even deeper into him, saw the passion and the need, the fantasies of limbs entwined and his hand around her throat, her body riding his, his mouth between her thighs. Strong hands holding her hips as he drove into her, gentler hands as he petted her down after a peak, kisses along her spine and on her throat.

Facing her now, her breasts crushed to his chest, his hand squeezing her flesh with proprietary passion.

His thoughts. His desires. For her.

Auden gasped, and knew he saw hers in turn. She felt no shame, no shyness. Because he was hers and she would allow him into any and every corner of her soul.

REMI'S head spun with the soft and the dangerous and the fierce and the protective. Pieces of Auden. She'd come to him as he held her in his arms. He'd barely felt her stir to wakefulness before she was inside him, a storm wind that brought him to his knees with her violent beauty and endless spirit.

She was love, such *love*. She was a warrior, ready to battle for her mate and her child. She was a lover who looked at him and saw raw masculine beauty. Images of him in motion in nothing but his skin, her hand stroking his cock, her lips kissing a path down his chest.

Then their fantasies tangled, became one, and they were kissing in a bond only mates would ever know, their hearts and minds forever linked.

Auden gasped against his chest even as tears of joy ran down Remi's face. He didn't fucking care. Because she'd given herself to him, now and forever. "Come on, little cat," he said. "Open those beautiful eyes."

Liberty made a happy little sound in the crib that sat next to Auden's bed.

"Yeah, your mama's back," he rumbled to the cub. "She's just taking her time to rise up out of her sleep."

Jaya, the empath who'd worked with Auden earlier that day had already left, but she'd done so with a smile that glowed against the dark brown hue of her skin. "She's tough, your Auden. I don't know how she did it, but she's literally rerouted her personality past any damage—and at a speed that should be impossible."

Because she's done it before, Remi had thought, his pride a wild thing. "Will she wake soon?"

"Within the day I'd say," Jaya had predicted, to the shock of Dr. Bashir, who'd predicted a coma of months if not years.

"I've never quite seen a mind like hers," Jaya had added. "There's . . ." A deep frown. "The link to her child is profound. It's beyond the usual maternal bond."

She'd shaken it off. "But it's nothing bad. Might simply be a result of the early trauma. I can continue to keep an eye on it if . . ." A fading of her smile, those empathic eyes soft with pain. "Hope, right? We have to have hope. I'm going to hope that the PsyNet has one last trick in its arsenal."

But Remi couldn't think about the impending catastrophe in this instant of joy clawed out of the grasp of nightmare. Trembling, he pressed his lips to Auden's curls at a time when it felt as if the whole world slept. "I miss you, Cupcake. Please wake up."

A rasp of breath.

He jerked his head down, saw Auden looking up at him. Her eyes were muddy and unfocused . . . but they cleared in a slow wave. Lips parting, she tried to speak, couldn't.

He grabbed the glass of water off the side table, helped her sip it, then put it aside and just held her tight while he fought to breathe.

Her hand spread on his heart. "How long?"

"Three days," he said. "Just three days." Even if it had felt like a lifetime. "You're a fucking miracle." He kissed those dry lips that were the most beautiful thing in the world to him. "I am so going to spank you for giving me such a fucking fright."

Her lips curved. "I love you, too."

He saw the knowledge of their bond in her eyes, in her smile before she said, "Liberty?"

"Hold on." Shifting off the bed, he picked the baby up from her crib and laid her in Auden's arms before taking his position on the bed beside her once again, his arm around her back. "You had bad internal bleeding, hemorrhages everywhere, but Bashir, that arrogant prick to whom I will forever be grateful, fixed those."

"Explains the body aches and exhaustion." But she was smiling and nuzzling at Liberty as she spoke. "Here I am, here I am. Yes, I know Mama was gone. I know. I'm sorry. I love you so much. I won't ever go away again." Her voice was soft and singsong in that way of parents with their cubs.

It melted his heart. "I'm going to make you pregnant every freaking year if you keep on being that adorable."

A sultry smile. "I saw your fantasies."

"I saw yours, too." He cupped her jaw, his heart yet thunder. "You have no idea how much I want to make every one of them raw, naked reality." Pleasure, play, whatever she wanted, he'd give her. But first of all, he'd hold her until his most primal core was convinced she'd woken, come back to him and Libby.

Auden's eyes bled to dark, but she glanced down suddenly, whispered, "She can't understand, can she?"

His shoulders shook as he cuddled both his girls close. "Her little ears are safe from our dirty talk, trust me." Nuzzling at her curls, he was about to whisper a few more sweet and dirty thoughts to her just because he could, because she was awake and alive, when she jolted.

Claws out, he searched the room for threats. "Auden?"

"The PsyNet. Something's wrong on the PsyNet." Her voice was fast, her pitch high. "It's falling. Crumbling. Oh my God, Liberty!"

. . .

AUDEN could see the Arrow shield above her mind, but it proved no barrier to the glittering blue spidersilk that was rising up from her own mind. It went through the shield as if it didn't exist . . . and so did Auden.

When she turned back and looked, her mind remained opaque . . . but the spidersilk was spreading across the starlit and fractured darkness of the PsyNet at impossible speed, with her the spider at the center. Because it *was* a web, with the perfect framework, each fine line followed by another and another.

Radial lines ran out in every direction, going as far as the eye could see, before fading away. "It's not me," she whispered on the physical plane, staring down at her sweet baby, whose brown eyes now glowed a glittering blue.

Remi growled. "What the fuck is happening?"

"I don't know," Auden admitted even as Liberty shook her fists with no indication of psychic stress or hurt. "It's Libby. She's doing something through me. I think . . . I think it needs an adult mind to work, but it's *her* power. I'm just the conduit." She brushed her fingers over her baby's soft cheek. "It's a web of glorious beauty, Remi. Like it's coated with crushed gemstones."

"It's a good thing?"

Despite her wonder, Auden frowned and considered it from every angle. "Yes," she said at last. "It's not doing harm. I think . . . I think it might be helping in a way I don't understand."

She looked at their daughter again. "What are you doing, my baby?"

But Liberty just yawned before rooting for her breast . . . and Auden's milk flowed so fast that it stained her T-shirt. Laughing, crying, she pulled down the loose neckline and fed her child while her mate—and Liberty's father—cradled them close and purred deep in his chest.

A nudge at the back of her mind, that desperate entity sighing in relief. The sensation was weak, the flowers it showered on her mind a cascade of luminous steel.

Chapter 48

I don't have empathy, Sahara. I can't feel for those who are going to die. It would be akin to asking a falcon to take flight when his wings had long been hacked off.

—Kaleb Krychek to Sahara Kyriakus (circa late 2081)

KALEB SAW THE line of spidersilk before it reached him. That blue . . .

The same blue as Shoshanna Scott's eyes.

Monster. Murderer. Spider.

The same blue as Auden Scott's eyes.

Protected by the NetMind itself, to the point that the neosentience had almost burned itself out sharing its own energy with her so she could heal.

It had nearly done the same a second time around, when it had screamed for Kaleb to help her.

The NetMind was ready to die for Auden Scott.

He allowed the spidersilk to touch his mind, anchor into it . . . and felt it at once, a subtle draw on his power. *Far* less, however, than he was expending in his brute force effort to hold the PsyNet from crumbling.

Because it turned out that he wasn't a black-hearted bastard after all.

Not when it came to children. He'd set himself up above the area where Sahara—in concert with local empaths—had corralled all the children in their region, his aim to protect their innocent minds as the PsyNet shattered.

Sahara stood next to him, hand in hand with him, her power his to use.

"Do you see the spidersilk?" he asked.

"It looks like a dream. Should I allow it in?"

"Yes," he said, remembering what the NetMind had shown him. "It's . . . a mirror of what Shoshanna did. She took and took and became bloated with it. I think this web is doing what Ivan's web does." Creating a closed system of energy using every mind in the PsyNet, strong and weak, old and young, broken and whole.

"Oh," Sahara whispered. "It's so . . . happy?" Tilting her head against his arm, she smiled. "It's gone now, but I could've sworn I felt the sweetest brush against my mind. This web is *young*."

Kaleb hadn't sensed any of that, but his emotions were twisted and calcified. He relied on Sahara when it came to knowing good from evil, dark from light. So, lifting her hand to his mouth, he pressed a kiss to her knuckles, then sent a telepathic blast through the PsyNet.

Accept the web. The NetMind designed it to hold the PsyNet together. It will not take by force. But the more minds in the web, the more energy it has to weave us back together.

The web spread at a phenomenal rate in a matter of seconds, and when he went to the mind he knew to be the center, it wasn't there. A glittering blue orb sat in its place, roiling with the energy of millions of minds linked in a biofeedback loop of inconceivable proportions.

Kaleb understood. The mind couldn't be seen, couldn't be known. It was too fragile. "It's a child," he said with confidence. "The being at the center of the web. Auden Scott's child."

Sahara met his gaze, her dark hair lifting in the breeze on their terrace. "Will you tell the others?"

"I think the Arrows must know. There was an Arrow shield around Auden Scott's mind the last time I saw it."

"Well, their ability to keep secrets is legendary."

"As for anyone else, no, I won't tell." The NetMind could make that call, decide who needed to know. "The child will be safe with the alpha I met." Clawed hands that even if they bled, wouldn't stop protecting.

Sahara's eyes glowed with a pulse of blue. "Kaleb, your eyes . . ."

"The web just pulsed," he said. "An overwhelming surge of energy in the network." Frowning, he looked in the PsyNet again, but could find nothing to explain it.

PAX felt his Scarabs slip out of his grasp one after the other. Terrified for them, he emerged into the Net . . . and saw the blue spiderweb that had entangled his broken people. He was afraid they were dead, but no, they lived.

Their chaotic energy was contained . . . and yet part of the system.

Flowers in his mind. Wilted and bruised, but held in cupped hands of radiant steel-gray alongside fresh blooms that were perfect.

Pax frowned, hands at the sides of his head. What was happening? Was he going mad?

The same image again. No. It was different this time. A glowing blue flower nestled deep inside the bouquet that was both fresh and decaying. Its light touched the edges of two of the twisted and bruised ones . . . and those blooms grew . . . not better, but less limp, more firm.

Pax stared at the glowing blue network as far as the eye could see. The tendril that had come to him just waited, floating in space. And he thought of what Kaleb Krychek had blasted out across the Net, his words carried in echoes created by thousands of minds.

No force. True choice.

Pax didn't trust anyone but his twin.

He shook his head, stepping back from the tendril.

. . .

ZAIRA had become entangled in the spidersilk at emergence, her mind having been the one that held the shield over Auden. Within minutes, she knew her shield was no longer necessary, Auden's mind engulfed by violent blue energy.

The spidersilk that had tangled her up fell away the instant she stepped back.

Aden's mind appeared beside her at the same time.

"What is this?" she asked.

"A much more powerful version of the same ability that allows Ivan to hold the Island." Aden touched a thread of spidersilk. "Young. Incredibly young. The infant."

"I don't believe in luck." Zaira folded her arms on the physical plane.

A bloated black spider, hovering over a glowing blue egg. It scratched at the egg with its legs, creating a crack, an opening . . . that sealed up with luminous steel before the spider could insert its face inside.

"What the hell in creepy fuck was that?" Zaira sent the stream of eerie images to the man who was her love and her soul.

"I think that's the NetMind telling us this has nothing to do with luck." Aden's voice held a taut satisfaction. "Whatever Shoshanna did to engineer Liberty, she gave the NetMind the perfect soil in which to plant a seed."

"It's using the baby?" Zaira would kill the damn neosentience.

"No, I think this is *exactly* what the child was designed to do—to supercharge Shoshanna's abilities to harvest energy from others. We all know it had to be her in that initial island where she was sucking the inhabitants dry, even if no one has proof."

Zaira had heard Ivan Mercant's description of the spider he'd encountered, and she'd read the reports on the genetic connection between Ivan and Shoshanna. That particular ability seemed to exist in only a single familial line. "Agreed."

Her lover's mind pulsed as he considered things in that calm way of his that fascinated her. "I don't think the NetMind did anything to either mother or child except help them win the battle against Shoshanna.

"It fixed the vulnerability that would've allowed Shoshanna to take control of Liberty, and there's a high chance it helped Auden heal from her earlier brain injuries so that she could protect her baby. It explains her recovery in a way nothing else comes close to doing."

"Hmm." Unconvinced, Zaira touched the spidersilk.

It twined around her psychic finger like the tiny child she'd petted in the infirmary, the feel of it purest innocence. "Ugh. Fine." When she accepted the bond, it settled into place like a cub snuggling into her.

Zaira refused to smile. "It's not a telepathic or psychic bond. No link between minds, no chance of information being siphoned out or pushed in. It's . . . a basic transfer of energy."

"It might mature as the child grows, but even if it never does, look at the PsyNet."

That was when Zaira realized: nothing had broken or crumbled or torn away since this began. The entire PsyNet was calm . . . was even being patched together in places as the excess energy from the network was sent into the psychic sphere to fix the battered fabric.

But Zaira had known happiness for only a short time and she saw the flaw. "One child," she said. "A fragile, breakable infant. The entire PsyNet cannot rest on those tiny shoulders. It's not fair to her, and it's not fair to the millions who need this network to survive."

A clock bloomed in her mind, the hand moving from midnight back to nine p.m.

"Got it," Zaira said, assuming the neosentience could hear her. "Thanks."

Black flowers showered on her head.

She scowled. "I don't remember it being so chatty before." Shaking away that question before Aden could answer, she said, "Did you see the clock?"

"Yes. This isn't permanent. It's a gift of time to allow us to rest and recover, and find the path forward." Aden paused again. "If I had to guess, I'd say the web is spread too thin. An emergency measure only. It can only hold for so long stretched across the entire PsyNet before it begins to break."

Zaira took his psychic hand. "We watch over the child."

"We watch over the child."

IT was hours later, when the first excitement had died down, that Kaleb received a visit from the NetMind. It was much stronger already, fed by the energy of a rejuvenated network. "How long?" he asked it, showing it an image of the web, alongside images of a baby, then a child of five, then of ten and so on.

He received the same nine o'clock image Aden had already shared with the Ruling Coalition, but the NetMind couldn't clarify whether each hour meant a month, a year, a decade, or more.

Given the extent of the damage, Kaleb was almost certain it would skew shorter.

"Will others be born who have the same ability as Ivan and the infant?" he asked, well aware the NetMind had the power to dabble with Psy in ways deep and unknowable.

A sense of sorrow, the image of a fractured line of steel gray.

It remained too weak, too damaged for such engineering.

Kaleb showered it in the flowers it so loved. "You've done enough, bought us time to fix what we spoiled." One hundred years of Silence couldn't be erased in a single beautiful night, but the NetMind loved its broken people enough to try to give them one final chance. "Thank you."

Fireworks lit up his mind.

Chapter 49

To be part of the birth of a pack? It's hard work, I won't lie. But the rewards—"astronomical" is about the right word. I helped build an aerie that will be used by generations, and I wouldn't give up even a single blister or callus that came from it.

But the best thing for me, the *absolute* best thing, is how close we are as a group. Our size means that we all connect on a daily basis, and honestly, this ornery old cat figured she'd go mad pretty damn fast as a result.

Instead, it turns out I love being in the center of the action, and I love that I can be part of everything. I just have to ask—there's always room for an extra pair of hands and someone ready to train you to the job.

As an example, a day before turning in this article, I spent two hours with my alpha on an important project. The project in question was an educational plan for our children.

We're now at the point where we're looking to set up a school and on the hunt for teachers who want to dive into life with an audacious young pack where adventure and discovery are a daily fact—alongside laughter, fun, and waking up to one of the most beautiful places on this planet each and every day.

P.S. I have been charged by the women of the pack to confirm that Remi is indeed scary but sexy, especially when he lets out that wicked smile of his. But he is also now very taken, wild women, so you'll have to aim for the other sexy unmated singles in the pack. I will be featuring them one by one in the column, never you worry. I know my responsibilities as a Wild Woman *columnist!*

—"The RainFire Diaries: Part 1" by Vesta Narin, in the December 2083 issue of *Wild Woman* magazine: "Skin Privileges, Style & Primal Sophistication"

. . .

"LIBBY IS *STILL* sleeping?" A disgusted Jojo threw up her tiny hands. "Babies!"

Biting the inside of her cheek to keep from laughing, Auden crouched down on the grass outside the aeries so Jojo could look down at Liberty's sleeping face. "Baby cubs sleep a lot," she acknowledged. "But look how cute she is. Sometimes she even snores." She imitated Liberty's adorable snuffle-snores.

Jojo giggled and touched her finger to Liberty's with the care taught to every cub in RainFire when it came to babies. "Hi, Libby," she whispered. "It's your friend Jojo." She pressed a soft kiss to Liberty's bare head.

It was an unseasonably warm day, the baby's glossy brown hair shining in the sunshine. No snow had fallen yet, but they all knew it was on the horizon.

She opened her eyes at her packmate's touch, those eyes a soft brown full of happiness. Liberty had been checked over by Finn, Dr. Bashir, and every empath known to either RainFire or the Arrow Squad.

The consensus was that she felt like she was just . . . being a baby. No strain, no tension, no special tiredness. Auden and Remi's cub simply had a brain that could act as the central processing plant for psychic energy.

Now that Auden knew Liberty was safe, she found grim pleasure in the fact that Shoshanna had inadvertently engineered a gift of hope for the very race she'd been trying to swallow up and control. Auden saw that hope each time she stepped into the PsyNet—to which she and Liberty were still connected, because Liberty was necessary to its survival.

Both of them were, however, also bonded to Remi—and that bond was unbreakable.

One was a bond of need by the PsyNet, the other a bond of love between a family.

As for Shoshanna's plans, Auden was still going through her mother's files, but it was clear that she'd been flat out insane by the end. Her whole plan of "transference" and "neural integration" had been the product of a disturbed mind from the start, but mercifully she'd had the sense to hire skilled M-Psy to engineer Liberty's DNA.

Auden had sent those particular files, as well as a sample of Liberty's DNA, to Ashaya Aleine. Mated to a DarkRiver sentinel, the scientist was the most top-tier and trustworthy specialist on the subject that Auden could've ever hoped to find. The other woman had examined the data with a fine-tooth comb.

"The M-Psy who worked on this took no dangerous risks," Ashaya had reported back. "I'd go so far as to say Shoshanna got lucky with the depth of Liberty's power—Psy have never been able to predict psychic strength beyond basic genetic matches. Most of the heavy lifting in this case was done by the Gradient levels involved."

A mother herself, the other woman had smiled. "Enjoy your cub, Auden. She's healthy and strong and from what I saw when we met, she's cherished by the entire pack and will grow up into a joyful and well-adjusted adult."

Auden intended to follow that advice.

"It's time for Liberty to go hang out with Finn now," Auden said to Jojo when Liberty yawned and closed her eyes again. "And hey"—she tapped Jojo on the nose—"isn't it a special dinner tonight?"

The cub lit up. "Pancakes!" Thus reminded of the promised breakfast-for-dinner night at the dining aerie, she ran off at speed.

Auden's heart filled to overflowing, as it so often did these days. Seven weeks after Liberty's birth and three weeks after her release from the pack's infirmary—to which she'd been shifted after Bashir agreed she was out of the critical danger zone—she felt more at home in Rain-Fire than she ever had in the Scott home.

Her stay in the infirmary had been nothing she could've imagined; she'd had a packmate or three drop by every single day. Each had brought stories or food or a funny show to watch with her. And her Remi had been with her through it all; he'd even snuck in cake and fed it to her bite after bite.

Smiling, she turned . . . and nearly ran into Kit.

"Can I hold her?" He made big, adorable eyes at her.

Rina's brother was ridiculously charming; they'd all miss him when he headed home next week. "I'm taking her to Finn." The healer had the night off because no one had managed to harm or otherwise injure themselves this past week, but instead of telling the pack to leave him alone, he'd volunteered to babysit while partaking of the communal meal.

"That's just how healers are," Lark had reassured her when Auden worried about Finn's lack of downtime. "This *is* his idea of downtime—chilling with the pack, cubs hanging off him. Also, trust me, he'll be less babysitting Libby and more keeping an eye on her while the pack cuddles her."

Liberty, Auden already knew, would thrive in the midst of the noise and conversation. Her and Remi's child might as well have been born half-changeling, she'd settled with such joy into the pack's communal way of life.

Kit held out his hands. "I'll take her. Promise I won't kidnap her and run away. Too scared of Remi's wrath."

Lips twitching, Auden gave the baby another cuddle before handing her over into those careful arms. Trust here, with these people, came easy. Not only because she was Remi's mate, but because each and every person here had watched over Liberty while she couldn't. Never would any of them harm her.

Kit's smile was that of a heartbreaker as he cuddled her close, his auburn hair falling over his forehead as he bent to nuzzle at the baby. "Hey, kitten."

Good thing Phoebe wasn't in range or the poor juvenile would surely have fainted. Her crush on Kit was sweet and young and made Auden smile—because to her, it showed the love in which Phoebe had been raised, that she felt safe crushing on a dangerous dominant. Auden wanted the same carefree sense of possibility for her baby.

"Does she need a bottle?" Kit looked up, the evening sunshine soft gold on his skin. "I could feed her."

"No, I just fed her." She'd done so sitting outside in the sun, under the wide canopy of an aerie tree.

No one had minded, smiles shot her way. Because she lived in a changeling pack, and breastfeeding a cub was nothing monumental on which to offer comment. Auden was still shy enough to use a shawl but her baby would grow up as wild and free as Jojo—who'd run naked through the closest stand of trees only the other day, while doing a warrior yell.

Three other equally naked cubs had followed, all of them echoing her cry.

Auden loved the thought of her child whooping it up after the assured ringleader of the cubs.

"But," she added when Kit's face fell, "I pumped more milk for later that's in the infirmary fridge. You can ask Finn if you can do her next feed." Because tonight, Auden was going out on a date with her mate.

Not only that, but she had, as of today, a full bill of health. Signed and sealed.

Finally.

Remington Denier was about to be pounced on by a very sexually frustrated woman who he'd managed to rouse to fever pitch night after night with his kisses and his stroking and his petting . . . and those oh-so-sexy words he purred in her ear.

Tonight, Auden intended to ride him to oblivion.

REMI almost swallowed his tongue when he saw Auden walking toward him. He'd asked her to meet him at the cabin. It had felt right that they'd consummate their relationship—at fucking last!—in the place where they'd first met.

Her hair was a halo of curls lustrous and lush that reached her shoulders, her lips plump and wet with gloss. And her body. "Fuck." It came out a croak.

She was wearing a little dress of shimmering bronze that ended high on her thighs; in between, it hugged every curve and scooped down to expose the upper curves of breasts lush and heavy. She'd paired it with ankle boots that allowed her to walk on the forest floor while around her neck dangled the gold chain he'd gifted her.

A gold chain with a tiny lock as a pendant.

A sensual and private game between mates.

"Hi, handsome," she said, coming to stand with one hand flat on his chest. "You clean up gorgeous, but tonight I want naked." A hint of heat on her cheeks. "Lots and lots of naked."

Smiling at her playfulness, he stroked his hand down to lie on the curve of her ass, and drew deep of the intoxication of her scent. "I want to eat you up," he growled.

"You did that last night." She ran her fingers down his black button-down shirt, which he'd paired with black pants. "Today, I get your cock."

That was another thing. His mate was a fast learner in bed, and had figured out that dirty talk from her drove him insane. Especially because she blushed and got all flustered in the aftermath.

Like now, her eyelashes lowering as she glanced down, and her feet doing a nervous movement.

Affection twined with lust, his adoration for her absolute. "You can have whatever you want," he said, "but first, how about I feed you the delicious meal I've put together for you?" He nuzzled at her, running his hand up her thigh and to the edge of her dress. "This dress is so short you can't bend over in front of anyone but me."

"I sat on your jacket while driving up," she whispered, undoing the buttons of his shirt. "I'm not wearing panties."

That was it. Remi only had so much endurance.

"Food can wait," he said and, fisting his hand in her hair, shoved up the hem of her dress to cup her between her thighs.

Her curls pressed into his palm, her flesh liquid silk in readiness.

Growling into her mouth, he worked one finger into her and felt her clench. She liked this. He knew because he'd done it two nights in a row.

One finger. Then two.

Getting her ready for tonight, for the much bigger, thicker intrusion into her body. He'd intended to go slow, take it easy, but she was pushing his shirt off his shoulders and moving on his fingers and kissing him all over his chest, and Remi needed to claim her more than he needed to breathe.

Removing his fingers from her, he threw her over his shoulder and spanked her exposed butt lightly as he carried her into the cabin. "You are messing up all my plans once again, Ms. Auden Denier."

Because she was a Denier now, as was Liberty, Scott a name that was tainted in Auden's eyes and that she didn't want to claim for either of them.

"I can't help it," she said. "I want you inside me. The need, it aches."

His own need to claim her a clawing within, he kicked the door shut behind himself before throwing her onto the bed with gentle arms. Her dress was shoved up around her waist, her lower body exposed and glistening, her breasts plumping up over her neckline. "Pull down the shoulders," he ordered as he tore off his shirt. "Shove the top of your dress down to the waist, too."

He was naked by the time she finished.

Cock in hand, he pumped once, twice.

Knees raised, she spread her thighs . . . and her arms.

He was lost, was *hers*. They'd play their sexy games later. Right now, he wanted to be inside his mate, wanted to mark her with his seed, and wanted her to mark him with her musk, her nails, her bite.

When he came over her, it was to kiss her with all the love inside his wild heart. She adored him in turn, her legs wrapping around his waist as he nudged at her entrance with his cock. Even though she was so slick, he took his time with this first dance.

The harder, rougher play could wait.

For his mate's first time, he'd show her nothing but patience even if it killed him.

It did. Almost. Kill him.

But his reward for the teeth-gritting will was Auden's pleasured gasp as she rode him exactly as she'd fantasized, her hands on his chest and her eyes locked with his before they hazed in an orgasm that clenched around him, breaking his control at last.

He came inside her. Marking and being marked.

LATER, much later, he fed her pastries while she sat naked on his lap, and music played through the speakers he'd brought up, while fairy lights twinkled all around them. He'd come up early to set it all up, give his mate the romance and the courtship she deserved—and he intended to keep it up. He planned to give her everything, permeate her world with joy.

Now he nuzzled and cuddled her, and bargained for future sexual favors with bites of cinnamon roll and salted caramel cupcake, and her giggles and kisses and happiness filled his heart to overflowing.

He was Remi Denier, Alpha, Father, and Mate.

And he was living a life far more extraordinary and joyous than could've been dreamed of by the lonely and grieving boy whose anger had once driven him to race and race in an effort to outrun his pain. There was no more need to run anywhere.

He was home.

In his pack.

In her arms.

Chapter 50

I am calling a meeting of the board at 11 a.m. Tuesday. Attendance is mandatory.

—Message from Auden Denier to the Scott
Board of Directors (17 January 2084)

AUDEN RAN HER hand down the lines of her sleek but comfortable dark pink shift one last time before she strode out of her office at the new Scott HQ in Sunset Falls and down the hall to the conference room where the board awaited—that included her uncle, who'd emerged from his kidnapping with a healthy fear of both changelings and Auden, and no actual memories of anything.

Auden might've felt sorry for him if she hadn't learned that, while she lay fighting for her life, he'd set a pack of lawyers to figuring out how to screw Liberty out of her birthright. After everything Shoshanna had done to Liberty before she was even born, Hayward didn't get to claim the one useful thing Shoshanna might have done for Auden's baby.

As Remi would say, *fuck that noise.*

She gave the entire board a cool look as she entered.

Then she took control with an ease and a depth of knowledge that had never been hers before her mother decided to invade her mind.

Bleedover.

She'd had two choices once it became clear that some of the bleed-over from Shoshanna's attempts at transference was permanent and embedded into her neurons: either rage against it in bitterness that would slowly turn toxic inside her . . . or own it.

Auden had chosen the latter option. Because even if Shoshanna had left information and skills behind in Auden's head, she hadn't left any traces of her personality or sense of self. Auden knew that beyond any doubt—because her mother had simply never had the capacity to love that bled through Auden's veins.

Remi had confirmed that her scent no longer showed any signs of cold metal, but her mate had also supported her desire to consult an empath, as well.

"The only person inside you is you," Vasic's mate, Ivy Jane Zen, had said. "I've worked with fragmented personalities before, and you're not one of them." She'd taken Auden's hands in her own. "Your mind is cohesive and your loyal, loving heart is a delight for an E—you're a *good* person, Auden, and you're very much your own person."

Ivy's little white dog had stood on Auden's feet just then, his tail wagging as he waited to be petted. "See," Ivy had said with a laugh, "Rabbit agrees with me, and he's the best judge of character around."

Shoshanna had played a high-stakes game—and lost.

Now, Auden *owned* this knowledge, and she'd decided to use it to seize control of her family.

"I have two options," she'd said to Remi once she was healed enough to head out into the world. "Surrender the family to its current path, or assume the CEO position and try to make them something better. I'm going for option two." Scott might not be a name Auden would ever again claim, for her or her child, but neither was she about to allow evil to win.

"I also feel bad for the young ones like my cousin Devlin," she'd added. "He's never had the chance to become anything but what Shoshanna, then Charisma shaped him to be. I think I can make a difference, give the next generation a shot at a life like our baby is going to have."

"You know I have your back," Remi had said. "I also know you'll kick ass."

Jaya, the empath who'd felt like a friend from the moment Auden first met her while conscious, had grimaced—but only because she knew what awaited Auden. "They'll try to manipulate you, poison your mind. Be wary."

"I will be," Auden had said, having no plans to be felled by arrogance. "But I have an advantage: all of my mother's strategic skills and memories." Shoshanna had been a grand master.

Jaya had held her gaze. "Power can be a kind of poison, too. Never forget that."

It was a warning Auden had heeded, and would continue to heed. What helped keep her centered and herself was that every night after she finished with her duties as the Scott CEO, she went home to Rain-Fire and to her mate and child. She'd also begun to hire staff unconnected to the family, shedding those she could never trust at the same time.

Her first hire had been an empath who could tell her which people were noxious.

Her second had been a teleport-capable telekinetic raised to be an Arrow but who'd gone freelance after the fall of Silence.

Zaira had vouched for him. Plus, while the nineteen-year-old was a grim-faced soldier when in front of her family, he turned into a big kid with the leopards. Turned out he was dating a RainFire juvenile around his own age.

She trusted him even with Liberty.

Who never ever left RainFire territory, and wouldn't without a guard until Auden had absolute control over this family.

"No," she said today in response to a proposal, her voice a blade of ice. "That will lead to a ten percent loss. The Suma projection came out three hours ago, altering the scope of the matter."

A rustle around the table as the others checked the projection. She permitted it, knowing that if she earned their respect, she'd hold it a lot longer than if she taught them to fear her. That was one good thing she'd learned at Shoshanna's knee; her mother had been an awful mother, and she'd taken the family in terrible directions—but once, long ago, she'd been a good CEO.

Her people had followed her because they trusted her.

Now the others agreed with Auden's decision, and when they began to discuss alternate options, she was ready with the best possible choice. She'd done her research, used every database at her disposal. This wasn't an easy job, would never be an easy job, but it was one she intended to conquer and hold.

Evil could only win if each person with a choice allowed it to win.

The meeting closed on a good note, with the board congratulating her on the outcome of another recent move, and one of the more senior members saying, "I hope you will excuse me for saying this, Auden, but you are proving to be your mother's daughter."

"I'm better." Auden rose to her feet. "My mother became interested in other things toward the end of her life, let the businesses and the family both get stagnant."

A ripple of nods around the table.

"I intend to take this family in fresh new directions," she said, now that she had their attention. "There is no room in my plan for dinosaurs who wish to do things as they've always been done."

Remi had laughed when she'd tried out this part of her intended speech on him. "That's my tough-as-nails little cat."

"Cupcake," she'd corrected. "A tough-as-nails iron cupcake."

Grinning, he'd crooked his finger at her from where he lounged on the floor cushions listening to her. "Come here, my gorgeous iron cupcake. I want to lick your frosting."

Needless to say, Auden had had an excellent night.

Today, as the board members looked at one another, she folded her arms. "Logic alone dictates that we can't make unethical decisions in a world full of empaths who are wide-awake and are working with many of our business associates. All the simulations I've run forecast a future where ethical businesses open to oversight by Es will outperform others by a considerable margin."

Oh, she had their attention now. And she *would* rub the dirt off the Scott name, even if it took her a lifetime. It was part of her baby's history, and she'd give her a history to be proud of.

WHEN she left the meeting to head downstairs, what she saw made little bubbles of happiness pop in her veins.

Remi stood behind the sliding glass doors of the entrance, his big body leaning up against a rugged vehicle that would take her up into the mountains and to RainFire. Camo green T-shirt, faded jeans, old boots, and sunglasses, he made her want to pounce on him and take a big bite.

"You could've at least washed the vehicle," she teased after she exited. "You probably gave the doorman an aneurysm."

"I washed myself," said the cat who was opening the passenger door for her. "Does that count?"

Since Auden was even then nuzzling his neck in open affection—because she would never again live a lie, not for anyone—she couldn't say anything but, "You are such a cat."

"Meow."

Laughing, she got into the passenger seat and was smiling as they drove away, heading home to their baby and their pack.

You will be happy.

Yes, her Remi kept his promises and always would.

No evil on earth could ever win against the power of his wild heart.